THE EVERYMAN
LIBRARY

*The Everyman Library was founded by J. M. Dent
in 1906. He chose the name Everyman because he wanted
to make available the best books ever written in every
field to the greatest number of people at the cheapest possible
price. He began with Boswell's 'Life of Johnson';
his one-thousandth title was Aristotle's 'Metaphysics',
by which time sales exceeded forty million.*

*Today Everyman paperbacks remain true to
J. M. Dent's aims and high standards, with a wide range
of titles at affordable prices in editions which address
the needs of today's readers. Each new text is reset to give
a clear, elegant page and to incorporate the latest thinking
and scholarship. Each book carries the pilgrim logo,
the character in 'Everyman', a medieval morality play,
a proud link between Everyman
past and present.*

Daniel Defoe

THE LIFE AND STRANGE
SURPRIZING ADVENTURES OF

ROBINSON CRUSOE,

OF YORK, MARINER:

*Who lived Eight and Twenty Years,
all alone in an un-inhabited Island on the Coast of
AMERICA, near the Mouth of the Great River of OROONOQUE;
Having been cast on Shore by Shipwreck, wherein
all the Men perished but himself.*

WITH

*An Account how he was at last as strangely
deliver'd by PYRATES.*

Written by Himself.

Edited by
JOHN MAN

EVERYMAN
j. M. DENT · LONDON
CHARLES E. TUTTLE
VERMONT

Introduction, chronology, notes and other critical apparatus
© J. M. Dent 1994

Robinson Crusoe first included in Everyman's Library in 1906
New Edition 1994
Reprinted 1996

J. M. Dent
Orion Publishing Group
Orion House, 5 Upper St Martin's Lane,
London WC2H 9EA
and
Charles E. Tuttle Co. Inc.
28 South Main Street,
Rutland, Vermont 05701, USA

Typeset by Spartan Press Ltd
Lymington, Hants
Printed in Great Britain by
The Guernsey Press Co. Ltd, Guernsey, C.I.

British Library Cataloguing-in-Publication Data
is available upon request.

ISBN 0 460 87439 X

CONTENTS

NOTE ON THE AUTHOR AND EDITOR

DANIEL DEFOE was born in 1660, the son of a tallow-chandler who became a Presbyterian. He was educated for the Presbyterian ministry at a dissenter's school until he was nineteen. He decided against the ministry and turned to trade, the first of several careers, involving a vast literary output, and a number of personal disasters. He spent some twenty years in business, first as a trader, until he went bankrupt in 1692, then as a brick-and-tile manufacturer. A second bankruptcy in 1703 ended his business career. He had married at the age of twenty-four, and had eight children. Business failure and his large family both ensured he was never free of financial demands. His poem, 'The True-Born Englishman', brought him fame, but his satire, *The Shortest Way with Dissenters*, landed him in prison (the cause of his second bankruptcy). He was released, and then backed by a Tory peer, Robert Harley, who employed him to report on matters of political interest. His life was now devoted to writing, concentrating at first on journalism. As 'the father of modern journalism', he was associated with twenty-six periodicals. One, the *Review*, he wrote and published himself (1703–14). His *Tour Through the Whole Island of Great Britain*, written in his old age, became a classic of reportage. His astringent political and religious views made him many enemies, and he was arrested several times. Throughout his life, Defoe explored a huge range of interests, not only in his hundreds of articles and pamphlets, but in books. They include works on trade, the education of children, the occult, pirates and travel.

In his late fifties, he turned to fiction. His first novel, *Robinson Crusoe*, was followed by six others, the best known of which are *Moll Flanders* and *A Journal of the Plague Year*. Several, like *Crusoe*, were written in the guise of fact. His contacts with criminals while in prison provided a particularly rich mine of information.

His last works were *A Plan of English Commerce* and *The*

Complete English Gentleman. He was still writing when he died at the age of seventy-one, in 1731.

JOHN MAN has a particular interest in the psychology of survival. In the early 1980s he made a six-part Channel 4 television documentary series, *Survive,* on human endurance in extreme circumstances. One of his contributors was the subject of his book *The Survival of Jan Little.* He wrote with Pin Ya-Thay *Stay Alive, My Son,* detailing Thay's escape from the Khmer Rouge. Other books include *Jungle Nomads of Ecuador: The Waorani.*

CHRONOLOGY OF DEFOE'S LIFE

Year	Age	Life
1660		Defoe's probable year of birth, in London. Son of James Foe, tallow-chandler
1662	2	The Foes become Presbyterians
1665	5	Taken to the country to avoid the Plague
1674(?) –1679	14–19	School in Newington Green, with view to becoming minister
1683	23	Sets up as hosiery merchant
1684	24	Marries Mary Tuffley, daughter of a rich cooper
1685	25	Takes part in Monmouth's rebellion and captured after the battle of Sedgemoor; eventually receives a royal pardon
1688	28	Writes in support of William III

CHRONOLOGY OF HIS TIMES

Year	Cultural Context	Historical Events
1660		End of Commonwealth: restoration of monarchy under Charles II
1665		Plague in London War with Holland begins (ends 1667)
1667	Milton, *Paradise Lost*	Fire of London
1672–8		War with Holland
1673		Test Act compels allegiance to Church of England
1678		Popish Plot: Catholics accused of planning regicide and coup
1682	Dryden, *Mac Flecknoe*	
1685		Death of Charles II; James II, a Roman Catholic, succeeds In France, Revocation of Edict of Nantes forces Huguenot (Protestant) emigration
1688	Pope born	Glorious Revolution; James flees on the invasion of William; William III of Orange and Mary II accede Toleration Act allows Non-conformists freedom of worship Bill of Rights bans Crown to Catholics

Year	Cultural Context	Historical Events
1689	Births of Richardson and Lady Mary Wertley Death of Aphra Behn	
1692		Massacre of Glencoe crushes Scots Salem witchcraft trials, Massachusetts Foundation of Bank of England
1694	Voltaire born	
1695		Death of Queen Mary
1700	Congreve, *Way of the World* Death of Dryden	
1701		French invade Holland Death of pretender James II; his son 'James III' recognised by Louis XIV War of Spanish Succession (1701–14)
1702		Act of Settlement (concerning Hanoverian line) Death of William III; accession of Queen Anne
1704	Swift, *Tale of a Tub* Newton, *Optics*	Battle of Blenheim
1707	Fielding born	Union of England with Scotland
1708		Further success for Allies under Marlborough in War of Spanish Succession
1709	Pope, *Pastorals* Johnson born Berkeley, *New Theory of Vision*	
1710		Sachverell trial; fall of Godolphin ministry; Harley succeeds

Year	Age	Life
1713	53	Arrested several times for debt and political writings and imprisoned in the Queen's Bench gaol
1715	55	*The Family Instructor* (I), didactic tales. Tried for libel but the case is dropped
1718	58	*The Family Instructor* (II)
1719	59	*Robinson Crusoe*, followed by its sequel, *The Farther Adventures of Robinson Crusoe*
1720	60	*Memoirs of a Cavalier*; *Captain Singleton*; *Serious Reflections . . . of Robinson Crusoe*
1722	62	*Moll Flanders*; *Religious Courtship*; *A Journal of the Plague Year*; *Colonel Jack*
1724	64	*Roxana*; *A General History of the Pyrates*; *A Tour Thro' the Whole Island of Great Britain*; *A New Voyage Round the World*
1725	65	*The Complete English Tradesman* (I)
1726	66	*The Political History of the Devil*
1726	67	*The History and Reality of Apparitions*; *The Complete English Tradesman* (II); *A System of Magic*; *A Plan of the English Commerce*
1731	71	Dies 'of a lethargy' in Ropemakers Alley, London, and buried Bunhill Fields (City Road, EC1), traditional dissenters' burial ground

Year	Cultural Context	Historical Events
1711	Addison and Steele, *Spectator* (runs until 1712) Pope, *Essay on Criticism*	
1712	Rousseau born Handel settles in England	
1713	Diderot born	Treaty of Utrecht
1714	Pope, *Rape of the Lock* in five cantos	Death of Queen Anne; succession of George I; fall of Harley
1715	Le Sage, *Gil Blas*, vols 1–2 Pope's translation of Homer's *Iliad*	Jacobite rising put down; death of Louis XIV
1717	Pope, *Works* collected	Triple Alliance
1719		Peerage Bill
1720		South Sea Bubble, following collapse of Mississippi scheme in Paris
1721		Walpole comes to power
1722		Atterbury's Jacobite plot uncovered Death of Marlborough
1724	Swift, *Drapier's Letters*	
1725	Pope, *Odyssey*	Death of Peter the Great, Russian Emperor Treaty of Hanover (England, France and Prussia)
1726	Swift, *Gulliver's Travels*	
1727	Newton, *Principia* Death of Newton	Death of George I, succeeded by George II
1728	Pope, *Dunciad* Gay, *Beggar's Opera*	
1729	Swift, *Modest Proposal*	
1730	Fielding, *Tom Thumb*	
1731	Prévost, *Manon Lescaut*	

INTRODUCTION

To begin with two little oddities about Defoe. The first is that he courted trouble in the glare of public life, yet kept part of himself hidden. A portrait would show a spare, hook-nosed, sharp-chinned man, with a mole near his mouth; but there is no portrait. He liked secrecy, and the motives for some of his actions are obscure still. The second is that, despite his towering reputation as an author, Defoe did not write an extended work, let alone a novel, until his forties, when he had already lived a life crammed with enough business, journalism and personal drama to fill several lives.

All of these factors, like his origins, were important ingredients in his work. His father, James Foe, turned Presbyterian, and wanted him to become a minister. Since Nonconformists, or dissenters – those Protestants who did not belong to the Church of England – were forbidden to attend university, his education ended when he left school at nineteen. His background left him with a chip on his shoulder. He felt himself to be an outsider, excluded. Perhaps it was this insecurity that led him to add 'de' to his father's name.

He had no urge to become a minister, though he retained a keen (if somewhat variable) sense of morality and a deep interest in religious matters. He turned instead to trade, at first in stockings, then branching into wine and other commodities. Even after he started writing, trade was his passion. 'Writing upon trade,' he said later, 'was the whore I really doted upon.'

He was not entirely suited to business. Throughout his life, he retained a volatility that drove him fluttering moth-like between different projects and subjects. In particular, he was drawn by politics and religion (then two sides to the same coin). His quick-silver intelligence, combined with a lack of hard-headed acumen, led him into backruptcy in 1692, when he was thirty-two. He set about honouring his debts, re-establishing himself with a brick-and-tile factory, but he never escaped the demands of creditors, a heavy burden for a man with a wife and family of eight.

Meanwhile, he remained in thrall to political and religious dispute. Cromwell, the Puritan destroyer of monarchy, had died in 1658, and in 1660 (the year of Defoe's birth), Charles II became king. The Crown restored – but with what powers? England remained in a ferment of debate. The central dispute – king vs. parliament – rippled outwards, engulfing class, religion and economic life. Town rivalled country; rising middle-class traders challenged land-owners for wealth and status; Anglicans assailed Non-conformists, while both opposed Catholics.

Defoe was deeply involved in this ferment of ideas and beliefs. In 1685, when the illegitimate son of Charles II, the Duke of Monmouth, made a mismanaged attempt to seize the throne from the new king, the Catholic James II, Defoe took a minor part in the rebellion. In the vicious reprisals that followed, Defoe was lucky to escape transportation or hanging.

James's attempts to impose Catholicism were scuppered when seven bishops offered the throne to James's daughter and her Protestant husband, the Dutchman William of Orange. When the 'Glorious Revolution' of 1688 ushered in a monarch constitutionally subservient to the state, Defoe was delighted. He became a propagandist both for William and his party, the Whigs. (Originally a Scottish term, 'Whig' came to describe those who rejected 'Tory' support for a hereditary monarchy. Increasingly, the Whig party represented the more liberal views, Tories the less tolerant attitudes typified by country gentry.)

The years after the 1688 revolution were heady ones for writers. Previously, the written word had been the domain of the scholar, poet, cleric and bureaucrat. Now, the new middle-class (of which Defoe was a part), fuelled by commerce, formed the first mass market. In its brief life (1711–12), revived in 1714, the most famous periodical, the *Spectator*, had a readership of perhaps 500,000 people, almost eight per cent of the whole population. To ensure they were read, journalists developed a popular, non-literary, chatty style which was a world apart from the courtly, academic elegance of their predecessors.

The debates raged not only in newspapers and periodicals – like the *Spectator*, the *Tatler* and their two hundred or more imitators – but in pamphlets, thousands of them every week, each typically a dozen or so pages, published and sold at street-stalls. For journalists like Defoe, these were the media. As yet, there were few novels.

Politics and commerce held only a part of Defoe's attention. He wrote poetry, lots of it, far too easily. His best – 'The True-Born Englishman' – was a sharp, witty satire on English weaknesses. His *Essay on Projects* (1698) reveals an astonishing depth of interests. He examined schemes for a national road system, a military academy, personal insurance, the education of women – all feasible, practical ideas, some of them well in advance of his time.

In 1702, when he was forty-two, his anti-establishment views brought the law down on him. The cause was a hoax, a pamphlet entitled *The Shortest Way with Dissenters*, presented as if it were by some anonymous High Church fanatic proposing to hang dissenters. His irony backfired. Too many people took it seriously. When the truth came out, he was arraigned for 'seditious libel,' and sentenced to an indefinite term in Newgate prison, with three turns in the pillory. Actually, this ordeal turned to triumph: the crowd refused to pelt him and garlanded him instead. But while he was inside, his brick-and-tile business failed and he was bankrupted a second time.

He was freed after five months only by the intercession of Robert Harley, Speaker of the House of Commons, who saw a use for Defoe's peculiar talents. Harley was a Tory, Defoe a Whig, but in these disputatious times both knew the value of give-and-take, of accurate information, and of public opinion.

Harley employed Defoe as a secret agent to report on the state of the nation. Plunging into a hectic round of travel and writing and furious controversy, he toured the country, observing, talking, reporting. His experiences later formed the basis for his *Tour thro' the Whole Island of Great Britain*, still considered a vital source of social information. His role suited him admirably. To merchants, he passed as a merchant; to lawyers, as a lawyer. Whig or Tory, he could fool them both. As part of his brief, he immersed himself in the debate in Scotland over the coming union with England, which came about in 1707.

It was probably with Harley's backing that Defoe also started a new periodical, the *Review*. It was supposedly independent, 'purg'd from the errors of partiality of newswriters and petty statesmen,' as its title page stated. Starting as a weekly, it eventually came out thrice weekly, for eleven years. Defoe wrote it all himself. As a Whig writing for a Tory, Defoe's position was delicate. He defended his stance as that of a moderate who cared nothing for parties, a speaker of truths, however disturbing. 'I write to please none of you, but to awaken you,' he declaimed grandly.

Perhaps. Or perhaps he trimmed his professional sails to whichever wind blew him towards solvency. He once wrote he was 'all to Every one that I may gain some.' It is this chameleon mentality that makes him a hard man to know. Mere deceiver, or, as he also claimed, deceiver for a high cause? In any event, such 'trimming' allowed him to indulge his gadfly mentality. He enjoyed courting trouble so much that in 1713 he turned in irony upon his own deeply-held belief that the throne should always be held by a Protestant monarch. Again, his irony backfired. Again, he was arrested. And again Harley intervened, obtaining a royal pardon.

When Queen Anne died in 1714, and George I became the first Hanoverian, Defoe might have been left high and dry. Harley had no office, and Defoe, caught between his mixed Whig and Tory loyalties, no *Review*, no protector, no job. In the event, the new Whig government knew their man. Defoe made a deal to work on three Tory periodicals. His brief was to subvert the editorial content, to make them 'pass as Tory papers, and yet be disabled and ennervated so as to do no mischief.' Defoe, both journalist and secret agent by inclination and profession, was ideally, probably uniquely, suited to the task.

He was now approaching sixty, with a rich life behind him. Another man might have considered retirement, or travel (strangely for one so active, Defoe never ventured abroad). But Defoe's active intellect, combined with his drive to produce and his inveterate habit of throwing himself in at the deep end, would not let him be. In addition to his frantic, stylish, informed work as a journalist, he now embarked on a wholly new career in writing: novelist.

Though he did not know it, he had before him an author's dream – a public hungry for fiction, and virtually no competition. All his experience seems a preparation for fiction. He had developed a novelistic style in the popular *True Relation of the Apparition of one Mrs Veal* (his first foray into another interest, the occult.) Now came some short stories in the *Review* and then a series of cautionary tales, *The Family Instructor* (1715; with a second volume in 1718). All the other elements of a novelist were in place: information galore, a passionate interest in the workings of life, an eye for detail, a flare for popular writing. Above all, his love of dissembling gave him an ability to assume the mantle of his own fictitious characters. It also inspired him to confront the still influential Puritan ethos that bracketed fiction with drama, as immoral invention, an objection Defoe avoided with another lie, presenting fiction as fact. That mix now combined to produce *Robinson Crusoe*.

Crusoe led on to two *Crusoe* sequels, *Moll Flanders, Roxana* and four other novels, work that stood him in good literary stead. The works of his old age, like the *Tour* (1724–26), have a relaxed narrative style and a novelist's flair for personal detail. Take his portrait of a family living in a cave in the Peak district. He spoke with the woman, who 'did not want manners, though she lived in a den like a wild body.' It amazed him that even in such poverty people could raise a healthy, happy family of five, and do so with a certain dignity. The cave had a chimney, and was neatly divided by curtains, with places to store food and pots, fronted by a garden-plot. It was a powerful lesson to Defoe: that happiness lies as much in effective work as in possessions. With that memory it would have been easy to imagine Crusoe's home.

Defoe died in 1731, aged seventy-one, most inappropriately, 'of a lethargy.'

THE BACKGROUND TO CRUSOE

One inspiration for *Crusoe* was the true story of Alexander Selkirk (1676–1721), a curmudgeonly sailor who had quarrelled with his captain and had himself been marooned for over four years on an uninhabited island. He survived the ordeal well, having become tough and fast enough to outrun the island's goats, left by previous visitors. His rescuer, Captain Woodes Rogers, wrote an account of Selkirk's survival in 1712, as did the journalist Steele the following year, both of whom Defoe would surely have read. Selkirk was in London in 1711. Possibly, Defoe could have met him and heard his story at first-hand.

Certainly there are parallels between Selkirk and Crusoe. Selkirk, like Crusoe, herded goats, suffered depression, ate turtles, dressed in goat-skin and preserved emotional stability with prayer. But it is stretching a point to claim Selkirk as the sole inspiration. Defoe wrote his story several years after Selkirk's became popular. He would have wished to distance himself from such a well-known tale, and anyway Selkirk's real-life adventures left a lot to be desired as the basis for fiction. His island, one of the Juan Fernandez group 350 miles off the coast of Chile in the Pacific, was a bleak little place, and he was left with remarkably little to aid survival.

To make a good tale, Defoe needed to provide greater variety. There were many other possible sources: romances, tales of crime, uplifting tracts, several other accounts of castaways, and travel books. Almost certainly he drew on the popular 'New Voyage Round the World' by the buccaneer and explorer William Dampier. He gave Crusoe a tropical Caribbean island, a ship-wreck to provide him with a good start and twenty-eight years of solitude.

DEFOE'S NARRATIVE SKILL

Crusoe's world is brilliantly convincing. In part, conviction comes from the use of detail – the objects taken from the wreck, the details of his abodes, his careful records, his defences, his crops. But conviction in story-telling – that bright filmic quality that turns words into images – is conveyed not by an overburden of detail, but by selectivity, often quite random. The only signs Crusoe sees of his drowned shipmates are 'three of their hats, one Cap, and two Shoes that were not fellows.' It would, of course, be a strange coincidence if the shoes had made a pair. But there is something touching in the image. It provides a sudden close-up. If that is real (says the reader's imagination), everything else must be as well. All disbelief is willingly suspended.

This is a device now well understood by writers, editors and critics. In its highest form, the trick of suggesting the whole with the part is described in terms of metaphor, simile and symbol. But it is also an essential element in popular writing. Those in the business of mass-marketing information call it 'colour.' General-isations and detail can both become tedious. What works is an interplay between the two. It is a technique, often used cynically in tabloid journalism. Whether high- or low-flown, though, it fulfils something fundamental in us: we absorb written information better in story form, and stories demand such details. Defoe, journalist, populist and stylist, master of the high and the low, used the technique to perfection.

It comes as something of a shock, then, to learn that this meticulous world is largely spurious, a fantasy, an *impression* of reality, not a 'realistic' view of desert-island life.

To take just a few examples:

There is no mention of defecation. This, as any camper knows, rapidly becomes a concern. For a long-term survivor, especially one committed to a fixed abode, it would be a major issue, to be solved by trips to the sea, or a handy stream, or the digging of one pit after another. Fortunately, Defoe either did not think of this, or ignored it. The stuff of practical camping is not the stuff of literature.

The novel has many such lapses of strict realism. Modern readers may find it odd that in twenty-eight years Crusoe (who later marries) is not bothered by a single sexual thought. No one who has lived in the tropics could contemplate dressing in a goat-skin suit, complete with goat-skin hat and goat-skin umbrella. (An *umbrella*? Had Defoe ever tried carrying a rain-soaked furry carpet above his head?) The heat would be unbearable, and the whole outfit would reek after days and perish in weeks. Finally, on the long return home, Friday has an extraordinary and entertaining encounter with a Pyrenean bear, which he kills, concluding with the words, 'so we kill Bear in my country.' In fact, there are no bears near the mouth of the Orinoco – the only South American bear is the retiring spectacled bear of the Andean foothills.

None of this matters, because Defoe's skill at creating Crusoe's fictional reality carries all before it. Nor is this mere narrative technique. It has a deeper purpose. Defoe, the novelist, uses Crusoe's survival to explore a reality very different from that of a shipwrecked mariner. The reality in which he is really interested is his own world and what makes it tick. In Defoe's time, there was a continuing debate about the nature of man and society. What were the original primeval conditions from which both sprang? Are we at heart reasonable? Religious? Or was life, in Hobbes's words written almost a century before, merely 'solitary, poor, nasty, brutish and short?' The island is a test-tube in which to perform a thought-experiment, and thus acquire and impart a deeper consideration of life as Defoe knew it. This is what gives the book its depth, its tangle of motive, theme, self-examination and symbol.

At first sight, for instance, Crusoe has a huge range of material goods with which to secure his survival. But the presence of some useful things points up the absence of others – needles, a spade, a sieve – which enable Defoe to open up a whole new level of thought (perhaps suggested to him after that conversation with a cave-woman in the Peak district): what are those things, he wonders, that are genuinely vital for a comfortable life?

The examination involves not only objects but skills. Crusoe, an expert sailor, still has to develop a whole range of skills vital for survival on his terms, which is to recreate his own world, in so far as he can. When the time comes for him to harvest bread, he has in effect to retrace the history of farming techniques in order to enjoy it, for he knows nothing of scything, winnowing, grinding or baking. Nor does he have a pot to cook in or store grain or bread in. How to make a pot? How to plant next year's crop, without a harrow?

Such questions lead deeper. Crusoe's cunning solutions impose human will on barbarous Nature. That in its turn leads him to master his own barbarous nature, and finally the barbarities of others. These are deep issues. They would never have arisen if Defoe had been 'realistic' – Selkirk, poor chap, had to be content with being a hunter gatherer.

CRUSOE THE MAN

The story appeals, then, partly because of the vividness; partly because of its thematic depth (more about that later); and partly because of the charm of the characters, particularly Crusoe himself.

Crusoe is an extraordinarily likeable man. He has a great range of emotional responses from the direst depression to near-ecstasy. He is a mix of interesting thought and decisive action (he sees how useless his money is, but who among his readers would wish him to throw it away? So he keeps it, and very useful it proves when rescue comes). He has a wry sense of humour, happily admitting how useless he is at unfamiliar tasks (like making a pot), and how ludicrous he must look with his goat-skin clothing and trailing moustache. He makes endearing mistakes, like building a boat so heavy he can't move it. He talks to himself. He is sometimes scared out of his wits. But he has an admirable ability to knuckle down and make the best of life. He is never depressed for long, and he takes us with him in his struggle for physical and emotional survival. He achieves a certain grandeur as the enlightened, but still self-critical despot of his little empire. So real does Crusoe seem, and so full of just the right combination of virtue and foible, of pluck, humour, feeling and thought that he could well have been an idealised self-portrait. This, surely, is how Defoe would have liked to be, an outsider who succeeds against all odds, mastering both himself and the world.

One aspect of Crusoe's character that will appeal less to modern readers is his attitude towards Friday. Crusoe saves Friday's life, but with an ulterior motive: to get help. He then sets about remoulding Friday in his own image. Friday is something of a cipher, a 'natural man,' a 'tabula rasa,' not to be taken seriously as a member of some real South American tribe. Crusoe never even asks his real name. He becomes one of Crusoe's attributes, like the goat-skin outfit, the parrot and the umbrella.

Defoe may not portray Friday with today's political correct-ness. How could he? He reflects the assumptions of his time, that the world was the white man's oyster, and "savages" were potential slaves. Dramatically, though, Friday is a brilliant creation, playing several roles, adding a new element to the story, testing and revealing Crusoe's maturing character. He is Defoe's proof that even the most benighted men are fundamentally virtuous and open to salvation – Crusoe converts him, as once he himself had been converted. Friday is a comic foil; the recipient and occasional critic of Crusoe's knowledge; and the perfect factotum. The variety of these roles, and his development in language, thought, loyalty and skill make him live, enough anyway to turn him into a type – in the 1970s companies advertised, rather disparagingly, for 'Girl Fridays' to help in offices.

CRUSOE'S INNER WORLD

Story and character may even be enough to carry modern readers along in the matter of Crusoe's religious conversion. In fact, if you stay with Crusoe, you will find that the religious elements are also part of the drama, a way of deepening emotion, thought and thus the reader's identification with Crusoe.

Religion was a matter closer to Defoe's contemporaries than to us, and it was certainly close to Defoe himself, the dissenter's son and intended minister. At the time, there were precedents galore for Defoe's interest, a whole literature of spiritual biography and autobiography. Crusoe owes more to Bunyan's Pilgrim than to Selkirk. Defoe was at school with one Timothy Cruso, who became famous enough as a cleric and writer of tracts for Defoe to borrow his name (though there is no evidence Defoe acknowledged the link).

It is perfectly natural, then, for Defoe to explore his version of the relationship between God and man. The young Crusoe, like the Prodigal Son, sins by ignoring his father's wishes, thus opposing the will of his heavenly Father. He lives a heedless life, and is punished by shipwreck, which leaves him like a hermit in a wilderness. Yet Providence also offers the chance of salvation. Indeed, few castaways can have been offered such a trove. He seizes the opportunity, by well-directed hard work. His labour turns inward, forcing spiritual progress. When the chance comes, he has the authority to impose himself on intruders, bend events to his own advantage, and thus escape. His final struggle through the Pyrenees ends in sort of commercial Promised Land – the estates he left behind twenty-eight years before have flourished in his absence. Both fathers would have approved.

Some critics insist this spiritual progress is Defoe's 'true' theme. If so, Defoe is too good a writer to let it overwhelm the story. God, too, is a character. At first the source of punishment, he becomes an ally as Crusoe learns to help himself. As Crusoe's mind expands, so does his range on the island: internal and external exploration mirror each other.

It may also be no coincidence, since the author had been in prison, that Crusoe's religious struggle is a classic survival technique. Loneliness, as those who impose or suffer solitary confinement know, can undermine personality. One way to hang onto a sense of self is to invent an alternative reality. Vladimir Bukovsky, the former Soviet dissident, is a case in point. He spent years in Moscow's Lubyanka Prison mentally building himself a castle in Scotland, in such detail that he was able to have a model of it made on his escape to the west. Indeed, his autobiography is called *To Build a Castle*. Crusoe's developing relationship with God is *his* castle.

This cannot, of course, be a nice, regular progression. It is full of agony and setbacks. The greatest shock of all comes when Crusoe finds The Footprint, an incident so well known, and so peculiar it deserves its capital letters. Who on earth made it? Not Friday – he arrives eight years later. One of the other 'savages'? Hardly. It is a very odd, almost surreal image: a print in tide-wet sand, yet without any other tracks; a print that endures the effects of tides for another week at least.

This is a very deliberate mystery, for it is the pivot of the novel. Crusoe had become a little cocksure, in need of a jolt. The Footprint is a supernatural event, a miracle, or at least a sort of apparition. (Defoe, remember, was fascinated by the occult). It is never explained, and therein lies its power. It induces a crisis in Crusoe. He reconnects himself to the great outside, imagines intruders, works through a whole cycle of emotional responses, reorders his whole life. When the intruders come, he is ready.

A BOOK WRITTEN AT SPEED

One aspect of Defoe's writing needs comment: his haste. *Crusoe* was probably written in a few weeks (its first sequel took three months). At one level, it is easy to criticise. The errors in *Crusoe* are notorious. To explore the wreck, Crusoe takes off all his clothes, swims out to the wreck, then fills his pockets with biscuits. The title page says Crusoe lived twenty-eight years on the island; in fact 30 Sept. 1659 to 19 December 1686 is nine months short of twenty-eight years. When rescue is at hand, the Spaniard tells him there are sixteen others; two pages later, there are fourteen. Towards the climactic battle, Crusoe keeps watch 'till near two in the morning,' though there was never a clock on the island (indeed, there could not have been. The sea-going chronometer was first tested in 1761). In a touching image, Crusoe/Defoe suggests that the parrot could well be on the island still, plaintively calling 'Robin Crusoe'; yet when Crusoe 'wrote' these words, he knew the truth—that he took the parrot with him when he left.

The whole book is thus a rough-and-ready piece of writing. There is one chapter-like sub-heading, 'The Journal,' which then begins. But it never ends. Defoe switches in and out of the journal quite at random, as best suits the story. He mixes past and present tense in a most ungrammatical way. He repeats himself. He promises to say more on a subject, and never does. He leaves holes, and fills them later ('And I must not forget that we had on the ship a dog and two cats,' he writes hastily, when about to introduce the dog, which we then learn had been with him for a while already).

Who cares about such deficiencies? Certainly not Defoe's many millions of readers, any more than they care about small factual errors, because readers perceive the errors not as Defoe's, but Crusoe's. The book is cast in the form of a journal, with Defoe as mere editor. Defoe's faults therefore become Crusoe's virtues. In our willing suspension of disbelief, we accept that Crusoe is an ill-educated sailor, that he was recording his terrible experiences under hard circumstances, that he was never writing for publication – the book only sees the light of day because Defoe somehow came across it. We may blame Defoe for not 'editing' better, but we certainly don't lose sympathy for or belief in Crusoe. On the contrary: Defoe's haste only increases the feeling of authenticity. The style balances neatly between the clarity of hindsight and the chaos of immediacy. Technical faults vanish beneath well-formulated virtues.

A MODERN MYTH, A PUBLISHING PHENOMENON

It is possible to 'explain' the novel in terms of Defoe's character and professional skills. But in literary terms, as a type of novel, it springs to life fully formed. No one before had written something like this: a vivid, real-seeming story of an ordinary man immersed in struggle. Afterwards, the type became popular. Defoe himself used similar techniques in his other novels. Richardson, Fielding, Smolett and Sterne all extended the range of the new novel within thirty years of Defoe's death.

Novelty alone seldom guarantees lasting success. And *Crusoe*'s success was, and is, out of all proportion with its stylistic novelty. It went through seven editions in Defoe's lifetime, and there have been over 700 since, 200 of them in English. It has been adapted into plays, an opera and several films. It inspired a whole genre of desert-island-castaway stories, so-called 'Robinsonads,' by analogy with 'The Aeneid' or 'The Iliad.' One nineteenth-century foreign spin-off, 'Swiss Family Robinson,' itself became a bestseller, and spawned its own imitators, in many languages. It has never sold as intensely as a modern bestseller – Harold Robbins has had sales of over 200 million – but in number of editions and in influence, *Crusoe* can claim to be the most successful novel ever written, in any language.

Why? An explanation of success on this scale owes only so much to technique and content. *Crusoe* touches something far more fundamental in the human psyche. It is the stuff of dream and fear and myth. Authors now constantly search for settings that allow conflict and character to emerge in raw simplicity. The struggle for survival is the most fundamental of human stories: a man alone, with only a remote chance of living and escaping. Settings for such stories are rare: an oasis, a desert march, a distant planet, a submarine. None, though, have quite the appeal of a desert island, and Defoe was the first to see it.

In this delightful yet frightening place, Crusoe becomes a universal 'I,' stripped of the usual supports of family and friends. There looms the fearful prospect of a lonely, painful death. Will I survive? Am I up to it? Yes, indeed. How pleasant, how flattering, how very reassuring to know that I can rise to the challenge, and by ingenuity, force of character and heroic labour survive, remake an image of the world I know, and escape! These are basic, simple, mythic issues.

Such subjects are by their nature rare. They are also extremely hard to capture in narrative form, especially a complex, involved narrative. Defoe struck gold. Understandably, he tried to repeat the trick, but failed. What Defoe missed in his two sequels, and what readers constantly derive from the book itself is that rare combination of an archetypal subject with a thematic complexity neatly carried by a simple, vivid story. That is something few manage, and that alone would make *Crusoe* extraordinary. The book's literary significance as 'the first great English novel' and its international success make it a wonder.

JOHN MAN

NOTE ON THE TEXT

Robinson Crusoe was published on 25 April, 1719. Three more editions appeared the same year, and another three before Defoe's death in 1731. Each edition had its own minor changes, mainly in spelling, punctuation, capitalisation and one-word alterations, amounting to some 14,000 in all. All, however, seem to have been made by printers and none by the author.

This edition, based on the first, retains a number of archaic features – haphazard spelling and capitalisation – as a reflection of Defoe's hasty, conversational style and of the time. (The first dictionary, by Dr Samuel Johnson, appeared only in 1755.)

THE
LIFE
AND
STRANGE SURPRIZING
ADVENTURES
OF
ROBINSON CRUSOE,
Of *YORK.* MARINER:

Who lived Eight and Twenty Years,
all alone in an un-inhabited Island on the
Coast of AMERICA, near the Mouth of
the Great River of OROONOQUE;

Having been cast on Shore by Shipwreck, wherein all the Men perished but himself.

WITH
An Account how he was at last as strangely deliver'd by PYRATES.

Written by Himself.

LONDON:
Printed for W. TAYLOR at the *Ship* in *Pater-Noster-
Row.* MDCCXIX.

THE
PREFACE.

IF ever the Story of any private Man's Adventures in the World were worth making Publick, and were acceptable when Publish'd, the Editor of this Account thinks this will be so.

The Wonders of this Man's Life exceed all that (he thinks) is to be found extant; the Life of one Man being scarce capable of a greater Variety.

The Story is told with Modesty, with Seriousness, and with a religious Application of Events to the Uses to which wise Men always

apply

The Preface.

apply them (viz.) to the Instruction of others by this Example, and to justify and honour the Wisdom of Providence in all the Variety of our Circumstances, let them happen how they will.

The Editor believes the thing to be a just History of Fact; neither is there any Appearance of Fiction in it: And however thinks, because all such things are dispatch'd, that the Improvement of it, as well to the Diversion, as to the Instruction of the Reader, will be the same; and as such, he thinks, without farther Compliment to the World, he does them o great Service in the Publication.

The Life and
Strange Surprizing
Adventures of
Robinson Crusoe,
of York, Mariner

THE LIFE AND STRANGE
SURPRIZING ADVENTURES OF ROBINSON CRUSOE,
OF YORK, MARINER

I was born in the year 1632, in the city of York, of a good family, tho' not of that country, my father being a foreigner of Bremen, who settled first at Hull. He got a good estate by merchandise, and leaving off his trade lived afterward at York, from whence he had married my mother, whose relations were named Robinson, a very good family, in that country, and from whom I was called Robinson Kreutznaer; but by the usual corruption of words in England, we are now called, nay, we call our selves and write our name, Crusoe, and so my companions always call'd me.

I had two elder brothers, one of which was lieutenant collonel to an English regiment of foot in Flanders, formerly commanded by the famous Coll. Lockhart, and was killed at the battle near Dunkirk against the Spaniards. What became of my second brother I never knew any more than my father or mother did know what was become of me.

Being the third son of the family and not bred to any trade, my head began to be fill'd very early with rambling thoughts. My father, who was very ancient, had given me a competent share of learning, as far as house-education and a country free-school generally goes, and design'd me for the law; but I would be satisfied with nothing but going to sea, and my inclination to this led me so strongly against the will, nay, the commands of my father, and against all the entreaties and perswasions of my mother and other friends, that there seem'd to be something fatal in that propension of nature tending directly to the life of misery which was to befal me.

My father, a wise and grave man, gave me serious and excellent counsel against what he foresaw was my design. He call'd me one morning into his chamber, where he was confined by the gout, and expostulated very warmly with me upon this subject. He ask'd me what reasons more than a meer wandring inclination I had for leaving my father's house and my native country, where I might be well introduced, and had a prospect of raising my fortune by application and industry, with a life of ease and pleasure. He told me it was for men of desperate fortunes on one hand, or of aspiring, superior fortune on the other, who went abroad upon adventures, to rise by enterprise, and make themselves famous in undertakings of a nature out of the common road; that these things were all either too far above me, or too far below me; that mine was the middle state, or what might be called the upper station of low life, which he had found by long experience was the best state in the world, the most suited to human happiness, not exposed to the miseries and hardships, the labour and sufferings of the mechanick part of mankind, and not embarass'd with the pride, luxury, ambition, and envy of the upper part of mankind. He told me I might judge of the happiness of this state by this one thing, viz. that this was the state of life which all other people envied, that kings have frequently lamented the miserable consequences of being born to great things, and wish'd they had been placed in the middle of the two extremes, between the mean and the great; that the wise man* gave his testimony to this as the just standard of true felicity, when he prayed to have neither poverty or riches.

He bid me observe it, and I should always find, that the calamities of life were shared among the upper and lower part of mankind; but that the middle station had the fewest disasters, and was not expos'd to so many vicissitudes as the higher or lower part of mankind; nay, they were not subjected to so many distempers and uneasinesses, either of body or mind, as those were who, by vicious living, luxury, and extravagancies on one hand, or by hard labour, want of necessaries, and mean or insufficient diet on the other hand, bring distempers upon themselves by the natural consequences of their way of living; that the middle station of life was calculated for all kinds of vertues and all kinds of enjoyments; that peace and plenty were the hand-maids of a middle fortune; that temperance, moderation, quietness, health, society, all agreeable diversions, and all desirable pleasures, were the blessings attending the middle station of life; that this way men went silently and smoothly thro' the world, and comfortably out of it, not embarass'd with the labours of the hands or of the head, not sold to the life of slavery for daily bread, or harrast with perplex'd circumstances, which rob the soul of peace, and the body of rest; not enrag'd with the passion of envy, or secret burning lust of ambition for great things; but in easy circumstances sliding gently thro' the world, and sensibly tasting the sweets of living without the bitter, feeling that they are happy, and learning by every day's experience to know it more sensibly.

After this, he press'd me earnestly, and in the most affectionate manner, not to play the young man, not to precipitate my self into miseries which nature and the station of life I was born in seem'd to have provided against; that I was under no necessity of seeking my bread; that he would do well for me and endeavour to enter me fairly into the station of life which he had been just recommending to me; and that if I was not very easy and happy in the world, it must be my meer* fate or fault that must hinder it, and that he should have nothing to answer for, having thus discharg'd his duty in warning me against measures which he knew would be to my hurt: in a word, that as he would do very kind things for me if I would stay and settle at home as he directed, so he would not have so much hand in my misfortunes as to give me any encouragement to go away: and to close all, he told me I had my elder brother for an example, to whom he had used the same earnest perswasions to keep him from going into the Low Country wars, but could not prevail, his young desires prompting him to run into the army, where he was kill'd; and tho' he said he would not cease to pray for me, yet he would venture to say to me, that if I did take this foolish step, God would not bless me, and I would have leisure hereafter to reflect upon having neglected his counsel when there might be none to assist in my recovery.

I observed in this last part of his discourse, which was truly prophetick, tho' I suppose my father did not know it to be so himself; I say, I observed the tears run down his face very plentifully, and especially when he spoke of my brother who was kill'd; and that when he spoke of my having leisure to repent, and none to assist me, he was so mov'd that he broke off the discourse, and told me his heart was so full he could say no more to me.

I was sincerely affected by this discourse, as indeed who could be otherwise? and I resolv'd not to think of going abroad any more, but to settle at home according to my father's desire. But alas! a few days wore it all off; and in short, to prevent any of my father's farther importunities, in a few weeks after, I resolv'd to run quite away from him. However, I did not act so hastily neither as my first heat of resolution prompted, but I took my mother, at a time when I thought her a little pleasanter than ordinary, and told her that my thoughts were so entirely bent upon seeing the world, that I should never settle to any thing with resolution enough to go through with it, and my father had better give me his consent than force me to go without it; that I was now eighteen years old, which was too late to go apprentice to a trade, or clerk to an attorney; that I was sure if I did, I should never serve out my time, and I should certainly run away from my master before my time was out, and go to sea; and if she would speak to my father to let me go but one voyage abroad, if I came home again and did not like it, I would go no more, and I would promise by a double diligence to recover that time I had lost.

This put my mother into a great passion. She told me she knew it would be to no purpose to speak to my father upon any such subject; that he knew too well what was my interest to give his consent to any thing so much for my hurt, and that she wondered how I could think of any such thing after such a discourse as I had had with my father, and such kind and tender expressions as she knew my father had us'd to me; and that in short, if I would ruine my self there was no help for me; but I might depend I should never have their consent to it: that for her part she would not have so much hand in my destruction; and I should never have it to say, that my mother was willing when my father was not.

Tho' my mother refused to move it to my father, yet as I have heard afterwards, she reported all the discourse to him, and that my father, after shewing a great concern at it, said to her with a sigh, 'That boy might be happy if he would stay at home, but if he goes abroad he will be the miserablest wretch that was ever born: I can give no consent to it.'

It was not till almost a year after this that I broke loose, tho' in the mean time I continued obstinately deaf to all proposals of settling to business, and frequently expostulating with my father and mother, about their being so positively determin'd against what they knew my inclinations prompted me to. But being one day at Hull, where I went casually, and without any purpose of making an elopement that time; but I say, being there, and one of my companions being going by sea to London in his father's ship, and prompting me to go with them, with the common allurement of seafaring men, viz. that it should cost me nothing for my passage, I consulted neither father or mother any more, nor so much as sent them word of it; but leaving them to hear of it as they might, without asking God's blessing, or my father's, without any consideration of circumstances or consequences, and in an ill hour, God knows, on the first of September 1651 I went on board a ship bound for London; never any young adventurer's misfortunes, I believe, began sooner, or continued longer, than mine. The ship was no sooner gotten out of the Humber, but the wind began to blow and the waves to rise in a most frightful manner; and as I had never been at sea before, I was most inexpressibly sick in body and terrify'd in my mind. I began now seriously to reflect upon what I had done, and how justly I was overtaken by the judgment of Heaven for my wicked leaving my father's house, and abandoning my duty; all the good counsel of my parents, my father's tears and my mother's entreaties, came now fresh into my mind; and my conscience, which was not yet come to the pitch of hardness to which it has been since, reproach'd me with the contempt of advice, and the breach of my duty to God and my father.

All this while the storm encreas'd, and the sea, which I had never been upon before, went very high, tho' nothing like what I have seen many times since; no, nor like what I saw a few days after: but it was enough to affect me then, who was but a young sailor, and had never known any thing of the matter. I expected every wave would have swallowed us up, and that every time the ship fell down, as I thought, in the trough or hollow of the sea, we should never rise more; and in this agony of mind I made many vows and resolutions, that if it would please God here to spare my life this one voyage, if ever I got once my foot upon dry land again, I would go directly home to my father, and never set it into a ship again while I liv'd; that I would take his advice, and never run my self into such miseries as these any more. Now I saw plainly the goodness of his observations about the middle station of life, how easy, how comfortably he had liv'd all his days, and never had been expos'd to tempests at sea or troubles on shore; and I resolv'd that I would, like a true repenting prodigal, go home to my father.

These wise and sober thoughts continued all the while the storm continued, and indeed some time after; but the next day the wind was abated and the sea calmer, and I began to be a little inur'd to it. However, I was very grave for all that day, being also a little sea-sick still; but towards night the weather clear'd up, the wind was quite over, and a charming fine evening follow'd; the sun went down perfectly clear and rose so the next morning; and having little or no wind and a smooth sea, the sun shining upon it, the sight was, as I thought, the most delightful that ever I saw.

I had slept well in the night, and was now no more sea-sick but very chearful, looking with wonder upon the sea that was so rough and terrible the day before, and could be so calm and so pleasant in so little time after. And now, least my good resolutions should continue, my companion, who had indeed entic'd me away, comes to me. 'Well, Bob,' says he, clapping me on the shoulder, 'how do you do after it? I warrant you were frighted, wa'n't you, last night, when it blew but a cap full of wind?' 'A cap full d' you call it?' said I, ' 'twas a terrible storm.' 'A storm, you fool, you,' replies he, 'do you call that a storm? Why, it was nothing at all; give us but a good ship and sea room, and we think nothing of such a squall of wind as that; but you're but a fresh water sailor, Bob; come, let us make a bowl of punch and we'll forget all that; d'ye see what charming weather 'tis now?' To make short this sad part of my story, we went the old way of all sailors, the punch was made, and I was made drunk with it, and in that one night's wickedness I drowned all my repentance, all my reflections upon my past conduct, and all my resolutions for my future. In a word, as the sea was returned to its smoothness of surface and settled calmness by the abatement of that storm, so the hurry of my thoughts being over, my fears and apprehensions of being swallow'd up by the sea being forgotten, and the current of my former desires return'd, I entirely forgot the vows and promises that I made in my distress. I found indeed some intervals of reflection, and the serious thoughts did, as it were, endeavour to return again sometimes, but I shook them off, and rouz'd my self from them as it were from a distemper, and applying my self to drink and company, soon mastered the return of those fits, for so I call'd them, and I had in five or six days got as compleat a victory over conscience as any young fellow that resolv'd not to be troubled with it could desire. But I was to have another trial for it still; and Providence, as in such cases generally it does, resolv'd to leave me entirely without excuse. For if I would not take this for a deliverance, the next was to be such a one as the worst and most harden'd wretch among us would confess both the danger and the mercy.

The sixth day of our being at sea we came into Yarmouth roads;* the wind having been contrary and the weather calm, we had made but little way since the storm. Here we were obliged to come to an anchor, and here we lay, the wind continuing contrary, viz. at south-west, for seven or eight days, during which time a great many ships from Newcastle came into the same roads, as the common harbour where the ships might wait for a wind for the river.

We had not, however, rid here so long, but should have tided it up the river, but that the wind blew too fresh, and, after we had lain four or five days, blew very hard. However, the roads being reckoned as good as a harbour, the anchorage good, and our ground-tackle very strong, our men were unconcerned, and not in the least apprehensive of danger, but spent the time in rest and mirth, after the manner of the sea; but the eighth day in the morning, the wind increased, and we had all hands at work to strike our top-masts and make every thing snug and close, that the ship might ride as easy as possible. By noon the sea went very high indeed, and our ship rid forecastle in, shipp'd several seas, and we thought once or twice our anchor had come home; upon which our master order'd out the sheet anchor;* to that we rode with two anchors a-head, and the cables vered out to the better end.*

By this time it blew a terrible storm indeed, and now I began to see terror and amazement in the faces even of the seamen themselves. The master, tho' vigilant to the business of preserving the ship, yet as he went in and out of his cabbin by me, I could hear him softly to himself say several times, 'Lord, be merciful to us, we shall be all lost, we shall be all undone'; and the like. During these first hurries I was stupid, lying still in my cabbin, which was in the steerage, and cannot describe my temper. I could ill re-assume the first penitence, which I had so apparently trampled upon and harden'd my self against: I thought the bitterness of death had been past, and that this would be nothing too, like the first. But when the master himself came by me, as I said just now, and said we should be all lost, I was dreadfully frighted. I got up out of my cabbin, and look'd out; but such a dismal sight I never saw: the sea went mountains high, and broke upon us every three or four minutes; when I could look about, I could see nothing but distress round us. Two ships that rid near us we found had cut their masts by the board, being deep loaden; and our men cry'd out that a ship which rid about a mile a-head of us was foundered. Two more ships, being driven from their anchors, were run out of the roads to sea at all adventures, and that with not a mast standing. The light ships fared the best, as not so much labouring in the sea; but two or three of them drove, and came close by us, running away with only their sprit-sail out before the wind.

Towards evening the mate and boat-swain begg'd the master of our ship to let them cut away the foremast, which he was very unwilling to: but the boat-swain protesting to him that if he did not, the ship would founder, he consented; and when they had cut away the foremast, the main-mast stood so loose, and shook the ship so much, they were obliged to cut her away also, and make a clear deck.

Any one may judge what a condition I must be in at all this, who was but a young sailor, and who had been in such a fright before at but a little. But if I can express at this distance the thoughts I had about me at that time, I was in tenfold more horror of mind upon account of my former convictions, and the having returned from them to the resolutions I had wickedly taken at first, than I was at death it self; and these, added to the terror of the storm, put me into such a condition, that I can by no words describe it. But the worst was not come yet; the storm continued with such fury, that the seamen themselves acknowledged they had never known a worse. We had a good ship, but she was deep loaden, and wallowed in the sea, that the seamen every now and then cried out she would founder. It was my advantage in one respect, and I did not know what they meant by 'founder' till I enquir'd. However, the storm was so violent, that I saw what is not often seen, the master, the boat-swain, and some others more sensible than the rest, at their prayers, and expecting every moment when the ship would go to the bottom. In the middle of the night, and under all the rest of our distresses, one of the men that had been down on purpose to see, cried out we had sprung a leak; another said there was four foot water in the hold. Then all hands were called to the pump. At that very word my heart, as I thought, died within me, and I fell backwards upon the side of my bed where I sat, into the cabbin. However, the men roused me, and told me that I that was able to do nothing before, was as well able to pump as another; at which I stirr'd up and went to the pump, and work'd very heartily. While this was doing, the master, seeing some light colliers, who not able to ride out the storm, were oblig'd to slip and run away to sea and would come near us, ordered to fire a gun as a signal of distress. I, who knew nothing what that meant, was so surprised that I thought the ship had broke, or some dreadful thing had happen'd. In a word, I was so surprised that I fell down in a swoon. As this was a time when every body had his own life to think of, no body minded me, or what was become of me; but another man stept up to the pump, and thrusting me aside with his foot, let me lye, thinking I had been dead; and it was a great while before I came to my self.

We work'd on, but the water encreasing in the hold, it was apparent that the ship would founder, and tho' the storm began to abate a little, yet as it was not possible she could swim till we might run into a port, so the master continued firing guns for help; and a light ship who had rid it out just ahead of us ventured a boat out to help us. It was with the utmost hazard the boat came near us, but it was impossible for us to get on board, or for the boat to lie near the ship side, till at last, the men rowing very heartily and venturing their lives to save ours, our men cast them a rope over the stern with a buoy to it, and then vered it out a great length, which they after great labour and hazard took hold of, and we hawl'd them close under our stern and got all into their boat. It was to no purpose for them or us after we were in the boat to think of reaching to their own ship, so all agreed to let her drive and only to pull her in towards shore as much as we could, and our master promised them that if the boat was stav'd upon shore he would make it good to their master; so partly rowing and partly driving, our boat went away to the norward sloaping towards the shore almost as far as Winterton Ness.*

We were not much more than a quarter of an hour out of our ship but we saw her sink, and then I understood for the first time what was meant by a ship foundering in the sea; I must acknowledge I had hardly eyes to look up when the seamen told me she was sinking; for from that moment they rather put me into the boat than that I might be said to go in, my heart was as it were dead within me, partly with fright, partly with horror of mind and the thoughts of what was yet before me.

While we were in this condition, the men yet labouring at the oar to bring the boat near the shore, we could see, when, our boat mounting the waves, we were able to see the shore, a great many people running along the shore to assist us when we should come near, but we made but slow way towards the shore, nor were we able to reach the shore, till being past the light-house at Winterton, the shore falls off to the westward towards Cromer, and so the land broke off a little the violence of the wind. Here we got in, and, tho' not without much difficulty, got all safe on shore, and walk'd afterwards on foot to Yarmouth, where, as unfortunate men, we were used with great humanity as well by the magistrates of the town, who assign'd us good quarters, as by particular merchants and owners of ships, and had money given us sufficient to carry us either to London or back to Hull, as we thought fit.

Had I now had the sense to have gone back to Hull, and have gone home, I had been happy, and my father, an emblem of our Blessed Saviour's parable, had even kill'd the fatted calf for me; for hearing the ship I went away in was cast away in Yarmouth road, it was a great while before he had any assurance that I was not drown'd.

But my ill fate push'd me on now with an obstinacy that nothing could resist; and tho' I had several times loud calls from my reason and my more composed judgment to go home, yet I had no power to do it. I know not what to call this, nor will I urge that it is a secret overruling decree that hurries us on to be the instruments of our own destruction, even tho' it be before us, and that we rush upon it with our eyes open. Certainly nothing but some such decreed unavoidable misery attending, and which it was impossible for me to escape, could have push'd me forward against the calm reasonings and perswasions of my most retired thoughts, and against two such visible instructions as I had met with in my first attempt.

My comrade, who had help'd to harden me before, and who was the master's son, was now less forward than I; the first time he spoke to me after we were at Yarmouth, which was not till two or three days, for we were separated in the town to several quarters; I say, the first time he saw me, it appear'd his tone was alter'd, and looking very melancholy and shaking his head, ask'd me how I did, and telling his father who I was, and how I had come this voyage only for a trial in order to go farther abroad; his father turning to me with a very grave and concern'd tone, 'Young man,' says he, 'you ought never to go to sea any more, you ought to take this for a plain and visible token that you are not to be a seafaring man.' 'Why, sir,' said I, 'will you go to sea no more?' 'That is another case,' said he, 'it is my calling, and therefore my duty; but as you made this voyage for a trial, you see what a taste Heaven has given you of what you are to expect if you persist; perhaps this is all befallen us on your account, like Jonah in the ship of Tarshish. Pray,' continues he, 'what are you? and on what account did you go to sea?' Upon that I told him some of my story; at the end of which he burst out with a strange kind of passion. 'What had I done,' says he, 'that such an unhappy wretch should come into my ship? I would not set my foot in the same ship with thee again for a thousand pounds.' This indeed was, as I said, an excursion of his spirits which were yet agitated by the sense of his loss, and was farther than he could have authority to go. However he afterwards talk'd very gravely to me, exhorted me to go back to my father, and not tempt Providence to my ruine; told me I might see a visible hand of Heaven against me, 'and, young man,' said he, 'depend upon it, if you do not go back, where-ever you go, you will meet with nothing but disasters and disappointments till your father's words are fulfilled upon you.'

We parted soon after, for I made him little answer, and I saw him no more; which way he went, I know not. As for me, having some money in my pocket, I travelled to London by land; and there, as well as on the road, had many struggles with my self, what course of life I should take, and whether I should go home or go to sea.

As to going home, shame opposed the best motions that offered to my thoughts; and it immediately occurr'd to me how I should be laugh'd at among the neighbours, and should be asham'd to see, not my father and mother only, but even every body clse; from whence I have since often observed, how incongruous and irrational the common temper of mankind is, especially of youth, to that reason which ought to guide them in such cases, viz. that they are not asham'd to sin, and yet are asham'd to repent; not asham'd of the action for which they ought justly to be esteemed fools, but are asham'd of the returning, which only can make them be esteem'd wise men.

In this state of life, however, I remained some time, uncertain what measures to take, and what course of life to lead. An irresistible reluctance continu'd to going home; and as I stay'd awhile, the remembrance of the distress I had been in wore off; and as that abated the little motion I had in my desires to a return wore off with it, till at last I quite lay'd aside the thoughts of it, and lookt out for a voyage.

That evil influence which carryed me first away from my father's house, that hurried me into the wild and indigested notion of raising my fortune, and that imprest those conceits so forcibly upon me, as to make me deaf to all good advice, and to the entreaties and even command of my father; I say the same influence, whatever it was, presented the most unfortunate of all enterprises to my view; and I went on board a vessel bound to the coast of Africa; or, as our sailors vulgarly call it, a voyage to Guinea.

It was my great misfortune that in all these adventures I did not ship my self as a sailor; whereby, tho' I might indeed have workt a little harder than ordinary, yet at the same time I had learn'd the duty and office of a fore-mast man; and in time might have quallified my self for a mate or lieutenant, if not for a master. But as it was always my fate to choose for the worse, so I did here; for having money in my pocket, and good cloaths upon my back, I would always go on board in the habit of a gentleman; and so I neither had any business in the ship, or learn'd to do any.

It was my lot first of all to fall into pretty good company in London, which does not always happen to such loose and unguided young fellows as I then was; the devil generally not omitting to lay some snare for them very early; but it was not so with me. I first fell acquainted with the master of a ship who had been on the coast of Guinea, and who, having had very good success there, was resolved to go again; and who, taking a fancy to my conversation, which was not at all disagreeable at that time, hearing me say I had a mind to see the world, told me if I wou'd go the voyage with him I should be at no expence; I should be his mess-mate and his companion, and if I could carry any thing with me, I should have all the advantage of it that the trade would admit; and perhaps I might meet with some encouragement.

I embrac'd the offer, and entring into a strict friendship with this captain, who was an honest and plain-dealing man, I went the voyage with him, and carried a small adventure with me, which by the disinterested honesty of my friend the captain I increased very considerably; for I carried about 40l. in such toys and trifles as the captain directed me to buy. This 40l. I had mustered together by the assistance of some of my relations whom I corresponded with, and who, I believe, got my father, or at least my mother, to contribute so much as that to my first adventure.

This was the only voyage which I may say was successful in all my adventures, and which I owe to the integrity and honesty of my friend the captain, under whom also I got a competent knowledge of the mathematicks and rules of navigation, learn'd how to keep an account of the ship's course, take an observation, and in short, to understand some things that were needful to be understood by a sailor: for, as he took delight to introduce me, I took delight to learn; and, in a word, this voyage made me both a sailor and a merchant; for I brought home 5 pounds 9 ounces of gold dust for my adventure, which yielded me in London at my return almost 300*l.*, and this fill'd me with those aspiring thoughts which have since so compleated my ruin.

Yet even in this voyage I had my misfortunes too; particularly, that I was continually sick, being thrown into a violent calenture* by the excessive heat of the climate; our principal trading being upon the coast, from the latitude of 15 degrees north even to the line it self.

I was now set up for a Guiney trader; and my friend, to my great misfortune, dying soon after his arrival, I resolved to go the same voyage again, and I embark'd in the same vessel with one who was his mate in the former voyage, and had now got the command of the ship. This was the unhappiest voyage that ever man made; for tho' I did not carry quite 100*l.* of my new gain'd wealth, so that I had 200 left, and which I lodg'd with my friend's widow, who was very just to me, yet I fell into terrible misfortunes in this voyage; and the first was this, viz: Our ship making her course towards the Canary Islands, or rather between those islands and the African shore, was surprised in the grey of the morning by a Turkish rover of Sallee,* who gave chase to us with all the sail she could make. We crowded also as much canvass as our yards would spread, or our masts carry, to have got clear; but finding the pirate gain'd upon us and would certainly come up with us in a few hours, we prepar'd to fight; our ship having 12 guns, and the rogue 18. About three in the afternoon he came up with us, and bringing to by mistake, just athwart our quarter, instead of athwart our stern, as he intended, we brought 8 of our guns to bear on that side, and pour'd in a broadside upon him, which made him sheer off again, after returning our fire, and pouring in also his small shot from near 200 men which he had on board. However, we had not a man touch'd, all our men keeping close. He prepar'd to attack us again, and we to defend our selves; but laying us on board the next time upon our other quarter, he entred 60 men upon our decks, who immediately fell to cutting and hacking the decks and rigging. We ply'd them with small-shot, half-pikes, powder-chests, and such like, and clear'd our deck of them twice. However, to cut short this melancholly part of our story, our ship being disabled, and three of our men kill'd, and eight wounded, we were obliged to yield, and were carry'd all prisoners into Sallee, a port belonging to the Moors.

The usage I had there was not so dreadful as at first I apprehended, nor was I carried up the country to the emperor's court, as the rest of our men were, but was kept by the captain of the rover as his proper prize, and made his slave, being young and nimble and fit for his business. At this surprising change of my circumstances from a merchant to a miserable slave, I was perfectly overwhelmed; and now I look'd back upon my father's prophetick discourse to me, that I should be miserable, and have none to relieve me, which I thought was now so effectually brought to pass that it could not be worse; that now the hand of Heaven had overtaken me, and I was undone without redemption. But alas! this was but a taste of the misery I was to go thro', as will appear in the sequel of this story.

As my new patron or master had taken me home to his house, so I was in hopes that he would take me with him when he went to sea again, believing that it would some time or other be his fate to be taken by a Spanish or Portugal man of war; and that then I should be set at liberty. But this hope of mine was soon taken away; for when he went to sea, he left me on shoar to look after his little garden, and do the common drudgery of slaves about his house; and when he came home again from his cruise, he order'd me to lye in the cabbin and look after the ship.

Here I meditated nothing but my escape, and what method I might take to effect it, but found no way that had the least probability in it. Nothing presented to make the supposition of it rational; for I had no body to communicate it to, that would embark with me; no fellow-slave, no Englishman, Irishman, or Scotsman there but my self; so that for two years, tho' I often pleased my self with the imagination, yet I never had the least encouraging prospect of putting it in practice.

After about two years an odd circumstance presented it self, which put the old thought of making some attempt for my liberty again in my head. My patron lying at home longer than usual, without fitting out his ship, which, as I heard, was for want of money, he used constantly, once or twice a week, sometimes oftener, if the weather was fair, to take the ship's pinnace, and go out into the road a-fishing; and as he always took me and a young Maresco* with him to row the boat, we made him very merry, and

I prov'd very dexterous in catching fish; insomuch that sometimes he would send me with a Moor, one of his kinsmen, and the youth, the Maresco as they call'd him, to catch a dish of fish for him.

It happen'd one time, that going a fishing in a stark calm morning, a fog rose so thick, that tho' we were not half a league from the shoar, we lost sight of it; and rowing we knew not whither or which way, we labour'd all day and all the next night, and when the morning came we found we had pull'd off to sea instead of pulling in for the shore, and that we were at least two leagues from the shoar. However, we got well in again, tho' with a great deal of labour, and some danger; for the wind began to blow pretty fresh in the morning; but particularly we were all very hungry.

But our patron, warn'd by this disaster, resolved to take more care of himself for the future; and having lying by him the long-boat of our English ship they had taken, he resolved he would not go a fishing any more without a compass and some provision; so he ordered the carpenter of his ship, who also was an English slave, to build a little state-room or cabin in the middle of the long boat, like that of a barge, with a place to stand behind it to steer and hale home the main-sheet, and room before for a hand or two to stand and work the sails; she sail'd with that we call a shoulder of mutton sail; and the boom gib'd over the top of the cabbin, which lay very snug and low, and had in it room for him to lye, with a slave or two, and a table to eat on, with some small lockers to put in some bottles of such liquor as he thought fit to drink; particularly his bread, rice, and coffee.

We went frequently out with this boat a fishing, and as I was most dextrous to catch fish for him, he never went without me. It happen'd that he had appointed to go out in this boat, either for pleasure or for fish, with two or three Moors of some distinction in that place, and for whom he had provided extraordinarily; and had therefore sent on board the boat, over night, a larger store of provisions than ordinary; and had order'd me to get ready three fuzees with powder and shot, which were on board his ship; for that they design'd some sport of fowling as well as fishing.

I got all things ready as he had directed, and waited the next morning with the boat, washed clean, her antient* and pendants out, and every thing to accommodate his guests; when by and by my patroon came on board alone, and told me his guests had put off going, upon some business that fell out, and order'd me with the man and boy, as usual, to go out with the boat and catch them some fish, for that his friends were to sup at his house; and commanded that as soon as I had got some fish I should bring it home to his house; all which I prepar'd to do.

This moment my former notions of deliverance darted into my thoughts, for now I found I was like to have a little ship at my command; and my master being gone, I prepar'd to furnish my self, not for a fishing business, but for a voyage; tho' I knew not, neither did I so much as consider, whither I should steer; for any where to get out of that place was my way.

My first contrivance was to make a pretence to speak to this Moor, to get something for our subsistance on board; for I told him we must not presume to eat of our patroon's bread; he said, that was true; so he brought a large basket of rusk or bisket of their kind, and three jarrs with fresh water into the boat; I knew where my patroon's case of bottles stood, which it was evident by the make were taken out of some English prize; and I convey'd them into the boat while the Moor was on shoar, as if they had been there before, for our master: I convey'd also a great lump of bees-wax into the boat, which weighed above half a hundred weight, with a parcel of twine or thread, a hatchet, a saw and a hammer, all which were of great use to us afterwards; especially the wax to make candles. Another trick I try'd upon him, which he innocently came into also; his name was Ismael, who they call Muly or Moely; so I call'd to him, 'Moely,' said I, 'our patroon's guns are on board the boat, can you not get a little powder and shot, it may be we may kill some alcamies (a fowl like our curlieus) for our selves, for I know he keeps the gunner's stores in the ship?' 'Yes,' says he, 'I'll bring some,' and accordingly he brought a great leather pouch which held about a pound and half of powder, or rather more; and another with shot, that had five or six pound, with some bullets; and put all into the boat. At the same time I had found some powder of my master's in the great cabbin, with which I fill'd one of the large bottles in the case, which was almost empty; pouring what was in it into another: and thus furnished with every thing needful, we sail'd out of the port to fish. The castle which is at the entrance of the port knew who we were, and took no notice of us; and we were not above a mile out of the port before we hal'd in our sail and set us down to fish. The wind blew from the N.N.E., which was contrary to my desire; for had it blown southerly I had been sure to have made the coast of Spain, and at last reacht to the bay of Cadiz; but my resolutions were, blow which way it would, I would be gone from that horrid place where I was, and leave the rest to fate.

After we had fisht some time and catcht nothing, for when I had fish on my hook, I would not pull them up, that he might not see them; I said to the Moor, 'This will not do, our master will not be thus serv'd, we must stand farther off.' He, thinking no harm, agreed, and being in the head of the boat set the sails; and as I had the helm I run the boat out a league farther, and then brought her too as if I would fish; when giving the boy the helm, I stept forward to where the Moor was, and making as if I stoopt for something behind him, I took him by surprise with my arm under his twist,* and tost him clear over-board into the sea; he rose immediately, for he swam like a cork, and call'd to me, begg'd to be taken in, told me he would go all over the world with me; he swam so strong after the boat that he would have reacht me very quickly, there being but little wind; upon which I stept into the cabbin, and fetching one of the fowling-pieces, I presented it at him, and told him I had done him no hurt, and if he would be quiet I would do him none; 'but,' said I, 'you swim well enough to reach to the shoar, and the sea is calm, make the best of your way to shoar and I will do you no harm, but if you come near the boat I'll shoot you thro' the head; for I am resolved to have my liberty'; so he turn'd himself about and swam for the shoar, and I make no doubt but he reacht it with ease, for he was an excellent swimmer.

I could ha' been content to ha' taken this Moor with me, and ha' drown'd the boy, but there was no venturing to trust him. When he was gone I turn'd to the boy, who they call'd Xury, and said to him, 'Xury, if you will be faithful to me I'll make you a great man, but if you will not stroak your face to be true to me,' that is, swear by Mahomet and his father's beard, 'I must throw you into the sea too.' The boy smil'd in my face and spoke so innocently that I could not mistrust him; and swore to be faithful to me, and go all over the world with me.

While I was in view of the Moor that was swimming, I stood out directly to sea with the boat, rather stretching to windward, that they might think me gone towards the straits-mouth (as indeed any one that had been in their wits must ha' been supposed to do), for who would ha' suppos'd we were saild on to the southward to the truly Barbarian coast, where whole nations of negroes were sure to surround us with their canoes, and destroy us; where we could ne'er once go on shoar but we should be devour'd by savage beasts, or more merciless savages of humane kind?

But as soon as it grew dusk in the evening, I chang'd my course, and steer'd directly south and by east, bending my course a little toward the east, that I might keep in with the shoar; and having a fair fresh gale of wind, and a smooth quiet sea, I made such sail that I believe by the next day at three a clock in the afternoon, when I first made the land, I could not be less than 150 miles south of Sallee; quite beyond the Emperor of Morocco's dominions, or indeed of any other king thereabouts, for we saw no people.

Yet such was the fright I had taken at the Moors, and the dreadful apprehensions I had of falling into their hands, that I would not stop, or go on shoar, or come to an anchor; the wind continuing fair, 'till I had sail'd in that manner five days; and then the wind shifting to the southward, I concluded also that if any of our vessels were in chase of me, they also would now give over; so I ventur'd to make to the coast, and came to an anchor in the mouth of a little river, I knew not what, or where; neither what latitude, what country, what nations, or what river: I neither saw, or desir'd to see, any people, the principal thing I wanted was fresh water. We came into this creek in the evening, resolving to swim on shoar as soon as it was dark, and discover the country; but as soon as it was quite dark, we heard such dreadful noises of the barking, roaring, and howling of wild creatures, of we knew not what kinds, that the poor boy was ready to die with fear, and beg'd of me not to go on shoar till day. 'Well, Xury,' said I, 'then I won't, but it may be we may see men by day, who will be as bad to us as those lyons.' 'Then we give them the shoot gun,' says Xury, laughing, 'make them run wey'; such English Xury spoke by conversing among us slaves. However, I was glad to see the boy so cheerful, and I gave him a dram (out of our patroon's case of bottles) to chear him up. After all, Xury's advice was good, and I took it. We dropt our little anchor and lay still at night; I say still, for we slept none! for in two or three hours we saw vast great creatures (we knew not what to call them) of many sorts, come down to the sea-shoar and run into the water, wallowing and washing themselves for the pleasure of cooling themselves; and they made such hideous howlings and yellings, that I never indeed heard the like.

Xury was dreadfully frighted, and indeed so was I too; but we were both more frighted when we heard one of these mighty creatures come swimming towards our boat; we could not see him, but we might hear him by his blowing to be a monstrous, huge, and furious beast; Xury said it was a lyon, and it might be so for ought I know; but poor Xury cryed to me to weigh anchor and row away. 'No,' says I, 'Xury, we can slip our cable with the buoy to it and go off to sea, they cannot follow us far.' I had no sooner said so, but I perceiv'd the creature (whatever it was) within two oars' length, which something surprized me; however, I immediately stept to the cabbin-door, and taking up my gun fir'd at him, upon which he immediately turn'd about and swam towards the shoar again.

But it is impossible to describe the horrible noises, and hideous cryes and howlings, that were raised, as well upon the edge of the shoar as higher within the country, upon the noise or report of the gun, a thing I have some reason to believe those creatures had never heard before. This convinc'd me that there was no going on shoar for us in the night upon that coast, and how to venture on shoar in the day was another question too; for to have fallen into the hands of any of the savages, had been as bad as to have fallen into the hands of lyons and tygers;* at least we were equally apprehensive of the danger of it.

Be that as it would, we were oblig'd to go on shoar somewhere or other for water, for we had not a pint left in the boat; when or where to get to it was the point. Xury said, if I would let him go on shoar with one of the jarrs, he would find if there was any water and bring some to me. I ask'd him why he would go; why I should not go and he stay in the boat; the boy answer'd with so much affection that made me love him ever after. Says he, 'If wild mans come, they eat me, you go wey.' 'Well, Xury,' said I, 'we will both go, and if the wild mans come we will kill them, they shall eat neither of us.' So I gave Xury a piece of rusk-bread to eat and a dram out of our patroon's case of bottles which I mentioned before; and we hal'd the boat in as near the shoar as we thought was proper, and so waded on shoar, carrying nothing but our arms and two jarrs for water.

I did not care to go out of sight of the boat, fearing the coming of canoes with savages down the river; but the boy seeing a low place about a mile up the country rambled to it; and by and by I saw him come running towards me. I thought he was pursued by some savage, or frighted with some wild beast, and I run forward towards him to help him, but when I came nearer to him, I saw something hanging over his shoulders which was a creature that he had shot, like a hare but different in colour, and longer legs; however, we were very glad of it, and it was very good meat; but the great joy that poor Xury came with, was to tell me he had found good water and seen no wild mans.

But we found afterwards that we need not take such pains for water, for a little higher up the creek where we were, we found the water fresh when the tide was out, which flowed but a little way up; so we filled our jarrs and feasted on the hare we had killed, and prepared to go on our way, having seen no foot-steps of any humane creature in that part of the country.

As I had been one voyage to this coast before, I knew very well that the islands of the Canaries, and the Cape de Verd Islands also, lay not far off from the coast. But as I had no instruments to take an observation to know what latitude we were in, and did not exactly know, or at least remember, what latitude they were in, I knew not where to look for them, or when to stand off to sea towards them; otherwise I might now easily have found some of these islands. But my hope was, that if I stood along this coast till I came to that part where the English traded, I should find some of their vessels upon their usual design of trade, that would relieve and take us in.

By the best of my calculation, that place where I now was, must be that country which, lying between the Emperor of Morocco's dominions and the negro's, lies wast and uninhabited, except by wild beasts; the negroes having abandon'd it and gone farther south for fear of the Moors; and the Moors not thinking it worth inhabiting, by reason of its barrenness; and indeed both forsaking it because of the prodigious numbers of tygers, lyons, leopards, and other furious creatures which harbour there; so that the Moors use it for their hunting only, where they go like an army, two or three thousand men at a time; and indeed for near an hundred miles together upon this coast, we saw nothing but a vast uninhabited country by day, and heard nothing but howlings and roaring of wild beasts by night.

Once or twice in the day time I thought I saw the Pico of Teneriffe, being the high top of the mountain Teneriffe in the Canaries, and had a great mind to venture out in hopes of reaching thither; but having tried twice I was forced in again by contrary winds, the sea also going too high for my little vessel, so I resolved to pursue my first design and keep along the shoar.

Several times I was obliged to land for fresh water after we had left this place; and once in particular, being early in the morning, we came to an anchor under a little point of land which was pretty high, and the tide beginning to flow, we lay still to go farther in; Xury, whose eyes were more about him than it seems mine were, calls softly to me, and tells me that we had best go farther off the shoar; 'for,' says he, 'look, yonder lies a dreadful monster on the side of that hillock fast asleep.' I look'd where he pointed, and saw a dreadful monster indeed, for it was a terrible great lyon that lay on the side of the shoar, under the shade of a piece of the hill that hung as it were a little over him. 'Xury,' says I, 'you shall go on shoar and kill him.' Xury look'd frighted, and said, 'Me kill! he eat me at one mouth'; one mouthful he meant; however, I said no more to the boy, but bad him lye still, and I took our biggest gun, which was almost musquet bore, and loaded it with a good charge of powder and with two slugs, and laid it down; then I loaded another gun with two bullets, and the third, for we had three pieces, I loaded with five smaller bullets. I took the best aim I could with the first piece to have shot him into the head, but he lay so with his leg rais'd a little above his nose, that the slugs hit his leg about the knee, and broke the bone. He started up growling at first, but finding his leg broke fell down again, and then got up upon three legs and gave the most hideous roar that ever I heard. I was a little surpriz'd that I had not hit him on the head; however, I took up the second piece immediately, and tho' he began to move off, fir'd again, and shot him into the head, and had the pleasure to see him drop, and make but little noise, but lay struggling for life. Then Xury took heart, and would have me let him go on shoar. 'Well, go,' said I; so the boy jump'd into the water, and taking a little gun in one hand swam to shoar with the other hand, and coming close to the creature, put the muzzle of the piece to his ear, and shot him into the head again, which dispatch'd him quite.

This was game indeed to us, but this was no food, and I was very sorry to lose three charges of powder and shot upon a creature that was good for nothing to us. However, Xury said he would have some of him; so he comes on board, and ask'd me to give him the hatchet. 'For what, Xury?' said I. 'Me cut off his head,' said he. However, Xury could not cut off his head, but he cut off a foot and brought it with him, and it was a monstrous great one.

I bethought my self, however, that perhaps the skin of him might one way or other be of some value to us, and I resolved to take off his skin if I could. So Xury and I went to work with him; but Xury was much the better workman at it, for I knew very ill how to do it. Indeed, it took us up both the whole day, but at last we got off the hide of him, and spreading it on the top of our cabbin, the sun effectually dried it in two days' time, and it afterwards serv'd me to lye upon.

After this stop we made on to the southward continually for ten or twelve days, living very sparing on our provisions, which began to abate very much, and going no oftner into the shoar than we were oblig'd to for fresh water; my design in this was to make the river Gambia or Senegall, that is to say, any where about the Cape de Verd, where I was in hopes to meet with some European ship, and if I did not, I knew not what course I had to take, but to seek out for the islands, or perish there among the negroes. I knew that all the ships from Europe, which sail'd either to the coast or Guiney, or to Brasil, or to the East-Indies, made this cape or those islands; and in a word, I put the whole of my fortune upon this single point, either that I must meet with some ship, or must perish.

When I had pursued this resolution about ten days longer, as I have said, I began to see that the land was inhabited, and in two or three places as we sailed by, we saw people stand upon the shoar to look at us; we could also perceive they were quite black and stark-naked. I was once inclin'd to ha' gone on shoar to them; but Xury was my better councellor, and said to me, 'No go, no go'; however, I hal'd in nearer the shoar that I might talk to them, and I found they run along the shoar by me a good way; I observ'd they had no weapons in their hands, except one who had a long slender stick, which Xury said was a lance, and that they would throw them a great way with good aim; so I kept at a distance, but talk'd with them by signs as well as I could, and particularly made signs for some thing to eat. They beckon'd to me to stop my boat, and that they would fetch me some meat; upon this I lower'd the top of my sail and lay by, and two of them run up into the country, and in less than half an hour came back and brought with them two pieces of dry flesh and some corn, such as is the produce of their country, but we neither knew what the one or the other was; however, we were willing to accept it, but how to come at it was our next dispute, for I was not for venturing on shore to them, and they were as much afraid of us; but they took a safe way for us all, for they brought it to the shore and laid it down, and went and stood a great way off till we fetch'd it on board, and then came close to us again.

We made signs of thanks to them, for we had nothing to make them amends; but an opportunity offer'd that very instant to oblige them wonderfully, for while we were lying by the shore, came two mighty creatures, one pursuing the other (as we took it) with great fury, from the mountains towards the sea; whether it was the male pursuing the female, or whether they were in sport or in rage, we could not tell, any more than we could tell whether it was usual or strange, but I believe it was the latter; because in the first place, those ravenous creatures seldom appear but in the night; and in the second place, we found the people terribly frighted, especially the women. The man that had the lance or dart did not fly from them, but the rest did; however, as the two creatures ran directly into the water, they did not seem to offer to fall upon any of the negroes, but plung'd themselves into the sea and swam about as if they had come for their diversion; at last one of them began to come nearer our boat than at first I expected, but I lay ready for him, for I had loaded my gun with all possible expedition, and bad Xury load both the others; as soon as he came fairly within my reach, I fir'd, and shot him directly into the head; immediately he sunk down into the water, but rose instantly and plung'd up and down as if he was struggling for life; and so indeed he was. He immediately made to the shore, but between the wound, which was his mortal hurt, and the strangling of the water, he dyed just before he reach'd the shore.

It is impossible to express the astonishment of these poor creatures at the noise and the fire of my gun; some of them were even ready to dye for fear, and fell down as dead with the very terror. But when they saw the creature dead and sunk in the water, and that I made signs to them to come to the shore, they took heart and came to the shore and began to search for the creature. I found him by his blood staining the water, and by the help of a rope which I slung round him and gave the negroes to hawl, they drag'd him on shore, and found that it was a most curious leopard, spotted and fine to an admirable degree, and the negroes held up their hands with admiration to think what it was I had kill'd him with.

The other creature, frighted with the flash of fire and the noise of the gun, swam on shore, and ran up directly to the mountains from whence they came, nor could I at that distance know what it was. I found quickly the negroes were for eating the flesh of this creature, so I was willing to have them take it as a favour from me, which when I made signs to them that they might take him, they were very thankful for, immediately they fell to work with him, and tho' they had no knife, yet with a sharpen'd piece of wood they took off his skin as readily and much more readily than we cou'd have done with a knife; they offer'd me some of the flesh, which I declined, making as if I would give it them, but made signs for the skin, which they gave me very freely, and brought me a great deal more of their provision, which tho' I did not understand, yet I accepted; then I made signs to them for some water, and held out one of my jarrs to them, turning it bottom upward, to shew that it was empty, and that I wanted to have it filled. They call'd immediately to some of their friends, and there came two women and brought a great vessel made of earth, and burnt as I suppose in the sun; this they set down for me, as before, and I sent Xury on shore with my jarrs, and filled them all three. The women were as stark naked as the men.

I was now furnished with roots and corn, such as it was, and water, and leaving my friendly negroes, I made forward for about eleven days more without offering to go near the shoar, till I saw the land run out a great length into the sea, at about the distance of four or five leagues before me, and the sea being very calm I kept a large offing to make this point; at length, doubling the point at about two leagues from the land, I saw plainly land on the other side to seaward; then I concluded, as it was most certain indeed, that this was the Cape de Verd, and those the islands call'd from thence Cape de Verd Islands. However, they were at a great distance, and I could not well tell what I had best to do, for if I should be taken with a fresh of wind I might neither reach one or other.

In this dilemma, as I was very pensive, I stept into the cabbin and sat me down, Xury having the helm, when on a suddain the boy cry'd out, 'Master, master, a ship with a sail,' and the foolish boy was frighted out of his wits, thinking it must needs be some of his master's ships sent to pursue us, when I knew we were gotten far enough out of their reach. I jump'd out of the cabbin, and immediately saw not only the ship, but what she was, viz. that it was a Portuguese ship, and as I thought was bound to the coast of Guinea for negroes. But when I observ'd the course she steer'd, I was soon convinc'd they were bound some other way, and did not design to come any nearer to the shoar; upon which I stretch'd out to sea as much as I could, resolving to speak with them if possible.

With all the sail I could make, I found I should not be able to come in their way, but that they would be gone by, before I could make any signal to them; but after I had crowded to the utmost, and began to despair, they it seems saw me by the help of their perspective-glasses,* and that it was some European boat, which as they supposed must belong to some ship that was lost, so they shortned sail to let me come up. I was encouraged with this, and as I had my patroon's antient on board, I made a waft of it to them for a signal of distress, and fir'd a gun, both which they saw, for they told me they saw the smoke, tho' they did not hear the gun; upon these signals they very kindly brought too, and lay by for me, and in about three hours time I came up with them.

They ask'd me what I was, in Portuguese, and in Spanish, and in French, but I understood none of them; but at last a Scots sailor who was on board call'd to me, and I answer'd him, and told him I was an Englishman, that I had made my escape out of slavery from the Moors at Sallee; then they bad me come on board, and very kindly took me in, and all my goods.

It was an inexpressible joy to me, that any one will believe, that I was thus deliver'd, as I esteem'd it, from such a miserable and almost hopeless condition as I was in, and I immediately offered all I had to the captain of the ship, as a return for my deliverance; but he generously told me he would take nothing from me, but that all I had should be deliver'd safe to me when I came to the Brasils , 'for' says he, 'I have sav'd your life on no other terms than I would be glad to be saved my self, and it may one time or other be my lot to be taken up in the same condition; besides,' said he, 'when I carry you to the Brasils, so great a way from your own country, if I should take from you what you have, you will be starved there, and then I only take away that life I have given. No, no, Seignor Inglese,' says he (Mr Englishman), 'I will carry you thither in charity, and those things will help you to buy your subsistance there and your passage home again.'

As he was charitable in his proposal, so he was just in the performance to a tittle, for he ordered the seamen that none should offer to touch any thing I had; then he took every thing into his own possession, and gave me back an exact inventory of them, that I might have them, even so much as my three earthen jarrs.

As to my boat, it was a very good one, and that he saw, and told me he would buy it of me for the ship's use, and ask'd me what I would have for it. I told him he had been so generous to me in every thing, that I could not offer to make any price of the boat, but left it entirely to him, upon which he told me he would give me a note of his hand to pay me 80 pieces of eight for it at Brasil, and when it came there, if any one offer'd to give more he would make it up; he offer'd me also 60 pieces of eight more for my boy Xury, which I was loath to take, not that I was not willing to let the captain have him, but I was very loath to sell the poor boy's liberty, who had assisted me so faithfully in procuring my own. However, when I let him know my reason, he own'd it to be just, and offer'd me this medium, that he would give the boy an obligation to set him free in ten years, if he turn'd Christian; upon this, and Xury saying he was willing to go to him, I let the captain have him.

We had a very good voyage to the Brasils, and arriv'd in the Bay de Todos los Santos, or All-Saints' Bay, in about twenty-two days after. And now I was once more deliver'd from the most miserable of all conditions of life, and what to do next with my self I was now to consider.

The generous treatment the captain gave me, I can never enough remember; he would take nothing of me for my passage, gave me twenty ducats for the leopard's skin, and forty for the lyon's skin which I had in my boat, and caused every thing I had in the ship to be punctually deliver'd me, and what I was willing to sell he bought, such as the case of bottles, two of my guns, and a piece of the lump of bees-wax, for I had made candles of the rest; in a word, I made about 220 pieces of eight of all my cargo, and with this stock I went on shoar in the Brasils.

I had not been long here, but being recommended to the house of a good honest man like himself, who had an *ingenio* as they call it, that is, a plantation and a sugar-house, I lived with him some time, and acquainted my self by that means with the manner of their planting and making of sugar; and seeing how well the planters liv'd, and how they grew rich suddenly, I resolv'd, if I could get licence to settle there, I would turn planter among them, resolving in the mean time to find out some way to get my money which I had left in London remitted to me. To this purpose getting a kind of a letter of naturalization, I purchased as much land that was uncur'd as my money would reach, and form'd a plan for my plantation and settlement, and such a one as might be suitable to the stock which I proposed to myself to receive from England.

I had a neighbour, a Portugueze of Lisbon, but born of English parents, whose name was Wells, and in much such circumstances as I was. I call him my neighbour, because his plantation lay next to mine, and we went on very sociably together. My stock was but low as well as his; and we rather planted for food than any thing else, for about two years. However, we began to increase, and our land began to come into order; so that the third year we planted some tobacco, and made each of us a large piece of ground ready for planting canes in the year to come; but we both wanted help, and now I found more than before, I had done wrong in parting with my boy Xury.

But alas! for me to do wrong that never did right, was no great wonder. I had no remedy but to go on; I was gotten into an employment quite remote to my genius, and directly contrary to the life I delighted in, and for which I forsook my father's house and broke thro' all his good advice; nay, I was coming into the very middle station, or upper degree of low life, which my father advised me to before; and which if I resolved to go on with, I might as well ha' staid at home, and never have fatigu'd my self in the world as I had done; and I used often to say to my self, I could ha' done this as well in England among my friends, as ha' gone 5,000 miles off to do it among strangers and savages in a wilderness, and at such a distance as never to hear from any part of the world that had the least knowledge of me.

In this manner I used to look upon my condition with the utmost regret. I had no body to converse with but now and then this neighbour; no work to be done but by the labour of my hands; and I used to say I liv'd just like a man cast away upon some desolate island, that has no body there but himself. But how just has it been, and how should all men reflect, that when they compare their present conditions with others that are worse,

Heaven may oblige them to make the exchange, and be convinc'd of their former felicity by their experience; I say, how just has it been, that the truly solitary life I reflected on an island of meer desolation should be my lot, who had so often unjustly compar'd it with the life which I then led, in which had I continued, I had in all probability been exceeding prosperous and rich.

I was in some degree settled in my measures for carrying on the plantation, before my kind friend, the captain of the ship that took me up at sea, went back; for the ship remained there in providing his loading, and preparing for his voyage, near three months, when telling him what little stock I had left behind me in London, he gave me this friendly and sincere advice: 'Seignior Inglese,' says he, for so he always called me, 'if you will give me letters, and a procuration here in form to me, with orders to the person who has your money in London, to send your effects to Lisbon, to such persons as I shall direct, and in such goods as are proper for this country, I will bring you the produce of them, God willing, at my return; but since human affairs are all subject to changes and disasters, I would have you give orders but for one hundred pounds sterling, which you say is half your stock, and let the hazard be run for the first; so that if it come safe, you may order the rest the same way; and if it miscarry, you may have the other half to have recourse to for your supply.'

This was so wholesom advice, and look'd so friendly, that I could not but be convinc'd it was the best course I could take; so I accordingly prepared letters to the gentlewoman with whom I had left my money, and a procuration to the Portuguese captain, as he desired.

I wrote the English captain's widow a full account of all my adventures, my slavery, escape, and how I had met with the Portugal captain at sea, the humanity of his behaviour, and in what condition I was now in, with all other necessary directions for my supply; and when this honest captain came to Lisbon, he found means by some of the English merchants there, to send over not the order only, but a full account of my story to a merchant at London, who represented it effectually to her; whereupon she not only delivered the money, but out of her own pocket sent the Portugal captain a very handsom present for his humanity and charity to me.

The merchant in London, vesting this hundred pounds in English goods, such as the captain had writ for, sent them directly to him at Lisbon, and he brought them all safe to me to the Brasils, among which, without my direction (for I was too young in my business to think of them), he had taken care to have all sorts of tools, iron-work, and utensils necessary for my plantation, and which were of great use to me.

When this cargo arrived, I thought my fortunes made, for I was surprised with the joy of it; and my good steward the captain had laid out the five pounds which my friend had sent him for a present for himself, to purchase and bring me over a servant under bond for six years' service, and would not accept of any consideration, except a little tobacco, which I would have him accept, being of my own produce.

Neither was this all; but my goods being all English manufactures, such as cloath, stuffs, bays, and things particularly valuable and desirable in the country, I found means to sell them to a very great advantage; so that I might say I had more than four times the value of my first cargo, and was now infinitely beyond my poor neighbour, I mean in the advancement of my plantation; for the first thing I did, I bought me a negro slave, and an European servant also; I mean another besides that which the captain brought me from Lisbon.

But as abus'd prosperity is oftentimes made the very means of our greatest adversity, so was it with me. I went on the next year with great success in my plantation. I raised fifty great rolls of tobacco on my own ground, more than I had disposed of for necessaries among my neighbours; and these fifty rolls being each of above a 100 wt were well cur'd and laid by against the return of the fleet from Lisbon: and now increasing in business and in wealth, my head began to be full of projects and undertakings beyond my reach; such as are indeed often the ruine of the best heads in business.

Had I continued in the station I was now in, I had room for all the happy things to have yet befallen me, for which my father so earnestly recommended a quiet retired life, and of which he had so sensibly describ'd the middle station of life to be full of; but other things attended me, and I was still to be the wilful agent of all my own miseries; and particularly to encrease my fault and double the reflections upon my self, which in my future sorrows I should have leisure to make; all these miscarriages were procured by my apparent obstinate adhering to my foolish inclination of wandring abroad and pursuing that inclination, in contradiction to the clearest views of doing my self good in a fair and plain pursuit of those prospects and those measures of life which nature and Providence concurred to present me with, and to make my duty.

As I had once done thus in my breaking away from my parents, so I could not be content now, but I must go and leave the happy view I had of being a rich and thriving man in my new plantation, only to pursue a rash and immoderate desire of rising faster than the nature of the thing admitted; and thus I cast my self down again into the deepest gulph of human misery that ever man fell into, or perhaps could be consistent with life and a state of health in the world.

To come then by the just degrees to the particulars of this part of my story; you may suppose, that having now lived almost four years in the Brasils, and beginning to thrive and prosper very well upon my plantation, I had not only learn'd the language, but had contracted acquaintance and friendship among my fellow-planters, as well as among the merchants at St. Salvadore, which was our port; and that in my discourses among them, I had frequently given them an account of my two voyages to the coast of Guinea, the manner of trading with the negroes there, and how easy it was to purchase upon the coast, for trifles, such as beads, toys, knives, scissars, hatchets, bits of glass, and the like, not only gold dust, Guinea grains, elephants' teeth, &c., but negroes, for the service of the Brasils, in great numbers.

They listened always very attentively to my discourses on these heads, but especially to that part which related to the buying negroes, which was a trade at that time not only not far entred into, but as far as it was, had been carried on by the assiento's, or permission of the kings of Spain and Portugal, and engross'd in the publick, so that few negroes were brought, and those excessive dear.

It happen'd, being in company with some merchants and planters of my acquaintance, and talking of those things very earnestly, three of them came to me the next morning, and told me they had been musing very much upon what I had discoursed with them of, the last night, and they came to make a secret proposal to me; and after enjoining me secrecy, they told me that they had a mind to fit out a ship to go to Guinea, that they had all plantations as well as I, and were straiten'd for nothing so much as servants; that as it was a trade that could not be carried on, because they could not publickly sell the negroes when they came home, so they desired to make but one voyage, to bring the negroes on shoar privately, and divide them among their own plantations; and in a word, the question was, whether I would go their super-cargo in the ship to manage the trading part upon the coast of Guinea. And they offer'd me that I should have my equal share of the negroes without providing any part of the stock.

This was a fair proposal, it must be confess'd, had it been made to any one that had not had a settlement and plantation of his own to look after, which was in a fair way of coming to be very considerable, and with a good stock upon it. But for me that was thus entered and established, and had nothing to do but go on as I had begun for three or four years more, and to have sent for the other hundred pound from England, and who in that time, and with that little addition, could scarce ha' fail'd of being worth three or four thousand pounds sterling, and that encreasing too; for me to think of such a voyage, was the most preposterous thing that ever man in such circumstances could be guilty of.

But I that was born to be my own destroyer, could no more resist the offer than I could restrain my first rambling designs, when my father's good counsel was lost upon me. In a word, I told them I would go with all my heart, if they would undertake to look after my plantation in my absence, and would dispose of it to such as I should direct if I miscarry'd. This they all engag'd to do, and entred into writings or convenants to do so; and I made a formal will, disposing of my plantation and effects, in case of my death, making the captain of the ship that had sav'd my life, as before, my universal heir, but obliging him to dispose of my effects as I had directed in my will, one half of the produce being to himself, and the other to be ship'd to England.

In short, I took all possible caution to preserve my effects, and keep up my plantation; had I used half as much prudence to have look'd into my own intrest, and have made a judgment of what I ought to have done and not to have done, I had certainly never gone away from so prosperous an undertaking, leaving all the probable views of a thriving circumstance, and gone upon a voyage to sea, attended with all its common hazards; to say nothing of the reasons I had to expect particular misfortunes to my self.

But I was hurried on, and obey'd blindly the dictates of my fancy rather than my reason; and accordingly the ship being fitted out, and the cargo furnished, and all things done as by agreement, by my partners in the voyage, I went on board in an evil hour, the first of September, 1659, being the same day eight year that I went from my father and mother at Hull, in order to act the rebel to their authority, and the fool to my own interest.

Our ship was about 120 tun burthen, carried 6 guns and 14 men, besides the master, his boy, and my self; we had on board no large cargo of goods, except of such toys as were fit for our trade with the negroes, such as beads, bits of glass, shells, and odd trifles, especially little looking-glasses, knives, scissars, hatchets, and the like.

The same day I went on board we set sail, standing away to the northward upon our own coast, with design to stretch over for the Affrican coast, when they came about 10 or 12 degrees of northern latitude, which it seems was the manner of their course in those days. We had very good weather, only excessive hot, all the way upon our own coast, till we came the height of Cape St. Augustino, from whence keeping farther off at sea we lost sight of land, and steer'd as if we was bound for the isle Fernand de Noronha, holding our course N.E. by N. and leaving those isles on the east; in this course we past the line in about 12 days' time, and were by our last observation in 7 degrees 22 min. northern latitude, when a violent tournado or hurricane took us quite out of our knowledge; it began from the south-east, came about to the north-west, and then settled into the north-east, from whence it blew in such a terrible manner, that for twelve days together we could do nothing but drive, and scudding away before it, let it carry us whither ever fate and the fury of the winds directed; and during these twelve days, I need not say that I expected every day to be swallowed up, nor indeed did any in the ship expect to save their lives.

In this distress, we had, besides the terror of the storm, one of our men dyed of the calenture, and one man and the boy wash'd over board; about the 12th day the weather abating a little, the master made an observation as well as he could, and found that he was in about 11 degrees north latitude, but that he was 22 degrees of longitude difference west from Cape St. Augustino; so that he found he was gotten upon the coast of Guinea, or the north part of Brasil, beyond the river Amozones, towards that of the river Oronoque,* commonly call'd the Great River, and began to consult with me what course he should take, for the ship was leaky and very much disabled, and he was going directly back to the coast of Brasil.

I was positively against that, and looking over the charts of the sea-coast of America with him, we concluded there was no inhabited country for us to have recourse to, till we came within the circle of the Carribbe-Islands, and therefore resolved to stand away for Barbadoes, which by keeping off at sea, to avoid the indraft of the bay or gulph of Mexico, we might easily perform, as we hoped, in about fifteen days' sail; whereas we could not possibly make our voyage to the coast of Affrica without some assistance, both to our ship and to our selves.

With this design we chang'd our course and steer'd away N.W. by W. in order to reach some of our English islands, where I hoped for relief; but our voyage was otherwise determined, for being in the latitude of 12 deg. 18 min. a second storm came upon us, which carry'd us away with the same impetuosity westward, and drove us so out of the very way of all humane commerce, that had all our lives been saved, as to the sea, we were rather in danger of being devoured by savages than ever returning to our own country.

In this distress, the wind still blowing very hard, one of our men early in the morning cry'd out, 'Land!' and we had no sooner run out of the cabbin to look out in hopes of seeing where abouts in the world we were, but the ship struck upon a sand, and in a moment, her motion being so stopp'd, the sea broke over her in such a manner that we expected we should all have perish'd immediately, and we were immediately driven into our close quarters to shelter us from the very foam and sprye of the sea.

It is not easy for any one, who has not been in the like condition, to describe or conceive the consternation of men in such circumstances; we knew nothing where we were, or upon what land it was we were driven, whether an island or the main, whether inhabited or not inhabited; and as the rage of the wind was still great, tho' rather less than at first, we could not so much as hope to have the ship hold many minutes without breaking in pieces, unless the winds by a kind of miracle should turn immediately about. In a word, we sat looking upon one another, and expecting death every moment, and every man acting accordingly, as preparing for another world, for there was little or nothing more for us to do in this; that which was our present comfort, and all the comfort we had was, that contrary to our expectation the ship did not break yet, and that the master said the wind began to abate.

Now tho' we thought that the wind did a little abate, yet the ship having thus struck upon the sand, and sticking too fast for us to expect her getting off, we were in a dreadful condition indeed, and had nothing to do but to think of saving our lives as well as we could; we had a boat at our stern just before the storm, but she was first stav'd by dashing against the ship's rudder, and in the next place she broke away, and either sunk or was driven off to sea, so there was no hope from her; we had another boat on board, but how to get her off into the sea was a doubtful thing; however, there was no room to debate, for we fancy'd the ship would break in pieces every minute, and some told us she was actually broken already.

In this distress the mate of our vessel lays hold of the boat, and with the help of the rest of the men, they got her slung over the ship's-side, and getting all into her, let go, and committed our selves, being eleven in number, to God's mercy and the wild sea; for tho' the storm was abated considerably, yet the sea went dreadful high upon the shore, and might well be call'd *den wild zee*, as the Dutch call the sea in a storm.

And now our case was very dismal indeed; for we all saw plainly, that the sea went so high that the boat could not live, and that we should be inevitably drowned. As to making sail, we had none, nor, if we had, could we ha' done any thing with it: so we work'd at the oar towards the land, tho' with heavy hearts, like men going to execution; for we all knew that when the boat came nearer the shore, she would be dash'd in a thousand pieces by the breach of the sea. However, we committed our souls to God in the most earnest manner, and the wind driving us towards the shore, we hasten'd our destruction with our own hands, pulling as well as we could towards land.

What the shore was, whether rock or sand, whether steep or shoal, we knew not; the only hope that could rationally give us the least shadow of expectation, was, if we might happen into some bay or gulph, or the mouth of some river, where by great chance we might have run our boat in, or got under the lee of the land, and perhaps made smooth water. But there was nothing of this appeared; but as we made nearer and nearer the shore, the land look'd more frightful than the sea.

After we had row'd, or rather driven, about a league and a half, as we reckon'd it, a raging wave, mountain-like, came rowling a-stern of us, and plainly bad us expect the *coup de grace*. In a word, it took us with such a fury, that it overset the boat at once; and separating us as well from the boat as from one another, gave us not time hardly to say, O God! for we were all swallowed up in a moment.

Nothing can describe the confusion of thought which I felt when I sunk into the water; for tho' I swam very well, yet I could not deliver my self from the waves so as to draw breath, till that wave having driven me, or rather carried me a vast way on towards the shore, and having spent it self, went back, and left me upon the land almost dry, but half-dead with the water I took in. I had so much presence of mind as well as breath left, that seeing my self nearer the main land than I expected, I got upon my feet, and endeavoured to make on towards the land as fast as I could, before another wave should return, and take me up again. But I soon found it was impossible to avoid it; for I saw the sea come after me as high as a great hill, and as furious as an enemy which I had no means or strength to contend with; my business was to hold my breath, and raise my self upon the water, if I could; and so by swimming to preserve my breathing, and pilot my self towards the shore, if possible; my greatest concern now being, that the sea, as it would carry me a great way towards the shore when it came on, might not carry me back again with it when it gave back towards the sea.

The wave that came upon me again, buried me at once 20 or 30 foot deep in its own body; and I could feel my self carried with a mighty force and swiftness towards the shore a very great way; but I held my breath, and assisted my self to swim still forward with all my might. I was ready to burst with holding my breath, when, as I felt my self rising up, so to my immediate relief, I found my head and hands shoot out above the surface of the water; and tho' it was not two seconds of time that I could keep my self so, yet it reliev'd me greatly, gave me breath and new courage. I was covered again with water a good while, but not so long but I held it out; and finding the water had spent it self, and began to return, I strook forward against the return of the waves, and felt ground again with my feet. I stood still a few moments to recover breath, and till the water went from me, and then took to my heels, and run with what strength I had farther towards the shore. But neither would this deliver me from the fury of the sea, which came pouring in after me again, and twice more I was lifted up by the waves and carried forwards as before, the shore being very flat.

The last time of these two had well near been fatal to me; for the
sea having hurried me along as before, landed me, or rather dash'd
me against a piece of a rock, and that with such force as it left me
senseless, and indeed helpless as to my own deliverance; for the
blow taking my side and breast, beat the breath as it were quite out
of my body; and had it returned again immediately, I must have
been strangled* in the water; but I recover'd a little before the
return of the waves, and seeing I should be cover'd again with the
water, I resolv'd to hold fast by a piece of the rock, and so to hold my
breath, if possible, till the wave went back; now as the waves were
not so high as at first, being nearer land, I held my hold till the wave
abated, and then fetch'd another run, which brought me so near the
shore, that the next wave, tho' it went over me, yet did not so
swallow me up as to carry me away, and the next run I took, I got to
the main land, where, to my great comfort, I clamber'd up the clifts
of the shore and sat me down upon the grass, free from danger, and
quite out of the reach of the water.

I was now landed and safe on shore, and began to look up and
thank God that my life was sav'd in a case wherein there was some
minutes before scarce any room to hope. I believe it is impossible to
express to the life what the extasies and transports of the soul are,
when it is so sav'd, as I may say, out of the very grave; and I do not
wonder now at that custom, viz. that when a malefactor who has
the halter about his neck, is tyed up, and just going to be turn'd off,*
and has a reprieve brought to him; I say, I do not wonder that they
bring a surgeon with it, to let him blood that very moment they tell
him of it, that the surprise may not drive the animal spirits from the
heart, and overwhelm him:

For sudden joys, like griefs, confound at first.

I walk'd about on the shore, lifting up my hands, and my whole
being, as I may say, wrapt up in the contemplation of my
deliverance, making a thousand gestures and motions which I
cannot describe, reflecting upon all my comrades that were
drown'd, and that there should not be one soul sav'd but my self;
for, as for them, I never saw them afterwards, or any sign of them,
except three of their hats, one cap, and two shoes that were not
fellows.

I cast my eyes to the stranded vessel, when the breach and froth of
the sea being so big, I could hardly see it, it lay so far off, and
considered, Lord! how was it possible I could get on shore?

After I had solac'd my mind with the comfortable part of my condition, I began to look round me to see what kind of place I was in, and what was next to be done, and I soon found my comforts abate, and that in a word I had a dreadful deliverance: for I was wet, had no clothes to shift me, nor any thing either to eat or drink to comfort me, neither did I see any prospect before me, but that of perishing with hunger, or being devour'd by wild beasts; and that which was particularly afflicting to me was that I had no weapon either to hunt and kill any creature for my sustenance, or to defend my self against any other creature that might desire to kill me for theirs. In a word, I had nothing about me but a knife, a tobacco-pipe, and a little tobacco in a box; this was all my provision, and this threw me into terrible agonies of mind, that for a while I run about like a mad-man. Night coming upon me, I began with a heavy heart to consider what would be my lot if there were any ravenous beasts in that country, seeing at night they always come abroad for their prey.

All the remedy that offer'd to my thoughts at that time was to get up into a thick bushy tree like a firr, but thorny, which grew near me, and where I resolv'd to sit all night, and consider the next day what death I should dye, for as yet I saw no prospect of life; I walk'd about a furlong from the shore, to see if I could find any fresh water to drink, which I did, to my great joy; and having drank and put a little tobacco in my mouth to prevent hunger, I went to the tree, and getting up into it, endeavour'd to place my self so, as that if I should sleep I might not fall; and having cut me a short stick, like a truncheon, for my defence, I took up my lodging, and having been excessively fatigu'd, I fell fast asleep and slept as comfortably as, I believe, few could have done in my condition, and found my self the most refresh'd with it that I think I ever was on such an occasion.

When I wak'd it was broad day, the weather clear, and the storm abated, so that the sea did not rage and swell as before: but that which surpris'd me most was that the ship was lifted off in the night from the sand where she lay, by the swelling of the tyde, and was driven up almost as far as the rock which I first mention'd, where I had been so bruis'd by the dashing me against it; this being within about a mile from the shore where I was, and the ship seeming to stand upright still, I wish'd my self on board, that, at least, I might save some necessary things for my use.

When I came down from my appartment in the tree, I look'd about me again, and the first thing I found was the boat, which lay as the wind and the sea had toss'd her up upon the land, about two miles on my right hand. I walk'd as far as I could upon the shore to have got to her, but found a neck or inlet of water between me and the boat, which was about half a mile broad, so I came back for the present, being more intent upon getting at the ship, where I hop'd to find something for my present subsistence.

A little after noon I found the sea very calm, and the tyde ebb'd so far out that I could come within a quarter of a mile of the ship; and here I found a fresh renewing of my grief, for I saw evidently, that if we had kept on board, we had been all safe, that is to say, we had all got safe on shore, and I had not been so miserable as to be left entirely destitute of all comfort and company, as I now was; this forc'd tears from my eyes again, but as there was little relief in that, I resolv'd, if possible, to get to the ship, so I pull'd off my clothes, for the weather was hot to extremity, and took the water, but when I came to the ship, my difficulty was still greater to know how to get on board, for she lay a ground, and high out of the water, there was nothing within my reach to lay hold of. I swam round her twice, and the second time I spy'd a small piece of a rope, which I wonder'd I did not see at first, hang down by the fore-chains so low, as that with great difficulty I got hold of it, and by the help of that rope, got up into the forecastle of the ship. Here I found that the ship was bulg'd, and had a great deal of water in her hold, but that she lay so on the side of a bank of hard sand, or rather earth, that her stern lay lifted up upon the bank, and her head low almost to the water; by this means all her quarter was free, and all that was in that part was dry; for you may be sure my first work was to search and to see what was spoil'd and what was free; and first I found that all the ship's provisions were dry and untouch'd by the water, and being very well dispos'd to eat, I went to the bread-room and fill'd my pockets with bisket, and eat it as I went about other things, for I had no time to lose; I also found some rum in the great cabbin, of which I took a large dram, and which I had indeed need enough of to spirit me for what was before me. Now I wanted nothing but a boat to furnish my self with many things which I foresaw would be very necessary to me.

It was in vain to sit still and wish for what was not to be had, and this extremity rouz'd my application. We had several spare yards, and two or three large sparrs of wood, and a spare top-mast

or two in the ship; I resolv'd to fall to work with these, and I flung
as many of them over board as I could manage for their weight,
tying every one with a rope that they might not drive away; when
this was done I went down the ship's side, and pulling them to me,
I ty'd four of them fast together at both ends as well as I could, in
the form of a raft, and laying two or three short pieces of plank
upon them crossways, I found I could walk upon it very well, but
that it was not able to bear any great weight, the pieces being too
light; so I went to work, and with the carpenter's saw I cut a spare
top-mast into three lengths, and added them to my raft, with a
great deal of labour and pains; but hope of furnishing my self with
necessaries encourag'd me to go beyond what I should have been
able to have done upon another occasion.

My raft was now strong enough to bear any reasonable weight;
my next care was what to load it with, and how to preserve what I
laid upon it from the surf of the sea, but I was not long considering
this. I first laid all the planks or boards upon it that I could get, and
having consider'd well what I most wanted, I first got three of the
seamen's chests, which I had broken open and empty'd, and
lower'd them down upon my raft; the first of these I fill'd with
provision, viz. bread, rice, three Dutch cheeses, five pieces of dry'd
goat's flesh, which we liv'd much upon, and a little remainder of
European corn which had been laid by for some fowls which we
brought to sea with us, but the fowls were kill'd; there had been
some barly and wheat together, but, to my great disappointment,
I found afterwards that the rats had eaten or spoil'd it all; as for
liquors, I found several cases of bottles belonging to our
skipper, in which were some cordial waters, and in all about five
or six gallons of rack;* these I stow'd by themselves, there being
no need to put them into the chest, nor no room for them. While I
was doing this, I found the tyde began to flow, tho' very calm, and
I had the mortification to see my coat, shirt, and wastcoat which I
had left on shore upon the sand, swim away; as for my breeches,
which were only linnen and open knee'd, I swam on board in them
and my stockings. However, this put me upon rummaging for
clothes, of which I found enough, but took no more than I wanted
for present use, for I had other things which my eye was more
upon, as first tools to work with on shore, and it was after long
searching that I found out the carpenter's chest, which was indeed
a very useful prize to me, and much more valuable than a ship
loading of gold would have been at that time; I got it down to my

raft, even whole as it was, without losing time to look into it, for I knew in general what it contain'd.

My next care was for some ammunition and arms; there were two very good fowling-pieces in the great cabbin, and two pistols; these I secur'd first, with some powder-horns, and a small bag of shot, and two old rusty swords; I knew there were three barrels of powder in the ship, but knew not where our gunner had stow'd them, but with much search I found them, two of them dry and good, the third had taken water; those two I got to my raft, with the arms; and now I thought my self pretty well freighted, and began to think how I should get to shore with them, having neither sail, oar, or rudder, and the least cap full of wind would have overset all my navigation.

I had three encouragements: 1, a smooth calm sea; 2, the tide rising, and setting in to the shore; 3, what little wind there was blew me towards the land; and thus, having found two or three broken oars belonging to the boat, and besides the tools which were in the chest, I found two saws, an axe, and a hammer, and with this cargo I put to sea. For a mile, or thereabouts, my raft went very well, only that I found it drive a little distant from the place where I had landed before, by which I perceiv'd that there was some indraft of the water, and consequently I hop'd to find some creek or river there, which I might make use of as a port to get to land with my cargo.

As I imagin'd, so it was, there appear'd before me a little opening of the land, and I found a strong current of the tide set into it, so I guided my raft as well as I could to keep in the middle of the stream. But here I had like to have suffer'd a second shipwreck, which, if I had, I think verily would have broke my heart, for knowing nothing of the coast, my raft run a-ground at one end of it upon a shoal, and not being a-ground at the other end, it wanted but a little that all my cargo had slip'd off towards that end that was a-float, and so fall'n into the water. I did my utmost by setting my back against the chests to keep them in their places, but could not thrust off the raft with all my strength, neither durst I stir from the posture I was in, but holding up the chests with all my might, stood in that manner near half an hour, in which time the rising of the water brought me a little more upon a level, and a little after, the water still rising, my raft floated again, and I thrust her off with the oar I had into the channel, and then driving up higher, I at length found my self in the mouth of a little river, with land on both sides, and a strong current or tide running up. I look'd on both sides for a proper place to get to shore, for I was not willing to be driven too high up the river, hoping in time to see some ship at sea, and therefore resolv'd to place my self as near the coast as I could.

At length I spy'd a little cove on the right shore of the creek, to which with great pain and difficulty I guided my raft, and at last got so near, as that, reaching ground with my oar, I could thrust her directly in; but here I had like to have dipt all my cargo in the sea again; for that shore lying pretty steep, that is to say sloping, there was no place to land but where one end of my float, if it run on shore, would lie so high, and the other sink lower as before, that it would endanger my cargo again. All that I could do was to wait 'till the tide was at the highest, keeping the raft with my oar like an anchor to hold the side of it fast to the shore, near a flat piece of ground, which I expected the water would flow over; and so it did. As soon as I found water enough, for my raft drew about a foot of water, I thrust her on upon that flat piece of ground, and there fasten'd or mor'd her by sticking my two broken oars into the ground, one on one side near one end, and one on the other side near the other end; and thus I lay 'till the water ebb'd away, and left my raft and all my cargoe safe on shore.

My next work was to view the country, and seek a proper place for my habitation, and where to stow my goods to secure them from whatever might happen; where I was, I yet knew not, whether on the continent or on an island, whether inhabited or not inhabited, whether in danger of wild beasts or not. There was a hill not above a mile from me, which rose up very steep and high, and which seem'd to over-top some other hills, which lay as in a ridge from it northward; I took out one of the fowling pieces, and one of the pistols, and an horn of powder, and thus arm'd I travell'd for discovery up to the top of that hill, where after I had with great labour and difficulty got to the top, I saw my fate to my great affliction, viz. that I was in an island environ'd every way with the sea, no land to be seen, except some rocks which lay a great way off, and two small islands less than this, which lay about three leagues to the west.

I found also that the island I was in was barren, and, as I saw good reason to believe, un-inhabited, except by wild beasts, of whom however I saw none, yet I saw abundance of fowls, but knew not their kinds, neither when I kill'd them could I tell what was fit for food, and what not; at my coming back, I shot at a great bird which I saw sitting upon a tree on the side of a great wood. I believe it was the first gun that had been fir'd there since the creation of the world; I had no sooner fir'd, but from all the parts of the wood there arose an innumerable number of fowls of many sorts, making a confus'd screaming, and crying every one according to his usual note; but not one of them of any kind that I knew. As for the creature I kill'd, I took it to be a kind of a hawk, its colour and beak resembling it, but had no talons or claws more than common; its flesh was carrion, and fit for nothing.

Contented with this discovery, I came back to my raft, and fell to work to bring my cargoe on shore, which took me up the rest of that day, and what to do with my self at night I knew not, nor indeed where to rest; for I was afraid to lie down on the ground, not knowing but some wild beast might devour me, tho', as I afterwards found, there was really no need for those fears.

However, as well as I could, I barricado'd my self round with the chests and boards that I had brought on shore, and made a kind of a hut for that night's lodging; as for food, I yet saw not which way to supply my self, except that I had seen two or three creatures like hares run out of the wood where I shot the fowl.

I now began to consider that I might yet get a great many things out of the ship, which would be useful to me, and particularly some of the rigging, and sails, and such other things as might come to land, and I resolv'd to make another voyage on board the vessel, if possible; and as I knew that the first storm that blew must necessarily break her all in pieces, I resolv'd to set all other things apart, 'till I got every thing out of the ship that I could get; then I call'd a council, that is to say, in my thoughts, whether I should take back the raft, but this appear'd impracticable; so I resolv'd to go as before, when the tide was down, and I did so, only that I stripp'd before I went from my hut, having nothing on but a chequer'd shirt, and a pair of linnen drawers, and a pair of pumps on my feet.

I got on board the ship, as before, and prepar'd a second raft, and having had experience of the first, I neither made this so unweildy, or loaded it so hard, but yet I brought away several things very useful to me; as first, in the carpenter's stores I found two or three bags full of nails and spikes, a great skrew-jack, a dozen or two of hatchets, and above all, that most useful thing call'd a grindstone; all these I secur'd together, with several things belonging to the gunner, particularly two or three iron crows, and two barrels of musquet bullets, seven musquets, and another fowling piece, with some small quantity of powder more; a large bag full of small shot, and a great roll of sheet lead. But this last was so heavy I could not hoise it up to get it over the ship's side.

Besides these things, I took all the men's cloaths that I could find, and a spare fore-top-sail, a hammock, and some bedding; and with this I loaded my second raft, and brought them all safe on shore to my very great comfort.

I was under some apprehensions during my absence from the land, that at least my provisions might be devour'd on shore; but when I came back, I found no sign of any visitor, only there sat a creature like a wild cat upon one of the chests, which when I came towards it, ran away a little distance, and then stood still; she sat very compos'd and unconcern'd, and look'd full in my face, as if she had a mind to be acquainted with me. I presented my gun at her, but as she did not understand it, she was perfectly unconcern'd at it, nor did she offer to stir away; upon which I toss'd her a bit of bisket, tho' by the way I was not very free of it, for my store was not great. However, I spar'd her a bit, I say, and she went to it, smell'd of it, and ate it, and look'd (as pleas'd) for more, but I thanked her, and could spare no more, so she march'd off.

Having got my second cargoe on shore, tho' I was fain to open the barrels of powder and bring them by parcels, for they were too heavy, being large casks, I went to work to make me a little tent with the sail and some poles which I cut for that purpose, and into this tent I brought every thing that I knew would spoil, either with rain or sun, and I piled all the empty chests and casks up in a circle round the tent, to fortify it from any sudden attempt, either from man or beast.

When I had done this I block'd up the door of the tent with some boards within, and an empty chest set up on end without, and spreading one of the beds upon the ground, laying my two pistols just at my head, and my gun at length by me, I went to bed for the first time, and slept very quietly all night, for I was very weary and heavy, for the night before I had slept little, and had labour'd very hard all day, as well to fetch all those things from the ship, as to get them on shore.

I had the biggest maggazin of all kinds now that ever were laid up, I believe, for one man, but I was not satisfy'd still; for while the ship sat upright in that posture, I thought I ought to get every thing out of her that I could; so every day at low water I went on board, and brought away something or other. But particularly the third time I went, I brought away as much of the rigging as I could, as also all the small ropes and rope-twine I could get, with a piece of spare canvass, which was to mend the sails upon occasion, the barrel of wet gunpowder: in a word, I brought away all the sails first and last, only that I was fain to cut them in pieces, and bring as much at a time as I could; for they were no more useful to be sails, but as meer canvass only.

But that which comforted me more still, was that at last of all, after I had made five or six such voyages as these, and thought I had nothing more to expect from the ship that was worth my medling with; I say, after all this, I found a great hogshead of bread and three large runlets* of rum or spirits, and a box of sugar, and a barrel of fine flower; this was surprizing to me, because I had given over expecting any more provisions, except what was spoil'd by the water: I soon empty'd the hogshead of that bread, and wrapt it up parcel by parcel in pieces of the sails, which I cut out; and in a word, I got all this safe on shore also.

The next day I made another voyage; and now having plunder'd the ship of what was portable and fit to hand out, I began with the cables; and cutting the great cable into pieces, such as I could move, I got two cables and a hawser on shore, with all the iron work I could get; and having cut down the spritsail-yard, and the missen-yard, and every thing I could to make a large raft, I loaded it with all those heavy goods, and came away. But my good luck began now to leave me; for this raft was so unweildy, and so overloaden, that after I was enter'd the little cove, where I had landed the rest of my goods, not being able to guide it so handily as I did the other, it overset, and threw me and all my cargoe into the water; as for my self it was no great harm, for I was near the shore; but as to my cargoe, it was great part of it lost, especially the iron, which I expected would have been of great use to me. However, when the tide was out, I got most of the pieces of cable ashore, and some of the iron, tho' with infinite labour; for I was fain to dip for it into the water, a work which fatigu'd me very much. After this I went every day on board, and brought away what I could get.

I had been now thirteen days on shore, and had been eleven times on board the ship; in which time I had brought away all that one pair of hands could well be suppos'd capable to bring, tho' I believe verily, had the calm weather held, I should have brought away the whole ship piece by piece. But preparing the 12th time to go on board, I found the wind begin to rise; however, at low water I went on board, and tho' I thought I had rumag'd the cabbin so effectually, as that nothing more could be found, yet I discover'd a locker with drawers in it, in one of which I found two or three razors, and one pair of large sizzers, with some ten or a dozen of good knives and forks; in another I found about thirty six pounds' value in money, some European coin, some Brasil, some pieces of eight, some gold, some silver.

I smil'd to myself at the sight of this money. 'O drug!' said I aloud, 'what are thou good for? Thou art not worth to me, no, not the taking off of the ground; one of those knives is worth all this heap; I have no manner of use for thee, e'en remain where thou art, and go to the bottom as a creature whose life is not worth saving.' However, upon second thoughts, I took it away, and wrapping all this in a piece of canvas, I began to think of making another raft, but while I was preparing this, I found the sky over-cast, and the wind began to rise, and in a quarter of an hour it blew a fresh gale from the shore; it presently occur'd to me that it was in vain to pretend to make a raft with the wind off shore, and that it was my business to be gone before the tide of flood began, otherwise I might not be able to reach the shore at all. Accordingly I let my self down into the water, and swam across the channel which lay between the ship and the sands, and even that with difficulty enough, partly with the weight of the things I had about me, and partly the roughness of the water, for the wind rose very hastily, and before it was quite high water it blew a storm.

But I was gotten home to my little tent, where I lay with all my wealth about me very secure. It blew very hard all that night, and in the morning when I look'd out, behold, no more ship was to be seen; I was a little supriz'd, but recover'd my self with this satisfactory reflection, viz. that I had lost no time, nor abated no dilligence to get every thing out of her that could be useful to me, and that indeed there was little left in her that I was able to bring away if I had had more time.

I now gave over any more thoughts of the ship, or of any thing out of her, except what might drive on shore from her wreck, as indeed divers pieces of her afterwards did; but those things were of small use to me.

My thoughts were now wholly employ'd about securing my self against either savages, if any should appear, or wild beasts, if any were in the island; and I had many thoughts of the method how to do this, and what kind of dwelling to make, whether I should make me a cave in the earth, or a tent upon the earth: and, in short, I resolv'd upon both, the manner and description of which it may not be improper to give an account of.

I soon found the place I was in was not for my settlement, particularly because it was upon a low moorish ground near the sea, and I believ'd would not be wholsome, and more particularly because there was no fresh water near it, so I resolv'd to find a more healthy and more convenient spot of ground.

I consulted several things in my situation which I found would be proper for me: 1st, health and fresh water I just now mention'd; 2dly, shelter from the heat of the sun; 3dly, security from ravenous creatures, whether men or beasts; 4thly, a view to the sea, that if God sent any ship in sight, I might not lose any advantage for my deliverance, of which I was not willing to banish all my expectation yet.

In search of a place proper for this, I found a little plain on the side of a rising hill, whose front towards this little plain was steep as a houseside, so that nothing could come down upon me from the top; on the side of this rock there was a hollow place worn a little way in like the entrance or door of a cave, but there was not really any cave or way into the rock at all.

On the flat of the green, just before this hollow place, I resolv'd to pitch my tent. This plain was not above a hundred yards broad, and about twice as long, and lay like a green before my door, and at the end of it descended irregularly every way down into the low-grounds by the sea side. It was on the N.N.W. side of the hill, so that I was shelter'd from the heat every day, till it came to a W. and by S. sun, or thereabouts, which in those countries is near the setting.

Before I set up my tent, I drew a half circle before the hollow place which took in about ten yards in its semi-diameter from the rock, and twenty yards in its diameter, from its beginning and ending.

In this half circle I pitch'd two rows of strong stakes, driving them into the ground till they stood very firm like piles, the biggest end being out of the ground about five foot and a half, and sharpen'd on the top. The two rows did not stand above six inches from one another.

Then I took the pieces of cable which I had cut in the ship, and I laid them in rows one upon another, within the circle, between these two rows of stakes, up to the top, placing other stakes in the in-side, leaning against them, about two foot and a half high, like a spurr to a post, and this fence was so strong that neither man or beast could get into it or over it. This cost me a great deal of time and labour, especially to cut the piles in the woods, bring them to the place, and drive them into the earth.

The entrance into this place I made to be not by a door, but by a short ladder to go over the top, which ladder, when I was in, I lifted over after me, and so I was compleatly fenc'd in, and fortify'd, as I thought, from all the world and consequently slept secure in the night, which otherwise I could not have done, tho', as it appear'd afterward, there was no need of all this caution from the enemies that I apprehended danger from.

Into this fence or fortress, with infinite labour, I carry'd all my riches, all my provisions, ammunition, and stores, of which you have the account above; and I made me a large tent, which, to preserve me from the rains that in one part of the year are very violent there, I made double, viz. one smaller tent within, and one larger tent above it, and cover'd the uppermost with a large tarpaulin which I had sav'd among the sails.

And now I lay no more for a while in the bed which I had brought on shore, but in a hammock, which was indeed a very good one, and belong'd to the mate of the ship.

Into this tent I brought all my provisions, and every thing that would spoil by the wet, and having thus enclos'd all my goods, I made up the entrance, which till now I had left open, and so pass'd and re-pass'd, as I said, by a short ladder.

When I had done this, I began to work my way into the rock, and bringing all the earth and stones that I dug down out thro' my tent, I laid 'em up within my fence in the nature of a terras, that so it rais'd the ground within about a foot and a half; and thus I made me a cave just behind my tent, which serv'd me like a cellar to my house.

It cost me much labour and many days before all these things were brought to perfection, and therefore I must go back to some other things which took up some of my thoughts. At the same time it happen'd, after I had laid my scheme for the setting up my tent and making the cave, that a storm of rain falling from a thick dark cloud, a sudden flash of lightning happen'd, and after that a great clap of thunder, as is naturally the effect of it; I was not so much surpris'd with the the lightning as I was with a thought which darted into my mind as swift as the lightning it self: O my powder! My very heart sunk within me when I thought that at one blast all my powder might be destroyed, on which not my defence only, but the providing me food, as I thought, entirely depended; I was nothing near so anxious about my own danger, tho' had the powder took fire, I had never known who had hurt me.

Such impression did this make upon me, that after the storm was over, I laid aside all my works, my building and fortifying, and apply'd my self to make bags and boxes to separate the powder, and keep it a little and a little in a parcel, in hope that whatever might come, it might not all take fire at once, and to keep it so apart that it should not be possible to make one part fire another. I finish'd this work in about a fortnight, and I think my powder, which in all was about 240 lb. weight, was divided in not less than a hundred parcels; as to the barrel that had been wet, I did not apprehend any danger from that, so I plac'd it in my new cave, which in my fancy I call'd my kitchin, and the rest I hid up and down in holes among the rocks, so that no wet might come to it, marking very carefully where I laid it.

In the interval of time while this was doing I went out once at least every day with my gun, as well to divert my self as to see if I could kill any thing fit for food, and as near as I could to acquaint my self with what the island produc'd. The first time I went out I presently discover'd that there were goats in the island, which was a great satisfaction to me; but then it was attended with this misfortune to me, viz. that they were so shy, so subtile, and so swift of foot, that it was the difficultest thing in the world to come at them. But I was not discourag'd at this, not doubting but I might now and then shoot one, as it soon happen'd, for after I had found their haunts a little, I laid wait in this manner for them: I observ'd if they saw me in the valleys, tho' they were upon the rocks, they would run away as in a terrible fright; but if they were feeding in the valleys, and I was upon the rocks, they took no notice of me, from whence I concluded that by the position of their opticks, their sight was so directed downward, that they did not readily see objects that were above them; so afterward I took this method, I always clim'd the rocks first to get above them, and then had frequently a fair mark. The first shot I made among these creatures, I kill'd a she-goat which had a little kid by her which she gave suck to, which griev'd me heartily; but when the old one fell, the kid stood stock still by her till I came and took her up, and not only so, but when I carry'd the old one with me upon my shoulders, the kid follow'd me quite to my enclosure, upon which I laid down the dam, and took the kid in my arms, and carry'd it over my pale, in hopes to have it bred up tame, but it would not eat, so I was forc'd to kill it and eat it my self; these two supply'd me with flesh a great while, for I eat sparingly, and sav'd my provisions (my bread especially) as much as possibly I could.

Having now fix'd my habitation, I found it absolutely necessary to provide a place to make a fire in, and fewel to burn; and what I did for that, as also how I enlarg'd my cave, and what conveniences I made, I shall give a full account of in its place. But I must first give some little account of my self, and of my thoughts about living, which it may well be suppos'd were not a few.

I had a dismal prospect of my condition, for as I was not cast away upon that island without being driven, as it said, by a violent storm quite out of the course of our intended voyage, and a great way, viz. some hundreds of leagues, out of the ordinary course of the trade of mankind, I had great reason to consider it as a determination of Heaven, that in this desolate place and in this desolate manner I should end my life; the tears would run plentifully down my face when I made these reflections, and sometimes I would expostulate with my self, why Providence should thus compleatly ruine its creatures, and render them so absolutely miserable, so without help abandon'd, so entirely depress'd, that it could hardly be rational to be thankful for such a life.

But something always return'd swift upon me to check these thoughts, and to reprove me; and particularly one day walking with my gun in my hand by the sea-side, I was very pensive upon the subject of my present condition, when reason as it were expostulated with me t'other way, thus: Well, you are in a desolate condition, 'tis true, but pray remember, where are the rest of you? Did not you come eleven of you into the boat? where are the ten? Why were not they sav'd and you lost? Why were you singled out: Is it better to be here or there? and then I pointed to the sea. All evils are to be considered with the good that is in them, and with what worse attends them.

Then it occurr'd to me again, how well I was furnish'd for my subsistence, and what would have been my case if it had not happen'd, which was an hundred thousand to one, that the ship floated from the place where she first struck and was driven so near to the shore that I had time to get all these things out of her. What would have been my case if I had been to have liv'd in the condition in which I at first came on shore, without necessaries of life, or necessaries to supply and procure them? Particularly, said I aloud (tho' to my self), what should I ha' done without a gun, without ammunition, without any tools to make any thing, or to work with, without clothes, bedding, a tent, or any manner of covering? and that now I had all these to a sufficient quantity, and was in a fair way to provide my self in such a manner, as to live without my gun when my ammunition was spent; so that I had a tollerable view of subsisting without any want as long as I liv'd; for I consider'd from the beginning how I would provide for the accidents that might happen, and for the time that was to come, even not only after my ammunition should be spent, but even after my health or strength should decay.

I confess I had not entertain'd any notion of my ammunition being destroy'd at one blast, I mean my powder being blown up by lightning, and this made the thought of it so surprising to me when it lighten'd and thunder'd, as I observ'd just now.

And now being to enter into a melancholy relation of a scene of silent life, such perhaps as was never heard of in the world before, I shall take it from its beginning, and continue it in its order. It was, by my account, the 30th of September when, in the manner as above said, I first set foot upon this horrid island, when the sun being, to us, in its autumnal equinox, was almost just over my head, for I reckon'd my self, by observation, to be in the latitude of 9 degrees 22 minutes north of the line.

After I had been there about ten or twelve days, it came into my thoughts that I should lose my reckoning of time for want of books and pen and ink, and should even forget the sabbath days from the working days; but to prevent this I cut it with my knife upon a large post, in capital letters, and making it into a great cross I set it up on the shore where I first landed, viz. 'I come on shore here on the 30th Sept. 1659.' Upon the sides of this square post I cut every day a notch with my knife, and every seventh notch was as long again as the rest, and every first day of the month as long again as that long one, and thus I kept my kalender, or weekly, monthly, and yearly reckoning of time.

In the next place we are to observe, that among the many things which I brought out of the ship in the several voyages, which, as above mention'd, I made to it, I got several things of less value, but not at all less useful to me, which I omitted setting down before; as in particular, pens, ink, and paper, several parcels in the captain's, mate's, gunner's, and carpenter's keeping, three or four compasses, some mathematical instruments, dials, perspectives, charts, and books of navigation, all which I huddled together, whether I might want them or no; also I found three very good Bibles which came to me in my cargo from England, and which I had pack'd up among my things; some Portugueze books also, and among them two or three popish prayer-books, and several other books, all which I carefully secur'd. And I must not forget that we had in the ship a dog and two cats, of whose eminent history I may have occasion to say something in its place; for I carry'd both the cats with me, and as for the dog, he jump'd out of the ship of himself, and swam on shore to me the day after I went on shore with my first cargo, and was a trusty servant to me many years; I wanted nothing that he could fetch me, nor any company that he could make up to me, I only wanted to have him talk to me, but that would not do. As I observ'd before, I found pen, ink, and paper, and I husbanded them to the utmost, and I shall shew, that while my ink lasted, I kept things very exact, but after that was gone I could not, for I could not make any ink by any means that I could devise.

And this put me in mind that I wanted many things, notwithstanding all that I had amass'd together, and of these, this of ink was one, as also spade, pick-axe, and shovel to dig or remove the earth, needles, pins, and thread; as for linnen, I soon learn'd to want that without much difficulty.

This want of tools made every work I did go on heavily, and it was near a whole year before I had entirely finish'd my little pale or surrounded habitation. The piles or stakes, which were as heavy as I could well lift, were a long time in cutting and preparing in the woods, and more by far in bringing home, so that I spent some times two days in cutting and bringing home one of those posts, and a third day in driving it into the ground; for which purpose I got a heavy piece of wood at first, but at last bethought my self of one of the iron crows, which however, tho' I found it, yet it made driving those posts or piles very laborious and tedious work.

But what need I ha' been concern'd at the tediousness of any thing I had to do, seeing I had time enough to do it in? nor had I any other employment if that had been over, at least that I could foresee, except the ranging the island to seek for food, which I did more or less every day.

I now began to consider seriously my condition, and the circumstance I was reduc'd to, and I drew up the state of my affairs in writing, not so much to leave them to any that were to come after me, for I was like to have but few heirs, as to deliver my thoughts from daily poring upon them, and afflicting my mind; and as my reason began now to master my despondency, I began to comfort my self as well as I could, and to set the good against the evil, that I might have something to distinguish my case from worse, and I stated it very impartially, like debtor and creditor, the comforts I enjoy'd against the miseries I suffer'd, thus:

EVIL	*GOOD*
I am cast upon a horrible desolate island, void of all hope of recovery.	*But I am alive, and not drown'd as all my ship's company was.*
I am singl'd out and separated, as it were, from all the world to be miserable.	*But I am singl'd out too from all the ship's crew to be spar'd from death; and He that miraculously sav'd me from death, can deliver me from this condition.*
I am divided from mankind, a solitaire, one banish'd from humane society.	*But I am not starv'd and perishing on a barren place, affording no sustenance.*
I have not clothes to cover me.	*But I am in a hot climate, where if I had clothes I could hardly wear them.*
I am without any defence or means to resist any violence of man or beast.	*But I am cast on an island, where I see no wild beasts to hurt me, as I saw on the coast of Africa; and what if I had been shipwreck'd there?*
I have no soul to speak to, or relieve me.	*But God wonderfully sent the ship in near enough to the shore, that I have gotten out so many necessary things as will either supply my wants, or enable me to supply my self even as long as I live.*

Upon the whole, here was an undoubted testimony, that there was scarce any condition in the world so miserable, but there was something negative or something positive to be thankful for in it; and let this stand as a direction from the experience of the most miserable of all conditions in this world, that we may always find in it something to comfort our selves from, and to set in the description of good and evil, on the credit side of the accompt.

Having now brought my mind a little to relish my condition, and given over looking out to sea to see if I could spy a ship; I say, giving over these things, I began to apply my self to accommodate my way of living, and to make things as easy to me as I could.

I have already describ'd my habitation, which was a tent under the side of a rock, surrounded with a strong pale of posts and cables, but I might now rather call it a wall, for I rais'd a kind of wall up against it of turfs, about two foot thick on the out-side, and after some time, I think it was a year and a half, I rais'd rafters from it leaning to the rock, and thatch'd or cover'd it with bows of trees, and such things as I could get to keep out the rain, which I found at some times of the year very violent.

I have already observ'd how I brought all my goods into this pale, and into the cave which I had made behind me. But I must observe too, that at first this was a confus'd heap of goods, which as they lay in no order, so they took up all my place, I had no room to turn my self; so I set my self to enlarge my cave and works farther into the earth, for it was a loose sandy rock, which yielded easily to the labour I bestow'd on it; and so when I found I was pretty safe as to beasts of prey, I work'd side-ways to the right hand into the rock, and then turning to the right again, work'd quite out and made me a door to come out, on the out-side of my pale or fortification.

This gave me not only egress and regress, as it were a back way to my tent and to my storehouse, but gave me room to stow my goods.

And now I began to apply my self to make such necessary things as I found I most wanted, as particularly a chair and a table; for without these I was not able to enjoy the few comforts I had in the world; I could not write, or eat, or do several things with so much pleasure without a table.

So I went to work; and here I must needs observe, that as reason is the substance and original of the mathematicks, so by stating and squaring every thing by reason, and by making the most rational judgment of things, every man may be in time master of every mechanick art. I had never handled a tool in my life, and yet in time, by labour, application, and contrivance, I found at last that I wanted nothing but I could have made it, especially if I had had tools; however, I made abundance of things, even without tools, and some with no more tools than an adze and a hatchet, which perhaps were never made that way before, and that with infinite labour. For example, if I wanted a board, I had no other way but to cut down a tree, set it on an edge before me, and hew it flat on either side with my axe, till I had brought it to be thin as a plank, and then dubb it smooth with my adze. It is true, by this method I could make but one board out of a whole tree, but this I had no remedy for but patience, any more than I had for the prodigious deal of time and labour which it took me up to make a plank or board. But my time or labour was little worth, and so it was as well employ'd one way as another.

However, I made my table and a chair, as I observ'd above, in the first place, and this I did out of the short pieces of boards that I brought on my raft from the ship. But when I had wrought out some boards, as above, I made large shelves of the breadth of a foot and a half one over another, all along one side of my cave, to lay all my tools, nails, and iron-work, and in a word, to separate every thing at large in their places, that I must come easily at them; I knock'd pieces into the wall of the rock to hang my guns and all things that would hang up.

So that had my cave been to be seen, it look'd like a general magazine of all necessary things, and I had every thing so ready at my hand, that it was a great pleasure to me to see all my goods in such order, and especially to find my stock of all necessaries so great.

And now it was when I began to keep a journal of every day's employment, for indeed at first I was in too much hurry, and not only hurry as to labour, but in too much discomposure of mind, and my journal would ha' been full of many dull things. For example, I must have said thus: 'Sept. the 30th. After I got to shore and had escap'd drowning, instead of being thankful to God for my deliverance, having first vomited with the great quantity of salt water which was gotten into my stomach, and recovering my self a little, I ran about the shore, wringing my hands and beating my head and face, exclaiming at my misery, and crying out, I was undone, undone, till tyr'd and faint I was forc'd to lye down on the ground to repose, but durst not sleep for fear of being devour'd.'

Some days after this, and after I had been on board the ship, and got all that I could out of her, yet I could not forbear getting up to the top of a little mountain and looking out to sea in hopes of seeing a ship, then fancy at a vast distance I spy'd a sail, please my self with the hopes of it, and then after looking steadily till I was almost blind, lose it quite, and sit down and weep like a child, and thus encrease my misery by my folly.

But having gotten over these things in some measure, and having settled my houshold stuff and habitation, made me a table and a chair, and all as handsome about me as I could, I began to keep my journal, of which I shall here give you the copy (tho' in it will be told all these particulars over again) as long as it lasted, for having no more ink I was forc'd to leave it off.

THE JOURNAL

September 30, 1659. I, poor miserable Robinson Crusoe, being ship-wreck'd, during a dreadful storm, in the offing, came on shore on this dismal unfortunate island, which I call'd the Island of Despair, all the rest of the ship's company being drown'd, and my self almost dead.

All the rest of that day I spent in afflicting my self at the dismal circumstances I was brought to, viz. I had neither food, house, clothes, weapon, or place to fly to, and in despair of any relief, saw nothing but death before me, either that I should be devour'd by wild beasts, murther'd by savages, or starv'd to death for want of food. At the approach of night, I slept in a tree for fear of wild creatures, but slept soundly tho' it rain'd all night.

October 1. In the morning I saw to my great surprise the ship had floated with the high tide, and was driven on shore again much nearer the island, which as it was some comfort on one hand, for seeing her sit upright, and not broken to pieces, I hop'd, if the wind abated, I might get on board, and get some food and necessaries out of her for my relief; so on the other hand, it renew'd my grief at the loss of my comrades, who I imagin'd if we had all staid on board might have sav'd the ship, or at least that they would not have been all drown'd as they were; and that had the men been sav'd, we might perhaps have built us a boat out of the ruins of the ship, to have carried us to some other part of the world. I spent a great part of this day in perplexing my self on these things; but at length seeing the ship almost dry, I went upon the sand as near as I could, and then swam on board; this day also it continu'd raining, tho' with no wind at all.

From the 1st of October to the 24th. All these days entirely spent in many several voyages to get all I could out of the ship, which I brought on shore, every tide of flood, upon rafts. Much rain also in these days, tho' with some intervals of fair weather: but, it seems, this was the rainy season.

Oct. 20. I overset my raft and all the goods I had got upon it, but being in shoal* water, and the things being chiefly heavy, I recover'd many of them when the tide was out.

Oct. 25. It rain'd all night and all day, with some gusts of wind, during which time the ship broke in pieces, the wind blowing a little harder than before, and was no more to be seen, except the wreck of her, and that only at low water. I spent this day in covering and securing the goods which I had sav'd, that the rain might not spoil them.

Oct. 26. I walk'd about the shore almost all day to find out a place to fix my habitation, greatly concern'd to secure my self from an attack in the night, either from wild beasts or men. Towards night I fix'd upon a proper place under a rock, and mark'd out a semi-circle for my encampment, which I resolv'd to strengthen with a work, wall, or fortification made of double piles, lin'd within with cables, and without with turf.

From the 26th to the 30th, I work'd very hard in carrying all my goods to my new habitation, tho' some part of the time it rain'd exceeding hard.

The 31st, in the morning I went out into the island with my gun to see for some food, and discover the country, when I kill'd a she-goat, and her kid follow'd me home, which I afterwards kill'd also because it would not feed.

November 1. I set up my tent under a rock, and lay there for the first night, making it as large as I could with stakes driven in to swing my hammock upon.

Nov. 2. I set up all my chests and boards, and the pieces of timber which made my rafts, and with them form'd a fence round me, a little within the place I had mark'd out for my fortification.

Nov. 3. I went out with my gun and kill'd two fowls like ducks, which were very good food. In the afternoon went to work to make me a table.

Nov. 4. This morning I began to order my times of work, of going out with my gun, time of sleep, and time for diversion, viz.: every morning I walk'd out with my gun for two or three hours if it did not rain, then employ'd my self to work till about eleven a-clock, then eat what I had to live on, and from twelve to two I lay down to sleep, the weather being excessive hot, and then in the evening to work again. The working part of this day and of the next were wholly employ'd in making my table, for I was yet but a very sorry workman, tho' time and necessity made me a compleat natural mechanick soon after, as I believe it would do any one else.

Nov. 5. This day went abroad with my gun and my dog, and kill'd a wild cat, her skin pretty soft, but her flesh good for nothing: every creature I kill'd I took off the skins and preserved them. Coming back by the sea shore, I saw many sorts of sea fowls which I did not understand, but was surpris'd and almost frighted with two or three seals,* which, while I was gazing at, not well knowing what they were, got into the sea and escap'd me for that time.

Nov. 6. After my morning walk I went to work with my table again, and finish'd it, tho' not to my liking; nor was it long before I learn'd to mend it.

Nov. 7. Now it began to be settled fair weather. The 7th, 8th, 9th, 10th, and part of the 12th (for the 11th was Sunday) I took wholly up to make me a chair, and with much ado brought it to a tolerable shape, but never to please me, and even in the making I pull'd it in pieces several times. *Note.* I soon neglected my keeping Sundays, for omitting my mark for them on my post, I forgot which was which.

Nov. 13. This day it rain'd, which refresh'd me exceedingly, and cool'd the earth, but it was accompany'd with terrible thunder and lightning, which frighted me dreadfully for fear of my powder; as soon as it was over, I resolv'd to separate my stock of powder into as many little parcels as possible, that it might not be in danger.

Nov. 14, 15, 16. These three days I spent in making little square chests or boxes, which might hold a pound or two pound, at most, of powder, and so putting the powder in, I stow'd it in places as secure and remote from one another as possible. On one of these three days I kill'd a large bird that was good to eat, but I know not what to call it.

Nov. 17. This day I began to dig behind my tent in to the rock to make room for my farther conveniency. *Note.* Three things I wanted exceedingly for this work, viz. a pick-axe, a shovel, and a wheel-barrow or basket; so I desisted from my work, and began to consider how to supply that want and make me some tools; as for a pick-axe, I made use of the iron crows, which were proper enough, tho' heavy; but the next thing was a shovel or spade; this was so absolutely necessary, that indeed I could do nothing effectually without it, but what kind of one to make I knew not.

Nov. 18. The next day in searching the woods I found a tree of that wood, or like it, which in the Brasils they call the iron tree, for its exceeding hardness; of this, with great labour and almost spoiling my axe, I cut a piece, and brought it home too with difficulty enough, for it was exceedingly heavy.

The excessive hardness of the wood, and having no other way, made me a long while upon this machine, for I work'd it effectually by little and little into the form of a shovel or spade, the handle exactly shap'd like ours in England, only that the broad part having no iron shod upon it at bottom, it would not last me so long; however, it serv'd well enough for the uses which I had occasion to put it to; but never was a shovel, I believe, made after that fashion, or so long a making.

I was still deficient, for I wanted a basket or a wheel-barrow; a basket I could not make by any means, having no such things as twigs that would bend to make wicker ware, at least none yet found out; and as to a wheel-barrow, I fancy'd I could make all but the wheel, but that I had no notion of, neither did I know how to go about it; besides, I had no possible way to make the iron gudgeons for the spindle or axis of the wheel to run in, so I gave it over, and so for carrying away the earth which I dug out of the cave, I made me a thing like a hodd, which the labourers carry morter in when they serve the bricklayers.

This was not so difficult to me as the making the shovel; and yet this, and the shovel, and the attempt which I made in vain to make a wheel-barrow, took me up no less than four days; I mean, always excepting my morning walk with my gun, which I seldom fail'd, and very seldom fail'd also bringing home something fit to eat.

Nov. 23. My other work having now stood still, because of my making these tools, when they were finish'd I went on, and working every day, as my strength and time allow'd, I spent eighteen days entirely in widening and deepening my cave, that it might hold my goods commodiously.

Note. During all this time, I work'd to make this room or cave spacious enough to accommodate me as a warehouse or magazin, a kitchen, a dining-room, and a cellar; as for my lodging, I kept to the tent, except that some times in the wet season of the year, it rain'd so hard that I could not keep my self dry, which caused me afterwards to cover all my place within my pale with long poles in the form of rafters leaning against the rock, and load them with flaggs* and large leaves of trees like a thatch.

December 10th. I began now to think my cave or vault finished, when on a sudden (it seems I had made it too large) a great quantity of earth fell down from the top and one side, so much, that in short it frighted me, and not without reason too; for if I had been under it I had never wanted a grave-digger. Upon this disaster I had a great deal of work to do over again; for I had the loose earth to carry out, and, which was of more importance, I had the seiling to prop up, so that I might be sure no more would come down.

Dec. 11. This day I went to work with it accordingly, and got two shores or posts pitch'd upright to the top, with two pieces of boards a-cross over each post; this I finish'd the next day; and setting more posts up with boards, in about a week more I had the roof secur'd, and the posts, standing in rows, serv'd me for partitions to part of my house.

Dec. 17. From this day to the twentieth I plac'd shelves, and knock'd up nails on the posts to hang every thing up that could be hung up, and now I began to be in some order within doors.

Dec. 20. Now I carry'd every thing into the cave, and began to furnish my house, and set up some pieces of boards, like a dresser, to order my victuals upon, but boards began to be very scarce with me; also I made me another table.

Dec. 24. Much rain all night and all day; no stirring out.

Dec. 25. Rain all day.

Dec. 26. No rain, and the earth much cooler than before, and pleasanter.

Dec. 27. Kill'd a young goat, and lam'd another so as that I catch'd it, and led it home in a string; when I had it home, I bound and splinter'd up its leg, which was broke. *N.B.* I took such care of it that it liv'd, and the leg grew well, and as strong as ever; but by my nursing it so long it grew tame, and fed upon the little green at my door, and would not go away. This was the first time that I entertain'd a thought of breeding up some tame creatures, that I might have food when my powder and shot was all spent.

Dec. 28, 29, 30. Great heats and no breeze; so that there was no stirring abroad, except in the evening for food; this time I spent in putting all my things in order within doors.

January 1. Very hot still, but I went abroad early and late with my gun, and lay still in the middle of the day. This evening, going farther into the valleys which lay towards the center of the island, I found there was plenty of goats, tho' exceeding shy and hard to come at; however I resolv'd to try if I could not bring my dog to hunt them down.

Jan. 2. Accordingly, the next day I went out with my dog, and set him upon the goats; but I was mistaken, for they all fac'd about the dog, and he knew his danger too well, for he would not come near them.

Jan. 3. I began my fence or wall; which, being still jealous of my being attack'd by some body, I resolv'd to make very thick and strong.

N.B. *This wall being describ'd before, I purposely omit what was said in the Journal; it is sufficient to observe that I was no less time than from the 3d of January to the 14th of April, working, finishing, and perfecting this wall, tho' it was no more than about 24 yards in length, being a half circle from one place in the rock to another place about eight yards from it, the door of the cave being in the center behind it.*

All this time I work'd very hard, and the rains hindering me many days, nay, sometimes weeks together; but I thought I should never be perfectly secure 'till this wall was finish'd; and it is scarce credible what inexpressible labour every thing was done with, especially the bringing piles out of the woods, and driving them into the ground, for I made them much bigger than I need to have done.

When this wall was finished, and the out-side double fenc'd with a turf-wall rais'd up close to it, I perswaded my self that if any people were to come on shore there, they would not perceive any thing like a habitation; and it was very well I did so, as may be observ'd hereafter upon a very remarkable occasion.

During this time, I made my rounds in the woods for game every day when the rain admitted me, and made frequent discoveries in these walks of something or other to my advantage; particularly I found a kind of wild pidgeons, who built not as wood pidgeons, in a tree, but rather as house pidgeons, in the holes of the rocks; and taking some young ones, I endeavoured to breed them up tame, and did so; but when they grew older they flew all away, which perhaps was at first for want of feeding them, for I had nothing to give them; however I frequently found their nests, and got their young ones, which were very good meat.

And now, in the managing my household affairs, I found my self wanting in many things, which I thought at first it was impossible for me to make, as indeed as to some of them it was; for instance, I could never make a cask to be hooped. I had a small runlet or two, as I observed before, but I could never arrive to the capacity of making one by them, tho' I spent many weeks about it; I could neither put in the heads, or joint the staves so true to one another as to make them hold water, so I gave that also over.

In the next place, I was at a great loss for candle; so that as soon as ever it was dark, which was generally by seven-a-clock, I was oblig'd to go to bed. I remembred the lump of bees-wax with which I made candles in my African adventure, but I had none of that now; the only remedy I had was, that when I had kill'd a goat, I sav'd the tallow, and with a little dish made of clay, which I bak'd in the sun, to which I added a wick of some oakum,* I made me a lamp; and this gave me light, tho' not a clear steady light like a candle. In the middle of all my labours it happen'd, that rummaging my things, I found a little bag, which, as I hinted before, had been fill'd with corn for the feeding of poultry, not for this voyage, but before, as I suppose, when the ship came from Lisbon. What little remainder of corn had been in the bag was all devour'd with the rats, and I saw nothing in the bag but husks and dust; and being willing to have the bag for some other use, I think it was to put powder in, when I divided it for fear of the lightning, or some such use, I shook the husks of corn out of it on one side of my fortification under the rock.

It was a little before the great rains, just now mention'd, that I threw this stuff away, taking no notice of any thing, and not so much as remembering that I had thrown any thing there; when about a month after, or thereabout, I saw some few stalks of something green shooting out of the ground, which I fancy'd might be some plant I had not seen; but I was surpriz'd and perfectly astonish'd, when, after a little longer time, I saw about ten or twelve ears come out, which were perfect green barley of the same kind as our European, nay, as our English barley.

It is impossible to express the astonishment and confusion of my thoughts on this occasion. I had hitherto acted upon no religious foundation at all; indeed, I had very few notions of religion in my head, or had entertain'd any sense of any thing that had befallen me, otherwise than as a chance, or, as we lightly say, what pleases God; without so much as enquiring into the end of Providence in these things, or His order in governing events in the world. But after I saw barley grow there, in a climate which I know was not proper for corn, and especially that I knew not how it came there, it startl'd me strangely, and I began to suggest that God had miraculously caus'd this grain to grow without any help of seed sown, and that it was so directed purely for my sustenance on that wild miserable place.

This touch'd my heart a little, and brought tears out of my eyes, and I began to bless my self that such a prodigy of nature should happen upon my account; and this was the more strange to me, because I saw near it still all along by the side of the rock, some other straggling stalks, which prov'd to be stalks of ryce, and which I knew, because I had seen it grow in Africa when I was ashore there.

I not only thought these the pure productions of Providence for my support, but not doubting but that there was more in the place, I went all over that part of the island where I had been before, peering in every corner, and under every rock, to see for more of it, but I could not find any; at last it occur'd to my thoughts, that I had shook a bag of chicken's meat out in that place, and then the wonder began to cease; and I must confess, my religious thankfulness to God's providence began to abate too, upon the discovering that all this was nothing but what was common; tho' I ought to have been as thankful for so strange and unforseen providence, as if it had been miraculous; for it was really the work of providence as to me, that should order or appoint, that 10 or 12 grains of corn should remain unspoil'd (when the rats had destroy'd all the rest) as if it had been dropt from heaven; as also, that I should throw it out in that particular place, where, it being in the shade of a high rock, it sprang up immediately; whereas, if I had thrown it anywhere else at that time, it had been burnt up and destroy'd.

I carefully sav'd the ears of this corn, you may be sure, in their season, which was about the end of June; and laying up every corn, I resolv'd to sow them all again, hoping in time to have some quantity sufficient to supply me with bread. But it was not till the 4th year that I could allow my self the least grain of this corn to eat, and even then but sparingly, as I shall say afterwards in its order; for I lost all that I sow'd the first season by not observing the proper time; for I sow'd it just before the dry season, so that it never came up at all, at least not as it would ha' done: of which in its place.

Besides this barley, there was, as above, 20 or 30 stalks of ryce, which I preserv'd with the same care, and whose use was of the same kind or to the same purpose, viz. to make me bread, or rather food; for I found ways to cook it up without baking, tho' I did that also after some time. But to return to my journal.

I work'd excessive hard these three or four months to get my wall done; and the 14th of April I closed it up, contriving to go into it, not by a door, but over the wall by a ladder, that there might be no sign in the out-side of my habitation.

April 16. I finish'd the ladder, so I went up with the ladder to the top, and then pull'd it up after me, and let it down in the in-side. This was a compleat enclosure to me; for within I had room enough, and nothing could come at me from without, unless it could first mount my wall.

The very next day after this wall was finish'd, I had almost had all my labour overthrown at once, and my self kill'd; the case was thus: As I was busy in the inside of it, behind my tent, just in the entrance into my cave, I was terribly frighted with a most dreadful surprising thing indeed; for all on a sudden I found the earth come crumbling down from the roof of my cave, and from the edge of the hill over my head, and two of the posts I had set up in the cave crack'd in a frightful manner; I was heartily scar'd, but thought nothing of what was really the cause, only thinking that the top of my cave was falling in, as some of it had done before; and for fear I shou'd be bury'd in it, I ran foreward to my ladder, and not thinking my self safe there neither, I got over my wall for fear of the pieces of the hill which I expected might roll down upon me: I was no sooner stepp'd down upon the firm ground, but I plainly saw it was a terrible earthquake, for the ground I stood on shook three times at about eight minutes' distance, with three such shocks as would have overturn'd the strongest building that could be suppos'd to have stood on the earth; and a great piece of the top of a rock, which stood about half a mile from me next the sea fell down with such a terrible noise as I never heard in all my life. I perceiv'd also, the very sea was put into violent motion by it; and I believe the shocks were stronger under the water than on the island.

I was so amaz'd with the thing it self, having never felt the like, or discours'd with any one that had, that I was like one dead or stupify'd; and the motion of the earth made my stomach sick like one that was toss'd at sea; but the noise of the falling of the rock awak'd me, as it were, and rousing me from the stupify'd condition I was in, fill'd me with horror, and I thought of nothing then but the hill falling upon my tent and all my houshold goods, and burying all at once; and this sunk my very soul within me a second time.

After the third shock was over, and I felt no more for some time, I began to take courage, and yet I had not heart enough to go over my wall again, for fear of being buried alive, but sat upon the ground, greatly cast down and disconsolate, not knowing what to do. All this while I had not the least serious religous thought, nothing but the common *Lord ha' mercy upon me*; and when it was over that went away too.

While I sat thus I found the air over-cast and grow cloudy as if it would rain; soon after that the wind rose by little and little, so that, in less than half an hour, it blew a most dreadful hurricane. The sea was all on a sudden cover'd over with foam and froth, the shore was cover'd with the breach of the water, the trees were torn up by the roots, and a terrible storm it was; and this held about three hours, and then began to abate, and in two hours more it was stark* calm, and began to rain very hard.

All this while I sat upon the ground very much terrify'd and dejected, when on a sudden it came into my thoughts, that these winds and rain being the consequences of the earthquake, the earthquake it self was spent and over, and I might venture into my cave again. With this thought my spirits began to revive, and the rain also helping to perswade me, I went in and sat down in my tent, but the rain was so violent, that my tent was ready to be beaten down with it, and I was forc'd to go into my cave, tho' very much afraid and uneasy for fear it should fall on my head.

This violent rain forc'd me to a new work, viz. to cut a hole thro' my new fortification like a sink to let the water go out, which would else have drown'd my cave. After I had been in my cave some time, and found still no more shocks of the earthquake follow, I began to be more compos'd; and now to support my spirits, which indeed wanted it very much, I went to my little store and took a small sup of rum, which, however, I did then and always very sparingly, knowing I could have no more when that was gone.

It continu'd raining all that night, and great part of the next day, so that I could not stir abroad, but my mind being more compos'd, I began to think of what I had best do, concluding that if the island was subject to these earthquakes, there would be no living for me in a cave, but I must consider of building me some little hut in an open place which I might surround with a wall as I had done here, and so make my self secure from wild beasts or men; but concluded, if I staid where I was, I should certainly, one time or other, be bury'd alive.

With these thoughts I resolv'd to remove my tent from the place where it stood, which was just under the hanging precipice of the hill, and which, if it should be shaken again, would certainly fall upon my tent. And I spent the two next days, being the 19th and 20th of April, in contriving where and how to remove my habitation.

The fear of being swallow'd up alive, made me that I never slept in quiet, and yet the apprehensions of lying abroad without any fence was almost equal to it; but still when I look'd about and saw how every thing was put in order, how pleasantly conceal'd I was, and how safe from danger, it made me very loath to remove.

In the mean time it occur'd to me that it would require a vast deal of time for me to do this, and that I must be contented to run the venture where I was, till I had form'd a camp for myself, and had secur'd it so as to remove to it; so with this resolution I compos'd my self for a time, and resolv'd that I would go to work with all speed to build me a wall with piles and cables, &c., in a circle as before, and set my tent up in it when it was finish'd, but that I would venture to stay where I was till it was finish'd and fit to remove to. This was the 21st.

April 22. The next morning I began to consider of means to put this resolve in execution, but I was at a great loss about my tools; I had three large axes and abundance of hatchets (for we carried the hatchets for traffick with the Indians), but with much chopping and cutting knotty hard wood, they were all full of notches and dull, and tho' I had a grindstone, I could not turn it and grind my tools too; this cost me as much thought as a statesman would have bestow'd upon a grand point of politicks, or a judge upon the life and death of a man. At length I contriv'd a wheel with a string, to turn it with my foot, that I might have both my hands at liberty. *Note.* I had never seen any such thing in England, or at least not to take notice how it was done, tho' since I have observ'd it is very common there: besides that, my grindstone was very large and heavy. This machine cost me a full week's work to bring it to perfection.

April 28, 29. These two whole days I took up in grinding my tools, my machine for turning my grindstone performing very well.

April 30. Having perceiv'd my bread had been low a great while, now I took a survey of it, and reduc'd my self to one bisket-cake a day, which made my heart very heavy.

May 1. In the morning, looking towards the sea-side, the tide being low, I saw something lye on the shore bigger than ordinary, and it look'd like a cask; when I came to it, I found a small barrel, and two or three pieces of the wreck of the ship, which were driven on shore by the late hurricane, and looking towards the wreck itself I thought it seem'd to lye higher out of the water than it us'd to do; I examin'd the barrel which was driven on shore, and soon found it was a barrel of gunpowder, but it had taken water, and the powder was cak'd as hard as a stone; however, I roll'd it farther on shore for the present, and went on upon the sands as near as I could to the wreck of the ship to look for more.

When I came down to the ship I found it strangely remov'd. The fore-castle, which lay before bury'd in sand, was heav'd up at least six foot, and the stern, which was broke to pieces and parted from the rest by the force of the sea soon after I had left rummaging her, was toss'd, as it were, up, and cast on one side, and the sand was thrown so high on that side next her stern, that whereas there was a great place of water before, so that I could not come within a quarter of a mile of the wreck without swimming, I could now walk quite up to her when the tide was out; I was surpris'd with this at first, but soon concluded it must be done by the earthquake, and as by this violence the ship was more broken open than formerly, so many things came daily on shore, which the sea had loosen'd, and which the winds and water rolled by degrees to the land.

This wholly diverted my thoughts from the design of removing my habitation; and I busied my self mightily that day especially, in searching whether I could make any way into the ship, but I found nothing was to be expected of that kind, for that all the in-side of the ship was choak'd up with sand. However, as I had learn'd not to despair of any thing, I resolv'd to pull every thing to pieces that I could of the ship, concluding that every thing I could get from her would be of some use or other to me.

May 3. I began with my saw and cut a piece of a beam thro', which I thought held some of the upper part or quarter-deck together, and when I had cut it thro', I clear'd away the sand as well as I could from the side which lay highest; but the tide coming in, I was oblig'd to give over for that time.

May 4. I went a fishing, but caught not one fish that I durst eat of, till I was weary of my sport, when just going to leave off, I caught a young dolphin. I had made me a long line of some rope yarn, but I had no hooks, yet I frequently caught fish enough, as much as I car'd to eat; all which I dry'd in the sun, and eat them dry.

May 5. Work'd on the wreck, cut another beam asunder, and brought three great fir planks off from the decks, which I ty'd together, and made swim on shore when the tide of flood came on.

May 6. Work'd on the wreck, got several iron bolts out of her, and other pieces of iron work; work'd very hard, and came home very much tyr'd, and had thoughts of giving it over.

May 7. Went to the wreck again, but with an intent not to work, but found the weight of the wreck had broke itself down, the beams being cut, that several pieces of the ship seem'd to lie loose, and the in-side of the hold lay so open that I could see into it, but almost full of water and sand.

May 8. Went to the wreck, and carry'd an iron crow to wrench up the deck, which lay now quite clear of the water or sand; I wrench'd open two planks, and brought them on shore also with the tide; I left the iron crow in the wreck for next day.

May 9. Went to the wreck, and with the crow made way into the body of the wreck, and felt several casks, and loosen'd them with the crow, but could not break them up; I felt also the roll of English lead, and could stir it, but it was too heavy to remove.

May 10, 11, 12, 13, 14. Went every day to the wreck, and got a great deal of pieces of timber, and boards, or plank, and 2 or 300 weight of iron.

May 15. I carry'd two hatchets to try if I could not cut a piece off of the roll of lead, by placing the edge of one hatchet, and driving it with the other; but as it lay about a foot and a half in the water, I could not make any blow to drive the hatchet.

May 16. It had blow'd hard in the night, and the wreck appear'd more broken by the force of the water; but I stay'd so long in the woods to get pidgeons for food, that the tide prevented me going to the wreck that day.

May 17. I saw some pieces of the wreck blown on shore, at a great distance, near two miles off me, but resolv'd to see what they were, and found it was a piece of the head, but too heavy for me to bring away.

May 24. Every day to this day I work'd on the wreck, and with hard labour I loosen'd some things so much with the crow, that the first blowing tide several casks floated out, and two of the seamen's chests; but the wind blowing from the shore, nothing came to land that day but pieces of timber and a hogshead which had some Brazil pork in it, but the salt-water and the sand had spoil'd it.

I continu'd this work every day to the 15th of June, except the time necessary to get food, which I always appointed, during this part of my employment, to be when the tide was up, that I might be ready when it was ebb'd out, and by this time I had gotten timber, and plank, and iron-work enough to have builded a good boat, if I had known how; and also I got, at several times and in several pieces, near 100 weight of the sheat-lead.

June 16. Going down to the sea-side, I found a large tortoise or turtle; this was the first I had seen, which it seems was only my misfortune, not any defect of the place, or scarcity; for had I happen'd to be on the other side of the island, I might have had hundreds of them every day, as I found afterwards; but perhaps had paid dear enough for them.

June 17. I spent in cooking the turtle; I found in her threescore eggs, and her flesh was to me at that time the most savoury and pleasant that ever I tasted in my life, having had no flesh, but of goats and fowls, since I landed in this horrid place.

June 18. Rain'd all day, and I stay'd within. I thought at this time the rain felt cold, and I was something chilly, which I knew was not usual in that latitude.

June 19. Very ill, and shivering, as if the weather had been cold.

June 20. No rest all night, violent pains in my head, and feverish.

June 21. Very ill, frighted almost to death with the apprehensions of my sad condition, to be sick, and no help; pray'd to God for the first time since the storm off of Hull, but scarce knew what I said, or why, my thoughts being all confused.

June 22. A little better, but under dreadful apprehensions of sickness.

June 23. Very bad again, cold shivering, and then a violent head-ach.

June 24. Much better.

June 25. An ague very violent; the fit held me seven hours, cold fit and hot, with faint sweats after it.

June 26. Better; and having no victuals to eat, took my gun, but found my self very weak; however, I kill'd a she-goat, and with much difficulty got it home, and broil'd some of it and eat; I wou'd fain have stew'd it and made some broath, but had no pot.

June 27. The ague again so violent that I lay a-bed all day, and neither eat or drank. I was ready to perish for thirst, but so weak, I had not strength to stand up, or to get my self any water to drink: pray'd to God again, but was light-headed, and when I was not, I was so ignorant that I knew not what to say; only I lay and cry'd, 'Lord look upon me, Lord pity me, Lord have mercy upon me.' I suppose I did nothing else for two or three hours, till the fit wearing off, I fell asleep, and did not wake till far in the night; when I wak'd, I found my self much refresh'd, but weak, and exceeding thirsty. However, as I had no water in my whole habitation, I was forc'd to lie till morning, and went to sleep again. In this second sleep, I had this terrible dream.

I thought that I was sitting on the ground on the outside of my wall, where I sat when the storm blew after the earthquake, and that I saw a man descend from a great black cloud, in a bright flame of fire, and light upon the ground. He was all over as bright as a flame, so that I could but just bear to look towards him; his countenance was most inexpressibly dreadful, impossible for words to describe; when he stepp'd upon the ground with his feet, I thought the earth trembl'd, just as it had done before in the earthquake, and all the air look'd, to my apprehension, as if it had been fill'd with flashes of fire.

He was no sooner landed upon the earth, but he moved forward towards me, with a long spear or weapon in his hand, to kill me; and when he came to a rising ground, at some distance, he spoke to me, or I heard a voice so terrible, that it is impossible to express the terror of it; all that I can say I understood, was this: 'Seeing all these things have not brought thee to repentance, now thou shalt die'; at which words, I thought he lifted up the spear that was in his hand, to kill me.

No one that shall ever read this account will expect that I should be able to describe the horrors of my soul at this terrible vision; I mean, that even while it was a dream, I even dreamed of those horrors; nor is it any more possible to describe the impression that remain'd upon my mind when I awak'd and found it was but a dream.

I had, alas! no divine knowledge; what I had received by the good instruction of my father was then worn out by an uninterrupted series, for 8 years, of seafaring wickedness, and a constant conversation with nothing but such as were like my self, wicked and prophane to the last degree. I do not remember that I had in all that time one thought that so much as tended either to looking upwards toward God, or inwards towards a reflection upon my own ways; but a certain stupidity of soul, without desire of good or conscience of evil, had entirely overwhelm'd me, and I was all that the most hardned, unthinking, wicked creature among our common sailors can be supposed to be, not having the least sense, either of the fear of God in danger, or of thankfulness to God in deliverances.

In the relating what is already past of my story, this will be the more easily believ'd, when I shall add, that thro' all the variety of miseries that had to this day befallen me, I never had so much as one thought of it being the hand of God, or that it was a just punishment for my sin; my rebellious behaviour against my father, or my present sins which were great; or so much as a punishment for the general course of my wicked life. When I was on the desperate expedition on the desart shores of Africa, I never had so much as one thought of what would become of me; or one wish to God to direct me whither I should go, or to keep me from the danger which apparently surrounded me, as well from voracious creatures as cruel savages: but I was meerly thoughtless of a God or a providence; acted like a meer brute from the principles of nature, and by the dictates of common sense only, and indeed hardly that.

When I was deliver'd and taken up at sea by the Portugal captain, well us'd, and dealt justly and honourably with, as well as charitably, I had not the least thankfulness on my thoughts. When again I was shipwreck'd, ruin'd, and in danger of drowning on this island, I was as far from remorse, or looking on it as a judgment; I only said to my self often, that I was an unfortunate dog, and born to be always miserable.

It is true, when I got on shore first here, and found all my ship's crew drown'd, and my self spar'd, I was surpriz'd with a kind of extasie, and some transports of soul, which, had the grace of God assisted, might have come up to true thankfulness; but it ended where it begun, in a meer common flight of joy, or as I may say, being glad I was alive, without the least reflection upon the distinguishing goodness of the hand which had preserv'd me, and had singled me out to be preserv'd, when all the rest were destroy'd; or an enquiry why Providence had been thus merciful to me; even just the same common sort of joy which seamen generally have after they are got safe ashore from a shipwreck, which they drown all in the next bowl of punch, and forget almost as soon as it is over; and all the rest of my life was like it.

Even when I was afterwards, on due consideration, made sensible of my condition, how I was cast on this dreadful place, out of the reach of humane kind, out of all hope of relief or prospect of redemption, as soon as I saw but a prospect of living, and that I should not starve and perish for hunger, all the sense of my affliction wore off, and I begun to be very easy, apply'd my self to the works proper for my preservation and supply, and was far enough from being afflicted at my condition, as a judgment from heaven, or as the hand of God against me; these were thoughts which very seldom enter'd into my head.

The growing up of the corn, as is hinted in my journal, had at first some little influence upon me, and began to affect me with seriousness, as long as I thought it had something miraculous in it; but as soon as ever that part of the thought was remov'd, all the impression which was rais'd from it wore off also, as I have noted already.

Even the earthquake, tho' nothing could be more terrible in its nature, or more immediately directing to the invisible power which alone directs such things, yet no sooner was the first fright over, but the impression it had made went off also. I had no more sense of God or His judgments, much less of the present affliction of my circumstances being from His hand, than if I had been in the most prosperous condition of life.

But now when I began to be sick, and a leisurely view of the miseries of death came to place itself before me, when my spirits began to sink under the burthen of a strong distemper, and nature was exhausted with the violence of the feaver, conscience, that had slept so long, begun to awake, and I began to reproach my self with my past life, in which I had so evidently, by uncommon wickedness, provok'd the justice of God to lay me under uncommon strokes, and to deal with me in so vindictive a manner.

These reflections oppress'd me for the second or third day of my distemper, and in the violence, as well of the feaver as of the dreadful reproaches of my conscience, extorted some words from me, like praying to God, tho' I cannot say they were either a prayer attended with desires or with hopes; it was rather the voice of meer fright and distress; my thoughts were confus'd, the convictions great upon my mind, and the horror of dying in such a miserable condition rais'd vapours into my head with the meer apprehensions; and in these hurries of my soul, I know not what my tongue might express: but it was rather exclamation, such as, 'Lord! what a miserable creature am I? If I should be sick, I shall certainly die for want of help, and what will become of me!' Then the tears burst out of my eyes, and I could say no more for a good while.

In this interval, the good advice of my father came to my mind, and presently his prediction which I mention'd at the beginning of this story, viz. that if I did take this foolish step, God would not bless me, and I would have leisure hereafter to reflect upon having neglected His counsel, when there might be none to assist in my recovery. 'Now,' said I aloud, 'my dear father's words are come to pass: God's justice has overtaken me, and I have none to help or hear me: I rejected the voice of Providence, which had mercifully put me in a posture or station of life wherein I might have been happy and easy; but I would neither see it my self, or learn to know the blessing of it from my parents; I left them to mourn over my folly, and now I am left to mourn under the consequences of it; I refus'd their help and assistance who wou'd have lifted me into the world, and wou'd have made every thing easy to me, and now I have difficulties to struggle with, too great even for nature itself to support, and no assistance, no help, no comfort, no advice.' Then I cry'd out, 'Lord, be my help, for I am in great distress.'

This was the first prayer, if I may call it so, that I had made for many years. But I return to my journal.

June 28. Having been somewhat refresh'd with the sleep I had had, and the fit being entirely off, I got up; and tho' the fright and terror of my dream was very great, yet I consider'd that the fit of the ague wou'd return again the next day, and now was my time to get something to refresh and support my self when I should be ill; and the first thing I did, I fill'd a large square case bottle with water, and set it upon my table, in reach of my bed; and to take off the chill or aguish disposition of the water, I put about a quarter of a pint of rum into it, and mix'd them together; then I got me a piece of the goat's flesh, and broil'd it on the coals, but could eat very little; I walk'd about, but was very weak, and withal very sad and heavy-hearted in the sense of my miserable condition; dreading the return of my distemper the next day; at night I made my supper of three of the turtle's eggs, which I roasted in the ashes, and eat, as we call it, in the shell; and this was the first bit of meat I had ever ask'd God's blessing to, even as I cou'd remember, in my whole life.

After I had eaten, I try'd to walk, but found my self so weak that I cou'd hardly carry the gun (for I never went out without that), so I went but a little way, and sat down upon the ground, looking out upon the sea, which was just before me, and very calm and smooth. As I sat here, some such thoughts as these occurred to me.

What is this earth and sea of which I have seen so much? Whence is it produc'd? And what am I and all the other creatures, wild and tame, humane and brutal? Whence are we?

Sure we are all made by some secret power, who form'd the earth and sea, the air and sky; and who is that?

Then it follow'd most naturally, It is God that has made it all. Well, but then it came on strangely, if God has made all these things, He guides and governs them all, and all things that concern them; for the power that could make all things must certainly have power to guide and direct them.

If so, nothing can happen in the great circuit of His works, either without His knowledge or appointment.

And if nothing happens without His knowledge, He knows that I am here, and am in this dreadful condition; and if nothing happens without His appointment, He has appointed all this to befal me.

Nothing occurr'd to my thought to contradict any of these conclusions; and therefore it rested upon me with the greater force that it must needs be, that God had appointed all this to befal me; that I was brought to this miserable circumstance by His direction, He having the sole power, not of me only, but of every thing that happen'd in the world. Immediately it follow'd:

Why has God done this to me? What have I done to be thus us'd?

My conscience presently check'd me in that enquiry, as if I had blasphem'd, and methought it spoke to me like a voice: 'WRETCH! dost thou ask what thou hast done? Look back upon a dreadful mis-spent life, and ask thy self what thou hast *not* done; ask, Why is it that thou wert not long ago destroy'd? Why wert thou not drown'd in Yarmouth roads? kill'd in the fight when the ship was taken by the Sallee man of war? devour'd by the wild beasts on the coast of Africa? or drown'd *here*, when all the crew perish'd but thy self? Dost thou ask, "What have I done?"'

I was struck dumb with these reflections, as one astonish'd, and had not a word to say, no, not to answer to my self, but rose up pensive and sad, walk'd back to my retreat, and went up over my wall, as if I had been going to bed, but my thoughts were sadly disturb'd, and I had no inclination to sleep; so I sat down in my chair and lighted my lamp, for it began to be dark. Now as the apprehension of the return of my distemper terrify'd me very much, it occurr'd to my thought, that the Brasilians take no physick but their tobacco for almost all distempers; and I had a piece of a roll of tobacco in one of the chests which was quite cur'd, and some also that was green and not quite cur'd.

I went, directed by Heaven, no doubt; for in this chest I found a cure, both for soul and body. I open'd the chest and found what I look'd for, viz. the tobacco; and as the few books I had sav'd lay there too, I took out one of the Bibles which I mention'd before, and which to this time I had not found leisure, or so much as inclination, to look into; I say, I took it out, and brought both that and the tobacco with me to the table.

What use to make of the tobacco I knew not, as to my distemper, or whether it was good for it or no; but I try'd several experiments with it, as if I was resolv'd it should hit one way or other. I first took a piece of a leaf, and chew'd it in my mouth, which indeed at first almost stupify'd my brain, the tobacco being green and strong, and that I had not been much us'd to it; then I took some and steeped it an hour or two in some rum, and resolv'd to take a dose of it when I lay down; and lastly, I burnt some upon a pan of coals, and held my nose close over the smoke of it as long as I could bear it, as well for the heat as almost for suffocation.

In the interval of this operation, I took up the Bible and began to read, but my head was too much disturb'd with the tobacco to bear reading, at least that time; only having opened the book casually, the first words that occur'd to me were these: *Call on me in the day of trouble, and I will deliver, and thou shalt glorify me.*

The words were very apt to my case, and made some impression upon my thoughts at the time of reading them, tho' not so much as they did afterwards; for as for being deliver'd, the word had no sound, as I may say, to me; the thing was so remote, so impossible in my apprehension of things, that I began to say as the children of Israel did, when they were promis'd flesh to eat: *Can God spread a table in the wilderness?* so I began to say, 'Can God Himself deliver me from this place?' and as it was not for many years that any hope appear'd, this prevail'd very often upon my thoughts; but, however, the words made a great impression upon me, and I mused upon them very often. It grew now late, and the tobacco had, as I said, doz'd my head so much, that I inclin'd to sleep; so I left my lamp burning in the cave, least I should want any thing in the night, and went to bed; but before I lay down, I did what I never had done in all my life, I kneel'd down and pray'd to God to fulfil the promise to me, that if I call'd upon Him in the day of trouble, He would deliver me; after my broken and imperfect prayer was over, I drunk the rum in which I had steep'd the tobacco, which was so strong and rank of the tobacco, that indeed I could scarce get it down; immediatly upon this I went to bed. I found presently it flew up in my head violently, but I fell into a sound sleep, and wak'd no more 'till by the sun it must necssarily be near three a-clock in the afternoon the next day; nay, to this hour, I'm partly of the opinion that I slept all the next day and night, and 'till almost three that day after; for otherwise I knew not how I should lose a day out of my reckoning in the days of the week, as it appear'd some years after I had done: for if I had lost it by crossing and re-crossing the line,* I should have lost more than one day. But certainly I lost a day in my accompt, and never knew which way.

Be that, however, one way or th' other, when I awak'd I found my self exceedingly refresh'd, and my spirits lively and chearful; when I got up, I was stronger than I was the day before, and my stomach better, for I was hungry; and in short, I had no fit the next day, but continu'd much alter'd for the better; this was the 29th.

The 30th was my well day of course, and I went abroad with my gun, but did not care to travel too far. I kill'd a sea fowl or two, something like a brand goose, and brought them home, but was not very forward to eat them; so I ate some more of the turtle's eggs, which were very good. This evening I renew'd the medicine which I had suppos'd did me good the day before, viz. the tobacco steep'd in rum, only I did not take so much as before, nor did I chew any of the leaf, or hold my head over the smoke; however I was not so well the next day, which was the first of July, as I hop'd I shou'd have been; for I had a little spice of the cold fit, but it was not much.

July 2. I renew'd the medicine all the three ways, and doz'd my self with it as at first; and doubled the quantity which I drank.

3. I miss'd the fit for good and all, tho' I did not recover my full strength for some weeks after; while I was thus gathering strength, my thoughts run exceedingly upon this scripture, *I will deliver thee*, and the impossibility of my deliverance lay much upon my mind in barr of my ever expecting it. But as I was discouraging my self with such thoughts, it occurr'd to my mind that I pored so much upon my deliverance from the main affliction, that I disregarded the deliverance I had receiv'd; and I was, as it were, made to ask my self such questions as these, viz. Have I not been deliver'd, and wonderfully too, from sickness? from the most distress'd condition that could be, and that was so frightful to me? and what notice had I taken of it? Had I done my part? God had deliver'd me, but I had not glorify'd Him; that is to day, I had not own'd and been thankful for that as a deliverance, and how cou'd I expect greater deliverance?

This touch'd my heart very much, and immediately I kneel'd down and gave God thanks aloud for my recovery from my sickness.

July 4. In the morning I took the Bible, and beginning at the New Testament, I began seriously to read it, and impos'd upon my self to read a while every morning and every night, not tying my self to the number of chapters, but as long as my thoughts shou'd engage me. It was not long after I set seriously to this work, but I found my heart more deeply and sincerely affected with the wickedness of my past life. The impression of my dream reviv'd, and the words, *All these things have not brought thee to repentance*, ran seriously in my thought. I was earnestly begging of God to give me repentance, when it happen'd providentially the very day that reading the scripture, I came to these words, *He is exalted a Prince and a Saviour, to give repentance, and to give remission.* I threw down the book, and with my heart as well as my hands lifted up to heaven, in a kind of extasy of joy, I cry'd out aloud, 'Jesu, thou son of David, Jesus, thou exalted Prince and Saviour, give me repentance!'

This was the first time that I could say, in the true sense of the words, that I pray'd in all my life; for now I pray'd with a sense of my condition, and with a true scripture view of hope founded on the encouragement of the word of God; and from this time, I may say, I began to have hope that God would hear me.

Now I began to construe the words mentioned above, *Call on me, and I will deliver you*, in a different sense from what I had ever done before; for then I had no notion of any thing being call'd deliverance, but my being deliver'd from the captivity I was in; for tho' I was indeed at large in the place, yet the island was certainly a prison to me, and that in the worst sense in the world; but now I learn'd to take it in another sense. Now I look'd back upon my past life with such horrour, and my sins appear'd so dreadful, that my soul sought nothing of God but deliverance from the load of guilt that bore down all my comfort: as for my solitary life, it was nothing; I did not so much as pray to be deliver'd from it, or think of it; it was all of no consideration in comparison to this. And I add this part here, to hint to whoever shall read it, that whenever they come to a true sense of things, they will find deliverance from sin a much greater blessing than deliverance from affliction.

But leaving this part, I return to my journal.

My condition began now to be, tho' not less miserable as to my way of living, yet much easier to my mind; and my thoughts being directed, by a constant reading the scripture and praying to God, to things of a higher nature, I had a great deal of comfort within, which till now I knew nothing of; also, as my health and strength returned, I bestirr'd my self to furnish my self with every thing that I wanted, and make my way of living as regular as I could.

From the 4th of July to the 14th, I was chiefly employ'd in walking about with my gun in my hand, a little and a little at a time, as a man that was gathering up his strength after a fit of sickness; for it is hardly to be imagin'd how low I was, and to what weakness I was reduc'd. The application which I made use of was perfectly new, and perhaps what had never cur'd an ague before, neither can I recommend it to any one to practise, by this experiment; and tho' it did carry off the fit, yet it rather contributed to weakening me; for I had frequent convulsions in my nerves and limbs for some time.

I learn'd from it also this in particular, that being abroad in the rainy season was the most pernicious thing to my health that could be, especially in those rains which came attended with storms and hurricanes of wind; for as the rain which came in the dry season was always most accompany'd with such storms, so I found that rain was much more dangerous than the rain which fell in September and October.

I had been now in this unhappy island above 10 months; all possibility of deliverance from this condition seem'd to be entirely taken from me; and I firmly believed that no humane shape had ever set foot upon that place. Having now secur'd my habitation, as I thought, fully to my mind, I had a great desire to make a more perfect discovery of the island, and to see what other productions I might find, which I yet knew nothing of.

It was the 15th of July that I began to take a more particular survey of the island it self. I went up the creek first, where, as I hinted, I brought my rafts on shore; I found, after I came about two miles up, that the tide did not flow any higher, and that it was no more than a little brook of running water, and very fresh and good; but this being the dry season, there was hardly any water in some parts of it, at least not enough to run in any stream so as it could be perceiv'd.

On the bank of this brook I found many pleasant savana's or meadows, plain, smooth, and cover'd with grass; and on the rising parts of them next to the higher grounds, where the water, as it might be supposed, never overflow'd, I found a great deal of tobacco, green, and growing to a great and very strong stalk; there were divers other plants which I had no notion of, or understanding about, and might perhaps have vertues of their own, which I could not find out.

I searched for the cassava root, which the Indians in all that climate make their bread of, but I could find none. I saw large plants of alloes, but did not then understand them. I saw several sugar canes, but wild and, for want of cultivation, imperfect. I contented my self with these discoveries for this time, and came back musing with my self what course I might take to know the vertue and goodness of any of the fruits or plants which I should discover; but could bring it to no conclusion; for, in short, I had made so little observation while I was in the Brasils, that I knew little of the plants in the field, at least very little that might serve me to any purpose now in my distress.

The next day, the 16th, I went up the same way again, and after going something farther than I had gone the day before, I found the brook, and the savana's began to cease, and the country became more woody than before; in this part I found different fruits, and particularly I found mellons upon the ground in great abundance, and grapes upon the trees; the vines had spread indeed over the trees, and the clusters of grapes were just now in their prime, very ripe and rich. This was a surprising discovery, and I was exceeding glad of them; but I was warn'd by my experience to eat sparingly of them, remembring that when I was ashore in Barbary, the eating of grapes kill'd several of our English men who were slaves there, by throwing them into fluxes and feavers. But I found an excellent use for these grapes, and that was to cure or dry them in the sun, and keep them as dry'd grapes or raisins are kept, which I thought would be, as indeed they were, as wholesom as agreeable to eat, when no grapes might be to be had.

I spent all that evening there, and went not back to my habitation, which, by the way, was the first night, as I might say, I had lain from home. In the night I took my first contrivance, and got up into a tree, where I slept well, and the next morning proceeded upon my discovery, travelling near four miles, as I might judge by the length of the valley, keeping still due north, with a ridge of hills on the south and north-side of me.

At the end of this march I came to an opening, where the country seem'd to descend to the west, and a little spring of fresh water, which issued out of the side of the hill by me, run the other way, that is, due east; and the country appear'd so fresh, so green, so flourishing, every thing being in a constant verdure or flourish of spring, that it looked like a planted garden.

I descended a little on the side of that delicious vale, surveying it with a secret kind of pleasure (tho' mixt with my other afflicting thoughts) to think that this was all my own, that I was king and lord of all this country indefeasibly, and had a right of possession; and if I could convey it, I might have it in inheritance as compleatly as any lord of a mannor in England. I saw here abundance of cocoa trees, orange, and lemon, and citron trees;

but all wild, and very few bearing any fruit, at least not then. However, the green limes that I gathered were not only pleasant to eat, but very wholesome; and I mix'd their juice afterwards with water, which made it very wholesome, and very cool and refreshing.

I found now I had business enough to gather and carry home; and I resolv'd to lay up a store, as well of grapes as limes and lemons, to furnish my self for the wet season, which I knew was approaching.

In order to this, I gather'd a great heap of grapes in one place, and a lesser heap in another place, and a great parcel of limes and lemons in another place; and taking a few of each with me, I travell'd homeward, and resolv'd to come again, and bring a bag or sack, or what I could make, to carry the rest home.

Accordingly, having spent three days in this journey, I came home; so I must now call my tent and my cave. But, before I got thither, the grapes were spoil'd; the richness of the fruits and the weight of the juice having broken them and bruis'd them, they were good for little or nothing; as to the limes, they were good, but I could bring but a few.

The next day, being the 19th, I went back having made me two small bags to bring home my harvest; but I was surpris'd, when coming to my heap of grapes, which were so rich and fine when I gather'd them, I found them all spread about, trod to pieces, and dragg'd about, some here, some there, and abundance eaten and devour'd. By this I concluded there were some wild creatures thereabouts which had done this; but what they were I knew not.

However, as I found that there was no laying them up on heaps, and no carrying them away in a sack, but that one way they would be destroy'd, and the other way they would be crush'd with their own weight, I took another course; for I gather'd a large quantity of the grapes, and hung them up upon the out branches of the trees, that they might cure and dry in the sun; and as for the limes and lemons, I carry'd as many back as I could well stand under.

When I came home from this journey, I contemplated with great pleasure the fruitfulness of that valley and the pleasantness of the situation, the security from storms on that side the water, and the wood, and concluded that I had pitch'd upon a place to fix my abode, which was by far the worst part of the country.

Upon the whole I began to consider of removing my habitation; and to look out for a place equally safe as where I now was, situate, if possible, in that pleasant fruitful part of the island.

This thought run long in my head, and I was exceeding fond of it for some time, the pleasantness of the place tempting me; but when I came to a nearer view of it, and to consider that I was now by the sea-side, where it was at least possible that something might happen to my advantage, and by the same ill fate that brought me hither, might bring some other unhappy wretches to the same place; and tho' it was scarce probable that any such thing should ever happen, yet to enclose my self among the hills and woods, in the center of the island, was to anticipate my bondage, and to render such an affair not only improbable, but impossible; and that therefore I ought not by any means to remove.

However, I was so enamour'd of this place, that I spent much of my time there for the whole remaining part of the month of July; and tho' upon second thoughts I resolv'd as above, not to remove, yet I built me a little kind of a bower, and surrounded it at a distance with a strong fence, being a double hedge, as high as I could reach, well stak'd, and fill'd between with brushwood; and here I lay very secure, sometimes two or three nights together, always going over it with a ladder, as before; so that I fancy'd now I had my country-house , and my sea-coast-house: and this work took me up to the beginning of August.

I had but newly finish'd my fence, and began to enjoy my labour, but the rains came on, and made me stick close to my first habitation; for tho' I had made me a tent like the other, with a piece of a sail, and spread it very well, yet I had not the shelter of a hill to keep me from storms, nor a cave behind me to retreat into, when the rains were extraordinary.

About the beginning of August, as I say, I had finish'd my bower, and began to enjoy my self. The third of August, I found the grapes I had hung up were perfectly dry'd, and indeed were excellent good raisins of the sun; so I began to take them down from the trees, and it was very happy that I did so; for the rains which follow'd would have spoil'd them, and I had lost the best part of my winter food; for I had above two hundred large bunches of them. No sooner had I taken them all down, and carry'd most of them home to my cave, but it began to rain, and from hence, which was the fourteenth of August, it rain'd more or less, every day, till the middle of October; and sometimes so violently that I could not stir out of my cave for several days.

In this season I was much surpris'd with the increase of my family. I had been concern'd for the loss of one of my cats, who run away from me, or, as I thought, had been dead, and I heard no more tale or tidings of her, till to my astonishment she came home about the end of August, with three kittens; this was the more strange to me, because tho' I had kill'd a wild cat, as I call'd it, with my gun, yet I thought it was a quite differing kind from our European cats; yet the young cats were the same kind of house breed like the old one; and both my cats being females, I thought it very strange. But from these three cats, I afterwards came to be so pester'd with cats, that I was forc'd to kill them like vermine or wild beasts, and to drive them from my house as much as possible.

From the fourteenth of August to the twenty sixth, incessant rain, so that I could not stir, and was now very careful not to be much wet. In this confinement I began to be straitned for food, but venturing out twice, I one day kill'd a goat, and the last day, which was the twenty-sixth, found a very large tortoise, which was a treat to me, and my food was regulated thus: I eat a bunch of raisins for my breakfast, a piece of the goat's flesh or of the turtle for my dinner, broil'd; for, to my great misfortune, I had no vessel to boil or stew any thing; and two or three of the turtle's eggs for my supper.

During this confinement in my cover by the rain, I work'd daily two or three hours at enlarging my cave, and be degrees work'd it on towards one side, till I came to the out-side of the hill, and made a door or way out, which came beyond my fence or wall, and so I came in and out this way; but I was not perfectly easy at lying so open; for as I had manag'd my self before, I was in a perfect enclosure, whereas now I thought I lay expos'd, and open for any thing to come in upon me; and yet I could not perceive that there was any living thing to fear, the biggest creature that I had yet seen upon the island being a goat.

September the thirtieth, I was now come to the unhappy anniversary of my landing. I cast up the notches on my post, and found I had been on shore three hundred and sixty five days. I kept this day as a solemn fast, setting it apart to religious exercise, prostrating my self on the ground with the most serious humiliation, confessing my sins to God, acknowledging His righteous judgments upon me, and praying to Him to have mercy on me, through Jesus Christ; and having not tasted the least refreshment for twelve hours, even till the going down of the sun, I then eat a bisket cake and a bunch of grapes, and went to bed, finishing the day as I began it.

I had all this time observ'd no sabbath-day; for as at first I had no sense of religion upon my mind, I had after some time omitted to distinguish the weeks, by making a longer notch than ordinary for the sabbath-day, and so did not really know what any of the days were; but now having cast up the days, as above, I found I had been there a year; so I divided it into weeks, and set apart every seventh day for a sabbath; though I found at the end of my account I had lost a day or two in my reckoning.

A little after this my ink began to fail me, and so I contented my self to use it more sparingly, and to write down only the most remarkable events of my life, without continuing a daily memorandum of other things.

The rainy season and the dry season began now to appear regular to me, and I learn'd to divide them so as to provide for them accordingly. But I bought all my experience before I had it; and this I am going to relate, was one of the most discouraging experiments that I made at all. I have mention'd that I had sav'd the few ears of barley and rice, which I had so surprisingly found spring up, as I thought, of themselves, and believe there was about thirty stalks of rice, and about twenty of barley; and now I thought it a proper time to sow it after the rains, the sun being in its southern position, going from me.

Accordingly I dug up a piece of ground as well as I could with my wooden spade, and dividing it into two parts, I sow'd my grain; but as I was sowing, it casually occur'd to my thoughts that I would not sow it all at first, because I did not know when was the proper time for it; so I sow'd about two thirds of the seed, leaving about a handful of each.

It was a great comfort to me afterwards that I did so, for not one grain of that I sow'd this time came to any thing; for the dry months following, the earth having had no rain after the seed was sown, it had no moisture to assist its growth, and never came up at all till the wet season had come again, and then it grew as if it had been but newly sown.

Finding my first seed did not grow, which I easily imagin'd was by the drought, I sought for a moister piece of ground to make another trial in, and I dug up a piece of ground near my new

bower and sow'd the rest of my seed in February, a little before
the vernal equinox; and this, having the rainy months of March
and April to water it, sprung up very pleasantly, and yielded a
very good crop; but having part of the seed left only, and not
daring to sow all that I had, I had but a small quantity at last, my
whole crop not amounting to above half a peck of each kind.

But by this experiment I was made master of my business, and
knew exactly when the proper season was to sow; and that I
might expect two seed times and two harvests every year.

While this corn was growing, I made a little discovery which
was of use to me afterwards. As soon as the rains were over, and
the weather began to settle, which was about the month of
November, I made a visit up the country to my bower, where
though I had not been some months, yet I found all things just as
I left them. The circle or double hedge that I had made was not
only firm and entire, but the stakes which I had cut out of some
trees that grew thereabouts were all shot out and grown with
long branches, as much as a willow-tree usually shoots the first
year after lopping its head. I could not tell what tree to call it that
these stakes were cut from. I was surpriz'd, and yet very well
pleas'd, to see the young trees grow; and I prun'd them, and led
them up to grow as much alike as I could; and it is scarce
credible how beautiful a figure they grew into in three years; so
that though the hedge made a circle of about twenty five yards in
diameter, yet the trees, for such I might now call them, soon
cover'd it; and it was a compleat shade, sufficient to lodge under
all the dry season.

This made me resolve to cut some more stakes, and make me a
hedge like this in a semicircle round my wall; I mean that of my
first dwelling, which I did; and placing the trees or stakes in a
double row, at about eight yards' distance from my first fence,
they grew presently, and were at first a fine cover to my
habitation, and afterwards serv'd for a defence also, as I shall
observe in its order.

I found now that the seasons of the year might generally be
divided, not into summer and winter, as in Europe, but into the
rainy seasons and the dry seasons, which were generally thus:

Half February ⎤
        March ⎬ Rainy, the sun being then on or near the equinox.
    Half April ⎦

Half April May June July Half August	Dry, the sun being then to the north of the line.
Half August September Half October	Rainy, the sun being then come back.
Half October November December January Half February	Dry, the sun being then to the south of the line.

The rainy season sometimes held longer or shorter, as the winds happen'd to blow; but this was the general observation I made. After I had found by experience the ill consequence of being abroad in the rain, I took care to furnish my self with provisions before hand, that I might not be oblig'd to go out; and I sat within doors as much as possible during the wet months.

This time I found much employment (and very suitable also to the time), for I found great occasion of many things which I had no way to furnish my self with, but by hard labour and constant application; particularly, I try'd many ways to make my self a basket, but all the twigs I could get for the purpose prov'd so brittle that they would do nothing. It prov'd of excellent advantage to me now, that when I was a boy, I used to take great delight in standing at a basket-maker's in the town where my father liv'd, to see them make their wicker-ware; and being, as boys usually are, very officious to help, and a great observer of the manner how they work'd those things, and sometimes lending a hand, I had by this means full knowledge of the methods of it, that I wanted nothing but the materials; when it came into my mind that the twigs of that tree from whence I cut my stakes that grew, might possibly be as tough as the sallows and willows and osiers in England, and I resolv'd to try.

Accordingly the next day, I went to my country-house, as I call'd it, and cutting some of the smaller twigs, I found them to my purpose as much as I could desire; whereupon I came the next time prepar'd with an hatchet to cut down a quantity, which I soon found, for there was great plenty of them; these I set up to dry within my circle or hedge, and when they were fit for use, I carry'd them to my cave, and here during the next season, I employ'd my self in making, as well as I could, a great many baskets, both to carry earth, or to carry or lay up any thing as I had occasion; and tho' I did not finish them very handsomly, yet I made them sufficiently serviceable for my purpose; and thus afterwards I took care never to be without them; and as my wicker-ware decay'd, I made more; especially I made strong deep baskets to place my corn in, instead of sacks, when I should come to have any quantity of it.

Having master'd this difficulty, and employ'd a world of time about it, I bestirr'd my self to see if possible how to supply two wants. I had no vessels to hold any thing that was liquid, except two runlets which were almost full of rum, and some glass-bottles, some of the common size, and others which were case-bottles, square, for the holding of waters, spirits, &c. I had not so much as a pot to boil any thing, except a great kettle, which I sav'd out of the ship, and which was too big for such use as I desired it, viz. to make broth and stew a bit of meat by it self. The second thing I would fain have had, was a tobacco-pipe, but it was impossible to make one; however, I found a contrivance for that too at last.

I employ'd my self in planting my second rows of stakes or piles, and in this wicker working, all the summer or dry season, when another business took me up more time than it could be imagin'd I could spare.

I mention'd before that I had a great mind to see the whole island, and that I had travell'd up the brook, and so on to where I built my bower, and where I had an opening quite to the sea on the other side of the island. I now resolv'd to travel quite cross to the sea-shore on that side; so taking my gun, a hatchet, and my dog, and a larger quantity of powder and shot than usual, with two bisket cakes and a great bunch of raisins in my pouch for my store, I began my journey. When I had pass'd the vale where my bower stood as above, I came within view of the sea, to the west, and it being a very clear day, I fairly descry'd land, whether an island or a continent, I could not tell; but it lay very high, extending from the west to the W.S.W. at a very great distance; by my guess it could not be less than fifteen or twenty leagues off.

I could not tell what part of the world this might be, otherwise than I knew it must be part of America, and, as I concluded by all my observations, must be near the Spanish dominions, and perhaps was all inhabited by savages, where if I should have landed, I had been in a worse condition than I was now; and therefore I acquiesced in the dispositions of Providence, which I began now to own and to believe order'd every thing for the best; I say, I quieted my mind with this, and left afflicting my self with fruitless wishes of being there.

Besides, after some pause upon this affair, I consider'd that if this land was the Spanish coast, I should certainly, one time or other, see some vessel pass or repass one way or other; but if not, then it was the savage coast between the Spanish country and Brasils, which are indeed the worst of savages; for they are cannibals, or men-eaters, and fail not to murther and devour all the humane bodies that fall into their hands.

With these considerations I walk'd very leisurely forward, I found that side of the island where I now was much pleasanter than mine, the open or savanna fields sweet, adorn'd with flowers and grass, and full of very fine woods. I saw abundance of parrots, and fain I would have caught one, if possible, to have kept it to be tame, and taught it to speak to me. I did, after some pains taking, catch a young parrot, for I knock'd it down with a stick, and having recover'd it, I brought it home; but it was some years before I could make him speak: however, at last I taught him to call me by my name very familiarly. But the accident that follow'd, tho' it be a trifle, will be very diverting in its place.

I was exceedingly diverted with this journey. I found in the low grounds hares, as I thought them to be, and foxes, but they differ'd greatly from all the other kinds I had met with; nor could I satisfy my self to eat them, tho' I kill'd several. But I had no need to be venturous; for I had no want of food, and of that which was very good too; especially these three sorts, viz. goats, pidgeons, and turtle or tortoise; which, added to my grapes, Leaden-hall Market could not have furnish'd a table better than I, in proportion to the company; and tho' my case was deplorable enough, yet I had great cause for thankfulness, that I was not driven to any extremities for food; but rather plenty, even to dainties.

I never travell'd in this journey above two miles outright in a day, or thereabouts; but I took so many turns and returns to see what discoveries I could make, that I came weary enough to the place where I resolv'd to sit down for all night; and then I either repos'd my self in a tree, or surrounded my self with a row of stakes set upright in the ground, either from one tree to another, or so as no wild creature could come at me without waking me.

As soon as I came to the sea shore, I was surpriz'd to see that I had taken up my lot on the worst side of the island; for here indeed the shore was cover'd with innumerable turtles, whereas on the other side I had found but three in a year and half. Here was also an infinite number of fowls of many kinds, some of which I had seen and some which I had not seen before, and many of them very good meat; but such as I knew not the names of, except those call'd penguins.

I could have shot as many as I pleas'd, but was very sparing of my powder and shot; and therefore had more mind to kill a she goat, if I could, which I could better feed on; and though there were many goats here more than on my side the island, yet it was with much more difficulty that I could come near them, the country being flat and even, and they saw me much sooner than when I was on the hill.

I confess this side of the country was much pleasanter than mine, but yet I had not the least inclination to remove; for as I was fix'd in my habitation, it became natural to me, and I seem'd all the while I was here to be as it were upon a journey, and from home. However, I travell'd along the shore of the sea towards the east, I suppose about twelve miles; and then setting up a great pole upon the shore for a mark, I concluded I would go home again; and that the next journey I took should be on the other side of the island, east from my dwelling, and so round till I came to my post again: of which in its place.

I took another way to come back than that I went, thinking I could easily keep all the island so much in my view that I could not miss finding my first dwelling by viewing the country; but I found my self mistaken; for being come about two or three miles, I found my self descended into a very large valley; but so surrounded with hills, and those hills cover'd with wood, that I could not see which was my way by any direction but that of the sun, nor even then, unless I knew very well the position of the sun at that time of the day.

It happen'd to my farther misfortune, that the weather prov'd hazey for three or four days while I was in this valley; and not being able to see the sun, I wander'd about very uncomfortably, and at last was oblig'd to find out the sea side, look for my post, and come back the same way I went; and then by easy journies I turn'd homeward, the weather being exceeding hot, and my gun, ammunition, hatchet, and other things very heavy.

In this journey my dog surpriz'd a young kid, and seiz'd upon it, and I running in to take hold of it, caught it, and sav'd it alive from the dog. I had a great mind to bring it home if I could; for I had often been musing whether it might not be possible to get a kid or two, and so raise a breed of tame goats, which might supply me when my powder and shot should be all spent.

I made a collar to this little creature, and with a string which I made of some rope-yarn, which I always carry'd about me, I led him along, tho' with some difficulty, till I came to my bower, and then I enclos'd him and left him; for I was very impatient to be at home, from whence I had been absent above a month.

I cannot express what a satisfaction it was to me, to come into my old hutch, and lye down in my hamock-bed. This little wandring journey, without settled place of abode, had been so unpleasant to me, that my own house, as I call'd it to my self, was a perfect settlement to me, compar'd to that; and it rendred every thing about me so comfortable, that I resolv'd I would never go a great way from it again, while it should be my lot to stay on the island.

I repos'd my self here a week, to rest and regale my self after my long journey; during which, most of the time was taken up in the weighty affair of making a cage for my Poll, who began now to be a meer domestick, and to be mighty well acquainted with me. Then I began to think of the poor kid, which I had penn'd in within my little circle, and resolv'd to go and fetch it home, or give it some food; accordingly I went, and found it where I left it, for indeed it could not get out, but almost starv'd for want of food, I went and cut bows of trees, and branches of such shrubs as I could find, and threw it over, and having fed it, I ty'd it as I did before, to lead it away; but it was so tame with being hungry, that I had no need to have ty'd it; for it follow'd me like a dog; and as I continually fed it, the creature became so loving, so gentle, and so fond, that it became from that time one of my domesticks also, and would never leave me afterwards.

The rainy season of the autumnal equinox was now come, and I kept the 30th of September in the same solemn manner as before, being the anniversary of my landing on the island, having now been there two years, and no more prospect of being deliver'd than the first day I came there. I spent the whole day in humble and thankful acknowledgments of the many wonderful mercies which my solitary condition was attended with, and without which it might have been infinitely more miserable. I gave humble and hearty thanks that God had been pleas'd to discover to me, even that it was possible I might be more happy in this solitary condition, than I should have been in a liberty of society, and in all the pleasures of the world; that He could fully make up to me the deficiences of my solitary state, and the want of humane society, by His presence and the communications of His grace to my soul, supporting, comforting, and encouraging me to depend upon His providence here, and hope for His eternal presence hereafter.

It was now that I began sensibly to feel how much more happy this life I now led was, with all its miserable circumstances, than the wicked, cursed, abominable life I led all the past part of my days; and now I chang'd both my sorrows and my joys; my very desires alter'd, my affections chang'd their gusts, and my delights were perfectly new from what they were at my first coming, or indeed for the two years past.

Before, as I walk'd about, either on my hunting, or for viewing the country, the anguish of my soul at my condition would break out upon me on a sudden, and my very heart would die within me, to think of the woods, the mountains, the desarts I was in; and how I was a prisoner, lock'd up with the eternal bars and bolts of the ocean, in an uninhabited wilderness, without redemption. In the midst of the greatest composures of my mind, this would break out upon me like a storm, and make me wring my hands and weep like a child. Sometimes it would take me in the middle of my work, and I would immediately sit down and sigh, and look upon the ground for an hour or two together; and this was still worse to me; for if I could burst out into tears, or vent my self by words, it would go off, and the grief having exhausted it self would abate.

But now I began to exercise my self with new thoughts; I daily read the word of God, and apply'd all the comforts of it to my present state. One morning, being very sad, I open'd the Bible upon these words, *I will never, never leave thee, nor forsake thee*; immediately it occurr'd that these words were to me; why else should they be directed in such a manner, just at the moment when I was mourning over my condition, as one forsaken of God and man? 'Well then,' said I, 'if God does not forsake me, of what ill consequence can it be, or what matters it, though the world should all forsake me, seeing, on the other hand, if I had all the world, and should lose the favour and blessing of God, there wou'd be no comparison in the loss?'

From this moment I began to conclude in my mind that it was possible for me to be more happy in this forsaken, solitary condition than it was probable I should ever have been in any other particular state in the world; and with this thought I was going to give thanks to God for bringing me to this place.

I know not what it was, but something shock'd my mind at that thought, and I durst not speak the words. 'How canst thou be such a hypocrite,' said I, even audibly, 'to pretend to be thankful for a condition, which however thou may'st endeavour to be contented with, thou would'st rather pray heartily to be deliver'd from?' So I stopp'd there; but though I could not say I thank'd God for being there, yet I sincerely gave thanks to God for opening my eyes, by whatever afflicting providences, to see the former condition of my life, and to mourn for my wickedness, and repent. I never open'd the Bible, or shut it, but my very soul within me bless'd God for directing my friend in England, without any order of mine, to pack it up among my goods; and for assisting me afterwards to save it out of the wreck of the ship.

Thus, and in this disposition of mind, I began my third year; and tho' I have not given the reader the trouble of so particular account of my works this year as the first, yet in general it may be observ'd that I was very seldom idle; but having regularly divided my time, according to the several daily employments that were before me, such as, first, my duty to God, and the reading the scriptures, which I constantly set apart some time for thrice every day; secondly, the going abroad with my gun for food, which generally took me up three hours in every morning, when it did not rain; thirdly, the ordering, curing, preserving, and cooking what I had kill'd or catch'd for my supply; these took up great part of the day; also it is to be considered that the middle of the day, when the sun was in the zenith, the violence of the heat was too great to stir out; so that about four hours in the evening was all the time I could be suppos'd to work in; with this exception, that sometimes I change'd my hours of hunting and working, and went to work in the morning, and abroad with my gun in the afternoon.

To this short time allow'd for labour, I desire may be added the exceeding laboriousness of my work; the many hours which, for want of tools, want of help, and want of skill, every thing I did took up out of my time. For example, I was full two and forty days making me a board for a long shelf, which I wanted in my cave; whereas two sawyers, with their tools and a saw-pit, would have cut six of them out of the same tree in half a day.

My case was this: It was to be a large tree which was to be cut down, because my board was to be a broad one. This tree I was three days a cutting down, and two more cutting off the bows, and reducing it to a log or piece of timber. With inexpressible hacking and hewing I reduc'd both sides of it into chips, till it begun to be light enough to move; then I turn'd it, and made one side of it smooth and flat as a board from end to end; then turning that side downward, cut the other side, till I brought the plank to be about three inches thick, and smooth on both sides. Any one may judge the labour of my hands in such a piece of work; but labour and patience carry'd me through that and many other things. I only observe this in particular, to shew the reason why so much of my time went away with so little work, viz. that what might be a little to be done with help and tools, was a vast labour, and requir'd a prodigious time to do alone and by hand.

But notwithstanding this, with patience and labour I went through many things; and indeed every thing that my circumstances made necessary to me to do, as will appear by what follows.

I was now, in the months of November and December, expecting my crop of barley and rice. The ground I had manur'd or dug up for them was not great; for as I observ'd, my seed of each was not above the quantity of half a peck; for I had lost one whole crop by sowing in the dry season; but now my crop promis'd very well, when on a sudden I found I was in danger of losing it all again by enemies of several sorts, which it was scarce possible to keep from it; as first, the goats, and wild creatures which I call'd hares, who tasting the sweetness of the blade, lay in it night and day, as soon as it came up, and eat it so close that it could get no time to shoot up into stalk.

This I saw no remedy for, but by making an enclosure about it with a hedge, which I did with a great deal of toil; and the more, because it requir'd speed. However, as my arable land was but small, suited to my crop, I got it totally well fenc'd in about three weeks' time; and shooting some of the creatures in the day time, I set my dog to guard it in the night, tying him up to a stake at the gate, where he would stand and bark all night long; so in a little time the enemies forsook the place, and the corn grew very strong and well, and began to ripen apace.

But as the beasts ruined me before, while my corn was in the blade, so the birds were as likely to ruin me now, when it was in the ear; for going along by the place to see how it throve, I saw my little crop surrounded with fowls of I know not how many sorts, who stood as it were watching till I should be gone. I immediately let fly among them (for I always had my gun with me). I had no sooner shot, but there rose up a little cloud of fowls, which I had not seen at all, from among the corn it self.

This touch'd me sensibly, for I foresaw that in a few days they would devour all my hopes, that I should be starv'd, and never be able to raise a crop at all, and what to do I could not tell. However, I resolv'd not to lose my corn, if possible, tho' I should watch it night and day. In the first place, I went among it to see what damage was already done, and found they had spoil'd a good deal of it, but that as it was yet too green for them, the loss was not so great, but that the remainder was like to be a good crop if it could be sav'd.

I staid by it to load my gun, and then coming away I could easily see the thieves sitting upon all the trees about me, as if they only waited till I was gone away, and the event proved it to be so; for as I walk'd off as if I was gone, I was no sooner out of their sight, but they dropt down one by one into the corn again. I was so provok'd that I could not have patience to stay till more came on, knowing that every grain that they eat now, was, as it might be said, a peck-load to me in the consequence; but coming up to the hedge I fir'd again, and kill'd three of them. This was what I wish'd for; so I took them up, and serv'd them as we serve notorious thieves in England, viz. hang'd them in chains for a terror to others. It is impossible to imagine almost, that this should have such an effect as it had; for the fowls wou'd not only not come at the corn, but in short they forsook all that part of the island, and I could never see a bird near the place as long as my scare-crows hung there.

This I was very glad of, you may be sure, and about the latter end of December, which was our second harvest of the year, I reap'd my crop.

I was sadly put to it for a scythe or a sicle to cut it down, and all I could do was to make one as well as I could out of one of the broad swords or cutlasses, which I sav'd among the arms out of the ship. However, as my first crop was but small, I had no great difficulty to cut it down; in short, I reap'd it my way, for I cut nothing off but the ears, and carry'd it away in a great basket which I had made, and so rubb'd it out with my hands; and at the end of all my harvesting, I found that out of my half peck of seed, I had near two bushels of rice, and above two bushels and half of barley; that is to say, by my guess, for I had no measure at that time.

However, this was a great encouragement to me, and I foresaw that in time it wou'd please God to supply me with bread. And yet here I was perplex'd again, for I neither knew how to grind or make meal of my corn, or indeed how to clean it and part it; nor if made into meal, how to make bread of it; and if how to make it, yet I knew not how to bake it. These things being added to my desire of having a good quantity for store, and to secure a constant supply, I resolv'd not to taste any of this crop, but to preserve it all for seed against the next season, and in the mean time to employ all my study and hours of working to accomplish this great work of providing my self with corn and bread.

It might be truly said, that now I work'd for my bread; 'tis a little wonderful, and what I believe few people have thought much upon, viz. the strange multitude of little things necessary in the providing, producing, curing, dressing, making, and finishing this one article of bread.

I that was reduced to a meer state of nature, found this to my daily discouragement, and was made more and more sensible of it every hour, even after I had got the first handful of seed-corn, which, as I have said, came up unexpectedly, and indeed to a surprize.

First, I had no plow to turn up the earth, no spade or shovel to dig it. Well, this I conquer'd, by making a wooden spade, as I observ'd before; but this did my work in but a wooden manner, and tho' it cost me a great many days to make it, yet for want of iron it not only wore out the sooner, but made my work the harder, and made it be perform'd much worse.

However, this I bore with, and was content to work it out with patience, and bear with the badness of the performance. When the corn was sow'd, I had no harrow, but was forced to go over it my self and drag a great heavy bough of a tree over it, to scratch it, as it may be call'd, rather than rake or harrow it.

When it was growing and grown, I have observ'd already how many things I wanted, to fence it, secure it, mow or reap it, cure and carry it home, thrash, part it from the chaff, and save it.

Then I wanted a mill to grind it, sieves to dress it, yeast and salt to make it into bread, and an oven to bake it, and yet all these things I did without, as shall be observ'd; and yet the corn was an inestimable comfort and advantage to me too. All this, as I said, made every thing laborious and tedious to me, but that there was no help for; neither was my time so much loss to me, because, as I had divided it, a certain part of it was every day appointed to these works; and as I resolv'd to use none of the corn for bread till I had a greater quantity by me, I had the next six months to apply my self wholly by labour and invention to furnish my self with utensils proper for the performing all the operations necessary for the making the corn (when I had it) fit for my use.

But first, I was to prepare more land, for I had now seed enough to sow above an acre of ground. Before I did this, I had a week's-work at least to make me a spade, which when it was done was but a sorry one indeed, and very heavy, and requir'd double labour to work with it; however, I went thro' that, and sow'd my seed in two large flat pieces of ground, as near my house as I could find them to my mind, and fenc'd them in with a good hedge, the stakes of which were all cut of that wood which I had set before, and knew it would grow, so that in one year's time I knew I should have a quick or living-hedge, that would want but little repair. This work was not so little as to take me up less than three months, because great part of that time was of the wet season, when I could not go abroad.

Within doors, that is, when it rained, and I could not go out, I found employment on the following occasions; always observing, that all the while I was at work I diverted my self with talking to my parrot, and teaching him to speak, and I quickly learn'd him to know his own name, and at last to speak it out pretty loud, POLL, which was the first word I ever heard spoken in the island by any mouth but my own. This, therefore, was not my work, but an assistant to my work, for now, as I said, I had a great employment upon my hands, as follows, viz. I had long study'd, by some means or other, to make my self some earthen vessels, which indeed I wanted sorely, but knew not where to come at them. However, considering the heat of the climate, I did not doubt but if I could find out any such clay, I might botch up some such pot as might, being dry'd in the sun, be hard enough and strong enough to bear handling, and to hold any thing that was dry and requir'd to be kept so; and as this was necessary in the preparing corn, meal,

&c., which was the thing I was upon, I resolv'd to make some as large as I could, and fit only to stand like jarrs to hold what should be put into them.

It would make the reader pity me, or rather laugh at me, to tell how many awkward ways I took to raise this paste, what odd mishapen ugly things I made, how many of them fell in, and how many fell out, the clay not being stiff enough to bear its own weight; how many crack'd by the over violent heat of the sun, being set out too hastily; and how many fell in pieces with only removing, as well before as after they were dry'd; and in a word, how after having labour'd hard to find the clay, to dig it, to temper it, to bring it home and work it, I could not make above two large earthen ugly things, I cannot call them jarrs, in about two months' labour.

However, as the sun bak'd these two very dry and hard, I lifted them very gently up, and set them down again in two great wicker-baskets which I had made on purpose for them, that they might not break, and as between the pot and the basket there was a little room to spare, I stuff'd it full of the rice and barley straw, and these two pots being to stand always dry, I thought would hold my dry corn, and perhaps the meal, when the corn was bruised.

Tho' I miscarried so much in my design for large pots, yet I made several smaller things with better success, such as little round pots, flat dishes, pitchers and pipkins, and any things my hand turn'd to, and the heat of the sun bak'd them strangely hard.

But all this would not answer my end, which was to get an earthen pot to hold what was liquid, and bear the fire, which none of these could do. It happen'd after some time, making a pretty large fire for cooking my meat, when I went to put it out after I had done with it, I found a broken piece of one of my earthen-ware vessels in the fire, burnt as hard as a stone, and red as a tile. I was agreeably surpris'd to see it, and said to my self, that certainly they might be made to burn whole if they would burn broken.

This set me to studying how to order my fire, so as to make it burn me some pots. I had no notion of a kiln, such as the potters burn in, or of glazing them with lead, tho' I had some lead to do it with; but I plac'd three large pipkins and two or three pots in a pile one upon another, and plac'd my fire-wood all round it with a great heap of embers under them; I ply'd the fire with fresh fuel round the out-side, and upon the top, till I saw the pots in the inside red hot quite thro', and observ'd that they did not crack at all; when I saw them clear red, I let them stand in that heat about 5 or 6 hours, till I found one of them, tho' it did not crack, did melt or run, for the sand which was mixed with the clay melted by the violence of the heat, and would have run into glass if I had gone on; so I slack'd my fire gradually till the pots began to abate of the red colour, and watching them all night, that I might not let the fire abate too fast, in the morning I had three very good, I will not say handsome, pipkins, and two other earthen pots, as hard burnt as cou'd be desir'd; and one of them perfectly glaz'd with the running of the sand.

After this experiment, I need not say that I wanted no sort of earthen ware for my use; but I must needs say, as to the shapes of them, they were very indifferent, as any one may suppose, when I had no way of making them but as the children make dirt-pies, or as a woman would make pies that never learn'd to raise paste.

No joy at a thing of so mean a nature was ever equal to mine, when I found I had made an earthen pot that would bear the fire; and I had hardly patience to stay till they were cold, before I set one upon the fire again, with some water in it, to boil me some meat, which it did admirably well; and with a piece of a kid I made some very good broth, though I wanted oatmeal, and several other ingredients requisite to make it so good as I would have had it been.

My next concern was to get me a stone mortar, to stamp or beat some corn in; for as to the mill, there was no thought at arriving to that perfection of art with one pair of hands. To supply this want I was at a great loss; for, of all trades in the world, I was as perfectly unqualify'd for a stone-cutter as for any whatever; neither had I any tools to go about it with. I spent many a day to find out a great stone big enough to cut hollow and make fit for a mortar, and could find none at all; except what was in the solid rock, and which I had no way to dig or cut out; nor indeed were the rocks in the island of hardness sufficient, but were all of a sandy crumbling stone, which neither would bear the weight of a heavy pestle, or would break the corn without filling it with sand; so after a great deal of time lost in searching for a stone, I gave it over, and resolv'd to look out for a great block of hard wood, which I found indeed much easier; and getting one as big as I had strength to stir, I rounded it, and form'd it in the out-side with my axe and hatchet, and then with the help of fire, and infinite labour, made a hollow place in it, as the Indians in Brasil make their canoes. After this, I made a great heavy pestle or beater, of the wood call'd the iron-wood, and this I prepar'd and laid by against I had my next crop of corn, when I propos'd to my self to grind, or rather pound, my corn into meal to make my bread.

My next difficulty was to make a sieve, or search,* to dress my meal, and to part it from the bran and the husk, without which I did not see it possible I could have any bread. This was a most difficult thing, so much as but to think on; for to be sure I had nothing like the necessary thing to make it; I mean fine thin canvas, or stuff, to search the meal through. And here I was at a full stop for many months; nor did I really know what to do; linnen I had none left, but what was meer rags; I had goat's hair, but neither knew I how to weave it or spin it; and had I known how, here was no tools to work it with; all the remedy that I found for this was, that at last I did remember I had among the seamen's cloaths which were sav'd out of the ship, some neckcloths of callicoe or muslin; and with some pieces of these I made three small sieves, but proper enough for the work; and thus I made shift for some years; how I did afterwards, I shall shew in its place.

The baking part was the next thing to be consider'd, and how I should make bread when I came to have corn; for first I had no yeast; as to that part, as there was no supplying the want, so I did not concern my self much about it; but for an oven, I was indeed in great pain. At length I found out an experiment for that also, which was this: I made some earthen vessels, very broad, but not deep; that is to say, about two foot diameter, and not above nine inches deep; these I burnt in the fire, as I had done the other, and laid them by; and when I wanted to bake, I made a great fire upon my hearth, which I had pav'd with some square tiles of my own making and burning also; but I should not call them square.

When the fire-wood was burnt pretty much into embers, or live coals, I drew them forward upon this hearth so as to cover it all over, and there I let them lye till the hearth was very hot; then sweeping away all the embers, I set down my loaf or loaves, and whelming down the earthen pot upon them, drew the embers all round the out-side of the pot, to keep in, and add to the heat; and thus, as well as in the best oven in the world, I bak'd my barley loaves, and became in little time a meer pastry-cook into the bargain; for I made my self several cakes of the rice, and puddings; indeed I made no pies, neither had I any thing to put into them, supposing I had, except the flesh either of fowls or goats.

It need not be wondred at, if all these things took me up most part of the third year of my abode here; for it is to be observ'd that in the intervals of these things, I had my new harvest and husbandry to manage; for I reap'd my corn in its season, and carry'd it home as well as I could, and laid it up in the ear in my large baskets, till I had time to rub it out; for I had no floor to thrash it on, or instrument to thrash it with.

And now indeed, my stock of corn increasing, I really wanted to build my barns bigger. I wanted a place to lay it up in; for the increase of the corn now yielded me so much, that I had of the barley about twenty bushels, and of the rice as much, or more; insomuch that now I resolv'd to begin to use it freely; for my bread had been quite gone a great while; also I resolv'd to see what quantity would be sufficient for me a whole year, and to sow but once a year.

Upon the whole, I found that the forty bushels of barley and rice was much more than I could consume in a year; so I resolv'd to sow just the same quantity every year that I sow'd the last, in hopes that such a quantity would fully provide me with bread, etc.

All the while these things were doing, you may be sure my thoughts run many times upon the prospect of land which I had seen from the other side of the island, and I was not without secret wishes that I were on shore there, fancying the seeing the main land, and in an inhabited country I might find some way or other to convey myself farther, and perhaps at last find some means of escape.

But all this while I made no allowance for the dangers of such a condition, and how I might fall into the hands of savages, and perhaps such as I might have reason to think far worse than the lions and tigers of Africa; that if I once came into their power, I should run a hazard more than a thousand to one of being kill'd, and perhaps of being eaten; for I had heard that the people of the Carribean coast were canibals, or man-eaters; and I knew by the latitude that I could not be far off from that shore. That suppose they were not canibals, yet that they might kill me, as many Europeans who had fallen into their hands had been serv'd, even when they had been ten or twenty together; much more I that was

but one, and could make little or no defence. All these things, I
say, which I ought to have consider'd well of, and did cast up in
my thoughts afterwards, yet took up none of my apprehensions at
first; but my head run mightily upon the thought of getting over to
the shore.

Now I wish'd for my boy Xury, and the long boat with the
shoulder of mutton sail, with which I sail'd above a thousand
miles on the coast of Africk; but this was in vain. Then I thought I
would go and look at our ship's boat, which, as I have said, was
blown up upon the shore, a great way in the storm, when we were
first cast away. She lay almost where she did at first, but not quite;
and was turn'd by the force of the waves and the winds almost
bottom upward, against a high ridge of beachy rough sand; but no
water about her as before.

If I had had hands to have refitted her, and to have launch'd her
into the water the boat would have done well enough, and I might
have gone back into the Brasils with her easily enough; but I might
have foreseen that I could no more turn her and set her upright
upon her bottom, than I could remove the island. However, I went
to the woods, and cut levers and rollers, and brought them to the
boat, resolv'd to try what I could do, suggesting to my self that if I
could but turn her down, I might easily repair the damage she had
received, and she would be a very good boat, and I might go to sea
in her very easily.

I spar'd no pains, indeed, in this piece of fruitless toil, and spent,
I think, three or four weeks about it; at last, finding it impossible
to heave it up with my little strength, I fell to digging away the
sand, to undermine it, and so to make it fall down, setting pieces
of wood to thrust and guide it right in the fall.

But when I had done this, I was unable to stir it up again, or to
get under it, much less to move it forward towards the water; so I
was forc'd to give it over; and yet, though I gave over the hopes of
the boat, my desire to venture over for the main increased, rather
than decreased, as the means for it seem'd impossible.

This at length put me upon thinking whether it was not possible
to make my self a canoe, or periagua,* such as the natives of those
climates make, even without tools, or, as I might say, without
hands, viz. of the trunk of a great tree. This I not only thought
possible, but easy, and pleas'd my self extreamly with the
thoughts of making it, and with my having much more
convenience for it than any of the negroes or Indians; but not at all

considering the particular inconveniences which I lay under, more than the Indians did, viz. want of hands to move it, when it was made, into the water, a difficulty much harder for me to surmount than all the consequences of want of tools could be to them; for what was it to me, that when I had chosen a vast tree in the woods, I might with much trouble cut it down, if after I might be able with my tools to hew and dub the out-side into the proper shape of a boat, and burn or cut out the in-side to make it hollow, so to make a boat of it, if, after all this, I must leave it just there where I found it, and was not able to launch it into the water?

One would have thought I could not have had the least reflection upon my mind of my circumstance while I was making this boat, but I should have immediately thought how I should get it into the sea; but my thoughts were so intent upon my voyage over the sea in it, that I never once consider'd how I should get it off of the land; and it was really in its own nature more easy for me to guide it over forty five miles of sea, than about forty five fathom of land, where it lay, to set it a float in the water.

I went to work upon this boat the most like a fool that ever man did, who had any of his senses awake. I pleas'd my self with the design, without determining whether I was ever able to undertake it; not but that the difficulty of launching my boat came often into my head; but I put a stop to my own enquiries into it, by this foolish answer which I gave myself, 'Let's first make it, I'll warrant I'll find some way or other to get it along when 'tis done.'

This was a most preposterous method; but the eagerness of my fancy prevail'd, and to work I went. I fell'd a cedar tree: I question much whether Solomon ever had such a one for the building of the temple at Jerusalem. It was five foot ten inches diameter at the lower part next the stump, and four foot eleven inches diameter at the end of twenty two foot, after which it lessen'd for a while, and then parted into branches. It was not without infinite labour that I fell'd this tree; I was twenty days hacking and hewing at it at the bottom; I was fourteen more getting the branches and limbs and the vast spreading head of it cut off, which I hack'd and hew'd through with axe and hatchet, and inexpressible labour; after this, it cost me a month to shape it, and dub it to a proportion, and to something like the bottom of a boat, that it might swim upright as it ought to do. It cost me near three months more to clear the in-side, and work it out so as to make an exact boat of it. This I did indeed without fire, by meer malett and chissel, and by the dint of hard labour, till I had brought it to be a very handsome periagua, and big enough to have carry'd six and twenty men, and consequently big enough to have carry'd me and all my cargo.

When I had gone through this work, I was extremely delighted with it. The boat was really much bigger than I ever saw a canoe or periagua, that was made of one tree, in my life. Many a weary stroke it had cost, you may be sure; and there remain'd nothing but to get it into the water; and had I gotten it into the water, I make no question but I should have began the maddest voyage, and the most unlikely to be perform'd, that ever was undertaken.

But all my devices to get it into the water fail'd me; tho' they cost me infinite labour too. It lay about one hundred yards from the water, and not more. But the first inconvenience was, it was up hill towards the creek; well, to take away this discouragement, I resolv'd to dig into the surface of the earth, and so make a declivity. This I begun, and it cost me a prodigious deal of pains; but who grutches* pains, that have their deliverance in view? But when this was work'd through, and this difficulty manag'd, it was still much at one; for I could no more stir the canoe than I could the other boat.

Then I measur'd the distance of ground, and resolv'd to cut a dock or canal, to bring the water up to the canoe, seeing I could not bring the canoe down to the water. Well, I began this work, and when I began to enter into it, and calculate how deep it was to be dug, how broad, how the stuff to be thrown out, I found that by the number of hands I had, being none but my own, it must have been ten or twelve years before I should have gone through with it: for the shore lay high, so that at the upper end it must have been at least twenty foot deep; so at length, tho' with great reluctancy, I gave this attempt over also.

This griev'd me heartily, and now I saw, tho' too late, the folly of beginning a work before we count the cost, and before we judge rightly of our own strength to go through with it.

In the middle of this work, I finish'd my fourth year in this place, and kept my anniversary with the same devotion, and with as much comfort as ever before; for by a constant study and serious application of the word of God, and by the assistance of His grace, I gain'd a different knowledge from what I had before. I entertain'd different notions of things. I look'd now upon the world as a thing remote, which I had nothing to do with, no expectation from, and indeed no desires about: in a word, I had nothing indeed to do with it, nor was ever like to have; so I thought it look'd as we may perhaps look upon it hereafter, viz. as a place I had liv'd in, but was come out of it; and well might I say, as Father Abraham to Dives, *Between me and thee is a great gulph fix'd*.

In the first place, I was remov'd from all the wickedness of the world here. I had neither *the lust of the flesh, the lust of the eye, or the pride of life*. I had nothing to covet; for I had all that I was now capable of enjoying; I was lord of the whole manor; or if I pleas'd, I might call my self king or emperor over the whole country which I had possession of. There were no rivals; I had no competitor, none to dispute sovereignty or command with me. I might have rais'd ship loadings of corn; but I had no use for it; so I let as little grow as I thought enough for my occasion. I had tortoise or turtles enough; but now and then one was as much as I could put to any use. I had timber enough to have built a fleet of ships. I had grapes enough to have made wine, or to have cur'd into raisins, to have loaded that fleet when they had been built.

But all I could make use of was all that was valuable. I had enough to eat and to supply my wants, and what was all the rest to me? If I kill'd more flesh than I could eat, the dog must eat it, or the vermin. If I sow'd more corn than I could eat, it must be spoil'd. The trees that I cut down were lying to rot on the ground. I could make no more use of them than for fewel; and that I had no occasion for, but to dress my food.

In a word, the nature and experience of things dictated to me, upon just reflection, that all the good things of this world are no farther good to us than they are for our use; and that whatever we may heap up indeed to give others, we enjoy just as much as we can use and no more. The most covetous griping miser in the world would have been cur'd of the vice of covetousness, if he had been in my case; for I possess'd infinitely more than I knew what to do with. I had no room for desire, except it was of things which I had not, and they were but trifles, though indeed of great use to me. I had, as I hinted before, a parcel of money, as well gold as silver, about thirty six pounds sterling. Alas! there the nasty sorry useless stuff lay; I had no manner of business for it; and I often thought with my self that I would have given a handful of it for a gross of tobacco-pipes, or for a hand-mill to grind my corn; nay, I would have given it all for six-pennyworth of turnip and carrot seed out of England, or for a handful of pease and beans, and a bottle of ink. As it was, I had not the least advantage by it, or benefit from it; but there it lay in a drawer, and grew mouldy with the damp of the cave in the wet season; and if I had had the drawer full of diamonds, it had been the same case; and they had been of no manner of value to me, because of no use.

I had now brought my state of life to be much easier in itself than it was at first, and much easier to my mind, as well as to my body. I frequently sat down to my meat with thankfulness, and admir'd the hand of God's providence, which had thus spread my table in the wilderness. I learn'd to look more upon the bright side of my condition, and less upon the dark side, and to consider what I enjoy'd, rather than what I wanted; and this gave me sometimes such secret comforts, that I cannot express them; and which I take notice of here, to put those discontented people in mind of it, who cannot enjoy comfortably what God has given them; because they see and covet something that He has not given them. All our discontents about what we want appear'd to me to spring from the want of thankfulness for what we have.

Another reflection was of great use to me, and doubtless would be so to any one that should fall into such distress as mine was; and this was, to compare my present condition with what I at first expected it should be; nay, with what it would certainly have been, if the good providence of God had not wonderfully order'd the ship to be cast up nearer to the shore, where I not only could come at her, but could bring what I got out of her to the shore, for my relief and comfort; without which, I had wanted for tools to work, weapons for defence, or gun-powder and shot for getting my food.

I spent whole hours, I may say whole days, in representing to my self in the most lively colours how I must have acted if I had got nothing out of the ship; how I could not have so much as got any food except fish and turtles; and that as it was long before I found any of them, I must have perish'd first; that I should have liv'd, if I had not perish'd, like a meer savage; that if I had kill'd a goat or a fowl, by any contrivance, I had no way to flea or open them, or part the flesh from the skin and the bowels, or to cut it up; but must gnaw it with my teeth and pull it with my claws like a beast.

These reflections made me very sensible of the goodness of Providence to me, and very thankful for my present condition, with all its hardships and misfortunes; and this part also I cannot but recommend to the reflection of those who are apt in their misery to say, 'Is any affliction like mine!' Let them consider how much worse the cases of some people are, and their case might have been, if Providence had thought fit.

I had another reflection which assisted me also to comfort my mind with hopes; and this was, comparing my present condition with what I had deserv'd, and had therefore reason to expect from the hand of Providence. I had liv'd a dreadful life, perfectly destitute of the knowledge and fear of God. I had been well instructed by father and mother; neither had they been wanting to me, in their early endeavours, to infuse a religious awe of God into my mind, a sense of my duty, and of what the nature and end of my being requir'd of me. But alas! falling early into the seafaring life, which of all the lives is the most destitute of the fear of God, though His terrors are always before them; I say, falling early into the seafaring life, and into seafaring company, all that little sense of religion which I had entertain'd was laugh'd out of me by my mess-mates, by a harden'd despising of dangers, and the views of death, which grew habitual to me by my long absence from all manner of opportunities to converse with any thing but what was like my self, or to hear any thing that was good or tended towards it.

So void was I of every thing that was good, or of the least sense of what I was, or was to be, that in the greatest deliverances I enjoy'd, such as my escape from Sallee, my being taken up by the Portuguese master of the ship, my being planted so well in the Brasils, my receiving the cargo from England, and the like, I never had once the word, 'Thank God,' so much as on my mind, or in my mouth; nor in the greatest distress, had I so much as a thought to pray to Him, or so much as to say, 'Lord have mercy upon me'; no, nor to mention the name of God, unless it was to swear by and blaspheme it.

I had terrible reflections upon my mind for many months, as I have already observ'd, on the account of my wicked and hardned life past; and when I look'd about me and considered what particular providences had attended me since my coming into this place, and how God had dealt bountifully with me; had not only punished me less than my iniquity had deserv'd, but had so plentifully provided for me; this gave me great hopes that my repentance was accepted, and that God had yet mercy in store for me.

With these reflections I work'd my mind up, not only to resignation to the will of God in the present disposition of my circumstances, but even to a sincere thankfulness for my condition, and that I, who was yet a living man, ought not to complain, seeing I had not the due punishment of my sins; that I enjoy'd so many mercies which I had no reason to have expected in that place; that I ought never more to repine at my condition, but to rejoyce, and to give daily thanks for that daily bread which nothing but a croud of wonders could have brought. That I ought to consider I had been fed even by miracle, even as great as that of feeding Elijah by ravens, nay, by a long series of miracles; and that I could hardly have nam'd a place in the unhabitable part of the world where I could have been cast more to my advantage; a place where, as I had no society, which was my affliction on one hand, so I found no ravenous beast, no furious wolves or tygers to threaten my life, no venomous creatures, or poisonous, which I might feed on to my hurt, no savages to murther and devour me.

In a word, as my life was a life of sorrow one way, so it was a life of mercy another; and I wanted nothing to make it a life of comfort, but to be able to make my sence of God's goodness to me, and care over me in this condition, be my daily consolation; and after I did make a just improvement of these things, I went away and was no more sad.

I had now been here so long that many things which I brought on shore for my help were either quite gone or very much wasted and near spent.

My ink, as I observed, had been gone some time, all but a very little, which I eek'd out with water a little and a little, till it was so pale it scarce left any appearane of black upon the paper. As long as it lasted, I made use of it to minute down the days of the month on which any remarkable thing happen'd to me, and first by casting up times past. I remember that there was a strange concurrence of days in the various providences which befel me; and which, if I had been superstitiously inclin'd to observe days as fatal or fortunate, I might have had reason to have look'd upon with a great deal of curiosity.

First, I had observed that the same day that I broke away from my father and my friends, and run away to Hull, in order to go to sea, the same day afterwards I was taken by the Sallee man of war, and made a slave.

The same day of the year that I escaped out of the wreck of that ship in Yarmouth roads, that same day-year afterwards I made my escape from Sallee in the boat.

The same day of the year I was born on, viz. the 30th of September, that same day I had my life so miraculously saved twenty-six year after,* when I was cast on shore in this island, so that my wicked life and my solitary life begun both on a day.

The next thing to my ink's being wasted, was that of my bread, I mean the bisket which I brought out of the ship; this I had husbanded to the last degree, allowing my self but one cake of bread a day for above a year, and yet I was quite without bread for near a year before I got any corn of my own, and great reason I had to be thankful that I had any at all, the getting it being, as has been already observed, next to miraculous.

My cloaths began to decay too mightily: as to linnen, I had had none a good while, except some chequer'd shirts which I found in the chests of the other seamen, and which I carefully preserved, because many times I could bear no other cloaths on but a shirt; and it was a very great help to me that I had among all the men's cloaths of the ship almost three dozen of shirts. There were also several thick watch-coats of the seamen's, which were left indeed, but they were too hot to wear; and tho' it is true that the weather was so violent hot that there was no need of cloaths, yet I could not go quite naked; no, tho' I had been inclin'd to it, which I was not, nor could not abide the thoughts of it, tho' I was all alone.

The reason why I could not go quite naked was, I could not bear the heat of the sun so well when quite naked as with some cloaths on; nay, the very heat frequently blistered my skin; whereas with a shirt on, the air itself made some motion and, whistling under that shirt, was twofold cooler than without it: no more could I ever bring my self to go out in the heat of sun without a cap or a hat; the heat of the sun, beating with such violence as it does in that place, would give me the head-ach presently, by darting so directly on my head, without a cap or hat on, so that I could not bear it, whereas, if I put on my hat, it would presently go away.

Upon those views I began to consider about putting the few rags I had, which I call'd cloaths, into some order; I had worn out all the wastcoats I had, and my business was now to try if I could not make jackets out of the great watch-coats which I had by me, and with such other materials as I had; so I set to work a taylering, or rather indeed a botching, for I made most piteous work of it. However, I made shift to make two or three new wastcoats, which I hoped wou'd serve me a great while; as for breeches or drawers, I made but a very sorry shift indeed, till afterward.

I have mentioned that I saved the skins of all the creatures that I kill'd, I mean four-footed ones, and I had hung them up stretched out with sticks in the sun, by which means some of them were so dry and hard that they were fit for little, but others, it seems, were very useful. The first thing I made of these was a great cap for my head, with the hair on the out side to shoot off the rain; and this I perform'd so well, that after this I made me a suit of cloaths wholly of these skins, that is to say, a wastcoat, and breeches open at knees, and both loose, for they were rather wanting to keep me cool than to keep me warm. I must not omit to acknowledge that they were wretchedly made; for if I was a bad carpenter, I was a worse taylor. However, they were such as I made very good shift with; and when I was abroad, if it happen'd to rain, the hair of my wastcoat and cap being outermost, I was kept very dry.

After this I spent a great deal of time and pains to make me an umbrella; I was indeed in great want of one, and had a great mind to make one; I had seen them made in the Brasils, where they are very useful in the great heats which are there; and I felt the heats every jot as great here, and greater too, being nearer the equinox; besides, as I was oblig'd to be much abroad, it was a most useful thing to me, as well for the rains as the heats. I took a world of pains at it, and was a great while before I could make anything likely to hold; nay, after I thought I had hit the way, I spoil'd two or three before I made one to my mind; but at last I made one that answer'd indifferently well. The main difficulty I found was to make it to let down. I could make it to spread, but if it did not let down too, and draw in, it was not portable for me any way but just over my head, which wou'd not do. However, at last, as I said, I made one to answer, and covered it with skins, the hair upwards, so that it cast off the rains like a penthouse, and kept off the sun so effectually, that I could walk out in the hottest of the weather with greater advantage than I could before in the coolest, and when I had no need of it, cou'd close it and carry it under my arm.

Thus I liv'd mighty comfortably, my mind being entirely composed by resigning to the will of God, and throwing my self wholly upon the disposal of His providence. This made my life better than sociable, for when I began to regret the want of conversation, I would ask my self whether thus conversing mutually with my own thoughts, and, as I hope I may say, with even God Himself by ejaculations, was not better than the utmost enjoyment of humane society in the world.

I cannot say that after this, for five years, any extraordinary thing happened to me, but I liv'd on in the same course, in the same posture and place, just as before; the chief things I was employ'd in, besides my yearly labour of planting my barley and rice, and curing my raisins, of both which I always kept up just enough to have sufficient stock of one year's provisions beforehand; I say, besides this yearly labour, and my daily labour of going out with my gun, I had one labour, to make me a canoe, which at last I finished; so that by digging a canal to it of six foot wide and four foot deep, I brought it into the creek, almost half a mile. As for the first, which was so vastly big, as I made it without considering before hand, as I ought to do, how I should be able to launch it; so, never being able to bring it to the water, or bring the water to it, I was oblig'd to let it lye where it was, as a memorandum to teach me to be wiser next time: indeed, the next time, tho' I could not get a tree proper for it, and in a place where I could not get the water to it at any less distance than, as I have said, nearly half a mile, yet as I saw it was practicable at last, I never gave it over; and though I was near two years about it, yet I never grutch'd my labour, in hopes of having a boat to go off to sea at last.

However, though my little periagua was finish'd, yet the size of it was not at all answerable to the design which I had in view when I made the first; I mean, of venturing over to the terra firma, where it was above forty miles broad; accordingly, the smallness of my boat assisted to put an end to that design, and now I thought no more of it: but as I had a boat, my next design was to make a tour round the island; for as I had been on the other side in one place, crossing, as I have already describ'd it, over the land, so the discoveries I made in that little journey made me very eager to see other parts of the coast; and now I had a boat, I thought of nothing but sailing round the island.

For this purpose, that I must do every thing with discretion and consideration, I fitted up a little mast to my boat, and made a sail to it out of some of the pieces of the ship's sail, which lay in store, and of which I had a great stock by me.

Having fitted my mast and sail, and try'd the boat, I found she would sail very well. Then I made little lockers, or boxes, at either end of my boat, to put provisions, necessaries, and ammunitions, &c., into, to be kept dry, either from rain or the sprye of the sea; and a little long hollow place I cut in the in-side of the boat, where

I could lay my gun, making a flap to hand down over it to keep it dry.

I fix'd my umbrella also in a step at the stern, like a mast, to stand over my head, and keep the heat of the sun off of me like an auning; and thus I every now and then took a little voyage upon the sea, but never went far out, nor far from the little creek; but at last, being eager to view the circumference of my little kingdom, I resolv'd upon my tour, and accordingly I victuall'd my ship for the voyage, putting in two dozen of my loaves (cakes I should rather call them) of barley bread, an earthen pot full of parch'd rice, a food I eat a great deal of, a little bottle of rum, half a goat, and powder and shot for killing more, and two large watch-coats, of those which, as I mention'd before, I had sav'd out of the seamen's chests; these I took, one to lye upon, and the other to cover me in the night.

It was the sixth of November, in the sixth year of my reign, or my captivity, which you please, that I set out on this voyage, and I found it much longer than I expected; for though the island it self was not very large, yet when I came to the east side of it, I found a great ledge of rocks lye out above two leagues into the sea, some above water, some under it; and beyond that, a shoal of sand, lying dry half a league more; so that I was oblig'd to go a great way out to sea to double the point.

When first I discover'd them, I was going to give over my enterprise, and come back again, not knowing how far it might oblige me to go out to sea; and above all, doubting how I should get back again; so I came to an anchor; for I had made me a kind of an anchor with a piece of a broken graplin which I got out of the ship.

Having secur'd my boat, I took my gun and went on shore, climbing up upon a hill which seem'd to overlook that point, where I saw the full extent of it, and resolv'd to venture.

In my viewing the sea from that hill where I stood, I perceiv'd a strong, and indeed a most furious current, which run to the east, and even came close to the point; and I took the more notice of it, because I saw there might be some danger; that when I came into it, I might be carry'd out to sea by the strength of it, and not be able to make the island again; and indeed, had I not gotten first up upon this hill, I believe it would have been so; for there was the same current on the other side the island, only that it set off at a farther distance; and I saw there was a strong eddy under the shore; so I had nothing to do but to get in out of the first current, and I should presently be in an eddy.

I lay here, however, two days; because the wind blowing pretty fresh at E.S.E., and that being just contrary to the said current, made a great breach of the sea upon the point; so that it was not safe for me to keep too close to the shore for the breach, nor to go too far off because of the stream.

The third day in the morning, the wind having abated over night, the sea was calm, and I ventur'd; but I am a warning piece again to all rash and ignorant pilots; for no sooner was I come to the point, when even I was not my boat's length from the shore, but I found my self in a great depth of water, and a current like the sluice of a mill: it carry'd my boat along with it with such violence that all I could do could not keep her so much as on the edge of it; but I found it hurry'd me farther and farther out from the eddy, which was on my left hand. There was no wind stirring to help me, and all I could do with my paddlers signify'd nothing, and now I began to give my self over for lost; for as the current was on both sides the island, I knew in a few leagues' distance they must joyn again, and then I was irrecoverably gone; nor did I see any possibility of avoiding it; so that I had no prospect before me but of perishing, not by the sea, for that was calm enough, but of starving for hunger. I had indeed found a tortoise on the shore, as big almost as I could lift, and had toss'd it into the boat; and I had a great jar of fresh water, that is to say, one of my earthen pots; but what was all this to being driven into the vast ocean, where, to be sure, there was no shore, no main land or island, for a thousand leagues at least?

And now I saw how easy it was for the providence of God to make the most miserable condition mankind could be in, worse. Now I look'd back upon my desolate solitary island as the most pleasant place in the world, and all the happiness my heart could wish for was to be but there again. I stretch'd out my hands to it with eager wishes. 'O happy desart,' said I, 'I shall never see thee more. O miserable creature,' said I, 'whither am I going?' Then I reproach'd my self with my unthankful temper, and how I had repin'd at my solitary condition; and now what would I give to be on shore there again! Thus we never see the true state of our condition till it is illustrated to us by its contraries, nor know how to value what we enjoy, but by the want of it. It is scarce possible to imagine the consternation I was now in, being driven from my beloved island (for so it appear'd to me now to be) into the wide ocean, almost two leagues, and in the utmost despair of ever recovering it again. However, I work'd hard, till indeed my strength was almost exhausted, and kept my boat as much to the northward, that is, towards the side of the current which the eddy lay on, as possibly I could; when about noon, as the sun pass'd the meridian, I thought I felt a little breeze of wind in my face, springing up from the S.S.E. This chear'd my heart a little, and especially when in about half an hour more it blew a pretty small gentle gale. By this time I was gotten at a frightful distance from the island, and had the least cloud of haizy weather interven'd, I had been undone another way too; for I had no compass on board, and should never have known how to have steer'd towards the island, if I had but once lost sight of it; but the weather continuing clear, I apply'd my self to get up my mast again, and spread my sail, standing away to the north as much as possible, to get out of the current.

Just as I had set my mast and sail, and the boat began to stretch away, I saw even by the clearness of the water some alteration of the current was near; for where the current was so strong, the water was foul; but perceiving the water clear, I found the current abate, and presently I found to the east, at about half a mile, a breach of the sea upon some rocks; these rocks I found caus'd the current to part again, and as the main stress of it ran away more southerly, leaving the rocks to the north-east, so the other return'd by the repulse of the rocks, and made a strong eddy, which run back again to the north-west, with a very sharp stream.

They who know what it is to have a reprieve brought to them upon the ladder, or to be rescued from thieves just a going to murther them, or who have been in such like extremities, may guess what my present surprise of joy was, and how gladly I put my boat into the stream of this eddy, and the wind also freshning, how gladly I spread my sail to it, running chearfully before the wind, and with a strong tide or eddy under foot.

This eddy carryed me about a league in my way back again directly towards the island, but about two leagues more to the northward than the current which carried me away at first; so that when I came near the island, I found my self open to the northern shore of it, that is to say, the other end of the island opposite to that which I went out from.

When I had made something more than a league of way by the help of this current or eddy, I found it was spent and serv'd me no farther. However, I found that being between the two great currents, viz. that on the south side which had hurried me away, and that on the north which lay about a league on the other side; I say, between these two, in the wake of the island, I found the water at least still and running no way, and having still a breeze of wind fair for me, I kept on steering directly for the island, tho' not making such fresh way as I did before.

About four a-clock in the evening, being then within about a league of the island, I found the point of the rocks which occasioned this disaster, stretching out as is describ'd before to the south-ward, and casting off the current more southwardly, had of course made another eddy to the north, and this I found very strong, but not directly setting the way my course lay, which was due west, but almost full north. However, having a fresh gale, I stretch'd a-cross this eddy slanting north-west, and in about an hour came within about a mile of the shore, where it being smooth water, I soon got to land.

When I was on shore I fell on my knees and gave God thanks for my deliverance, resolving to lay aside all thoughts of my deliverance by my boat; and refreshing my self with such things as I had, I brought my boat close to the shore in a little cove that I had spy'd under some trees, and lay'd me down to sleep, being quite spent with the labour and fatigue of the voyage.

I was now at a great loss which way to get home with my boat. I had run so much hazard, and knew too much the case, to think of attempting it by the way I went out, and what might be at the other side (I mean the west side) I knew not, nor had I any mind to run any more ventures; so I only resolved in the morning to make my way westward along the shore and to see if there was no creek where I might lay up my frigate in safety, so as to have her again if I wanted her; in about three mile or thereabout, coasting the shore, I came to a very good inlet or bay about a mile over, which narrowed till it came to a very little rivulet or brook, where I found a very convenient harbour for my boat, and where she lay as if she had been in a little dock made on purpose for her. Here I put in, and having stow'd my boat very safe, I went on shore to look about me and see where I was.

I soon found I had but a little past by the place where I had been before, when I travell'd on foot to that shore; so taking nothing out of my boat but my gun and my umbrella, for it was exceeding hot, I began my march. The way was comfortable enough after such a voyage as I had been upon, and I reach'd my old bower in the evening, where I found every thing standing as I left it; for I always kept it in good order, being, as I said before, my country house.

I got over the fence, and laid me down in the shade to rest my limbs, for I was very weary, and fell asleep. But judge you, if you can, that read my story, what a surprize I must be in, when I was wak'd out of my sleep by a voice calling me by my name several times, 'Robin, Robin, Robin Crusoe, poor Robin Crusoe, where are you, Robin Crusoe? Where are you? Where have you been?'

I was so dead asleep at first, being fatigu'd with rowing, or paddling, as it is call'd, the first part of the day, and with walking the latter part, that I did not wake thoroughly, but dozing between sleeping and waking, thought I dream'd that some body spoke to me: but as the voice continu'd to repeat 'Robin Crusoe, Robin Crusoe,' at last I began to wake more perfectly, and was at first dreadfully frighted, and started up in the utmost consternation. But no sooner were my eyes open, than I saw my Poll sitting on the top of the hedge, and immediately knew that it was he that spoke to me; for just in such bemoaning language I had used to talk to him and teach him; and he had learn'd it so perfectly, that he would sit upon my finger, and lay his bill close to my face, and cry, 'Poor Robin Crusoe, where are you? Where have you been? How come you here?' and such things as I had taught him.

However, even though I knew it was the parrot, and that indeed it could be no body else, it was a good while before I could compose my self. First, I was amazed how the creature got thither, and then, how he should just keep about the place, and no where else: but as I was well satisfied it could be no body but honest Poll, I got it over; and holding out my hand, and calling him by his name, Poll, the sociable creature came to me, and sat upon my thumb, as he used to do, and continu'd talking to me, Poor Robin Crusoe! and how did I come here? and where had I been? just as if he had been overjoy'd to see me again; and so I carry'd him home along with me.

I had now had enough of rambling to sea for some time, and had enough to do for many days to sit still, and reflect upon the danger I had been in. I would have been very glad to have had my boat again on my side of the island; but I knew not how it was practicable to get it about. As to the east side of the island, which I had gone round, I knew well enough there was no venturing that way; my very heart would shrink, and my very blood run chill, but to think of it: and as to the other side of the island, I did not know how it might be there; but supposing the current ran with the same force against the shore at the east as it pass'd by it on the other, I might run the same risk of being driven down the stream, and carry'd by the island, as I had been before of being carry'd away from it; so with these thoughts I contented my self to be without any boat, though it had been the product of so many months' labour to make it, and of so many more to get in unto the sea.

In this government of my temper I remain'd near a year, liv'd a very sedate, retir'd life, as you may well suppose; and my thoughts being very much composed as to my condition, and fully comforted in resigning my self to the dispositions of Providence, I thought I liv'd really very happily in all things, except that of society.

I improv'd myself in this time in all the mechanick exercises which my necessities put me upon applying my self to, and I believe cou'd, upon occasion, make a very good carpenter, especially considering how few tools I had.

Besides this, I arriv'd at an unexpected perfection in my earthen ware, and contriv'd well enough to make them with a wheel, which I found infinitely easyer and better; because I made things round and shapable, which before were filthy things indeed to look on. But I think I was never more vain of my own performance, or more joyful for any thing I found out, than for my being able to make a tobacco-pipe. And tho' it was a very ugly clumsy thing when it was done, and only burnt red like other earthen ware, yet as it was hard and firm, and would draw the smoke, I was exceedingly comforted with it, for I had been always used to smoke, and there were pipes in the ship, but I forgot them at first, not knowing that there was tobacco in the island; and afterwards, when I search'd the ship again, I could not come at any pipes at all.

In my wicker ware also I improved much, and made abundance of necessary baskets, as well as my invention shew'd me, tho' not very handsome, yet they were such as were very handy and convenient for my laying things up in, or fetching things home in. For example, if I kill'd a goat abroad, I could hang it up in a tree, flea it and dress it, and cut it in pieces, and bring it home in a basket; and the like by a turtle; I could cut it up, take out the eggs and a piece or two of the flesh, which was enough for me, and bring them home in a basket, and leave the rest behind me. Also large deep baskets were my receivers for my corn, which I always rubb'd out as soon as it was dry, and cured, and kept it in great baskets.

I began now to perceive my powder abated considerably, and this was a want which it was impossible for me to supply, and I began seriously to consider what I must do when I should have no more powder; that is to say, how I should do to kill any goat. I had, as is observ'd in the third year of my being here, kept a young kid, and bred her up tame, and I was in hope of getting a he-goat, but I could not by any means bring it to pass, 'till my kid grew an old goat; and I could never find it in my heart to kill her, till she dy'd at last of meer age.

But being now in the eleventh year of my residence and, as I have said, my ammunition growing low, I set my self to study some art to trap and snare the goats, to see whether I could not catch some of them alive, and particularly I wanted a she-goat great with young.

To this purpose I made snares to hamper them, and I do believe they were more than once taken in them, but my tackle was not good, for I had no wire, and I always found them broken, and my bait devoured.

At length I resolved to try a pit-fall; so I dug several large pits in the earth, in places where I had observ'd the goats used to feed, and over these pits I plac'd hurdles, of my own making too, with a great weight upon them; and several times I put ears of barley and dry rice, without setting the trap, and I could easily perceive that the goats had gone in and eaten up the corn, for I could see the mark of their feet. At length I set three traps in one night, and going the next morning I found them all standing, and yet the bait eaten and gone; this was very discouraging. However, I alter'd my trap, and, not to trouble you with particulars, going one morning to see my trap, I found in one of them a large old he-goat, and in one of the other three kids, a male and two females.

As to the old one, I knew not what to do with him, he was so fierce I durst not go into the pit to him; that is to say, to go about to bring him away alive, which was what I wanted. I could have kill'd him, but that was not my business, nor would it answer my end. So I e'en let him out, and he ran away as if he had been frighted out of his wits: but I had forgot then what I learn'd afterwards, that hunger will tame a lyon. If I had let him stay there three or four days without food, and then have carry'd him some water to drink, and then a little corn, he would have been as tame as one of the kids, for they are mighty sagacious, tractable creatures where they are well used.

However, for the present I let him go, knowing no better at that time; then I went to the three kids, and taking them one by one, I tyed them with strings together, and with some difficulty brought them all home.

It was a good while before they wou'd feed, but throwing them some sweet corn, it tempted them and they began to be tame; and now I found that if I expected to supply my self with goat-flesh when I had no powder or shot left, breeding some up tame was my only way, when perhaps I might have them about my house like a flock of sheep.

But then it presently occurr'd to me, that I must keep the tame from the wild, or else they would always run wild when they grew up, and the only way for this was to have some enclosed piece of ground, well fenc'd either with hedge or pale, to keep them in so effectually, that those within might not break out, or those without break in.

This was a great undertaking for one pair of hands, yet as I saw there was an absolute necessity of doing it, my first piece of work was to find out a proper piece of ground, viz. where there was likely to be herbage for them to eat, water for them to drink, and cover to keep them from the sun.

Those who understand such enclosures will think I had very little contrivance, when I pitch'd upon a place very proper for all these, being a plain open piece of meadow-land, or savanna (as our people call it in the western collonies), which had two or three little drills of fresh water in it, and at one end was very woody; I say, they will smile at my forecast, when I shall tell them I began my enclosing of this piece of ground in such a manner that my hedge or pale must have been at least two mile about. Nor was the madness of it so great as to the compass, for if it was ten mile about I was like to have time enough to do it in. But I did not consider that my goats would be as wild in so much compass as if they had had the whole island, and I should have so much room to chace them in, that I should never catch them.

My hedge was begun and carry'd on, I believe, about fifty yards,

when this thought occur'd to me; so I presently stopt short, and
for the first beginning I resolv'd to enclose a piece of about 150
yards in length and 100 yards in breadth, which as it would
maintain as many as I should have in any reasonable time, so, as
my flock encreased, I could add more ground to my enclosure.

This was acting with some prudence, and I went to work with
courage. I was about three months hedging in the first piece, and
till I had done it I tether'd the three kids in the best part of it, and
us'd them to feed as near me as possible to make them familiar;
and very often I would go and carry them some ears of barley, or a
handful of rice, and feed them out of my hand; so that after my
enclosure was finished, and I let them loose, they would follow me
up and down, bleating after me for a handful of corn.

This answer'd my end, and in about a year and half I had a flock
of about twelve goats, kids and all; and in two years more I had
three and forty, besides several that I took and kill'd for my food.
And after that I enclosed five several pieces of ground to feed them
in, with little pens to drive them into, to take them as I wanted,
and gates out of one piece of ground into another.

But this was not all, for now I not only had goat's flesh to feed
on when I pleas'd, but milk too, a thing which indeed in my
beginning I did not so much as think of, and which, when it came
into my thoughts, was really an agreeable surprize. For now I set
up my dairy, and had sometimes a gallon or two of milk in a day.
And as nature, who gives supplies of food to every creature,
dictates even naturally how to make use of it; so I that had never
milk'd a cow, much less a goat, or seen butter or cheese made, very
readily and handily, tho' after a great many essays and
miscarriages, made me both butter and cheese at last, and never
wanted it afterwards.

How mercifully can our great Creator treat His creatures, even
in those conditions in which they seem'd to be overwhelm'd in
destruction! How can He sweeten the bitterest providences, and
give us cause to praise Him for dungeons and prisons! What a
table was here spread for me in a wilderness, where I saw nothing
at first but to perish for hunger!

It would have made a stoick smile to have seen me and my little
family sit down to dinner; there was my majesty the prince and
lord of the whole island; I had the lives of all my subjects at my
absolute command; I could hang, draw, give liberty, and take it
away, and no rebels among all my subjects.

Then to see how like a king I din'd too, all alone, attended by my servants. Poll, as if he had been my favourite, was the only person permitted to talk to me. My dog, who was now grown very old and crazy, and had found no species to multiply his kind upon, sat always at my right hand, and two cats, one on one side the table, and one on the other, expecting now and then a bit from my hand, as a mark of special favour.

But these were not the two cats which I brought on shore at first, for they were both of them dead, and had been interr'd near my habitation by my own hand; but one of them having multiply'd by I know not what kind of creature, these were two which I had preserv'd tame, whereas the rest run wild in the woods, and became indeed troublesom to me at last; for they would often come into my house, and plunder me too, till at last I was obliged to shoot them, and did kill a great many; at length they left me. With this attendance and in this plentiful manner I lived; neither could I be said to want any thing but society, and of that, in some time after this, I was like to have too much.

I was something impatient, as I have observ'd, to have the use of my boat; though very loath to run any more hazards; and therefore sometimes I sat contriving ways to get her about the island, and at other times I sat my self down contented enough without her. But I had a strange uneasiness in my mind to go down to the point of the island, where, as I have said, in my last ramble, I went up the hill to see how the shore lay, and how the current set, that I might see what I had to do. This inclination encreas'd upon me every day, and at length I resolv'd to travel thither by land, following the edge of the shore. I did so: but had any one in England been to meet such a man as I was, it must either have frighted them, or rais'd a great deal of laughter; and as I frequently stood still to look at my self, I could not but smile at the notion of my travelling through Yorkshire with such an equipage, and in such a dress. Be pleas'd to take a sketch of my figure, as follows.

I had a great high shapeless cap, made of a goat's skin, with a flap hanging down behind, as well to keep the sun from me as to shoot the rain off from running into my neck; nothing being so hurtful in these climates as the rain upon the flesh under the cloaths.

I had a short jacket of goat-skin, the skirts coming down to about the middle of my thighs, and a pair of open-knee'd breeches of the same; the breeches were made of the skin of an old he-goat, whose hair hung down such a length on either side that like pantaloons it reach'd to the middle of my legs; stockings and shoes I had none, but had made me a pair of somethings, I scare know what to call them, like buskins, to flap over my legs and lace on either side like spatter-dashes; but of a most barbarous shape, as indeed were all the rest of my cloaths.

I had on a broad belt of goat's-skin dry'd, which I drew together with two thongs of the same, instead of buckles, and in a kind of a frog* on either side of this, instead of a sword and a dagger, hung a little saw and a hatchet, one on one side, one on the other. I had another belt not so broad, and fasten'd in the same manner, which hung over my shoulder; and at the end of it, under my left arm, hung two pouches, both made of goat's-skin too; in one of which hung my powder, in the other my shot. At my back I carry'd my basket, on my shoulder my gun, and over my head a great clumsy ugly goat-skin umbrella, but which, after all, was the most necessary thing I had about me, next to my gun. As for my face, the colour of it was really not so moletta-like as one might expect from a man not at all careful of it, and living within nine or ten degrees of the equinox. My beard I had once suffer'd to grow till it was about a quarter of a yard long; but as I had both scissars and razors sufficient, I had cut it pretty short, except what grew on my upper lip, which I had trimm'd into a large pair of Mahometan whiskers, such as I had seen worn by some Turks who I saw at Sallee; for the Moors did not wear such, tho' the Turks did; of these mustachioes or whiskers I will not say they were long enough to hang my hat upon them; but they were of a length and shape monstrous enough, and such as in England would have pass'd for frightful.

But all this is by the by; for as to my figure, I had so few to observe me that it was of no manner of consequence; so I say no more to that part. In this kind of figure I went my new journey, and was out five or six days. I travell'd first along the sea shore, directly to the place where I first brought my boat to an anchor, to get up upon the rocks; and having no boat now to take care of, I went over the land a nearer way to the same height that I was upon before, when looking forward to the point of the rocks which lay out, and which I was oblig'd to double with my boat, as is said above, I was surpriz'd to see the sea all smooth and quiet, no ripling, no motion, no current, any more there than in other places.

I was at a strange loss to understand this, and resolv'd to spend some time in the observing it, to see if nothing from the sets of the tide had occasion'd it; but I was presently convinc'd how it was, viz. that the tide of ebb setting from the west, and joyning with the current of waters from some great river on the shore, must be the occasion of this current; and that according as the wind blew more forcibly from the west or from the north, this current came nearer or went farther from the shore; for waiting thereabouts till evening, I went up to the rock again, and then the tide of ebb being made, I plainly saw the current again as before, only that it run farther off, being near half a league from the shore; whereas in my case, it set close upon the shore, and hurry'd me and my canoe along with it, which at another time it would not have done.

This observation convinc'd me that I had nothing to do but to observe the ebbing and the flowing of the tide, and I might very easily bring my boat about the island again: but when I began to think of putting it in practice, I had such a terror upon my spirit at the remembrance of the danger I had been in, that I could not think of it again with any patience; but on the contrary, I took up another resolution which was more safe, though more laborious; and this was that I would build, or rather make me, another periagua or canoe; and so have one for one side of the island and one for the other.

You are to understand that now I had, as I may call it, two plantations in the island; one my little fortification or tent, with the wall about it under the rock, with the cave behind me, which by this time I had enlarg'd into several apartments or caves, one within another. One of these, which was the dryest and largest, and had a door out beyond my wall or fortification, that is to say, beyond where my wall joyn'd to the rock, was all fill'd up with the large earthen pots, of which I have given an account, and with fourteen or fifteen great baskets, which would hold five or six bushels each, where I laid up my stores of provision, especially my corn, some in the ear cut off short from the straw, and the other rubb'd out with my hand.

As for my wall, made, as before, with long stakes or piles, those piles grew all like trees, and were by this time grown so big, and spread so very much, that there was not the least appearance to any one's view of any habitation behind them.

Near this dwelling of mine, but a little farther within the land, and upon lower ground, lay my two pieces of corn-ground, which

I kept duly cultivated and sow'd, and which duly yielded me their harvest in its season; and whenever I had occasion for more corn, I had more land adjoyning as fit as that.

Besides this, I had my country seat, and I had now a tollerable plantation there also; for first, I had my little bower, as I call'd it, which I kept in repair; that is to say, I kept the hedge which circled it in constantly fitted up to its usual height, the ladder standing always in the inside; I kept the trees, which at first were no more than my stakes, but were now grown very firm and tall; I kept them always so cut, that they might spread and grow thick and wild, and make the more agreeable shade, which they did effectually to my mind. In the middle of this I had my tent always standing, being a piece of a sail spread over poles set up for that purpose, and which never wanted any repair or renewing; and under this I had made me a squab or couch, with the skins of the creatures I had kill'd, and with other soft things, and a blanket laid on them, such as belong'd to our sea-bedding, which I had saved, and a great watch-coat to cover me; and here, whenever I had occasion to be absent from my chief seat, I took up my country habitation.

Adjoyning to this I had my enclosures for my cattle, that is to say, my goats. And as I had taken an inconceivable deal of pains to fence and enclose this ground, so I was so uneasy to see it kept entire, lest the goats should break thro', that I never left off till with infinite labour I had stuck the out-side of the hedge so full of small stakes, and so near to one another, that it was rather a pale than a hedge, and there was scarce room to put a hand thro' between them, which afterwards when those stakes grew, as they all did in the next rainy season, made the enclosure strong like a wall, indeed stronger than any wall.

This will testify for me that I was not idle, and that I spared no pains to bring to pass whatever appear'd necessary for my comfortable support; for I consider'd the keeping up a breed of tame creatures thus at my hand would be a living magazine of flesh, milk, butter, and cheese for me as long as I liv'd in the place, if it were to be forty years; and that keeping them in my reach depended entirely upon my perfecting my enclosures to such a degree that I might be sure of keeping them together; which by this method indeed I so effectually secur'd that, when these little stakes began to grow, I had planted them so very thick, I was forced to pull some of them up again.

In this place also I had my grapes growing, which I principally depended on for my winter store of raisins, and which I never fail'd to preserve very carefully, as the best and most agreeable dainty of my whole diet; and indeed they were not agreeable only, but physical, wholesome, nourishing, and refreshing to the last degree.

As this was also about half way between my other habitation and the place where I had laid up my boat, I generally stay'd and lay here in my way thither; for I used frequently to visit my boat, and I kept all things about or belonging to her in very good order; sometimes I went out in her to divert my self, but no more hazardous voyages would I go, nor scarce ever above a stone's cast or two from the shore, I was so apprehensive of being hurry'd out of my knowledge again by the currents, or winds, or any other accident. But now I come to a new scene of my life.

It happen'd one day about noon going towards my boat, I was exceedingly surpriz'd with the print of a man's naked foot on the shore, which was very plain to be seen in the sand. I stood like one thunder-struck, or as if I had seen an apparition; I listen'd, I look'd round me, I could hear nothing, nor see any thing; I went up to a rising ground to look farther; I went up the shore and down the shore, but it was all one, I could see no other impression but that one. I went to it again to see if there were any more, and to observe if it might not be my fancy; but there was no room for that, for there was exactly the very print of a foot, toes, heel, and every part of a foot; how it came thither I knew not, nor could in the least imagine. But after innumerable fluttering thoughts, like a man perfectly confus'd and out of my self, I came home to my fortification, not feeling, as we say, the ground I went on, but terrify'd to the last degree, looking behind me at every two or three steps, mistaking every bush and tree, and fancying every stump at a distance to be a man; nor is it possible to describe how many various shapes affrighted imagination represented things to me in, how many wild ideas were found every moment in my fancy, and what strange unaccountable whimsies came into my thoughts by the way.

When I came to my castle, for so I think I call'd it ever after this, I fled into it like one pursued; whether I went over by the ladder as first contriv'd, or went in at the hole in the rock which I call'd a door, I cannot remember; no, nor could I remember the next morning, for never frighted hare fled to cover, or fox to earth, with more terror of mind than I to this retreat.

I slept none that night; the farther I was from the occasion of my fright, the greater my apprehensions were, which is something contrary to the nature of such things, and especially to the usual practice of all creatures in fear: but I was so embarrass'd with my own frightful ideas of the thing, that I form'd nothing but dismal imaginations to my self, even tho' I was now a great way off of it. Sometimes I fancy'd it must be the devil; and reason joyn'd with me upon this supposition; for how should any other thing in human shape come into the place? Where was the vessel that brought them? What marks was there of any other footsteps? And how was it possible a man should come there? But then to think that Satan should take human shape upon him in such a place where there could be no manner of occasion for it, but to leave the print of his foot behind him, and that even for no purpose too, for he could not be sure I should see it; this was an amusement the other way; I consider'd that the devil might have found out abundance of other ways to have terrify'd me than this of the single print of a foot; that as I liv'd quite on the other side of the island, he would never have been so simple to leave a mark in a place where 'twas ten thousand to one whether I should ever see it or not, and in the sand too, which the first surge of the sea upon a high wind would have defac'd entirely. All this seem'd inconsistent with the thing it self, and with all the notions we usually entertain of the subtilty of the devil.

Abundance of such things as these assisted to argue me out of all apprehensions of its being the devil: and I presently concluded then, that it must be some more dangerous creature, viz. that it must be some of the savages of the main land over-against me, who had wander'd out to sea in their canoes, and, either driven by the currents or by contrary winds, had made the island; and had been on shore, but were gone away again to sea, being as loth, perhaps, to have stay'd in this desolate island as I would have been to have had them.

While these reflections were rowling upon my mind, I was very thankful in my thoughts that I was so happy as not to be thereabouts at that time, or that they did not see my boat, by which they would have concluded that some inhabitants had been in the place, and perhaps have search'd farther for me. Then terrible thoughts rack'd my imagination about their having found my boat, and that there were people here; and that if so, I should certainly have them come again in greater numbers, and devour me; that if it should happen so that they should not find me, yet they would find my enclosure, destroy all my corn, carry away all my flock of tame goats, and I should perish at last for meer want.

Thus my fear banish'd all my religious hope; all that former confidence in God, which was founded upon such wonderful experience as I had had in His goodness, now vanished, as if He that had fed me by miracle hitherto, could not preserve by His power the provision which He had made for me by His goodness. I reproach'd myself with my easiness, that would not sow any more corn one year than would just serve me till the next season, as if no accident could intervene to prevent my enjoying the crop that was upon the ground; and this I thought so just a reproof, that I resolv'd for the future to have two or three years' corn beforehand, so that whatever might come, I might not perish for want of bread.

How strange a chequer work of providence is the life of man! and by what secret differing springs are the affections hurry'd about as differing circumstances present! To day we love what to morrow we hate; to day we seek what to morrow we shun; to day we desire what to morrow we fear, nay, even tremble at the apprehensions of; this was exemplify'd in me at this time in the most lively manner imaginable; for I whose only affliction was, that I seem'd banished from human society, that I was alone, circumscrib'd by the boundless ocean, cut off from mankind, and condemn'd to what I call'd silent life; that I was as one who Heaven thought not worthy to be number'd among the living, or to appear among the rest of His creatures; that to have seen one of my own species would have seem'd to me a raising me from death to life, and the greatest blessing that Heaven it self, next to the supreme blessing of salvation, could bestow; I say, that I should now tremble at the very apprehensions of seeing a man, and was ready to sink into the ground at but the shadow or silent appearance of a man's having set his foot in the island.

Such is the uneven state of human life; and it afforded me a great many curious speculations afterwards, when I had a little recover'd my first surprize; I consider'd that this was the station of life the infinitely wise and good providence of God had determin'd for me, that as I could not foresee what the ends of divine wisdom might be in all this, so I was not to dispute His sovereignty, who, as I was His creature, had an undoubted right by creation to govern and dispose of me absolutely as He thought fit; and who, as I was a creature who had offended Him, had likewise a judicial right to condemn me to what punishment He thought fit; and that it was my part to submit to bear His indignation, because I had sinn'd against Him.

I then reflected that God, who was not only righteous but omnipotent, as He had thought fit thus to punish and afflict me, so He was able to deliver me; that if He did not think fit to do it, 'twas my unquestion'd duty to resign my self absolutely and entirely to His will; and on the other hand, it was my duty also to hope in Him, pray to Him, and quietly to attend the dictates and directions of His daily providence.

These thoughts took me up many hours, days, nay, I may say weeks and months; and one particular effect of my cogitations on this occasion I cannot omit, viz.: One morning early, lying in my bed, and fill'd with thought about my danger from the appearance of savages, I found it discompos'd me very much, upon which those words of the scripture came into my thoughts, *Call upon me in the day of trouble, and I will deliver, and thou shalt glorify me.*

Upon this, rising chearfully out of my bed, my heart was not only comforted, but I was guided and encourag'd to pray earnestly to God for deliverance. When I had done praying, I took up my Bible, and opening it to read, the first words that presented to me were, *Wait on the Lord, and be of good cheer, and he shall strengthen thy heart; wait, I say, on the Lord.* It is impossible to express the comfort this gave me. In answer, I thankfully laid down the book, and was no more sad, at least, not on that occasion.

In the middle of these cogitations, apprehensions, and reflections, it came into my thought one day, that all this might be a meer chimera of my own, and that this foot might be the print of my own foot, when I came on shore from my boat. This chear'd me up a little too, and I began to perswade my self it was all a delusion; that it was nothing else but my own foot, and why might not I come that way from the boat, as well as I was going that way to the boat? Again, I consider'd also that I could by no means tell for certain where I had trod, and where I had not; and that if at last this was only the print of my own foot, I had play'd the part of those fools who strive to make stories of spectres and apparitions, and then are frighted at them more than any body.

Now I began to take courage, and to peep abroad again; for I had not stirr'd out of my castle for three days and nights; so that I began to starve for provision; for I had little or nothing within doors but some barley cakes and water. Then I knew that my goats wanted to be milk'd too which usually was my evening diversion; and the poor creatures were in great pain and inconvenience for want of it; and indeed, it almost spoil'd some of them, and almost dry'd up their milk.

Heartning my self therefore with the belief that this was nothing but the print of one of my own feet, and so I might be truly said to start at my own shadow, I began to go abroad again, and went to my country house to milk my flock; but to see with what fear I went forward, how often I look'd behind me, how I was ready every now and then to lay down my basket and run for my life, it would have made any one have thought I was haunted with an evil conscience, or that I had been lately most terribly frighted, and so indeed I had.

However, as I went down thus two or three days, and having seen nothing, I began to be a little bolder, and to think there was really nothing in it but my own imagination: but I cou'd not perswade my self fully of this till I should go down to the shore again, and see this print of a foot, and measure it by my own, and see if there was any similitude or fitness, that I might be assur'd it was my own foot. But when I came to the place, first, it appear'd evidently to me, that when I laid up my boat, I could not possibly be on shore any where there about; secondly, when I came to measure the mark with my own foot, I found my foot not so large by a great deal. Both these things fill'd my head with new imaginations, and gave me the vapours again to the highest degree; so that I shook with cold, like one in an ague; and I went home again, fill'd with the belief that some man or men had been on shore there; or in short, that the island was inhabited, and I might be surpriz'd before I was aware; and what course to take for my security I knew not.

O what ridiculous resolution men take, when possess'd with fear! It deprives them of the use of those means which reason offers for their relief. The first thing I propos'd to my self was, to throw down my enclosures and turn all my tame cattle wild into the woods, that the enemy might not find them, and then frequent the island in prospect of the same or the like booty; then to the simple thing of digging up my two corn fields, that they might not find such a grain there, and still be prompted to frequent the island; then to demolish my bower and tent, that they might not see any vestiges of habitation, and be prompted to look farther, in order to find out the persons inhabiting.

These were the subject of the first night's cogitation, after I was come home again, while the apprehensions which had so over-run my mind were fresh upon me, and my head was full of vapours, as above. Thus fear of danger is ten thousand times more terrifying than danger it self when apparent to the eyes; and we find the burthen of anxiety greater by much than the evil which we are anxious about; and, which was worse than all this, I had not that relief in this trouble from the resignation I used to practise, that I hop'd to have. I look'd, I thought, like Saul, who complain'd not only that the Philistines were upon him, but that God had forsaken him; for I did not now take due ways to compose my mind, by crying to God in my distress, and resting upon His providence, as I had done before, for my defence and deliverance; which if I had done, I had at least been more cheerfully supported under this new surprise, and perhaps carry'd through it with more resolution.

This confusion of my thoughts kept me waking all night; but in the morning I fell asleep, and having, by the amusement of my mind, been as it were tyr'd, and my spirits exhausted, I slept very soundly, and wak'd much better compos'd than I had ever been before; and now I began to think sedately; and upon the utmost debate with my self, I concluded that this island, which was so exceeding pleasant, fruitful, and no farther from the main land than as I had seen, was not so entirely abandon'd as I might imagine; that altho' there were no stated inhabitants who liv'd on the spot, yet that there might sometimes come boats off from the shore, who either with design, or perhaps never but when they were driven by cross winds, might come to this place.

That I had liv'd here fifteen years now, and had not met with the least shadow or figure of any people yet; and that if at any time they should be driven here, it was probable they went away again as soon as ever they could, seeing they had never thought fit to fix there upon any occasion, to this time.

That the most I cou'd suggest any danger from, was from any such casual accidental landing of straggling people from the main, who, as it was likely if they were driven hither, were here against their wills, so they made no stay here, but went off again with all possible speed, seldom staying one night on shore, least they should not have the help of the tides and day-light back again; and that therefore I had nothing to do but to consider of some safe retreat, in case I should see any savages land upon the spot.

Now I began sorely to repent that I had dug my cave so large as to bring a door through again, which door, as I said, came out beyond where my fortification joyn'd to the rock; upon maturely considering this therefore, I resolv'd to draw me a second fortification, in the same manner of a semicircle, at a distance from my wall just where I had planted a double row of trees about twelve years before, of which I made mention. These trees having been planted so thick before, they wanted but a few piles to be driven between them, that they should be thicker and stronger, and my wall would be soon finish'd.

So that I had now a double wall, and my outer wall was thickned with pieces of timber, old cables, and every thing I could think of, to make it strong; having in it seven little holes, about as big as I might put my arm out at. In the in-side of this, I thickned my wall to above ten foot thick, with continual bringing earth out of my cave, and laying it at the foot of the wall, and walking upon it; and through the seven holes I contriv'd to plant the musquets, of which I took notice that I got seven on shore out of the ship; these, I say, I planted like my cannon, and fitted them into frames that held them like a carriage, that so I could fire all the seven guns in two minutes' time. This wall I was many a weary month a finishing, and yet never thought my self safe till it was done.

When this was done, I stuck all the ground without my wall, for a great way every way, as full with stakes or sticks of the osier-like wood, which I found so apt to grow, as they could well stand; insomuch that I believe I might set in near twenty thousand of them, leaving a pretty large space between them and my wall, that I might have room to see an enemy, and they might have no shelter from the young trees, if they attempted to approach my outer wall.

Thus in two years' time I had a thick grove, and in five or six years' time I had a wood before my dwelling, growing so monstrous thick and strong, that it was indeed perfectly impassable; and no men of what kind soever would ever imagine that there was any thing beyond it, much less a habitation. As for the way which I propos'd to my self to go in and out, for I left no avenue, it was setting two ladders, one to a part of the rock which was low, and then broke in, and left room to place another ladder upon that; so when the two ladders were taken down, no man living could come down to me without mischieving himself; and if they had come down they were still on the out-side of my outer wall.

Thus I took all the measures humane prudence could suggest for my own preservation; and it will be seen at length that they were not altogether without just reason; though I foresaw nothing at that time, more than my meer fear suggested to me.

While this was doing, I was not altogether careless of my other affairs; for I had a great concern upon me for my little herd of goats; they were not only a present supply to me upon every occasion, and began to be sufficient to me without the expence of powder and shot, but also without the fatigue of hunting after the wild ones, and I was loth to lose the advantage of them, and to have them all to nurse up over again.

To this purpose, after long consideration, I could think of but two ways to preserve them; one was to find another convenient place to dig a cave under-ground, and to drive them into it every night; and the other was to enclose two or three little bits of land, remote from one another and as much conceal'd as I could, where I might keep about half a dozen young goats in each place: so that if any disaster happen'd to the flock in general, I might be able to raise them again with little trouble and time: and this, tho' it would require a great deal of time and labour, I thought was the most rational design.

Accordingly I spent some time to find out the most retir'd parts of the island; and I pitch'd upon one which was as private indeed as my heart could wish for; it was a little damp piece of ground in the middle of the hollow and thick woods, where, as is observ'd, I almost lost my self once before, endeavouring to come back that way from the eastern part of the island. Here I found a clear piece of land near three acres, so surrounded with woods that it was almost an enclosure by nature, at least it did not want near so much labour to make it so as the other pieces of ground I had work'd so hard at.

I immediately went to work with this piece of ground, and in less than a month's time I had so fenc'd it round, that my flock or herd, call it which you please, who were not so wild now as at first they might be supposed to be, were well enough secur'd in it. So, without any farther delay, I removed ten young she-goats and two he-goats to this piece; and when they were there, I continued to perfect the fence till I had made it as secure as the other, which, however, I did at more leisure, and it took me up more time by a great deal.

All this labour I was at the expence of, purely from my apprehensions on the account of the print of a man's foot which I had seen; for as yet I never saw any human creature come near the island, and I had now liv'd two years under these uneasinesses, which indeed made my life much less comfortable than it was before; as may well be imagin'd by any who know what it is to live in the constant snare of the fear of man; and this I must observe with grief too, that the discomposure of my mind had too great impressions also upon the religious part of my thoughts, for the dread and terror of falling into the hands of savages and canibals lay so upon my spirits, that I seldom found my self in a due temper for application to my Maker, at least not with the sedate calmness and resignation of soul which I was wont to do; I rather pray'd to God as under great affliction and pressure of mind, surrounded with danger, and in expectation every night of being murther'd and devour'd before morning; and I must testify from my experience, that a temper of peace, thankfulness, love and affection is much more the proper frame for prayer than that of terror and discomposure; and that under the dread of mischief impending, a man is no more fit for a comforting performance of the duty of praying to God, than he is for repentance on a sick bed: for these discomposures affect the mind as the others do the body; and the discomposure of the mind must necessarily be as great a disability as that of the body, and much greater, praying to God being properly an act of the mind, not of the body.

But to go on. After I had thus secur'd one part of my little living stock, I went about the whole island, searching for another private place, to make such another deposit; when wandring more to the west point of the island than I had ever gone yet, and looking out to sea, I thought I saw a boat upon the sea, at a great distance; I had found a prospective glass or two in one of the seamen's chests, which I sav'd out of our ship; but I had it not about me, and this was so remote that I could not tell what to make of it, though I look'd at it till my eyes were not able to hold to look any longer; whether it was a boat or not, I do not know; but as I descended from the hill, I could see no more of it, so I gave it over; only I resolv'd to go no more out without a prospective glass in my pocket.

When I was come down the hill to the end of the island, where indeed I had never been before, I was presently convinc'd that the seeing the print of a man's foot was not such a strange thing in the island as I imagin'd; and but that it was a special providence that I was cast upon the side of the island where the savages never came, I should easily have known that nothing was more frequent than for the canoes from the main, when they happen'd to be a little too far out at sea, to shoot over to that side of the island for harbour; likewise as they often met and fought in their canoes, the victors, having taken any prisoners, would bring them over to this shore, where according to their dreadful customs, being all canibals, they would kill and eat them; of which hereafter.

When I was come down the hill to the shore, as I said above, being the S.W. point of the island, I was perfectly confounded and amaz'd; nor is it possible for me to express the horror of my mind, at seeing the shore spread with skulls, hands, feet, and other bones of humane bodies; and particularly I observ'd a place where there had been a fire made, and a circle dug in the earth, like a cockpit, where it is suppos'd the savage wretches had sat down to their inhumane feastings upon the bodies of their fellow-creatures.

I was so astonish'd with the sight of these things, that I entertain'd no notions of any danger to my self from it for a long while; all my apprehensions were bury'd in the thoughts of such a pitch of inhuman, hellish brutality, and the horror of the degeneracy of humane nature; which, though I had heard of often, yet I never had so near a view of before; in short, I turn'd away my face from the horrid spectacle; my stomach grew sick, and I was just at the point of fainting, when nature discharg'd the disorder from my stomach, and having vomited with an uncommon violence, I was a little reliev'd, but cou'd not bear to stay in the place a moment; so I gat me up the hill again with all the speed I cou'd, and walk'd on towards my own habitation.

When I came a little out of that part of the island, I stood still a while as amaz'd; and then recovering my self, I looked up with the utmost affection of my soul, and with a flood of tears in my eyes, gave God thanks that had cast my first lot in a part of the world where I was distinguish'd from such dreadful creatures as these; and that, though I had esteem'd my present condition very miserable, had yet given me so many comforts in it, that I had still more to give thanks for than to complain of; and this above all, that I had even in this miserable condition been comforted with the knowledge of Himself, and the hope of His blessing, which was a felicity more than sufficiently equivalent to all the misery which I had suffer'd, or could suffer.

In this frame of thankfulness, I went home to my castle, and began to be much easier now, as to the safety of my circumstances, than ever I was before; for I observ'd that these wretches never came to this island in search of what they could get; perhaps not seeking, not wanting, or not expecting any thing here; and having often, no doubt, been up in the cover'd woody part of it, without finding any thing to their purpose. I knew I had been here now almost eighteen years, and never saw the least foot-steps of humane creature there before; and I might be here eighteen more, as entirely conceal'd as I was now, if I did not discover my self to them, which I had no manner of occasion to do, it being my only business to keep my self entirely conceal'd where I was, unless I found a better sort of creatures than canibals to make my self known to.

Yet I entertain'd such an abhorrence of the savage wretches that I have been speaking of, and of the wretched inhuman custom of their devouring and eating one another up, that I continu'd pensive and sad, and kept close within my own circle for almost two years after this. When I say my own circle, I mean by it my three plantations, viz. my castle, my country seat, which I call'd my bower, and my enclosure in the woods; nor did I look after this for any other use than as an enclosure for my goats; for the aversion which nature gave me to these hellish wretches was such, that I was fearful of seeing them as of seeing the devil himself; nor did I so much as go to look after my boat in all this time, but began rather to think of making me another; for I cou'd not think of ever making any more attempts to bring the other boat round the island to me, least I should meet with some of these creatures at sea, in which if I had happen'd to have fallen into their hands, I knew what would have been my lot.

Time, however, and the satisfaction I had that I was in no danger of being discover'd by these people, began to wear off my uneasiness about them; and I began to live just in the same compos'd manner as before; only with this difference, that I used more caution, and kept my eyes more about me than I did before, least I should happen to be seen by any of them; and particularly, I was more cautious of firing my gun, least any of them being on the island should happen to hear of it: and it was therefore a very good providence to me, that I had furnish'd my self with a tame breed of goats, that I needed not hunt any more about the woods, or shoot at them; and if I did catch any of them after this, it was by

traps and snares, as I had done before; so that for two years after
this, I believe I never fir'd my gun once off, though I never went
out without it; and, which was more, as I had sav'd three pistols
out of the ship, I always carry'd them out with me, or at least
two of them, sticking them in my goat-skin belt; also I furbish'd
up one of the great cutlashes that I had out of the ship, and made
me a belt to put it on also; so that I was now a most formidable
fellow to look at when I went abroad, if you add to the former
description of my self, the particular of two pistols, and a great
broad sword hanging at my side in a belt, but without a
scabbard.

Things going on thus, as I have said, for some time, I seem'd,
excepting these cautions, to be reduc'd to my former calm,
sedate way of living. All these things tended to shewing me more
and more how far my condition was from being miserable,
compar'd to some others; nay, to many other particulars of life,
which it might have pleased God to have made my lot. It put me
upon reflecting how little repining there would be among
mankind at any condition of life, if people would rather compare
their condition with those that are worse, in order to be
thankful, than be always comparing them with those which are
better, to assist their murmurings and complainings.

As in my present condition there were not really many things
which I wanted, so indeed I thought that the frights I had been in
about these savage wretches, and the concern I had been in for
my own preservation, had taken off the edge of my invention for
my own conveniences; and I had dropp'd a good design, which I
had once bent my thoughts too much upon; and that was, to try
if I could not make some of my barley into malt, and then try to
brew my self some beer. This was really a whimsical thought,
and I reprov'd my self often for the simplicity of it; for I
presently saw there would be the want of several things
necessary to the making my beer, that it would be impossible for
me to supply; as first, casks to preserve it in, which was a thing
that, as I have observ'd already, I cou'd never compass; no,
though I spent not many days, but weeks, nay, months in
attempting it, but to no purpose. In the next place, I had no hops
to make it keep, no yeast to make it work, no copper or kettle to
make it boil; and yet all these things notwithstanding, I verily
believe, had not these things interven'd, I mean the frights and
terrors I was in about the savages, I had undertaken it, and

perhaps brought it to pass too; for I seldom gave any thing over without accomplishing it, when I once had it in my head enough to begin it.

But my invention now run quite another way; for night and day I could think of nothing but how I might destroy some of these monsters in their cruel bloody entertainment, and, if possible, save the victim they should bring hither to destroy. It would take up a larger volume than this whole work is intended to be, to set down all the contrivances I hatch'd, or rather brooded upon in my thought, for the destroying these creatures, or at least frightening them, so as to prevent their coming hither any more; but all was abortive, nothing could be possible to take effect, unless I was to be there to do it my self; and what could one man do among them, when perhaps there mght be twenty or thirty of them together, with their darts, or their bows and arrows, with which they could shoot as true to a mark as I could with my gun?

Sometimes I contriv'd to dig a hole under the place where they made their fire, and put in five or six pound of gun-powder, which when they kindled their fire, would consequently take fire, and blow up all that was near it; but as in the first place I should be very loth to wast so much powder upon them, my store being now within the quantity of one barrel, so neither could I be sure of its going off at any certain time, when it might surprise them; and at best, that it would do little more than just blow the fire about their ears and fright them, but not sufficient to make them forsake the place; so I laid it aside, and then propos'd that I would place my self in ambush in some convenient place, with my three guns, all double loaded, and, in the middle of their bloody ceremony, let fly at them, when I should be sure to kill or wound perhaps two or three at every shoot; and then falling in upon them with my three pistols and my sword, I made no doubt but that if there was twenty I should kill them all. This fancy pleas'd my thoughts for some weeks, and I was so full of it that I often dream'd of it, and sometimes that I was just going to let fly at them in my sleep.

I went so far with it in my imagination, that I employ'd my self several days to find out proper places to put my self in ambuscade, as I said, to watch for them; and I went frequently to the place it self, which was now grown more familiar to me; and especially while my mind was thus fill'd with thoughts of revenge, and of a bloody putting twenty or thirty of them to the sword, as I may call it, the horror I had at the place, and at the signals of the barbarous wretches devouring one another, abated* my malice.

Well, at length I found a place in the side of the hill, where I was satisfy'd I might securely wait till I saw any of their boats coming, and might then, even before they would be ready to come on shore, convey my self unseen into thickets of trees, in one of which there was a hollow large enough to conceal me entirely; and where I might sit and observe all their bloody doings, and take my full aim at their heads, when they were so close together as that it would be next to impossible that I should miss my shoot, or that I could fail wounding three or four of them at the first shoot.

In this place then I resolv'd to fix my design, and accordingly I prepar'd two muskets and my ordinary fowling piece. The two muskets I loaded with a brace of slugs each, and four or five smaller bullets, about the size of pistol bullets; and the fowling piece I loaded with near a handful of swan-shot, of the largest size; I also loaded my pistols with about four bullets each; and in this posture, well provided with ammunition for a second and third charge, I prepar'd my self for my expedition.

After I had thus laid the scheme of my design, and in my imagination put it in practice, I continually made my tour every morning up to the top of the hill, which was from my castle, as I call'd it, about three miles or more, to see if I cou'd observe any boats upon the sea, coming near the island, or standing over towards it; but I began to tire of this hard duty, after I had for two or three months constantly kept my watch, but came always back without any discovery, there having not in all that time been the least appearance, not only on or near the shore, but not on the whole ocean, so far as my eyes or glasses could reach every way.

As long as I kept up my daily tour to the hill to look out, so long also I kept up the vigour of my design, and my spirits seem'd to be all the while in a suitable form for so outragious an execution as the killing twenty or thirty naked savages, for an offence which I had not at all entred into a discussion of in my thoughts, any farther than my passions were at first fir'd by the horror I conceiv'd at the unnatural custom of that people of the country, who it seems had been suffer'd by Providence, in His wide disposition of the world, to have no other guide than that of their own abominable and vitiated passions; and consequently were left, and perhaps had been so for some ages, to act such horrid things, and receive such dreadful customs, as nothing but nature entirely abandon'd of Heaven, and acted by some hellish degeneracy, could have run them into. But now, when, as I have said, I began to be weary of the fruitless excursion, which I had made so long, and so far, every morning in vain, so my opinion of the action it self began to alter, and I began with cooler and calmer thoughts to consider what it was I was going to engage in; what authority or call I had, to pretend to be judge and executioner upon these men as criminals, whom Heaven had thought fit for so many ages to suffer unpunish'd, to go on, and to be, as it were, the executioners of His judgments one upon another; how far these people were offenders against me, and what right I had to engage in the quarrel of that blood which they shed promiscuously one upon another. I debated this very often with my self thus: How do I know what God Himself judges in this particular case? It is certain these people either do not commit this as a crime; it is not against their own consciences reproving, or their light reproaching them. They do not know it be an offence, and then commit it in defiance of divine justice, as we do in almost all the sins we commit. They think it no more a crime to kill a captive taken in war, than we do to kill an ox; nor to eat humane flesh, than we do to eat mutton.

When I had consider'd this a little, it follow'd necessarily that I was certainly in the wrong in it, that these people were not murtherers in the sense that I had before condemn'd them in my thoughts; any more than those Christians were murtherers who often put to death the prisoners taken in battle; or more frequently, upon many occasions, put whole troops of men to the sword, without giving quarter, though they threw down their arms and submitted.

In the next place it occurr'd to me, that albeit the usage they thus gave one another was thus brutish and inhumane, yet it was really nothing to me: these people had done me no injury. That if they attempted me, or I saw it necessary for my immediate preservation to fall upon them, some thing might be said for it; but that as I was yet out of their power, and they had really no knowledge of me, and consequently no design upon me; and therefore it could not be just for me to fall upon them. That this would justify the conduct of the Spaniards in all their barbarities practis'd in America, where they destroy'd millions of these people, who, however they were idolaters and barbarians, and had several bloody and barbarious rites in their customs, such as sacrificing human bodies to their idols, were yet, as to the Spaniards, very innocent people; and that the rooting them out of the country is spoken of with the utmost abhorrence and detestation by even the Spaniards themselves at this time, and by all other Christian nations of Europe, as a meer butchery, a bloody and unnatural piece of cruelty, unjustifiable either to God or man; and such, as for which the very name of a Spaniard is reckon'd to be frightful and terrible to all people of humanity, or of Christian compassion; as if the kingdom of Spain were particularly eminent for the product of a race of men who were without principles of tenderness, or the common bowels of pity to the miserable, which is reckon'd to be a mark of generous temper in the mind.

These considerations really put me to a pause, and to a kind of a full-stop; and I began by little and little to be off of my design, and to conclude I had taken wrong measures in my resolutions to attack the savages; that it was not my business to meddle with them, unless they first attack'd me, and this it was my business if possible to prevent; but that if I were discover'd and attack'd, then I knew my duty.

On the other hand, I argu'd with my self, that this really was the way not to deliver my self, but entirely to ruin and destroy my self; for unless I was sure to kill every one that not only should be on shore at that time, but that should ever come on shore afterwards, if but one of them escap'd to tell their country people what had happen'd, they would come over again by thousands to revenge the death of their fellows, and I should only bring upon my self a certain destruction, which at present I had no manner of occasion for.

Upon the whole I concluded that neither in principle or in policy, I ought one way or other to concern my self in this affair. That my business was by all possible means to conceal my self from them, and not to leave the least signal to them to guess by, that there were any living creatures upon the island; I mean of humane shape.

Religion joyn'd in with this prudential, and I was convinc'd now many ways, that I was perfectly out of my duty when I was laying all my bloody schemes for the destruction of innocent creatures, I mean innocent as to me. As to the crimes they were guilty of towards one another, I had nothing to do with them; they were national, and I ought to leave them to the justice of God, who is the governour of nations, and knows how by national punishments to make a just retribution for national offences; and to bring publick judgments upon those who offend in a publick manner, by such ways as best pleases Him.

This appear'd so clear to me now, that nothing was a greater satisfaction to me, than that I had not been suffer'd to do a thing which I now saw so much reason to believe would have been no less a sin than that of wilful murther, if I had committed it; and I gave most humble thanks on my knees to God, that had thus deliver'd me from blood-guiltiness; beseeching Him to grant me the protection of His providence, that I might not fall into the hands of the barbarians; or that I might not lay my hands upon them, unless I had a more clear call from Heaven to do it, in defence of my own life.

In this disposition I continu'd for near a year after this; and so far was I from desiring an occasion for falling upon these wretches, that in all that time I never once went up the hill to see whether there were any of them in sight, or to know whether any of them had been on shore there or not, that I might not be tempted to renew any of my contrivances against them, or be provok'd by any advantage which might present it self, to fall upon them; only this I did, I went and remov'd my boat, which I had on the other side the island, and carry'd it down to the east end of the whole island, where I ran it into a little cove which I found under some high rocks, and where I knew, by reason of the currents, the savages durst not, at least would not come with their boats, upon any account whatsoever.

With my boat I carry'd away every thing that I had left there belonging to her, though not necessary for the bare going thither, viz. a mast and sail which I had made for her, and a thing like an anchor, but indeed which could not be call'd either anchor or grapling; however, it was the best I could make of its kind. All this I remov'd, that there might not be the least shadow of any discovery, or any appearance of any boat or of any human habitation upon the island.

Besides this, I kept my self, as I said, more retir'd than ever, and seldom went from my cell, other than upon my constant employment, viz. to milk my she-goats, and manage my little flock in the wood; which, as it was quite on the other part of the island, was quite out of danger; for certain it is, that these savage people who sometimes haunted this island never came with any thoughts of finding any thing here; and consequently never wandred off from the coast; and I doubt not, but they might have been several times on shore after my apprehensions of them had made me cautious, as well as before; and indeed, I look'd back with some horror upon the thoughts of what my condition would have been, if I had chop'd upon them and been discover'd before that, when naked* and unarm'd, except with one gun, and that loaden often only with small shot, I walk'd every where peeping and peeping about the island to see what I could get; what a surprise should I have been in, if when I discover'd the print of a man's foot, I had instead of that seen fifteen or twenty savages, and found them pursuing me, and by the swiftness of their running, no possibility of my escaping them.

The thoughts of this sometimes sunk my very soul within me, and distress'd my mind so much, that I could not soon recover it, to think what I should have done, and how I not only should not have been able to resist them, but even should not have had presence of mind enough to do what I might have done; much less, what now after so much consideration and preparation I might be able to do. Indeed, after serious thinking of these things, I should be very melancholy; and sometimes it would last a great while; but I resolv'd it at last all into thankfulness to that Providence, which had deliver'd me from so many unseen dangers, and had kept me from those mischiefs which I could no way have been the agent in delivering my self from; because I had not the least notion of any such thing depending, or the least supposition of it being possible.

This renew'd a contemplation which often had come to my thoughts in former time, when first I began to see the merciful dispositions of Heaven in the dangers we run through in this life; how wonderfully we are deliver'd when we know nothing of it; how when we are in a quandary, as we call it, a doubt or hesitation, whether to go this way or that way, a secret hint shall direct us this way, when we intended to go that way; nay, when sense, our own inclination, and perhaps business has call'd to go the other way, yet a strange impression upon the mind, from we know not what springs, and by we know not what power, shall over-rule us to go this way; and it shall afterwards appear that had we gone that way which we should have gone, and even to our imagination ought to have gone, we should have been ruin'd and lost. Upon these and many like reflections, I afterwards made it a certain rule with me, that whenever I found those secret hints or pressings of my mind, to doing or not doing any thing that presented, or to going this way or that way, I never fail'd to obey the secret dictate; though I knew no other reason for it than that such a pressure or such a hint hung upon my mind. I could give many examples of the success of this conduct in the course of my life; but more especially in the latter part of my inhabiting this unhappy island; besides many occasions which it is very likely I might have taken notice of, if I had seen with the same eyes then, that I saw with now. But 'tis never too late to be wise; and I cannot but advise all considering men, whose lives are attended with such extraordinary incidents as mine, or even though not so extraordinary, not to slight such secret intimations of providence, let them come from what invisible intelligence they will, that I shall not discuss, and perhaps cannot account for; but certainly they are a proof of the converse of spirits, and the secret communication between those embody'd and those unembody'd; and such a proof as can never be withstood. Of which I shall have occasion to give some very remarkable instances in the remainder of my solitary residence in this dismal place.

I believe the clean reader of this will not think strange if I confess that these anxieties, these constant dangers I liv'd in, and the concern that was now upon me, put an end to all invention, and to all the contrivances that I had laid for my future accommodations and conveniences. I had the care of my safety more now upon my hands than that of my food. I car'd not to drive a nail or chop a stick of wood now, for fear the noise I should make should be heard; much less would I fire a gun, for the same reason; and above all, I was intollerably uneasy at making any fire, least the smoke which is visible at a great distance in the day should betray me; and for this reason I remov'd that part of my business which requir'd fire, such as burning of pots and pipes, &c., into my new apartment in the woods, where, after I had been some time, I found, to my unspeakable consolation, a meer natural cave in the earth, which went in a vast way, and where, I dare say, no savage, had he been at the mouth of it, would be so hardy as to venture in, nor indeed would any man else, but one who, like me, wanted nothing so much as a safe retreat.

The mouth of this hollow was at the bottom of a great rock,

where by meer accident (I would say, if I did not see abundant reason to ascribe all such things now to providence) I was cutting down some thick branches of trees, to make charcoal; and before I go on, I must observe the reason of my making this charcoal; which was thus:

I was afraid of making a smoke about my habitation, as I said before; and yet I could not live there without baking my bread, cooking my meat, &c., so I contriv'd to burn some wood here, as I had seen done in England, under turf, till it became chark,* or dry coal; and then putting the fire out, I preserv'd the coal to carry home, and perform the other services which fire was wanting for at home without danger of smoke.

But this is by the by. While I was cutting down some wood here, I perceiv'd that behind a very thick branch of low brushwood, or underwood, there was a kind of hollow place; I was curious to look into it, and getting with difficulty into the mouth of it, I found it was pretty large; that is to say, sufficient for me to stand upright in it, and perhaps another with me; but I must confess to you, I made more hast out than I did in, when looking farther into the place, and which was perfectly dark, I saw two broad shining eyes of some creature, whether devil or man I knew not, which twinkl'd like two stars, the dim light from the cave's mouth shining directly in and making the reflection.

However, after some pause, I recover'd my self, and began to call my self a thousand fools, and tell my self, that he that was afraid to see the devil was not fit to live twenty years in an island all alone; and that I durst to believe there was nothing in this cave that was more frightful than my self; upon this, plucking up my courage, I took up a great firebrand, and in I rush'd again, with the stick flaming in my hand. I had not gone three steps in, but I was almost as much frighted as I was before; for I heard a very loud sigh, like that of a man in some pain, and it was follow'd by a broken noise, as if of words half express'd, and then a deep sigh again. I stepp'd back, and was indeed struck with such a surprize, that it put me into a cold sweat; and if I had had a hat on my head, I will not answer for it, that my hair might not have lifted it off. But still plucking up my spirits as well as I could, and encouraging my self a little with considering that the power and presence of God was every where, and was able to protect me; upon this I stepp'd forward again, and by the light of the firebrand, holding it up a little over my head, I saw lying on the ground a most monstrous frightful old he-goat, just making his will, as we say, and gasping for life, and dying indeed of meer old age.

I stirr'd him a little to see if I could get him out, and he essay'd to get up, but was not able to raise himself; and I thought with my self, he might even lie there; for if he had frighted me so, he would certainly fright any of the savages, if any of them should be so hardy as to come in there, while he had any life in him.

I was now recover'd from my surprize, and began to look round me, when I found the cave was but very small, that is to say, it might be about twelve foot over, but in no manner of shape, either round or square, no hands having ever been employ'd in making it but those of meer nature. I observ'd also, that there was a place at the farther side of it, that went in farther, but was so low that it requir'd me to creep upon my hands and knees to go into it, and whither I went I knew not; so having no candle, I gave it over for some time; but resolv'd to come again the next day, provided with candles and a tinder-box, which I had made of the lock of one of the muskets, with some wild-fire* in the pan.

Accordingly, the next day I came provided with six large candles of my own making; for I made very good candles now of goat's tallow; and going into this low place, I was oblig'd to creep upon all fours, as I have said, almost ten yards; which, by the way, I thought was a venture bold enough, considering that I knew not how far it might go, nor what was beyond it. When I was got through the strait, I found the roof rose higher up, I believe near twenty foot; but never was such a glorious sight seen in the island, I dare say, as it was to look round the sides and roof of this vault or cave; the walls reflected 100 thousand lights to me from my two candles; what it was in the rock, whether diamonds, or any other precious stones, or gold, which I rather suppos'd it to be, I knew not.

The place I was in was a most delightful cavity or grotto of its kind, as could be expected, though perfectly dark; the floor was dry and level, and had a sort of small loose gravel upon it, so that there was no nauseous or venomous creature to be seen, neither was there any damp or wet on the sides or roof. The only difficulty in it was the entrance, which, however, as it was a place of security, and such a retreat as I wanted, I thought that was a convenience; so that I was really rejoyc'd at the discovery, and resolv'd without any delay to bring some of those things which I was most anxious about, to this place; particulary, I resolv'd to bring hither my magazine of powder, and all my spare arms, viz. two fowling-pieces, for I had three in all; and three muskets, for of them I had eight in all; so I kept at my castle only five, which stood ready mounted like pieces of cannon on my out-most fence, and were ready also to take out upon any expedition.

Upon this occasion of removing my ammunition, I took occasion to open the barrel of powder which I took up out of the sea, and which had been wet; and I found that the water had penetrated about three or four inches into the powder on every side, which caking and growing hard, had preserv'd the inside like a kernel in a shell; so that I had near sixty pound of very good powder in the center of the cask, and this was an agreeable discovery to me at that time; so I carry'd all away thither, never keeping above two or three pound of powder with me in my castle, for fear of a surprize of any kind: I also carried thither all the lead I had left for bullets.

I fancy'd my self now like one of the ancient giants, which are said to live in caves and holes in the rocks, where none could come at them; for I perswaded my self while I was here, if five hundred savages were to hunt me, they could never find me out; or if they did, they would not venture to attack me here.

The old goat who I found expiring, dy'd in the mouth of the cave, the next day after I made this discovery; and I found it much easier to dig a great hole there, and throw him in and cover him with earth, than to drag him out; so I interr'd him there, to prevent the offence to my nose.

I was now in my twenty third year of residence in this island, and was so naturaliz'd to the place, and to the manner of living, that could I have but enjoy'd the certainty that no savages would come to the place to disturb me, I could have been content to have capitulated for spending the rest of my time there, even to the last moment, till I had laid me down and dy'd, like the old goat in the cave. I had also arriv'd to some little diversions and amusements, which made the time pass more pleasantly with me a great deal than it did before; as first, I had taught my Poll, as I noted before, to speak; and he did it so familiarly and talk'd so articulately and plain, that it was very pleasant to me; and he liv'd with me no less than six and twenty years: how long he might live afterwards, I know not; though I know they have a notion in the Brasils that they live a hundred years; perhaps poor Poll may be alive there still, calling after poor Robin Crusoe to this day. I wish no English man the ill luck to come there and hear him; but if he did, he would certainly believe it was the devil. My dog was a very pleasant and loving companion to me for no less than sixteen years of my time, and then dy'd of meer old age; as for my cats, they multiply'd as I have observ'd to that degree, that I was oblig'd to shoot several of them at first, to keep them from devouring me and all I had; but at length, when the two old ones I had brought with me were gone, and after some time continually driving them from me, and letting them have no provision with me, they all ran wild into the woods, except two or three favourites, which I kept tame, and whose young, when they had any, I always drown'd; and these were part of my family. Besides these, I always kept two or three household kids about me, who I taught to feed out of my hand; and I had two more parrots which talk'd pretty well, and would all call Robin Crusoe; but none like my first; nor indeed did I take the pains with any of them that I had done with him. I had also several tame sea-fowls, whose names I know not, who I caught upon the shore, and cut their wings; and the little stakes which I had planted before my castle wall being now grown up to a good thick grove, these fowls all liv'd among these low trees, and bred there, which was very agreeable to me; so that, as I said above, I began to be very well contented with the life I led, if it might but have been secur'd from the dread of the savages.

But it was otherwise directed; and it may not be amiss for all people who shall meet with my story, to make this just observation from it, viz. how frequently, in the course of our lives, the evil which in it self we seek most to shun, and which when we are fallen into it is the most dreadful to us, is oftentimes the very means or door of our deliverance, by which alone we can be rais'd again from the affliction we are fallen into. I cou'd give many examples of this in the course of my unaccountable life; but in nothing was it more particularly remarkable, than in the circumstances of my last years of solitary residence in this island.

It was now the month of December, as I said above, in my twenty third year; and this being the southern solstice, for winter I cannot call it, was the particular time of my harvest, and requir'd my being pretty much abroad in the fields; when going out pretty early in the morning, even before it was thorow day-light, I was surpriz'd with seeing a light of some fire upon the shore, at a distance from me of about two mile towards the end of the island, where I had observ'd some savages had been as before; but not on the other side; but to my great affliction, it was on my side of the island.

I was indeed terribly surpriz'd at the sight, and stopp'd short within my grove, not daring to go out, least I might be surpriz'd; and yet I had no more peace within, from the apprehensions I had that if these savages, in rambling over the island, should find my corn standing or cut, or any of my works and improvements, they would immediately conclude that there were people in the place, and would then never give over till they had found me out. In this extremity I went back directly to my castle, pull'd up the ladder after me, and made all things without look as wild and natural as I could.

Then I prepar'd my self within, putting my self in a posture of defence; I loaded all my cannon, as I call'd them, that is to say, my muskets which were mounted upon my new fortification, and all my pistols, and resolv'd to defend my self to the last gasp, not forgetting seriously to commend my self to the divine protection, and earnestly to pray to God to deliver me out of the hands of the barbarians; and in this posture I continu'd about two hours; but began to be mighty impatient for intelligence abroad, for I had no spies to send out.

After sitting a while longer, and musing what I should do in this case, I was not able to bear sitting in ignorance any longer; so setting up my ladder to the side of the hill, where there was a flat place, as I observ'd before, and then pulling the ladder up after me, I set it up again, and mounted to the top of the hill; and pulling out my perspective glass, which I had taken on purpose, I laid me down flat on my belly on the ground, and began to look for the place; I presently found there was no less than nine naked savages, sitting round a small fire they had made, not to warm them, for they had no need of that, the weather being extreme hot; but, as I suppos'd, to dress some of their barbarous diet of humane flesh, which they had brought with them, whether alive or dead I could not know.

They had two canoes with them, which they had haled up upon the shore; and as it was then tide of ebb, they seem'd to me to wait for the return of the flood, to go away again; it is not easy to imagine what confusion this sight put me into, especially seeing them come on my side the island, and so near me too; but when I observ'd their coming must always be with the current of the ebb, I began afterwards to be more sedate in my mind, being satisfy'd that I might go abroad with safety all the time of the tide of flood, if they were not on shore before: and having made this observation, I went abroad about my harvest work with the more composure.

As I expected, so it proved; for as soon as the tide made to the westward, I saw them all take boat, and row (or paddle as we call it) all away. I should have observ'd, that for an hour and more before they went off, they went to dancing, and I could easily discern their postures and gestures by my glasses: I could not perceive, by my nicest* observation, but that they were stark naked, and had not the least covering upon them; but whether they were men or women, that I could not distinguish.

As soon as I saw them shipp'd and gone, I took two guns upon my shoulders, and two pistols at my girdle, and my great sword by my side, without a scabbard, and with all the speed I was able to make, I went away to the hill, where I had discover'd the first appearance of all; and as soon as I gat thither, which was not less than two hours (for I could not go apace, being so loaden with arms as I was), I perceiv'd there had been three canoes more of savages on that place; and looking out farther, I saw they were all at sea together, making over for the main.

This was a dreaful sight to me, especially when going down to the shore, I could see the marks of horror which the dismal work they had been about had left behind it, viz. the blood, the bones, and part of the flesh of humane bodies, eaten and devour'd by those wretches, with merriment and sport. I was so fill'd with indignation at the sight, that I began now to premeditate the destruction of the next that I saw there, let them be who or how many soever.

It seem'd evident to me that the visits which they thus make to this island are not very frequent; for it was above fifteen months before any more of them came on shore there again; that is to say, I neither saw them, or any footsteps or signals of them, in all that time; for as to the rainy seasons, then they are sure not to come abroad, at least not so far; yet all this while I liv'd uncomfortably, by reason of the constant apprehensions I was in of their coming upon me by surprize; from whence I observe, that the expectation of evil is more bitter than the suffering, especially if there is no room to shake off that expectation or those apprehensions.

During all this time I was in the murthering humour; and took up most of my hours, which should have been better employ'd, in contriving how to circumvent and fall upon them, the very next time I should see them; especially if they should be divided, as they were the last time, into two parties; nor did I consider at all, that if I kill'd one party, suppose ten or a dozen, I was still the next day, or week, or month, to kill another, and so another, even *ad infinitum*, till I should be at length no less a murtherer than they were in being man-eaters; and perhaps much more so.

I spent my days now in great perplexity and anxiety of mind, expecting that I should one day or other fall into the hands of these merciless creatures; and if I did at any time venture abroad, it was not without looking round me with the greatest care and caution imaginable; and now I found, to my great comfort, how happy it was that I provided for a tame flock or herd of goats; for I durst not upon any account fire my gun, especially near that side of the island where they usually came, least I should alarm the savages; and if they had fled from me now, I was sure to have them come back again, with perhaps two or three hundred canoes with them, in a few days, and then I knew what to expect.

However, I wore out a year and three months more, before I ever saw any more of the savages, and then I found them again, as I shall soon observe. It is true, they might have been there once or twice; but either they made no stay, or at least I did not hear them; but in the month of May, as near as I could calculate, and in my four and twentieth year, I had a very strange encounter with them, of which in its place.

The perturbation of my mind, during this fifteen or sixteen months' interval, was very great; I slept unquiet, dream'd always frightful dreams, and often started out of my sleep in the night: in the day great troubles overwhelm'd my mind, and in the night I dream'd often of killing the savages, and of the reasons why I might justify the doing of it; but to wave all this for a while, it was in the middle of May, on the sixteenth day I think, as well as my poor wooden calendar would reckon; for I markt all upon the post still; I say, it was the sixteenth of May, that it blew a very great storm of wind all day, with a great deal of lightning and thunder, and a very foul night it was after it; I know not what was the particular occasion of it, but as I was reading in the Bible, and taken up with very serious thoughts about my present condition, I was surpriz'd with a noise of a gun, as I thought, fir'd at sea.

This was to be sure a surprize of a quite different nature from any I had met with before; for the notions this put into my thoughts were quite of another kind. I started up in the greatest hast imaginable, and in a trice clapt my ladder to the middle place of the rock, and pull'd it after me, and mounting it the second time, got to the top of the hill the very moment that a flash of fire bid me listen for a second gun, which accordingly in about half a minute I heard, and by the sound knew that it was from that part of the sea where I was driven down the current in my boat.

I immediately consider'd that this must be some ship in distress, and that they had some comrade, or some other ship in company, and fir'd these guns for signals of distress, and to obtain help. I had this presence of mind at that minute, as to think that though I could not help them, it may be they might help me; so I brought together all the dry wood I could get at hand, and making a good handsome pile, I set it on fire upon the hill; the wood was dry, and blaz'd freely; and though the wind blew very hard, yet it burnt fairly out; that I was certain, if there was any such thing as a ship, they must needs see it, and no doubt they did; for as soon as ever my fire blaz'd up, I heard another gun, and after that several others, all from the same quarter; I ply'd my fire all night long, till day broke; and when it was broad day, and the air clear'd up, I saw something at a great distance at sea, full east of the island, whether a sail or a hull I could not distinguish, no, not with my glasses, the distance was so great, and the weather still something haizy also; at least it was so out at sea.

I look'd frequently at it all that day, and soon perceiv'd that it did not move; so I presently concluded that it was a ship at an anchor, and being eager, you may be sure, to be satisfy'd, I took my gun in my hand, and run toward the south side of the island, to the rocks where I had formerly been carry'd away with the current; and getting up there, the weather by this time being perfectly clear, I could plainly see, to my great sorrow, the wreck of a ship cast away in the night upon those concealed rocks which I found when I was out in my boat; and which rocks, as they check'd the violence of the stream and made a kind of counter-stream or eddy, were the occasion of my recovering from the most desperate hopeless condition that ever I had been in in all my life.

Thus what is one man's safety is another man's destruction; for it seems these men, whoever they were, being out of their knowledge, and the rocks being wholly under water, had been driven upon them in the night, the wind blowing hard at E. and E.N.E. Had they seen the island, as I must necessarily suppose they did not, they must, as I thought, have endeavour'd to have sav'd themselves on shore by the help of their boat; but their firing of guns for help, especially when they saw, as I imagin'd, my fire, fill'd me with many thoughts. First, I imagin'd that upon seeing my light, they might have put themselves into their boat, and have endeavour'd to make the shore; but that the sea going very high, they might have been cast away; other times I imagin'd that they might have lost their boat before, as might be the case many ways; as particularly by the breaking of the sea upon their ship, which many times obliges men to stave or take in pieces their boat, and sometimes to throw it over-board with their own hands; other times I imagin'd they had some other ship or ships in company, who, upon the signals of distress they had made, had taken them up and carry'd them off; other whiles I fancy'd they were all gone off to sea in their boat, and being hurry'd away by the current that I had been formerly in, were carry'd out into the great ocean, where there was nothing but misery and perishing; and that perhaps they might by this time think of starving, and of being in a condition to eat one another.

As all these were but conjectures at best, so in the condition I was in, I could do no more than look on upon the misery of the poor men, and pity them, which had still this good effect on my side that it gave me more and more cause to give thanks to God who had so happily and comfortably provided for me in my desolate condition; and that of two ships' companies who were now cast away upon this part of the world, not one life should be spar'd but mine. I learn'd here again to observe, that it is very rare that the providence of God casts us into any condition of life so low, or any misery so great, but we may see something or other to be thankful for, and may see others in worse circumstances than our own.

Such certainly was the case of these men, of whom I could not so much as see room to suppose any of them were sav'd; nothing could make it rational so much as to wish or expect that they did not all perish there; except the possibility only of their being taken up by another ship in company, and this was but meer possibility indeed; for I saw not the least signal or appearance of any such thing.

I cannot explain by any possible energy of words what a strange longing or hankering of desires I felt in my soul upon this sight; breaking out sometimes thus: 'O that there had been but one or two; nay, or but one soul sav'd out of this ship, to have escap'd to me, that I might but have had one companion, one fellow-creature to have spoken to me, and to have convers'd with!' In all the time of my solitary life, I never felt so earnest, so strong a desire after the society of my fellow-creatures, or so deep a regret at the want of it.

There are some secret moving springs in the affections, which when they are set a going by some object in view, or be it some object, though not in view, yet rendred present to the mind by the power of imagination, that motion* carries out the soul by its impetuosity to such violent eager embracings of the object, that the absence of it is insupportable.

Such were these earnest wishings that but one man had been sav'd! 'O that it had been but one!' I believe I repeated the words, 'O that it had been but one!' a thousand times; and the desires were so mov'd by it, that when I spoke the words, my hands would clinch together, and my fingers press the palms of my hands, that if I had had any soft thing in my hand, it would have crusht it involuntarily; and my teeth in my head wou'd strike together, and set against one another so strong, that for some time I could not part them again.

Let the naturalists* explain these things, and the reason and manner of them; all I can say to them is, to describe the fact, which was even surprising to me when I found it; though I knew not from what it should proceed; it was doubtless the effect of ardent wishes, and of strong ideas form'd in my mind, realizing the comfort which the conversation of one of my fellow-Christians would have been to me.

But it was not to be; either their fate or mine, or both, forbid it; for till the last year of my being on this island, I never knew whether any were saved out of that ship or no; and had only the affliction, some days after, to see the corps of a drownded boy come on shore, at the end of the island which was next the shipwreck. He had on no cloaths but a seaman's wastcoat, a pair of open knee'd linnen drawers, and a blew linnen shirt; but nothing to direct me so much as to guess what nation he was of. He had nothing in his pocket but two pieces of eight, and a tobacco-pipe; the last was to me of ten times more value than the first.

It was now calm, and I had a great mind to venture out in my boat to this wreck; not doubting but I might find something on board that might be useful to me; but that did not altogether press me so much as the possibility that there might be yet some living creature on board, whose life I might not only save, but might, by saving that life, comfort my own to the last degree; and this thought clung so to my heart, that I could not be quiet, night or day, but I must venture out in my boat on board this wreck; and committing the rest to God's providence, I thought the impression was so strong upon my mind, that it could not be resisted, that it must come from some invisible direction, and that I should be wanting to my self if I did not go.

Under the power of this impression, I hasten'd back to my castle, prepar'd every thing for my voyage, took a quantity of bread, a great pot for fresh water, a compass to steer by, a bottle of rum, for I had still a great deal of that left, a basket full of raisins; and thus loading my self with every thing necessary, I went down to my boat, got the water out of her, and got her afloat, loaded all my cargo in her, and then went home again for more; my second cargo was a great bag full of rice, the umbrella to set up over my head for shade, another large pot full of fresh water, and about two dozen of my small loaves or barley cakes, more than before, with a bottle of goat's-milk and a cheese; all which, with great labour and sweat, I brought to my boat; and praying to God to direct my voyage, I put out, and rowing or padling the canoe along the shore, I came at last to the utmost point of the island on that side, viz. N.E. And now I was to launch out into the ocean, and either to venture, or not to venture. I look'd on the rapid currents which ran constantly on both sides of the island at a distance, and which were very terrible to me, from the remembrance of the hazard I had been in before, and my heart began to fail me; for I foresaw that if I was driven into either of those currents, I should be carry'd a vast way out to sea, and perhaps out of my reach, or sight of the island again; and that then, as my boat was but small, if any little gale of wind should rise, I should be inevitably lost.

These thoughts so oppress'd my mind that I began to give over my enterprize, and having haled my boat into a little creek on the shore, I stept out, and sat me down upon a little rising bit of ground, very pensive and anxious, between fear and desire about my voyage; when, as I was musing, I could perceive that the tide was turn'd, and the flood come on, upon which my going was for so many hours impracticable; upon this presently it occurr'd to me that I should go up to the highest piece of ground I could find, and observe, if I could, how the sets of the tide or currents lay when the flood came in, that I might judge whether, if I was driven one way out, I might not expect to be driven another way home, with the same rapidness of the currents. This thought was no sooner in my head, but I cast my eye upon a little hill, which sufficiently overlook'd the sea both ways, and from whence I had a clear view of the currents, or sets of the tide, and which way I was to guide my self in my return; here I found, that as the current of the ebb set out close by the south point of the island, so the current of the flood set in close by the shore of the north side, and that I had nothing to do but to keep to the north of the island in my return, and I should do well enough.

Encourag'd with this observation, I resolv'd the next morning to set out with the first of the tide; and reposing my self for the night in the canoe, under the great watch-coat I mention'd, I launched out. I made first a little out to sea full north, till I began to feel the benefit of the current, which set eastward, and which carry'd me at a great rate, and yet did not so hurry me as the southern side current had done before, and so as to take from me all government of the boat; but having a strong steerage with my paddle, I went at a great rate directly for the wreck, and in less than two hours I came up to it.

It was a dismal sight to look at: the ship, which by its building was Spanish, stuck fast, jaum'd in between two rocks; all the stern and quarter of her was beaten to pieces with the sea; and as her forecastle, which stuck in the rocks, had run on with great violence, her mainmast and foremast were brought by the board, that is to say, broken short off; but her bolt-sprit* was sound and the head and bow appear'd firm. When I came close to her, a dog appear'd upon her, who seeing me coming, yelp'd and cry'd; and as soon as I call'd him, jump'd into the sea, to come to me, and I took him into the boat, but found him almost dead for hunger and thirst. I gave him a cake of my bread, and he eat it like a ravenous wolf, that had been starving a fortnight in the snow. I then gave the poor creature some fresh water, with which, if I would have let him, he would have burst himself.

After this I went on board; but the first sight I met with was two men drown'd in the cook-room or forecastle of the ship, with their arms fast about one another. I concluded, as is indeed probable, that when the ship struck, it being in a storm, the sea broke so high and so continually over her, that the men were not able to bear it, and were strangled with the constant rushing in of the water, as much as if they had been under water. Besides the dog, there was nothing left in the ship that had life; nor any goods that I could see, but what were spoil'd by the water. There were some casks of liquor, whether wine or brandy I knew not, which lay lower in the hold, and which, the water being ebb'd out, I could see; but they were too big to meddle with. I saw several chests, which I believ'd belong'd to some of the seamen; and I got two of them into the boat, without examining what was in them.

Had the stern of the ship been fix'd, and the forepart broken off, I am perswaded I might have made a good voyage; for by what I found in these two chests, I had room to suppose the ship had a great deal of wealth on board; and if I may guess by the course she steer'd, she must have been bound from the Buenos Ayres, or the Rio de la Plata, in the south part of America, beyond the Brasils, to the Havana, in the Gulph of Mexico, and so perhaps to Spain. She had no doubt a great treasure in her, but of no use at the time to any body; and what became of the rest of her people, I then knew not.

I found, besides these chests, a little cask full of liquor, of about twenty gallons, which I got into my boat with much difficulty; there were several muskets in a cabin, and a great powder-horn, with about 4 pounds of powder in it; as for the muskets, I had no occasion for them; so I left them, but took the powder-horn. I took a fire shovel and tongs, which I wanted extremely; as also two little brass kettles, a copper pot to make chocolate, and a gridiron; and with this cargo, and the dog, I came away, the tide beginning to make home again; and the same evening, about an hour within night, I reach'd the island again, weary and fatigu'd to the last degree.

I repos'd that night in the boat, and in the morning I resolved to harbour what I had gotten in my new cave, not to carry it home to my castle. After refreshing my self, I got all my cargo on shore, and began to examine the particulars. The cask of liquor I found to be a kind of rum, but not such as we had at the Brasils; and in a word, not at all good; but when I came to open the chests, I found several things of great use to me: for example, I found in one a fine case of bottles, of an extraordinary kind, and fill'd with cordial waters, fine and very good; the bottles held about three pints each, and were tipp'd with silver: I found two pots of very good succades* or sweetmeats, so fastned also on top that the salt water had not hurt them; and two more of the same, which the water had spoil'd: I found some very good shirts, which were very welcome to me; and about a dozen and half of linnen white handkerchiefs and colour'd neckcloths; the former were also very welcome, being exceeding refreshing to wipe my face in a hot day. Besides this, when I came to the till in the chest, I found there three great bags of pieces of eight, which held about eleven hundred pieces in all; and in one of them, wrapt up in a paper, six doubloons of gold, and some small bars of wedges of gold; I suppose they might all weigh near a pound.

The other chest I found had some cloaths in it, but of little value; but by the circumstances it must have belong'd to the gunner's mate; though there was no powder in it but about two pound of fine glaz'd powder, in three small flasks, kept, I suppose, for charging their fowling-pieces on occasion. Upon the whole, I got very little by this voyage that was of any use to me; for as to the money, I had no manner of occasion for it: 'twas to me as the dirt under my feet; and I would have given it all for three or four pair of English shoes and stockings, which were things I greatly wanted, but had not had on my feet now for many years: I had indeed gotten two pair of shoes now, which I took off of the feet of the two drown'd men who I saw in the wreck; and I found two pair more in one of the chests, which were very welcome to me; but they were not like our English shoes, either for ease or service; being rather what we call pumps than shoes. I found in this seaman's chest about fifty pieces of eight in ryals, but no gold; I suppose this belong'd to a poorer man than the other, which seem'd to belong to some officer.

Well, however, I lugg'd this money home to my cave, and laid it up, as I had done that before which I brought from our own ship; but it was great pity, as I said, that the other part of this ship had not come to my share; for I am satisfy'd I might have loaded my canoe several times over with money, which, if I had ever escap'd to England, would have lain here safe enough, till I might have come again and fetch'd it.

Having now brought all my things on shore, and secur'd them, I went back to my boat, and row'd or paddled her along the shore to her old harbour, where I laid her up, and made the best of my way to my old habitation, where I found everything safe and quiet; so I began to repose my self, live after my old fashion, and take care of my family affairs; and for a while, I liv'd easy enough;

only that I was more vigilant than I us'd to be, look'd out oftner, and did not go abroad so much; and if at any time I did stir with any freedom, it was always to the east part of the island, where I was pretty well satisfy'd the savages never came, and where I could go without so many precautions, and such a load of arms and ammunition as I always carry'd with me if I went the other way.

I liv'd in this condition near two years more; but my unlucky head, that was always to let me know it was born to make my body miserable, was all this two years fill'd with projects and designs, how, if it were possible, I might get away from this island; for sometimes I was for making another voyage to the wreck, though my reason told me that there was nothing left there worth the hazard of my voyage; sometimes for a ramble one way, sometimes another; and I believe verily, if I had had the boat that I went from Sallee in, I should have ventur'd to sea, bound any where, I knew not whither.

I have been in all my circumstances a memento to those who are touched with the general plague of mankind, whence, for ought I know, one half of their miseries flow; I mean that of not being satisfy'd with the station wherein God and nature has plac'd them; for not to look back upon my primitive condition, and the excellent advice of my father, the opposition to which was, as I may call it, my original sin, my subsequent mistakes of the same kind had been the means of my coming into this miserable condition; for had that providence, which so happily had seated me at the Brasils as a planter, bless'd me with confin'd desires, and I could have been contented to have gone on gradually, I might have been by this time, I mean, in the time of my being in this island, one of the most considerable planters in the Brasils; nay, I am perswaded that by the improvements I had made in that little time I liv'd there, and the encrease I should probably have made if I had stay'd, I might have been worth an hundred thousand moydors;* and what business had I to leave a settled fortune, a well stock'd plantation, improving and encreasing, to turn supra-cargo to Guinea, to fetch negroes, when patience and time would have so encreas'd our stock at home, that we could have bought them at our own door, from those whose business it was to fetch them? and though it had cost us something more, yet the difference of that price was by no means worth saving at so great a hazard.

But as this is ordinarily the fate of young heads, so reflection upon the folly of it is as ordinarily the exercise of more years, or of the dear bought experience of time; and so it was with me now; and yet so deep had the mistake taken root in my temper, that I could not satisfy my self in my station, but was continually poring upon the means and possibility of my escape from this place; and that I may, with the greater pleasure to the reader, bring on the remaining part of my story, it may not be improper to give some account of my first conceptions on the subject of this foolish scheme for my escape; and how, and upon what foundation I acted.

I am now to be suppos'd retir'd into my castle, after my late voyage to the wreck, my frigate laid up and secur'd under water, as usual, and my condition restor'd to what it was before. I had more wealth indeed than I had before, but was not at all the richer; for I had no more use for it than the Indians of Peru had before the Spaniards came here.

It was one of the nights in the rainy season in March, the four and twentieth year of my first setting foot in this island of solitariness; I was lying in my bed, or hammock, awake, very well in health, had no pain, no distemper, no uneasiness of body; no, nor any uneasiness of mind, more than ordinary; but could by no means close my eyes, that is, so as to sleep; no, not a wink all night long, otherwise than as follows:

It is as impossible as needless to set down the innumerable crowd of thoughts that whirl'd through the great thorow-fare of the brain, the memory, in this night's time: I run over the whole history of my life in miniature, or by abridgement, as I may call it, to my coming to this island, and also of the part of my life since I came to this island. In my reflections upon the state of my case since I came on shore on this island, I was comparing the happy posture of my affairs in the first years of my habitation here, compar'd to the life of anxiety, fear, and care which I had liv'd ever since I had seen the print of a foot in the sand; not that I did not believe the savages had frequented the island even all the while, and might have been several hundreds of them at times on shore there; but I had never known it, and was incapable of any apprehensions about it; my satisfaction was perfect, though my danger was the same; and I was as happy in not knowing my danger, as if I had never really been expos'd to it. This furnish'd my thoughts with many very profitable reflections, and particularly this one, how infinitely good that providence is, which has provided in its government of mankind such narrow bounds to his sight and knowledge of things; and though he walks in the midst of so many thousand dangers, the sight of which, if discover'd to him, would distract his mind and sink his spirits, he is kept serene and calm, by having the events of things hid from his eyes and knowing nothing of the dangers which surround him.

After these thoughts had for some time entertain'd me, I came to reflect seriously upon the real danger I had been in for so many years, in this very island; and how I had walk'd about in the greatest security, and with all possible tranquillity; even when perhaps nothing but a brow of a hill, a great tree, or the casual approach of night had been between me and the worst kind of destruction, viz. that of falling into the hands of cannibals and savages, who would have seiz'd on me with the same view as I did of a goat or a turtle, and have thought it no more a crime to kill and devour me, than I did of a pidgeon or a curlieu. I would unjustly slander my self, if I should say I was not sincerely thankful to my great Preserver, to whose singular protection I acknowledg'd, with great humility, that all these unknown deliverances were due; and without which, I must inevitably have fallen into their merciless hands.

When these thoughts were over, my head was for some time taken up in considering the nature of these wretched creatures, I mean the savages; and how it came to pass in the world, that the wise Governour of all things should give up any of His creatures to such inhumanity, nay, to something so much before even brutality itself, as to devour its own kind; but as this ended in some (at that time fruitless) speculations, it occurr'd to me to enquire what part of the world these wretches liv'd in; how far off the coast was from whence they came; what they ventur'd over so far from home for; what kind of boats they had; and why I might not order my self and my business so, that I might be able to go over thither as they were to come to me.

I never so much as troubl'd my self to consider what I should do with my self when I came thither; what would become of me, if I fell into the hands of the savages; or how I should escape from them, if they attempted me; no, nor so much as how it was possible for me to reach the coast, and not to be attempted by some or other of them, without any possibility of delivering my self; and if I should not fall into their hands, what I should do for provision, or whither I should bend my course; none of these thoughts, I say, so much as came in my way; but my mind was wholly bent upon the notion of my passing over in my boat to the main land. I look'd back upon my present condition as the most miserable that could possibly be, that I was not able to throw my self into any thing but death, that could be call'd worse; that if I reached the shore of the main, I might perhaps meet with relief, or I might coast along, as I did on the shore of Africk, till I came to some inhabited country, and where I might find some relief; and after all, perhaps I might fall in with some Christian ship that might take me in; and if the worse came to the worst, I could but die, which would put an end to all these miseries at once. Pray note, all this was the fruit of a disturb'd mind, an impatient temper, made as it were desperate by the long continuance of my troubles and the disappointments I had met in the wreck I had been on board of; and where I had been so near the obtaining what I so earnestly long'd for, viz. some-body to speak to, and to learn some knowledge from of the place where I was, and of the probable means of my deliverance; I say, I was agitated wholly by these thoughts. All my calm of mind in my resignation to providence, and waiting the issue of the dispositions of Heaven, seem'd to be suspended, and I had, as it were, no power to turn my thoughts to any thing, but to the project of a voyage to the main, which came upon me with such force, and such an impetuosity of desire, that it was not to be resisted.

When this had agitated my thoughts for two hours or more, with such violence, that it set my very blood into a ferment, and my pulse beat as high as if I had been in a feaver, meerly with the extraordinary fervour of my mind about it; nature, as if I had been fatigued and exhausted with the very thought of it, threw me into a sound sleep; one would have thought I should have dream'd of it, but I did not, nor of any thing relating to it; but I dream'd that as I was going out in the morning as usual from my castle, I saw upon the shore two canoes and eleven savages coming to land, and that they brought with them another savage, who they were going to kill, in order to eat him; when on a sudden, the savage that they were going to kill, jumpt away, and ran for his life; and I thought, in my sleep, that he came running into my little thick grove before my fortification, to hide himself; and that I seeing him alone, and not perceiving that the other sought him that way, show'd my self to him, and smiling upon him, encourag'd him;

that he kneel'd down to me, seeming to pray me to assist him; upon which I shew'd my ladder, made him go up, and carry'd him into my cave, and he became my servant; and that as soon as I had gotten this man, I said to my self, 'Now I may certainly venture to the main land; for this fellow will serve me as a pilot, and will tell me what to do, and whether to go for provisions; and whether not to go for fear of being devoured, what places to venture into, and what to escape.' I wak'd with this thought, and was under such inexpressible impressions of joy at the prospect of my escape in my dream, that the disappointments which I felt upon coming to my self and finding it was no more than a dream, were equally extravagant the other way, and threw me into a very great dejection of spirit.

Upon this, however, I made this conclusion, that my only way to go about an attempt for an escape was, if possible, to get a savage into my possession; and if possible, it should be one of their prisoners, who they had condemned to be eaten, and should being thither to kill; but these thoughts still were attended with this difficulty, that it was impossible to effect this, without attacking a whole caravan of them, and killing them all; and this was not only a very desperate attempt, and might miscarry; but on the other hand, I had greatly scrupled the lawfulness of it to me; and my heart trembled at the thoughts of shedding so much blood, tho' it was for my deliverance. I need not repeat the arguments which occurr'd to me against this, they being the same mention'd before; but tho' I had other reasons to offer now, viz. that those men were enemies to my life, and would devour me, if they could; that it was self-preservation in the highest degree, to deliver my self from this death of a life, and was acting in my own defence as much as if they were actually assaulting me, and the like; I say, tho' these things argued for it, yet the thoughts of shedding humane blood for my deliverance were very terrible to me, and such as I could by no means reconcile my self to, a great while.

However, at last, after many secret disputes with my self, and after great perplexities about it, for all these arguments one way and another struggl'd in my head a long time, the eager prevailing desire of deliverance at length master'd all the rest; and I resolved, if possible, to get one of those savages into my hands, cost what it would. My next thing then was to contrive how to do it, and this indeed was very difficult to resolve on. But as I could pitch upon no probable means for it, so I resolv'd to put my self upon the watch, to see them when they came on shore, and leave the rest to the event, taking such measures as the opportunity should present, let be what would be.

With these resolutions in my thoughts, I set my self upon the scout as often as possible, and indeed so often till I was heartily tir'd of it, for it was above a year and a half that I waited, and for great part of that time went out to the west end, and to the south west corner of the island, almost every day, to see for canoes, but none appear'd. This was very discouraging, and began to trouble me much, tho' I cannot say that it did in this case, as it had done some time before that, viz. wear off the edge of my desire to the thing. But the longer it seem'd to be delay'd, the more eager I was for it; in a word, I was not at first so careful to shun the sight of these savages, and avoid being seen by them, as I was now eager to be upon them.

Besides, I fancied my self able to manage one, nay, two or three savages, if I had them, so as to make them entirely slaves to me, to do whatever I should direct them, and to prevent their being able at any time to do me any hurt. It was a great while that I pleas'd my self with this affair, but nothing still presented; all my fancies and schemes came to nothing, for no savages came near me for a great while.

About a year and a half after I had entertain'd these notions, and, by long musing, had as it were resolved them all into nothing, for want of an occasion to put them in execution, I was surpriz'd one morning early, with seeing no less than five canoes all on shore together on my side the island; and the people who belong'd to them all landed, and out of my sight. The number of them broke all my measures, for seeing so many, and knowing that they always came four or six, or sometimes more in a boat, I could not tell what to think of it, or how to take my measures to attack twenty or thirty men single handed; so I lay still in my castle, perplex'd and discomforted; however, I put my self into all the same postures for an attack that I had formerly provided, and was just ready for action, if any thing had presented. Having waited a good while, listening to hear if they made any noise, at length, being very impatient, I set my guns at the foot of my ladder, and clamber'd up to the top of the hill, by my two stages as usual; standing so, however, that my head did not appear above the hill, so that they could not perceive me by any means; here I observ'd, by the help of my perspective glass, that they were no less than thirty in number, that they had a fire kindled, that they had had meat dress'd. How they had cook'd it, that I knew not, or what it was; but they were all dancing in I know not how many barbarous gestures and figures, their own way, round the fire.

While I was thus looking on them, I perceived by my perspective two miserable wretches dragg'd from the boats, where it seems they were laid by, and were now brought out for the slaughter. I perceived one of them immediately fell, being knock'd down, I suppose with a club or wooden sword, for that was their way, and two or three others were at work immediately cutting him open for their cookery, while the other victim was left standing by himself, till they should be ready for him. In that very moment this poor wretch seeing himself a little at liberty, nature inspir'd him with hopes of life, and he started away from them, and ran with incredible swiftness along the sands directly towards me, I mean towards that part of the coast where my habitation was.

I was dreadfully frighted (that I must acknowledge) when I perceived him to run my way, and especially when, as I thought, I saw him pursued by the whole body; and now I expected that part of my dream was coming to pass, and that he would certainly take shelter in my grove; but I could not depend by any means upon my dream for the rest of it, viz. that the other savages would not pursue him thither, and find him there. However, I kept my station, and my spirits began to recover when I found that there was not above three men that follow'd him, and still more was I encourag'd when I found that he outstrip'd them exceedingly in running, and gain'd ground of them, so that if he could but hold it for half an hour, I saw easily he would fairly get away from them all.

There was between them and my castle the creek which I mention'd often at the first part of my story, when I landed my cargoes out of the ship; and this, I saw plainly, he must necessarily swim over, or the poor wretch would be taken there. But when the savage escaping came thither, he made nothing of it, tho' the tide was then up, but plunging in, swam thro' in about thirty strokes or thereabouts, landed, and ran on with exceeding strength and swiftness; when the three persons came to the creek, I found that two of them could swim, but the third cou'd not, and that standing on the other side, he look'd at the other, but went no further, and soon after went softly back again, which, as it happen'd, was very well for him in the main.

I observ'd that the two who swam were yet more than twice as long swimming over the creek as the fellow was that fled from them. It came now very warmly upon my thoughts, and indeed irresistibly, that now was my time to get me a servant, and perhaps a companion or assistant; and that I was call'd plainly by Providence to save this poor creature's life; I immediately run down the ladders with all possible expedition, fetch'd my two guns, for they were both but at the foot of the ladders, as I observ'd above; and getting up again, with the same haste, to the top of the hill, I cross'd toward the sea; and having a very short cut, and all down hill, clapp'd my self in the way between the pursuers and the pursu'd; hallowing aloud to him that fled, who looking back, was at first perhaps as much frighted at me as at them; but I beckon'd with my hand to him to come back; and in the mean time, I slowly advanc'd towards the two that follow'd; then rushing at once upon the foremost, I knock'd him down with the stock of my piece; I was loath to fire, because I would not have the rest hear; though at that distance it would not have been easily heard, and being out of sight of the smoke too, they wou'd not have easily known what to make of it. Having knock'd this fellow down, the other who pursu'd with him stopp'd, as if he had been frighted; and I advanc'd a-pace towards him; but as I came nearer, I perceiv'd presently he had a bow and arrow, and was fitting it to shoot at me; so I was then necessitated to shoot at him first, which I did, and kill'd him at the first shoot; the poor savage who fled, but had stopp'd, though he saw both his enemies fallen and kill'd, as he thought, yet was so frighted with the fire and noise of my piece, that he stood stock still, and neither came forward or went backward, tho' he seem'd rather enclin'd to fly still than to come on; I hollow'd again to him, and made signs to come forward, which he easily understood, and came a little way, then stopp'd again, and then a little further, and stopp'd again, and I cou'd then perceive that he stood trembling, as if he had been taken prisoner, and had just been to be kill'd, as his two enemies were. I beckon'd him again to come to me, and gave him all the signs of encouragement that I could think of, and he came nearer and nearer, kneeling down every ten or twelve steps in token of acknowledgement for my saving his life. I smil'd at him, and look'd pleasantly, and beckon'd to him to come still nearer; at length he came close to me, and then he kneel'd down again, kiss'd the ground, and laid his head upon the ground, and taking me by the foot, set my foot upon his head; this it seems was in token of swearing to be my slave for ever; I took him up, and made much of him, and encourag'd him all I could. But there was more work to do yet, for I perceived the savage who I knock'd down was not kill'd, but stunn'd with the blow, and began to come to himself; so I pointed to him, and showing him the savage, that he was not dead; upon this he spoke some words to me, and though I could not understand them, yet I thought they were pleasant to hear, for they were the first sound of a man's voice that I had heard, my own excepted, for above twenty five years. But there was no time for such reflections now; the savage who was knock'd down recover'd himself so far as to sit upon the ground, and I perceived that my savage began to be afraid; but when I saw that, I presented my other piece at the man, as if I would shoot him; upon this my savage, for so I call him now, made a motion to me to lend him my sword, which hung naked in a belt by my side; so I did: he no sooner had it, but he runs to his enemy, and at one blow cut off his head as cleaverly, no executioner in Germany could have done it sooner or better; which I thought very strange, for one who I had reason to believe never saw a sword in his life before, except their own wooden swords; however, it seems, as I learn'd afterwards, they make their wooden swords so sharp, so heavy, and the wood is so hard, that they will cut off heads even with them, ay and arms, and that at one blow too; when he had done this, he comes laughing to me in sign of triumph, and brought me the sword again, and with abundance of gestures which I did not understand, laid it down with the head of the savage that he had kill'd, just before me.

But that which astonish'd him, most, was to know how I had kill'd the other Indian so far off; so pointing to him, he made signs to me to let him go to him, so I bad him go, as well as I could; when he came to him, he stood like one amaz'd, looking at him, turn'd him first on one side, then on t'other, look'd at the wound the bullet had made, which it seems was just in his breast, where it had made a hole, and no great quantity of blood had follow'd, but he had bled inwardly, for he was quite dead. He took up his bow and arrows, and came back, so I turn'd to go away, and beckon'd to him to follow me, making signs to him that more might come after them.

Upon this he sign'd to me that he should bury them with sand, that they might not be seen by the rest if they follow'd; and so I made signs again to him to do so; he fell to work, and in an instant he had scrap'd a hole in the sand with his hands, big enough to bury the first in, and then dragg'd him into it, and cover'd him, and did so also by the other; I believe he had bury'd them both in a quarter of an hour; then calling him away, I carry'd him not to my castle, but quite away to my cave, on the farther part of the island; so I did not let my dream come to pass in that part, viz. that he came into my grove for shelter.

Here I gave him bread, and a bunch of raisins to eat, and a draught of water, which I found he was indeed in great distress for, by his running; and having refresh'd him, I made signs for him to go lie down and sleep; pointing to a place where I had laid a great parcel of rice straw, and a blanket upon it, which I used to sleep upon my self sometimes; so the poor creature laid down, and went to sleep.

He was a comely handsome fellow, perfectly well made; with straight strong limbs, not too large; tall and well shap'd, and, as I reckon, about twenty six years of age. He had a very good countenance, not a fierce and surly aspect; but seem'd to have something very manly in his face, and yet he had all the sweetness and softness of an European in his countenance too, especially when he smil'd. His hair was long and black, not curl'd like wool; his forehead very high and large, and a great vivacity and sparkling sharpness in his eyes. The colour of his skin was not quite black, but very tawny; and yet not of an ugly yellow nauseous tawny, as the Brasilians, and Virginians, and other natives of America are; but of a bright kind of a dun olive colour, that had in it something very agreeable, tho' not very easy to describe. His face was round and plump; his nose small, not flat like the negroes, a very good mouth, thin lips, and his fine teeth well set, and white as ivory. After he had slumber'd, rather than slept, about half an hour, he wak'd again, and comes out of the cave to me; for I had been milking my goats, which I had in the enclosure just by; when he espy'd me, he came running to me, laying himself down again upon the ground, with all the possible signs of an humble thankful disposition, making a many antick gestures to show it. At last he lays his head flat upon the ground, close to my foot, and sets my other foot upon his head, as he had done before; and after this, made all the signs to me of subjection, servitude, and submission imaginable, to let me know how he would serve me as long as he liv'd. I understood him in many things, and let him know I was very well pleas'd with him; in a little time I began to speak to him, and teach him to speak to me; and first, I made him know his name should be Friday, which was the day I sav'd his life; I call'd him so for the memory of the time; I likewise taught him to say Master, and then let him know, that was to be my name; I likewise taught him to say yes and no, and to know the meaning of them; I gave him some milk in an earthen pot, and let him see me drink it before him, and sop my bread in it; and I gave him a cake of bread to do the like, which he quickly comply'd with, and made signs that it was very good for him.

I kept there with him all that night; but as soon as it was day, I beckon'd to him to come with me, and let him know I would give him some cloaths, at which he seem'd very glad, for he was stark naked. As we went by the place where he had bury'd the two men, he pointed exactly to the place, and shew'd me the marks that he had made to find them again, making signs to me that we should dig them up again, and eat them; at this I appear'd very angry, express'd my abhorrence of it, made as if I would vomit at the thoughts of it, and beckon'd with my hand to him to come away, which he did immediately, with great submission. I then led him up to the top of the hill, to see if his enemies were gone; and pulling out my glass, I look'd, and saw plainly the place where they had been, but no appearance of them, or of their canoes; so that it was plain they were gone, and had left their two comrades behind them, without any search after them.

But I was not content with this discovery; but having now more courage, and consequently more curiosity, I took my man Friday with me, giving him the sword in his hand, with the bow and arrows at his back, which I found he could use very dextrously, making him carry one gun for me, and I two for my self, and away we march'd to the place where these creatures had been; for I had a mind now to get some fuller intelligence of them. When I came to the place, my very blood ran chill in my veins, and my heart sunk within me, at the horror of the spectacle: indeed it was a dreadful sight, at least it was so to me; though Friday made nothing of it. The place was cover'd with humane bones, the ground dy'd with their blood, great pieces of flesh left here and there, half eaten, mangl'd and scorch'd; and in short, all the tokens of the triumphant feast they had been making there, after a victory over their enemies. I saw three skulls, five hands, and the bones of three or four legs and feet, and abundance of other parts of the bodies; and Friday, by his signs, made me understand that they brought over four prisoners to feast upon; that three of them were eaten up, and that he, pointing to himself, was the fourth; that there had been a great battle between them and their next king, whose subjects it seems he had been one of; and that they had taken a great number of prisoners, all which were carry'd to several places by those that had taken them in the fight, in order to feast upon them, as was done here by these wretches upon those they brought hither.

I caus'd Friday to gather all the skulls, bones, flesh, and whatever remain'd, and lay them together on a heap, and make a great fire upon it, and burn them all to ashes: I found Friday had still a hankering stomach after some of the flesh, and was still a cannibal in his nature; but I discover'd so much abhorrence at the very thoughts of it, and at the least appearance of it, that he durst not discover it; for I had by some means let him know that I would kill him if he offer'd it.

When we had done this, we came back to our castle, and there I fell to work for my man Friday; and first of all, I gave him a pair of linnen drawers, which I had out of the poor gunner's chest I mentioned, and which I found in the wreck; and which with a little alteration fitted him very well; then I made him a jerkin of goat's-skin, as well as my skill would allow; and I was now grown a tollerable good taylor; and I gave him a cap, which I had made of a hare-skin, very convenient, and fashionable enough; and thus he was cloath'd for the present, tollerably well, and was mighty well pleas'd to see himself almost as well cloath'd as his master. It is true, he went awkwardly in these things at first; wearing the drawers was very awkward to him, and the sleeves of the wastcoat gall'd his shoulders and the inside of his arms; but a little easing them where he complain'd they hurt him, and using himself to them, at length he took to them very well.

The next day after I came home to my hutch with him, I began to consider where I should lodge him; and that I might do well for him, and yet be perfectly easy my self, I made a little tent for him in the vacant place between my two fortifications, in the inside of the last, and in the outside of the first; and as there was a door or entrance there into my cave, I made a formal fram'd door case, and a door to it of boards, and set it up in the passage, a little

within the entrance; and causing the door to open on the inside, I
barr'd it up in the night, taking in my ladders too; so that Friday
could no way come at me in the inside of my innermost wall,
without making so much noise in getting over, that it must needs
waken me; for my first wall had now a compleat roof over it of
long poles, covering all my tent, and leaning up to the side of the
hill, which was again laid cross with smaller sticks instead of
laths, and then thatch'd over a great thickness with the rice
straw, which was strong like reeds; and at the hole or place
which was left to go in or out by the ladder, I had plac'd a kind
of trap-door, which if it had been attempted on the outside,
would not have open'd at all, but would have fallen down and
made a great noise; and as to weapons, I took them all in to my
side every night.

But I needed none of all this precaution; for never man had a
more faithful, loving, sincere servant, than Friday was to me;
without passions, sullenness, or designs, perfectly oblig'd and
engag'd; his very affections were ty'd to me, like those of a child
to a father; and I dare say he would have sacrific'd his life for the
saving mine upon any occasion whatsoever; the many
testimonies he gave me of this, put it out of doubt, and soon
convinc'd me that I needed to use no precautions as to my safety
on his account.

This frequently gave me occasion to observe, and that with
wonder, that however it had pleas'd God, in His providence, and
in the government of the works of His hands, to take from so
great a part of the world of His creatures, the best uses to which
their faculties and the powers of their souls are adapted; yet that
He has bestow'd upon them the same powers, the same reason,
the same affections, the same sentiments of kindness and
obligation, the same passions and resentments of wrongs, the
same sense of gratitude, sincerity, fidelity, and all the capacities
of doing good and receiving good, that He has given to us; and
that when He pleases to offer to them occasions of exerting
these, they are as ready, nay, more ready to apply them to the
right uses for which they were bestowed, than we are: and this
made me very melancholly sometimes, in reflecting as the several
occasions presented, how mean a use we make of all these, even
though we have these powers enlighten'd by the great lamp of
instruction, the spirit of God, and by the knowledge of His
word, added to our understanding; and why it has pleas'd God

to hide the like saving knowledge from so many millions of souls, who, if I might judge by this poor savage, would make a much better use of it than we did.

From hence, I sometimes was led too far to invade the soverainty of Providence, and as it were arraign the justice of so arbitrary a disposition of things, that should hide that light from some, and reveal it to others, and yet expect a like duty from both. But I shut it up, and check'd my thoughts with this conclusion, (1st) that we did not know by what light and law these should be condemn'd; but that as God was necessarily, and by the nature of His being, infinitely holy and just, so it could not be, but that if these creatures were all sentenc'd to absence from Himself, it was on account of sinning against that light which, as the scripture says, was a law to themselves, and by such rules as their consciences would acknowledge to be just, tho' the foundation was not discover'd to us: and (2d) that still as we are all the clay in the hand of the potter, no vessel could say to Him, Why hast Thou form'd me thus?

But to return to my new companion: I was greatly delighted with him, and made it my business to teach him every thing that was proper to make him useful, handy, and helpful; but especially to make him speak, and understand me when I spake, and he was the aptest schollar that ever was, and particularly was so merry, so constantly diligent, and so pleas'd, when he cou'd but understand me, or make me understand him, that it was very pleasant to me to talk to him; and now my life began to be so easy, that I began to say to my self, that could I but have been safe from more savages, I cared not if I was never to remove from the place while I lived.

After I had been two or three days return'd to my castle, I thought that, in order to bring Friday off from his horrid way of feeding, and from the relish of a cannibal's stomach, I ought to let him taste other flesh; so I took him out with me one morning to the woods. I went indeed intending to kill a kid out of my own flock, and bring him home and dress it; but as I was going, I saw a she goat lying down in the shade, and two young kids sitting by her. I catch'd hold of Friday. 'Hold,' says I, 'stand still,' and made signs to him not to stir; immediately I presented my piece, shot and kill'd one of the kids. The poor creature, who had at a distance indeed seen me kill the savage his enemy, but did not know or could imagine how it was done, was sensibly surpriz'd, trembled and shook, and look'd so amaz'd that I thought he would have sunk down. He did not see the kid I shot at, or perceive I had kill'd it, but ripp'd up his wastcoat to feel if he was not wounded, and as I found, presently thought I was resolv'd to kill him; for he came and kneel'd down to me, and embraceing my knees, said a great many things I did not understand; but I could easily see that the meaning was to pray me not to kill him.

I soon found a way to convince him that I would do him no harm, and taking him up by the hand, laugh'd at him, and pointed to the kid which I had kill'd, beckoned to him to run and fetch it, which he did; and while he was wondering and looking to see how the creature was kill'd, I loaded my gun again, and by and by I saw a great fowl like a hawk sit upon a tree within shot; so to let Friday understand a little what I would do, I call'd him to me again, pointed at the fowl, which was indeed a parrot, tho' I thought it had been a hawk; I say, pointing to the parrot, and to my gun, and to the ground under the parrot, to let him see I would make it fall, I made him understand that I would shoot and kill that bird; according I fir'd and bad him look, and immediately he saw the parrot fall, he stood like one frighted again, notwithstanding all I had said to him; and I found he was the more amaz'd because he did not see me put any thing into the gun; but thought that there must be some wonderful fund of death and destruction in that thing, able to kill man, beast, bird, or any thing near or far off, and the astonishment this created in him was such as could not wear off for a long time; and I believe, if I would have let him, he would have worshipp'd me and my gun. As for the gun it self, he would not so much as touch it for several days after; but would speak to it, and talk to it, as if it had answer'd him, when he was by himself; which, as I afterwards learn'd of him, was to desire it not to kill him.

Well, after his astonishment was a little over at this, I pointed to him to run and fetch the bird I had shot, which he did, but stay'd some time; for the parrot, not being quite dead, was flutter'd away a good way off from the place where she fell; however, he found her, took her up, and brought her to me; and as I had perceiv'd his ignorance about the gun before, I took this advantage to charge the gun again, and not let him see me do it, that I might be ready for any other mark that might present; but nothing more offer'd at that time; so I brought home the kid, and the same evening I took the skin off, and cut it out as well as I could; and having a pot for that purpose, I boil'd or stew'd some of the flesh, and made some very good broth; and after I had begun to eat some, I gave some to my man, who seem'd very glad of it, and lik'd it very well; but that which was strangest to him was to see me eat salt with it; he made a sign to me that the salt was not good to eat, and putting a little into his own mouth, he seem'd to nauseate it, and would spit and sputter at it, washing his mouth with fresh water after it; on the other hand, I took some meat in my mouth without salt, and I pretended to spit and sputter for want of salt, as fast as he had done at the salt; but it would not do, he would never care for salt with his meat or in his broth; at least not a great while, and then but a very little.

Having thus fed him with boil'd meat and broth, I was resolv'd to feast him the next day with roasting a piece of the kid; this I did by hanging it before the fire on a string, as I had seen many people do in England, setting two poles up, one on each side the fire, and one cross on the top, and tying the string to the cross-stick, letting the meat turn continually. This Friday admir'd very much; but when he came to taste the flesh, he took so many ways to tell me how well he lik'd it, that I could not but understand him; and at last he told me he would never eat man's flesh any more, which I was very glad to hear.

The next day I set him to work to beating some corn out, and sifting it in the manner I us'd to do, as I observ'd before, and he soon understood how to do it as well as I, especially after he had seen what the meaning of it was, and that it was to make bread of; for after that I let him see me make my bread, and bake it too, and in a little time Friday was able to do all the work for me, as well as I could do it myself.

I begun now to consider, that having two mouths to feed instead of one, I must provide more ground for my harvest, and plant a larger quantity of corn than I us'd to do; so I mark'd out a larger piece of land, and began the fence in the same manner as before, in which Friday not only work'd very willingly and very hard, but did it very chearfully, and I told him what it was for; that it was for corn to make more bread, because he was now with me, and that I might have enough for him and my self too. He appear'd very sensible of that part, and let me know that he thought I had much more labour upon me on his account than I had for my self; and that he would work the harder for me, if I would tell him what to do.

This was the pleasantest year of all the life I led in this place;

Friday began to talk pretty well, and understand the names of almost every thing I had occasion to call for, and of every place I had to send him to, and talk'd a great deal to me; so that, in short, I began now to have some use for my tongue again, which indeed I had very little occasion for before; that is to say, about speech; besides the pleasures of talking to him, I had a singular satisfaction in the fellow himself; his simple unfeign'd honesty appear'd to me more and more every day, and I began really to love the creature; and on his side, I believe he lov'd me more than it was possible for him ever to love any thing before.

I had a mind once to try if he had any hankering inclination to his own country again, and having learn'd him English so well that he could answer me almost any questions, I ask'd him whether the nation that he belong'd to never conquer'd in battle; at which he smil'd, and said, 'Yes, yes, we always fight the better'; that is, he meant always get the better in fight; and so we began the following discourse: 'You always fight the better,' said I, 'how came you to be taken prisoner then, Friday?'

Friday: My nation beat much, for all that.

Master: How beat? if your nation beat them, how came you to be taken?

Friday: They more many than my nation in the place where me was; they take one, two, three, and me; my nation over-beat them in the yonder place, where me no was; there my nation take one, two, great thousand.

Master: But why did not your side recover you from the hands of your enemies then?

Friday: They run one, two, three, and me, and make go in the canoe; my nation have no canoe that time.

Master: Well, Friday, and what does your nation do with the men they take, do they carry them away and eat them, as these did?

Friday: Yes, my nation eat mans too, eat all up.

Master: Where do they carry them?

Friday: Go to other place where they think.

Master: Do they come hither?

Friday: Yes, yes, they come hither; come other else place.

Master: Have you been here with them?

Friday: Yes, I been here. [*Points to the N.W. side of the island, which, it seems, was their side.*]

By this I understood, that my man Friday had formerly been

among the savages who us'd to come on shore on the farther part of the island, on the same man eating occasions that he was now brought for; and sometime after, when I took the courage to carry him to that side, being the same I formerly mention'd, he presently knew the place, and told me he was there once when they eat up twenty men, two women, and one child; he could not tell twenty in English; but he numbred them by laying so many stones on a row, and pointing to me to tell them over.

I have told this passage, because it introduces what follows; that after I had had this discourse with him, I ask'd him how far it was from our island to the shore, and whether the canoes were not often lost; he told me there was no danger, no canoes ever lost; but that after a little way out to the sea, there was a current, and wind, always one way in the morning, the other in the afternoon.

This I understood to be no more than the sets of the tide, as going out or coming in; but I afterwards understood it was occasion'd by the great draft and reflux of the mighty river Oroonooko; in the mouth or the gulph of which river, as I found afterwards, our island lay; and this land which I perceiv'd to the W. and N.W. was the great island Trinidad, on the north point of the mouth of the river. I ask'd Friday a thousand questions about the country, the inhabitants, the sea, the coast, and what nations were near; he told me all he knew with the greatest openness imaginable; I ask'd him the name of the several nations of his sort of people; but could get no other name than Caribs; from whence I easily understood that these were the Caribbees, which our maps place on the part of America which reaches from the mouth of the river Oroonooko to Guiana, and onwards to St Martha. He told me that up a great way beyond the moon, that was, beyond the setting of the moon, which must be W. from their country, there dwelt white bearded men, like me; and pointed to my great whiskers, which I mention'd before; and that they had kill'd 'much mans,' that was his word; by all which I understood, he meant the Spaniards, whose cruelties in America had been spread over the whole countries, and was remember'd by all the nations from father to son.

I enquir'd if he could tell me how I might come from this island, and get among those white men; he told me, yes, yes, I might go 'in two canoe'; I could not understand what he meant, or make him describe to me what he meant by 'two canoe,' till at

last, with great difficulty, I found he meant it must be in a large
great boat, as big as two canoes.

This part of Friday's discourse began to relish with me very
well, and from this time I entertain'd some hopes, that one time or
other, I might find an opportunity to make my escape from this
place; and that this poor savage might be a means to help me to
do it.

During the long time that Friday had now been with me, and
that he began to speak to me and understand me, I was not
wanting to lay a foundation of religious knowledge in his mind;
particularly I ask'd him one time who made him. The poor
creature did not understand me at all, but thought I had ask'd him
who was his father; but I took it by another handle, and ask'd him
who made the sea, the ground we walk'd on, and the hills, and
woods; he told me it was one old Benamuckee, that liv'd beyond
all. He could describe nothing of this great person, but that he was
very old; much older, he said, than the sea or the land, than the
moon or the stars. I ask'd him then, if this old person had made all
things, why did not all things worship him; he look'd very grave,
and with a perfect look of innocence said, 'All things do say O* to
him.' I ask'd him if the people who die in his country went away
any where. He said, yes, they all went to Benamuckee; then I ask'd
him whether these they eat up went thither too. He said yes.

From these things I began to instruct him in the knowledge of
the true God. I told him that the great Maker of all things liv'd up
there, pointing up towards heaven; that He governs the world by
the same power and providence by which He had made it; that He
was omnipotent, could do every thing for us, give every thing to
us, take every thing from us; and thus by degrees I open'd his eyes.
He listned with great attention, and receiv'd with pleasure the
notion of Jesus Christ being sent to redeem us, and of the manner
of making our prayers to God, and His being able to hear us, even
into heaven. He told me one day, that if our God could hear us up
beyond the sun, He must needs be a greater god than their
Benamuckee, who liv'd but a little way off, and yet could not hear
till they went up to the great mountains where he dwelt to speak to
him. I ask'd him if ever he went thither to speak to him; he said no,
they never went that were young men; none went thither but the
old men, who he call'd their *oowocakee*, that is, as I made him
explain it to me, their religious, or clergy, and that they went to
say O (so he call'd saying prayers) and then came back, and told

them what Benamuckee said. By this I observ'd that there is priestcraft even amongst the most blinded ignorant pagans in the world; and the policy of making a secret religion, in order to preserve the veneration of the people to the clergy, is not only to be found in the Roman, but perhaps among all religions in the world, even among the most brutish and barbarous savages.

I endeavour'd to clear up this fraud to my man Friday, and told him that the pretence of their old men going up the mountains to say O to their god Benamuckee was a cheat, and their bringing word from thence what he said was much more so; that if they met with any answer, or spake with any one there, it must be with an evil spirit. And then I entred into a long discourse with him about the devil, the original of him, his rebellion against God, his enmity to man, the reason of it, his setting himself up in the dark parts of the world to be worship'd instead of God, and as God; and the many stratagems he made use of to delude mankind to his ruine; how he had a secret access to our passions and to our affections, to adapt his snares so to our inclinations, as to cause us even to be our own tempters, and to run upon our destruction by our own choice.

I found it was not so easie to imprint right notions in his mind about the devil, as it was about the being of a God. Nature assisted all my arguments to evidence to him even the necessity of a great First Cause and over-ruling governing Power, a secret directing Providence, and of the equity and justice of paying homage to Him that made us, and the like. But there appeared nothing of all this in the notion of an evil spirit; of his original, his being, his nature, and above all of his inclination to do evil, and to draw us in to do so too; and the poor creature puzzl'd me once in such a manner, by a question meerly natural and innocent, that I scarce knew what to say to him. I had been talking a great deal to him of the power of God, His omnipotence, His dreadful nature to sin, His being a consuming fire to the workers of iniquity; how, as He had made us all, He could destroy us and all the world in a moment; and he listen'd with great seriousness to me all the while.

After this, I had been telling him how the devil was God's enemy in the hearts of men, and used all his malice and skill to defeat the good designs of Providence, and to ruine the kingdom of Christ in the world; and the like. 'Well,' says Friday, 'but you say, God is so strong, so great, is He not much strong, much might as the devil?' 'Yes, yes,' says I, 'Friday, God is stronger than the devil, God is above the devil, and therefore we pray to God to tread him down under our feet, and enable us to resist his temptations and quench his fiery darts. 'But,' says he again, 'if God much strong, much might as the devil, why God no kill the devil, so make him no more do wicked?'

I was strangely surpriz'd at his question, and after all, tho' I was now an old man, yet I was but a young doctor, and ill enough quallified for a casuist, or a solver of difficulties; and at first I could not tell what to say, so I pretended not to hear him, and ask'd him what he said. But he was too earnest for an answer to forget his question; so that he repeated it in the very same broken words, as above. By this time I had recovered my self a little, and I said, 'God will at last punish him severely; he is reserv'd for the judgment, and is to be cast into the bottomless-pit, to dwell with everlasting fire.' This did not satisfie Friday, but he returns upon me, repeating my words, 'Reserve, at last, me no understand; but why not kill the devil now, not kill great ago?' 'You may as well ask me,' said I, 'why God does not kill you and I, when we do wicked things here that offend Him. We are preserv'd to repent and be pardon'd.' He muses a while at this. 'Well, well,' says he, mighty affectionately, 'that well; so you, I, devil, all wicked, all preserve, repent, God pardon all.' Here I was run down again by him to the last degree, and it was a testimony to me, how the meer notions of nature, though they will guide reasonable creatures to the knowledge of a God, and of a worship or homage due to the supreme Being, of God as the consequence of our nature; yet nothing but divine revelation can form the knowledge of Jesus Christ, and of a redemption purchas'd for us, of a Mediator of the new covenant, and of an Intercessor at the foot-stool of God's throne; I say, nothing but a revelation from heaven can form these in the soul, and that therefore the gospel of our Lord and Saviour Jesus Christ, I mean, the word of God, and the spirit of God promis'd for the guide and sanctifier of His people, are the absolutely necessary instructors of the souls of men, in the saving knowledge of God, and the means of salvation.

I therefore diverted the present discourse between me and my man, rising up hastily, as upon some sudden occasion of going out; then sending him for something a good way off, I seriously pray'd to God that He would enable me to instruct savingly this poor savage, assisting by His spirit the heart of the poor ignorant creature, to receive the light of the knowledge of God in Christ, reconciling him to Himself, and would guide me to speak so to him from the word of God, as his conscience might be convinc'd, his eyes open'd, and his soul sav'd. When he came again to me, I entred into a long discourse with him upon the subject of the redemption of man by the Saviour of the world, and of the doctrine of the gospel preach'd from heaven, viz. of repentance towards God, and faith in our blessed Lord Jesus. I then explain'd to him, as well as I could, why our blessed Redeemer took not on Him the nature of angels, but the seed of Abraham, and how for that reason the fallen angels had no share in the redemption; that he came only to the lost sheep of the house of Israel and the like.

I had, God knows, more sincerity than knowledge, in all the methods I took for this poor creature's instruction, and must acknowledge what I believe all that act upon the same principle will find, that in laying things open to him, I really inform'd and instructed myself in many things that either I did not know, or had not fully consider'd before, but which occurr'd naturally to my mind, upon my searching into them for the information of this poor savage; and I had more affection* in my enquiry after things upon this occasion, than ever I felt before; so that whether this poor wild wretch was the better for me or no, I had great reason to be thankful that ever he came to me. My grief set lighter upon me, my habitation grew comfortable to me beyond measure; and when I reflected that in this solitary life which I had been confin'd to, I had not only been moved my self to look up to heaven, and to seek to the hand that had brought me there, but was now to be made an instrument under Providence to save the life, and, for ought I knew, the soul of a poor savage, and bring him to the true knowledge of religion, and of the Christian doctrine, that he might know Christ Jesus, to know whom is life eternal; I say, when I reflected upon all these things, a secret joy run through every part of my soul, and I frequently rejoyc'd that ever I was brought to this place, which I had so often thought the most dreadful of all afflictions that could possibly have befallen me.

In this thankful frame I continu'd all the remainder of my time, and the conversation which employ'd the hours between Friday and I was such as made the three years which we liv'd there together perfectly and compleatly happy, if any such thing as compleat happiness can be form'd in a sublunary state. The savage was now a good Christian, a much better than I; though I have reason to hope, and bless God for it, that we were equally penitent, and comforted restor'd penitents; we had here the word of God to read, and no farther off from His spirit to instruct, than if we had been in England.

I always apply'd my self in reading the scripture, to let him know, as well as I could, the meaning of what I read; and he again, by his serious enquiries and questionings, made me, as I said before, a much better scholar in the scripture knowledge than I should ever have been by my own private meer reading. Another thing I cannot refrain from observing here also from experience, in this retir'd part of my life, viz. how infinite and inexpressible a blessing it is, that the knowledge of God, and of the doctrine of salvation by Christ Jesus, is so plainly laid down in the word of God, so easy to be receiv'd and understood, that as the bare reading the scripture made me capable of understanding enough of my duty to carry me directly on to the great work of sincere repentance for my sins, and laying hold of a Saviour for life and salvation, to a stated reformation in practice, and obedience to all God's commands, and this without any teacher or instructer; I mean, humane; so the same plain instruction sufficiently serv'd to the enlightning this savage creature, and bringing him to be such a Christian, as I have known few equal to him in my life.

As to all the disputes, wranglings, strife, and contention, which has happen'd in the world about religion, whether niceties in doctrines, or schemes of church government, they were all perfectly useless to us; as for ought I can yet see, they have been to all the rest of the world. We had the sure guide to heaven, viz. the word of God; and we had, blessed be God, comfortable views of the spirit of God teaching and instructing us by His word, leading us into all truth, and making us both willing and obedient to the instruction of His word, and I cannot see the least use that the greatest knowledge of the disputed points in religion which have made such confusions in the world would have been to us, if we could have obtain'd it; but I must go on with the historical part of things, and take every part in its order.

After Friday and I became more intimately acquainted, and that he could understand almost all I said to him, and speak fluently, though in broken English, to me, I acquainted him with my own story, or at least so much of it as related to my coming into the place, how I had liv'd there, and how long. I let him into the mystery, for such it was to him, of gunpowder and bullet, and taught him how to shoot; I gave him a knife, which he was wonderfully delighted with, and I made him a belt, with a frog hanging to it, such as in England we wear hangers in; and in the frog, instead of a hanger, I gave him a hatchet, which was not only as good a weapon in some cases, but much more useful upon other occasions.

I describ'd to him the country of Europe, and particularly England, which I came from; how we liv'd, how we worshipp'd God, how we behav'd to one another; and how we traded in ships to all parts of the world. I gave him an account of the wreck which I had been on board of, and shew'd him as near as I could the place where she lay; but she was all beaten in pieces before, and gone.

I shew'd him the ruins of our boat, which we lost when we escap'd, and which I could not stir with my whole strength then, but was now fallen almost to pieces. Upon seeing this boat, Friday stood musing a great while, and said nothing; I ask'd him what it was he study'd upon; at last says he, 'Me see such boat like come to place at my nation.'

I did not understand him a good while; but at last, when I had examin'd farther into it, I understood by him that a boat, such as that had been, came on shore upon the country where he liv'd; that is, as he explain'd it, was driven thither by stress of weather. I presently imagin'd that some European ship must have been cast away upon their coast, and the boat might get loose, and drive a shore; but was so dull, that I never once thought of men making escape from a wreck thither, much less whence they might come; so I only inquir'd after a description of the boat.

Friday describ'd the boat to me well enough; but brought me better to understand him, when he added with some warmth, 'We save the white mans from drown.' Then I presently ask'd him if there was any white mans, as he call'd them, in the boat. 'Yes,' he said, 'the boat full white mans.' I ask'd him how many; he told upon his fingers seventeen. I ask'd him then what become of them; he told me, 'They live, they dwell at my nation.'

This put new thoughts into my head; for I presently imagin'd that these might be the men belonging to the ship that was cast away in sight of my island, as I now call it; and who after the ship was struck on the rock, and they saw her inevitably lost, had sav'd themselves in their boat, and were landed upon that wild shore among the savages.

Upon this, I enquir'd of him more critically what was become of them. He assur'd me they lived still there; that they had been there about four years; that the savages let them alone, and gave them victuals to live. I ask'd him how it came to pass they did not kill them and eat them. He said, 'No, they make brother with them'; that is, as I understood him, a truce: and then he added, 'They no eat mans but when makes the war fight'; that is to say, they never eat any men but such as come to fight with them, and are taken in battle.

It was after this some considerable time, that being upon the top of the hill, at the east side of the island, from whence, as I have said, I had in a clear day discover'd the main or continent of America; Friday, the weather being very serene, looks very earnestly towards the main land, and in a kind of surprise, falls a jumping and dancing, and calls out to me, for I was at some distance from him. I ask'd him what was the matter. 'O joy!' says he, 'O glad! There see my country, there my nation!'

I observ'd an extraordinary sense of pleasure appear'd in his face, and his eyes sparkled, and his countenance discover'd a strange eagerness as if he had a mind to be in his own country again; and this observation of mine put a great many thoughts into me, which made me at first not so easy about my new man Friday as I was before; and I made no doubt but that if Friday could get back to his own nation again, he would not only forget all his religion, but all his obligation to me; and would be forward enough to give his countrymen an account of me, and come back perhaps with a hundred or two of them, and make a feast upon me, at which he might be as merry as he us'd to be with those of his enemies when they were taken in war.

But I wrong'd the poor honest creature very much, for which I was very sorry afterwards. However, as my jealousy encreased, and held me some weeks, I was a little more circumspect, and not so familiar and kind to him as before; in which I was certainly in the wrong too, the honest grateful creature having no thought about it, but what consisted with the best principles, both as a religious Christian, and as a grateful friend, as appeared afterwards to my full satisfaction.

While my jealousy of him lasted, you may be sure I was every day pumping him to see if he would discover any of the new thoughts, which I suspected were in him; but I found every thing he said was so honest and so innocent, that I could find nothing to nourish my suspicion; and in spight of all my uneasiness he made me at last entirely his own again, nor did he in the least perceive that I was uneasie, and therefore I could not suspect him of deceit.

One day walking up the same hill, but the weather being haizy at sea, so that we could not see the continent, I call'd to him, and said, 'Friday, do not you wish your self in your own country, your own nation?' 'Yes,' he said, 'he be much O glad to be at his own nation.' 'What would you do there?' said I, 'would you turn wild again, eat men's flesh again, and be a savage as you were before?' He lookt full of concern, and shaking his head said, 'No, no, Friday tell them to live good, tell them to pray God, tell them to eat corn bread, cattle-flesh, milk, no eat man again.' 'Why then,' said I to him, 'they will kill you.' He look'd grave at that, and then said, 'No, they no kill me, they willing love learn.' He meant by this, they would be willing to learn. He added, they learn'd much of the bearded-mans that come in the boat. Then I ask'd him if he would go back to them. He smil'd at that, and told me he could not swim so far. I told him I would make a canoe for him. He told me he would go, if I would go with him. 'I go!' says I, 'why, they will eat me if I come there.' 'No, no,' says he, 'me make they no eat you; me make they much love you.' He meant he would tell them how I had kill'd his enemies, and sav'd his life, and so he would make them love me; then he told me as well as he could, how kind they were to seventeen white-men, or bearded-men, as he call'd them, who came on shore there in distress.

From this time I confess I had a mind to venture over, and see if I could possibly joyn with these bearded-men, who I made no doubt were Spaniards or Portuguese; not doubting but if I could we might find some method to escape from thence, being upon the continent, and a good company together; better than I could from an island 40 miles off the shore, and alone without help. So after some days I took Friday to work again, by way of discourse, and told him I would give him a boat to go back to his own nation; and accordingly I carry'd him to my frigate which lay on the other side of the island, and having clear'd it of water, for I always kept it sunk in the water, I brought it out, shewed it him, and we both went into it.

I found he was a most dextrous fellow at managing it, would make it go almost as swift and fast again as I could; so when he was in, I said to him, 'Well now, Friday, shall we go to your nation?' He look'd very dull at my saying so, which it seems was because he thought the boat too small to go so far. I told him then I had a bigger; so the next day I went to the place where the first boat lay which I had made, but which I could not get into water. He said that was big enough; but then as I had taken no care of it, and it had lain two or three and twenty years there, the sun had split and dry'd it, that it was in a manner rotten. Friday told me such a boat would do very well, and would carry 'much enough vittle, drink, bread,' that was his way of talking.

Upon the whole, I was by this time so fix'd upon my design of going over with him to the continent, that I told him we would go and make one as big as that, and he should go home in it. He answer'd not one word, but look'd very grave and sad. I ask'd him what was the matter with him. He ask'd me again thus, 'Why you angry mad with Friday, what me done?' I ask'd him what he meant; I told him I was not angry with him at all. 'No angry! No angry!' says he, repeating the words several times, 'why send Friday home away to my nation?' 'Why,' says I, 'Friday, did you not say you wish'd you were there?' 'Yes, yes,' says he, 'wish be both there, no wish Friday there, no master there.' In a word, he would not think of going there without me. 'I go there! Friday,' says I, 'what shall I do there?' He turn'd very quick upon me at this: 'You do great deal much good,' says he, 'you teach wild mans be good sober tame mans; you tell them know God, pray God, and live new life.' 'Alas! Friday,' says I, 'thou knowest not what thou sayest, I am but an ignorant man my self.' 'Yes, yes,' says he, 'you teachee me good, you teachee them good.' 'No, no, Friday,' says I, 'you shall go without me, leave me here to live by my self, as I did before.' He look'd confus'd again at that word, and running to one of the hatchets which he used to wear, he takes it up hastily, comes and gives it me. 'What must I do with this?' says I to him. 'You take, kill Friday,' says he. 'What must I kill you for?' said I again. He returns very quick, 'What you send Friday away for? take, kill Friday, no send Friday away?' This he spoke so earnestly, that I saw tears stand in his eyes. In a word, I so plainly discover'd the utmost affection in him to me, and a firm resolution in him, that I told him then, and often after, that I would never send him away from me, if he was willing to stay with me.

Upon the whole, as I found by all his discourse a settled affection to me, and that nothing should part him from me, so I found all the foundation of his desire to go to his own country was laid in his ardent affection to the people, and his hopes of my doing them good; a thing which as I had no notion of my self, so I had not the least thought or intention or desire of undertaking it. But still I found a strong inclination to my attempting an escape as above, founded on the supposition gather'd from the discourse, viz. that there were seventeen bearded men there; and therefore, without any more delay, I went to work with Friday to find out a great tree proper to fell, and make a large periagua or canoe to undertake the voyage. There were trees enough in the island to have built a little fleet, not of periagua's and canoes, but even of good large vessels. But the main thing I look'd at, was to get one so near the water that we might launch it when it was made, to avoid the mistake I committed at first.

At last, Friday pitch'd upon a tree, for I found he knew much better than I what kind of wood was fittest for it, nor can I tell to this day what wood to call the tree we cut down, except that it was very like the tree we call fustic,* or between that and the Nicaragua wood,* for it was much the same colour and smell. Friday was for burning the hollow or cavity of this tree out to make it for a boat. But I shew'd him how rather to cut it out with tools, which, after I had shew'd him how to use, he did very handily, and in about a month's hard labour we finished it, and made it very handsome, especially when with our axes, which I shew'd him how to handle, we cut and hew'd the out-side into the true shape of a boat; after this, however, it cost us near a fortnight's time to get her along as it were inch by inch upon great rowlers into the water. But when she was in, she would have carry'd twenty men with great ease.

When she was in the water, and tho' she was so big, it amazed me to see with what dexterity and how swift my man Friday would manage her, turn her, and paddle her along; so I ask'd him if he would, and if we might venture over in her. 'Yes,' he said, 'he venture over in her very well, tho' great blow wind.' However, I had a farther design that he knew nothing of, and that was to make a mast and sail and to fit her with an anchor and cable. As to a mast, that was easy enough to get; so I pitch'd upon a strait young cedar-tree, which I found near the place, and which there was great plenty of in the island, and I set Friday to work to cut it down, and gave him directions how to shape and order it. But as to the sail, that was my particular care; I knew I had old sails, or rather pieces of old sails enough; but as I had had them now six and twenty years by me, and had not been very careful to preserve them, not imagining that I should ever have this kind of use for them, I did not doubt but they were all rotten, and indeed most of them were so; however, I found two pieces which appear'd pretty good, and with these I went to work, and with a great deal of pains and awkward tedious stitching (you may be sure) for want of needles, I at length made a three corner'd ugly thing, like what we call in England a shoulder of mutton sail, to go with a boom at bottom, and a little short sprit at the top, such as usually our ships' long-boats sail with, and such as I best knew how to manage; because it was such a one as I had to the boat in which I made my escape from Barbary, as related in the first part of my story.

I was near two months performing this last work, viz. rigging and fitting my mast and sails; for I finish'd them very compleat, making a small stay, and a sail or fore-sail to it, to assist, if we should turn to windward; and which was more than all, I fix'd a rudder to the stern of her, to steer with; and though I was but a bungling shipwright, yet as I knew the usefulness, and even necessity of such a thing, I apply'd my self with so much pains to do it, that at last I brought it to pass; though considering the many dull contrivances I had for it that fail'd, I think it cost me almost as much labour as making the boat.

After all this was done too, I had my man Friday to teach as to what belong'd to the navigation of my boat; for though he knew very well how to paddle a canoe, he knew nothing what belong'd to a sail and a rudder; and was the most amaz'd, when he saw me work the boat to and again in the sea by the rudder, and how the sail gyb'd, and fill'd this way or that way, as the course we sail'd chang'd; I say, when he saw this, he stood like one astonish'd and amaz'd. However, with a little use, I made all these things familiar to him; and he became an expert sailor, except that as to the compass, I could make him understand very little of that. On the other hand, as there was very little cloudy weather, and seldom or never any fogs in those parts, there was the less occasion for a compass, seeing the stars were always to be seen by night, and the shore by day, except in the rainy seasons, and then no body car'd to stir abroad, either by land or sea.

I was now entred on the seven and twentieth year of my captivity in this place; though the three last years that I had this creature with me ought rather to be left out of the account, my habitation being quite of another kind than in all the rest of the time. I kept the anniversary of my landing there with the same thankfulness to God for His mercies, as at first; and if I had such cause of acknowledgment at first, I had much more so now, having such additional testimonies of the care of Providence over me, and the great hopes I had of being effectually and speedily deliver'd; for I had an invincible impression upon my thoughts, that my deliverance was at hand, and that I should not be another year in this place. However, I went on with my husbandry, digging, planting, fencing, as usual; I gather'd and cur'd my grapes, and did every necessary thing as before.

The rainy season was in the mean time upon me, when I kept more within doors than at other times; so I had stow'd our new vessel as secure as we could, bringing her up into the creek, where as I said, in the beginning I landed my rafts from the ship, and haling her up to the shore at high water mark, I made my man Friday dig a little dock, just big enough to hold her, and just deep enough to give her water enough to float in; and then when the tide was out, we made a strong dam cross the end of it, to keep the water out; and so she lay dry, as to the tide from the sea; and to keep the rain off, we laid a great many boughs of trees, so thick that she was as well thatch'd as a house; and thus we waited for the month of November and December, in which I design'd to make my adventure.

When the settled season began to come in, as the thought of my design return'd with the fair weather, I was preparing daily for the voyage; and the first thing I did was to lay by a certain quantity of provisions, being the stores for our voyage; and intended, in a week or a fortnight's time, to open the dock and launch out our boat. I was busy one morning upon some thing of this kind, when I call'd to Friday, and bid him go to the sea shore, and see if he could find a turtle or tortoise, a thing which we generally got once a week, for the sake of the eggs as well as the flesh. Friday had not been long gone, when he came running back, and flew over my outer wall, or fence, like one that felt not the ground, or the steps he set his feet on; and before I had time to speak to him, he cries out to me, 'O master! O master! O sorrow! O bad!' 'What's the matter, Friday?' says I. 'O yonder, there,' says he, 'one, two, three canoe! one, two, three!' By his way of speaking, I concluded there were six; but on inquiry, I found it was but three. 'Well, Friday,' says I, 'do not be frighted'; so I heartned him up as well as I could. However, I saw the poor fellow was most terribly scar'd; for nothing ran in his head but that they were come to look for him, and would cut him in pieces and eat him; and the poor fellow

trembled so, that I scarce knew what to do with him. I comforted
him as well as I could, and told him I was in as much danger as he,
and that they would eat me as well as him; 'but,' says I, 'Friday, we
must resolve to fight them; can you fight, Friday?' 'Me shoot,' says
he, 'but there come many great number.' 'No matter for that,' said
I again, 'our guns will fright them that we do not kill'; so I ask'd
him whether if I resolv'd to defend him, he would defend me, and
stand by me, and do just as I bid him. He said, 'Me die, when you
bid die, master'; so I went and fetch'd a good dram of rum, and
gave him; for I had been so good a husband of my rum, that I had a
great deal left. When he had drank it, I made him take the two
fowling-pieces, which we always carry'd, and load them with
large swan-shot, as big as small pistol bullets; then I took four
muskets, and loaded them with two slugs and five small bullets
each; and my two pistols I loaded with a brace of bullets each; I
hung my great sword as usual, naked by my side, and gave Friday
his hatchet.

When I had thus prepar'd my self, I took my perspective-glass,
and went up to the side of the hill, to see what I could discover;
and I found quickly, by my glass, that there were one and twenty
savages, three prisoners, and three canoes; and that their whole
business seem'd to be the triumphant banquet upon these three
humane bodies (a barbarous feast indeed), but nothing more than
as I had observ'd was usual with them.

I observ'd also, that they were landed not where they had done
when Friday made his escape, but nearer to my creek, where the
shore was low, and where a thick wood came close almost down
to the sea. This, with the abhorrence of the inhumane errand these
wretches came about, fill'd me with such indignation that I came
down again to Friday, and told him I was resolv'd to go down to
them, and kill them all; and ask'd him if he would stand by me. He
was now gotten over his fright, and his spirits being a little rais'd
with the dram I had given him, he was very chearful, and told me
as before, he would die, when I bid die.

In this fit of fury, I took first and divided the arms which I had
charg'd, as before, between us; I gave Friday one pistol to stick in
his girdle, and three guns upon his shoulder; and I took one pistol
and the other three my self; and in this posture we march'd out. I
took a small bottle of rum in my pocket, and gave Friday a large
bag, with more powder and bullet; and as to orders, I charg'd him
to keep close behind me, and not to stir, or shoot, or do any thing,

till I bid him; and in the mean time, not to speak a word. In this posture I fetch'd a compass* to my right-hand, of near a mile, as well to get over the creek as to get into the wood; so that I might come within shoot of them before I should be discover'd, which I had seen by my glass it was easy to do.

While I was making this march, my former thoughts returning, I began to abate my resolution; I do not mean that I entertain'd any fear of their number; for as they were naked, unarm'd wretches, 'tis certain I was superior to them; nay, though I had been alone; but it occur'd to my thoughts, what call, what occasion, much less what necessity I was in to go and dip my hands in blood, to attack people who had neither done, or intended me any wrong, who as to me were innocent, and whose barbarous customs were their own disaster, being in them a token indeed of God's having left them, with the other nations of that part of the world, to such stupidity, and to such inhumane courses; but did not call me to take upon me to be a judge of their actions, much less an executioner of His justice; that whenever He thought fit, He would take the cause into His own hands, and by national vengeance punish them as a people, for national crimes; but that in the mean time, it was none of my business; that it was true, Friday might justify it, because he was a declar'd enemy, and in a state of war with those very particular people; and it was lawful for him to attack them; but I could not say the same with respect to me. These things were so warmly press'd upon my thoughts, all the way as I went, that I resolv'd I would only go and place my self near them, that I might observe their barbarous feast, and that I would act then as God should direct; but that unless something offer'd that was more a call to me than yet I knew of, I would not meddle with them.

With this resolution I enter'd the wood, and with all possible wariness and silence, Friday following close at my heels, I march'd till I came to the skirt of the wood, on the side which was next to them; only that one corner of the wood lay between me and them; here I call'd softly to Friday, and shewing him a great tree, which was just at the corner of the wood, I bad him go to the tree, and bring me word if he could see there plainly what they were doing; he did so, and came immediately back to me, and told me they might be plainly view'd there; that they were all about their fire, eating the flesh of one of their prisoners; and that another lay bound upon the sand, a little from them, which he said they would kill next, and which fir'd all the very soul within me; he told me it was not one of their nation, but one of the bearded men, who he had told me of, that came to their country in the boat. I was fill'd with horror at the very naming the white bearded man, and going to the tree, I saw plainly by my glass a white man who lay upon the beach of the sea, with his hands and his feet ty'd, with flags, or things like rushes; and that he was an European, and had cloaths on.

There was another tree, and a little thicket beyond it, about fifty yards nearer to them than the place where I was, which by going a little way about, I saw I might come at undiscover'd, and that then I should be within half shot of them; so I with-held my passion, though I was indeed enrag'd to the highest degree, and going back about twenty paces, I got behind some bushes, which held all the way till I came to the other tree; and then I came to a little rising ground, which gave me a full view of them, at the distance of about eighty yards.

I had now not a moment to lose; for nineteen of the dreadful wretches sat upon the ground, all close huddled together, and had just sent the other two to butcher the poor Christian, and bring him perhaps limb by limb to their fire, and they were stoop'd down to untie the bands at his feet; I turn'd to Friday. 'Now, Friday,' said I, 'do as I bid thee'; Friday said he would; 'Then, Friday,' says I, 'do exactly as you see me do, fail in nothing'; so I set down one of the muskets and the fowling-piece upon the ground, and Friday did the like by his; and with the other musket I took my aim at the savages, bidding him do the like; then asking him if he was ready, he said yes. 'Then fire at them,' said I; and the same moment I fir'd also.

Friday took his aim so much better than I, that on the side that he shot, he kill'd two of them, and wounded three more; and on my side, I kill'd one, and wounded two. They were, you may be sure, in a dreadful consternation; and all of them, who were not hurt, jump'd up upon their feet, but did not immediately know which way to run, or which way to look; for they knew not from whence their destruction came. Friday kept his eyes close upon me, that as I had bid him, he might observe what I did; so as soon as the first shot was made, I threw down the piece, and took up the fowling-piece, and Friday did the like; he see me cock and present, he did the same again. 'Are you ready, Friday?' said I; 'Yes,' says he; 'Let fly then,' says I, 'in the name of God,' and with that I fir'd again among the amaz'd wretches, and so did Friday; and as our pieces were now loaden with what I call'd swan-shot, or small pistol bullets, we found only two drop; but so many were wounded, that they run about yelling and skreaming like mad creatures, all bloody, and miserably wounded, most of them; whereof three more fell quickly after, though not quite dead.

'Now, Friday,' says I, laying down the discharg'd pieces, and taking up the musket which was yet loaden, 'follow me,' says I; which he did, with a great deal of courage; upon which I rush'd out of the wood, and shew'd my self, and Friday, close at my foot; as soon as I perceiv'd they saw me, I shouted as loud as I could, and bad Friday do so too; and running as fast as I could, which by the way, was not very fast, being loaden with arms as I was, I made directly towards the poor victim, who was, as I said, lying upon the beach or shore, between the place where they sat and the sea. The two butchers who were just going to work with him, had left him at the surprize of our first fire, and fled in a terrible fright to the sea side, and had jump'd into a canoe, and three more of the rest made the same way; I turn'd to Friday, and bid him step forwards, and fire at them; he understood me immediately, and running about forty yards, to be near them, he shot at them, and I thought he had kill'd them all; for I see them all fall of a heap into the boat; though I saw two of them up again quickly: however, he kill'd two of them, and wounded the third; so that he lay down in the bottom of the boat, as if he had been dead.

While my man Friday fir'd at them, I pull'd out my knife, and cut the flags that bound the poor victim, and loosing his hands and feet, I lifted him up, and ask'd him in the Portuguese tongue what he was. He answer'd in Latin, 'Christianus'; but was so weak and faint, that he could scarce stand or speak; I took my bottle out of my pocket, and gave it him, making signs that he should drink, which he did; and I gave him a piece of bread, which he eat; then I ask'd him what countryman he was, and he said, 'Espagniole'; and being a little recover'd, let me know by all the signs he could possibly make, how much he was in my debt for his deliverance. 'Seignior,' said I, with as much Spanish as I could make up, 'we will talk afterwards; but we must fight now; if you have any strength left, take this pistol and sword, and lay about you.' He took them very thankfully, and no sooner had he the arms in his hands, but as if they had put new vigour into him, he flew upon his murtherers like a fury, and had cut two of them in pieces in an instant; for the truth is, as the whole was a surprize to them, so the poor creatures were so much frighted with the noise of our pieces, that they fell down for meer amazement and fear; and had no more power to attempt their own escape, than their flesh had to resist our shot; and that was the case of those five that Friday shot at in the boat; for as three of them fell with the hurt they receiv'd, so the other two fell with the fright.

I kept my piece in my hand still, without firing, being willing to keep my charge ready, because I had given the Spaniard my pistol and sword; so I call'd to Friday, and bad him run up to the tree from whence we first fir'd, and fetch the arms which lay there, that had been discharg'd, which he did with great swiftness; and then giving him my musket, I sat down my self to load all the rest again, and bad them come to me when they wanted. While I was loading these pieces, there happen'd a fierce engagement between the Spaniard and one of the savages, who made at him with one of their great wooden swords, the same weapon that was to have kill'd him before, if I had not prevented it. The Spaniard, who was as bold and as brave as could be imagin'd, though weak, had fought this Indian a good while, and had cut him two great wounds on his head; but the savage being a stout lusty fellow, closing in with him, had thrown him down (being faint) and was wringing my sword out of his hand, when the Spaniard, tho' undermost, wisely quitting the sword, drew the pistol from his girdle, shot the savage through the body, and kill'd him upon the spot, before I, who was running to help him, could come near him.

Friday, being now left to his liberty, pursu'd the flying wretches with no weapon in his hand but his hatchet; and with that he dispatch'd those three who, as I said before, were wounded at first and fallen, and all the rest he could come up with, and the Spaniard coming to me for a gun, I gave him one of the fowling-pieces, with which he pursu'd two of the savages, and wounded them both; but as he was not able to run, they both got from him into the wood, where Friday pursu'd them, and kill'd one of them; but the other was too nimble for him, and though he was wounded, yet had plunged himself into the sea, and swam with all his might off to those two who were left in the canoe, which three in the canoe, with one wounded, who we know not whether he dy'd or no, were all that escap'd our hands of one and twenty. The account of the rest is as follows:

3 kill'd at our first shot from the tree.
2 kill'd at the next shot.
2 kill'd by Friday in the boat.
2 kill'd by ditto, of those at first wounded.
1 kill'd by ditto, in the wood.
3 kill'd by the Spaniard.
4 kill'd, being found dropp'd here and there of their wounds, or kill'd
   by Friday in his chase of them.
4 escap'd in the boat, whereof one wounded if not dead.
—
21 in all.
—

Those that were in the canoe work'd hard to get out of gun-shot; and though Friday made two or three shot at them, I did not find that he hit any of them. Friday would fain have had me took one of their canoes, and pursu'd them; and indeed I was very anxious about their escape, least carrying the news home to their people, they should come back perhaps with two or three hundred of their canoes, and devour us by meer multitude; so I consented to pursue them by sea, and running to one of their canoes, I jump'd in, and bad Friday follow me; but when I was in the canoe, I was surpriz'd to find another poor creature lye there alive, bound hand and foot, as the Spaniard was, for the slaughter, and almost dead with fear, not knowing what the matter was; for he had not been able to look up over the side of the boat, he was ty'd so hard, neck and heels, and had been ty'd so long that he had really but little life in him.

I immediately cut the twisted flags or rushes which they had bound him with, and would have helped him up; but he could not stand or speak, but groan'd most piteously, believing it seems still that he was only unbound in order to be kill'd.

When Friday came to him, I bade him speak to him, and tell him of his deliverance, and pulling out my bottle, made him give the poor wretch a dram, which, with the news of his being deliver'd, reviv'd him, and he sat up in the boat; but when Friday came to hear him speak, and look in his face, it would have mov'd any one to tears, to have seen how Friday kiss'd him, embrac'd him, hugg'd him, cry'd, laugh'd, hollow'd, jump'd about, danc'd, sung, and then cry'd again, wrung his hands, beat his own face and head, and then sung and jump'd about again, like a distracted creature. It was a good while before I could make him speak to me, or tell me what was the matter; but when he came a little to himself, he told me that it was his father.

It is not easy for me to express how it mov'd me to see what extasy and filial affection had work'd in this poor savage, at the sight of his father, and of his being deliver'd from death; nor indeed can I describe half the extravagancies of his affection after this; for he went into the boat and out of the boat a great many times. When he went in to him, he would sit down by him, open his breast, and hold his father's head close to his bosom, half an hour together, to nourish it; then he took his arms and ankles, which were numb'd and stiff with the binding, and chaffed and rubbed them with his hands, and I perceiving what the case was, gave him some rum out of my bottle to rub them with, which did them a great deal of good.

This action put an end to our pursuit of the canoe with the other savages, who were now gotten almost out of sight; and it was happy for us that we did not; for it blew so hard within two hours after, and before they could be gotten a quarter of their way, and continued blowing so hard all night, and that from the north-west, which was against them, that I could not suppose their boat could live, or that they ever reach'd to their own coast.

But to return to Friday, he was so busy about his father, that I could not find in my heart to take him off for some time: but after I thought he could leave him a little, I call'd him to me, and he came jumping and laughing, and pleas'd to the highest extream; then I ask'd him if he had given his father any bread. He shook his head, and said, 'None: ugly dog eat all up self'; so I gave him a cake of bread out of a little pouch I carry'd on purpose; I also gave him a dram for himself, but he would not taste it, but carry'd it to his father. I had in my pocket also two or three bunches of my raisins, so I gave him a handful of them for his father. He had no sooner given his father these raisins, but I saw him come out of the boat, and run away, as if he had been bewitch'd, he run at such a rate; for he was the swiftest fellow of his foot that ever I saw; I say, he run at such a rate, that he was out of sight, as it were, in an instant; and though I call'd, and hollow'd too, after him, it was all one, away he went, and in a quarter of an hour I saw him come back again, though not so fast as he went; and as he came nearer, I found his pace was slacker because he had something in his hand.

When he came up to me, I found he had been quite home for an earthen jugg or pot to bring his father some fresh water, and that he had got two more cakes or loaves of bread: the bread he gave me, but the water he carry'd to his father: however, as I was very thirsty too, I took a little sup of it. This water reviv'd his father more than all the rum or spirits I had given him; for he was just fainting with thirst.

When his father had drank, I call'd to him to know if there was any water left; he said yes; and I bad him give it to the poor Spaniard, who was in as much want of it as his father; and I sent one of the cakes, that Friday brought, to the Spaniard too, who was indeed very weak, and was reposing himself upon a green place under the shade of a tree; and whose limbs were also very stiff, and very much swell'd with the rude bandage he had been ty'd with. When I saw that upon Friday's coming to him with the water, he sat up and drank, and took the bread, and began to eat, I went to him and gave him a handful of raisins; he look'd up in my face with all the tokens of gratitude and thankfulness that could appear in any countenance; but was so weak, notwithstanding he had so exerted himself in the fight, that he could not stand up upon his feet; he try'd to do it two or three times, but was really not able, his ankles were so swell'd and so painful to him; so I bad him sit still, and caused Friday to rub his ankles, and bathe them with rum, as he had done his father's.

I observ'd the poor affectionate creature every two minutes, or perhaps less, all the while he was here, turn'd his head about, to see if his father was in the same place and posture as he left him sitting; and at last he found he was not to be seen; at which he started up, and without speaking a word, flew with that swiftness to him, that one could scarce perceive his feet to touch the ground as he went. But when he came, he only found he had laid himself down to ease his limbs; so Friday came back to me presently, and I then spoke to the Spaniard to let Friday help him up if he could, and lead him to the boat, and then he should carry him to our dwelling, where I would take care of him. But Friday, a lusty strong fellow, took the Spaniard quite up upon his back, and carry'd him away to the boat, and set him down softly upon the side or gunnel of the canoe, with his feet in the inside of it, and then lifted him quite in, and set him close to his father, and presently stepping out again, launched the boat off, and paddled it along the shore faster than I could walk, tho' the wind blew pretty hard too; so he brought them both safe into our creek; and leaving them in the boat, runs away to fetch the other canoe. As he pass'd me, I spoke to him, and ask'd him whither he went; he told me, 'Go fetch more boat'; so away he went like the wind; for sure never man or horse run like him, and he had the other canoe in the creek, almost as soon as I got to it by land; so he wafted me over, and then went to help our new guests out of the boat, which he did; but they were neither of them able to walk; so that poor Friday knew not what to do.

To remedy this, I went to work in my thought, and calling to Friday to bid them sit down on the bank while he came to me, I soon made a kind of hand-barrow to lay them on, and Friday and I carry'd them up both together upon it between us. But when we got them to the outside of our wall or fortification, we were at a worse loss than before; for it was impossible to get them over; and I was resolv'd not to break it down: so I set to work again; and Friday and I, in about 2 hours' time, made a very handsom tent, cover'd with old sails, and above that with boughs of trees, being in the space without our outward fence, and between that and the grove of young wood which I had planted: and here we made them two beds of such things as I had, viz. of good rice-straw, with blankets laid upon it to lye on, and another to cover them on each bed.

My island was now peopled, and I thought my self very rich in subjects; and it was a merry reflection which I frequently made, how like a king I look'd. First of all, the whole country was my own meer property; so that I had an undoubted right of dominion. 2dly, my people were perfectly subjected: I was absolute lord and lawgiver; they all owed their lives to me, and were ready to lay down their lives, if there had been occasion of it, for me. It was remarkable too, we had but three subjects, and they were of three different religions. My man Friday was a Protestant, his father was a pagan and a cannibal, and the Spaniard was a Papist: however, I allow'd liberty of conscience throughout my dominions. But this is by the way.

As soon as I had secur'd my two weak rescued prisoners, and given them shelter, and a place to rest them upon, I began to think of making some provision for them. And the first thing I did, I order'd Friday to take a yearling goat, betwixt a kid and a goat, out of my particular flock, to be kill'd, when I cut off the hinder quarter, and chopping it into small pieces, I set Friday to work to boiling and stewing, and made them a very good dish, I assure you, of flesh and broth, having put some barley and rice also into the broth; and as I cook'd it without doors, for I made no fire within my inner wall, so I carry'd it all into the new tent; and having set a table there for them, I sat down and eat my own dinner also with them, and, as well as I could, chear'd them and encourag'd them; Friday being my interpreter, especially to his father, and indeed to the Spaniard too; for the Spaniard spoke the language of the savages pretty well.

After we had dined, or rather supped, I order'd Friday to take one of the canoes, and go and fetch our muskets and other fire-arms, which for want of time we had left upon the place of battle, and the next day I order'd him to go and bury the dead bodies of the savages, which lay open to the sun, and would presently be offensive; and I also ordered him to bury the horrid remains of their barbarous feast, which I knew were pretty much, and which I could not think of doing my self; nay, I could not bear to see them, if I went that way: all which he punctually performed, and defaced the very appearance of the savages being there; so that when I went again, I could scarce know where it was, otherwise than by the corner of the wood pointing to the place.

I then began to enter into a little conversation with my two new subjects; and first I set Friday to enquire of his father, what he thought of the escape of the savages in that canoe, and whether we might expect a return of them with a power too great for us to resist. His first opinion was, that the savages in the boat never could live out the storm which blew that night they went off, but must of necessity be drowned or driven south to those other shores, where they were as sure to be devoured as they were to be drowned if they were cast away; but as to what they would do if they came safe on shore, he said he knew not; but it was his opinion that they were so dreadfully frighted with the manner of their being attack'd, the noise and the fire, that he believed they would tell their people they were all kill'd by thunder and lightning, not by the hand of man, and that the two which appear'd, viz. Friday and me, were two heavenly spirits or furies, come down to destroy them, and not men with weapons. This he said he knew, because he heard them all cry out so in their language to one another, for it was impossible to them to conceive that a man could dart fire, and speak thunder, and kill at a distance without lifting up the hand, as was done now. And this old savage was in the right, for, as I understood since by other hands, the savages never attempted to go over to the island afterwards; they were so terrified with the accounts given by those four men (for it seems they did escape the sea), that they believ'd whoever went to that enchanted island would be destroy'd with fire from the gods.

This however I knew not, and therefore was under continual apprehensions for a good while, and kept always upon my guard, me and all my army; for as we were now four of us, I would have ventur'd upon a hundred of them fairly in the open field at any time.

In a little time, however, no more canoes appearing, the fear of their coming wore off, and I began to take my former thoughts of a voyage to the main into consideration, being likewise assur'd by Friday's father, that I might depend upon good usage from their nation on his account, if I would go.

But my thoughts were a little suspended when I had a serious discourse with the Spaniard, and when I understood that there were sixteen* more of his countrymen and Portuguese, who having been cast away, and made their escape to that side, liv'd there at peace indeed with the savages, but were very sore put to it for necessaries, and indeed for life. I ask'd him all the particulars of their voyage, and found they were a Spanish ship bound from the Rio de la Plata to the Havana, being directed to leave their loading there, which was chiefly hides and silver, and to bring back what European goods they could meet with there; that they had five Portuguese seamen on board, who they took out of another wreck; that five of their own men were drowned when the first ship was lost, and that these escaped thro' infinite dangers and hazards, and arriv'd almost starv'd on the cannibal coast, where they expected to have been devour'd every moment.

He told me they had some arms with them, but they were perfectly useless, for that they had neither powder or ball, the washing of the sea having spoil'd all their powder but a little, which they used at their first landing to provide themselves some food.

I ask'd him what he thought would become of them there, and if they had form'd no design of making any escape. He said they had many consultations about it, but that having neither vessel, or tools to build one, or provisions of any kind, their councils always ended in tears and despair.

I ask'd him how he thought they would receive a proposal from me, which might tend towards an escape, and whether, if they were all here, it might not be done. I told him with freedom, I fear'd mostly their treachery and ill usage of me, if I put my life in their hands; for that gratitude was no inherent virtue in the nature of man; nor did men always square their dealings by the obligations they had receiv'd, so much as they did by the advantages they expected. I told him it would be very hard that I should be the instrument of their deliverance, and that they should afterwards make me their prisoner in New Spain, where an English man was certain to be made a sacrifice, what necessity, or what accident soever, brought him thither; and that I had rather be deliver'd up to the savages, and be devour'd alive, than fall into the merciless claws of the priests, and be carry'd into the Inquisition. I added, that otherwise I was perswaded, if they were all here, we might, with so many hands, build a bark large enough to carry us all away, either to the Brasils south-ward, or to the islands or Spanish coast north-ward; but that if in requital they should, when I had put weapons into their hands, carry me by force among their own people, I might be ill used for my kindness to them, and make my case worse than it was before.

He answer'd with a great deal of candor and ingenuity, that their condition was so miserable, and they were so sensible of it, that he believed they would abhor the thought of using any man unkindly that should contribute to their deliverance; and that, if I pleased, he would go to them with the old man, and discourse with them about it, and return again, and bring me their answer: that he would make conditions with them upon their solemn oath, that they should be absolutely under my leading, as their commander and captain, and that they should swear upon the holy sacraments and the Gospel, to be true to me, and to go to such Christian country as that I should agree to, and no other; and to be directed wholly and absolutely by my orders, 'till they were landed safely in such country as I intended; and that he would bring a contract from under their hands for that purpose.

Then he told me he would first swear to me himself that he would never stir from me as long as he liv'd, 'till I gave him orders; and that he would take my side to the last drop of his blood, if there should happen the least breach of faith among his country-men.

He told me they were all of them very civil honest men, and they were under the greatest distress imaginable, having neither weapons or cloaths, nor any food, but at the mercy and discretion of the savages; out of all hopes of ever returning to their own country; and that he was sure, if I would undertake their relief, they would live and die by me.

Upon these assurances, I resolv'd to venture to relieve them, if possible, and to send the old savage and this Spaniard over to them to treat. But when we had gotten all things in a readiness to go, the Spaniard himself started an objection, which had so much prudence in it on one hand, and so much sincerity on the other hand, that I could not but be very well satisfy'd in it; and by his advice, put off the deliverance of his comerades for at least half a year. The case was thus:

He had been with us now about a month; during which time I had let him see in what manner I had provided, with the assistance of Providence, for my support; and he saw evidently what stock of corn and rice I had laid up; which as it was more than sufficient for my self, so it was not sufficient, at least without good husbandry, for my family, now it was encreas'd to number four: but much less would it be sufficient, if his country-men, who were, as he said, fourteen still alive, should come over. And least of all should it be sufficient to victual our vessel, if we should build one, for a voyage to any of the Christian colonies of America. So he told me, he thought it would be more advisable to let him and the two other dig and cultivate some more land, as much as I could spare seed to sow; and that we should wait another harvest, that we might have a supply of corn for his country-men when they should come; for want might be a temptation to them to disagree, or not to think themselves delivered, otherwise than out of one difficulty into another. 'You know,' says he, 'the children of Israel, though they rejoyc'd at first for their being deliver'd out of Egypt, yet rebell'd even against God Himself that deliver'd them, when they came to want bread in the wilderness.'

His caution was so seasonable, and his advice so good, that I could not but be very well pleased with his proposal, as well as I was satisfy'd with his fidelity. So we fell to digging all four of us, as well as the wooden tools we were furnish'd with permitted; and in about a month's time, by the end of which it was seed time, we had gotten as much land cur'd and trim'd up, as we sowed 22 bushels of barley on, and 16 jarrs of rice, which was in short all the seed we had to spare; nor indeed did we leave our selves barley sufficient for our own food, for the six months that we had to expect our crop, that is to say, reckoning from the time we set our seed aside for sowing; for it is not to be supposed it is six months in the ground in the country.

Having now society enough, and our number being sufficient to put us out of fear of the savages, if they had come, unless their number had been very great, we went freely all over the island, where-ever we found occasion; and as here we had our escape or deliverance upon our thoughts, it was impossible, at least for me, to have the means of it out of mine; to this purpose, I mark'd out several trees which I thought fit for our work, and I set Friday and his father to cutting them down; and then I caused the Spaniard, to whom I imparted my thought on that affair, to oversee and direct their work. I shewed them with what indefatigable pains I had hewed a large tree into single planks, and I caused them to do the like, till they had made about a dozen large planks of good oak,* near 2 foot broad, 35 foot long, and from 2 inches to 4 inches thick: what prodigious labour it took up, any one may imagine.

At the same time I contrived to encrease my little flock of tame goats as much as I could; and to this purpose, I made Friday and the Spaniard go out one day, and my self with Friday the next day; for we took our turns: and by this means we got above 20 young kids to breed up with the rest; for when-ever we shot the dam, we saved the kids, and added them to our flock. But above all, the season for curing the grapes coming on, I caused such a prodigious quantity to be hung up in the sun, that I believe, had we been at Alicant, where the raisins of the sun are cur'd, we could have fill'd 60 or 80 barrels; and these with our bread was a great part of our food, and very good living too, I assure you; for it is an exceeding nourishing food.

It was now harvest, and our crop in good order; it was not the most plentiful encrease I had seen in the island, but, however, it was enough to answer our end; for from our 22 bushels of barley we brought in and thrashed out above 220 bushels; and the like in proportion of the rice, which was store enough for our food to the next harvest, tho' all the 16 Spaniards had been on shore with me; or if we had been ready for a voyage, it would very plentifully have victualled our ship, to have carry'd us to any part of the world, that is to say, of America.

When we had thus hous'd and secur'd our magazine of corn, we fell to work to make more wicker work, viz. great baskets in which we kept it; and the Spaniard was very handy and dexterous at this part, and often blam'd me that I did not make some things, for defence, of this kind of work; but I saw no need of it.

And now having a full supply of food for all the guests I expected, I gave the Spaniard leave to go over to the main, to see what he could do with those he had left behind him there. I gave him a strict charge in writing* not to bring any man with him, who would not first swear in the presence of himself and of the old savage that he would no way injure, fight with, or attack the person he should find in the island, who was so kind to send for them in order to their deliverance; but that they would stand by and defend him against all such attempts, and where-ever they went, would be entirely under and subjected to his commands; and that this should be put in writing, and signed with their hands. How we were to have this done, when I knew they had neither pen or ink, that indeed was a question which we never asked.

Under these instructions, the Spaniard and the old savage, the father of Friday, went away in one of the canoes, which they might be said to come in, or rather were brought in, when they came as prisoners to be devour'd by the savages.

I gave each of them a musket with a firelock on it, and about eight charges of powder and ball, charging them to be very good husbands of both, and not to use either of them but upon urgent occasion.

This was a chearful work, being the first measures used by me in view of my deliverance for now 27 years and some days. I gave them provisions of bread, and of dry'd grapes, sufficient for themselves for many days, and sufficient for all their country-men for about eight days' time; and wishing them a good voyage, I see them go, agreeing with them about a signal they should hang out at their return, by which I should know them again, when they came back, at a distance, before they came on shore.

They went away with a fair gale on the day that the moon was at full by my account, in the month of October: but as for an exact reckoning of days, after I had once lost it, I could never recover it again; nor had I kept even the number of years so punctually as to be sure that I was right, tho' as it prov'd, when I afterwards examin'd my account, I found I had kept a true reckoning of years.

It was no less than eight days I had waited for them, when a strange and unforeseen accident interven'd, of which the like has not perhaps been heard of in history. I was fast asleep in my hutch one morning, when my man Friday came running in to me, and call'd aloud, 'Master, master, they are come, they are come.'

I jump'd up, and regardless of danger, I went out, as soon as I could get my cloaths on, thro' my little grove, which by the way was by this time grown to be a very thick wood; I say, regardless of danger, I went without my arms, which was not my custom to do: but I was surpriz'd, when turning my eyes to the sea, I presently saw a boat at about a league and an half's distance, standing in for the shore, with a shoulder of mutton sail, as they call it; and the wind blowing pretty fair to bring them in; also I observ'd presently that they did not come from that side which the shore lay on, but from the southernmost end of the island. Upon this I call'd Friday in, and bid him lie close, for these were not the people we look'd for, and that we might not know yet whether they were friends or enemies.

In the next place, I went in to fetch my perspective glass, to see what I could make of them; and having taken the ladder out, I climb'd up to the top of the hill, as I used to do when I was apprehensive of any thing, and to take my view the plainer without being discover'd.

I had scarce set my foot on the hill, when my eye plainly discover'd a ship lying at an anchor, at about two leagues and an half's distance from me south-south-east, but not above a league and an half from the shore. By my observation it appear'd plainly to be an English ship, and the boat appear'd to be an English long-boat.

I cannot express the confusion I was in, tho' the joy of seeing a ship, and one who I had reason to believe was mann'd by my own country-men, and consequently friends, was such as I cannot describe; but yet I had some secret doubts hung about me, I cannot tell from whence they came, bidding me keep upon my guard. In the first place, it occurr'd to me to consider what business an English ship could have in that part of the world, since it was not the way to or from any part of the world where the English had any traffick; and I knew there had been no storms to drive them in there, as in distress; and that if they were English really, it was most probable that they were here upon no good design; and that I had better continue as I was, than fall into the hands of thieves and murtherers.

Let no man despise the secret hints and notices of danger, which sometimes are given him, when he may think there is no possibility of its being real. That such hints and notices are given us, I believe few that have made any observations of things can deny; that they are certain discoveries of an invisible world, and a converse of spirits, we cannot doubt; and if the tendency of them seems to be to warn us of danger, why should we not suppose they are from some friendly agent, whether supreme, or inferior, and subordinate, is not the question; and that they are given for our good?

The present question abundantly confirms me in the justice of this reasoning; for had I not been made cautious by this secret admonition, come it from whence it will, I had been undone inevitably, and in a far worse condition than before, as you will see presently.

I had not kept my self in this posture, but I saw the boat draw near the shore, as if they look'd for a creek to thrust in at for the convenience of landing; however, as they did not come quite far enough, they did not see the little inlet where I formerly landed my rafts; but run their boat on shore upon the beach, at about half a mile from me, which was very happy for me; for otherwise they would have landed just, as I may say, at my door, and would soon have beaten me out of my castle, and perhaps have plunder'd me of all I had.

When they were on shore I was fully satisfy'd that they were English men; at least, most of them; one or two I thought were Dutch, but it did not prove so. They were in all eleven men, whereof three of them I found were unarm'd, and, as I thought, bound; and when the first four or five of them were jump'd on shore, they took those three out of the boat as prisoners. One of the three I could perceive using the most passionate gestures of entreaty, affliction, and despair, even to a kind of extravagance; the other two I could perceive lifted up their hands sometimes, and appear'd concern'd indeed, but not to such a degree as the first.

I was perfectly confounded at the sight, and knew not what the meaning of it should be. Friday call'd out to me in English, as well as he could, 'O master! you see English mans eat prisoner as well as savage mans.' 'Why,' says I, 'Friday, do you think they are a going to eat them then?' 'Yes,' says Friday, 'they will eat them.' 'No, no,' says I, 'Friday, I am afraid they will murther them indeed, but you may be sure they will not eat them.'

All this while I had no thought of what the matter really was, but stood trembling with the horror of the sight, expecting every moment when the three prisoners should be kill'd; nay, once I saw one of the villains lift up his arm with a great cutlash, as the seamen call it, or sword, to strike one of the poor men; and I expected to see him fall every moment, at which all the blood in my body seem'd to run chill in my veins.

I wish'd heartily now for my Spaniard, and the savage that was gone with him; or that I had any way to have come undiscover'd within shot of them, that I might have rescu'd the three men; for I saw no fire arms they had among them; but it fell out to my mind another way.

After I had observ'd the outrageous usage of the three men by the insolent seamen, I observ'd the fellows run scattering about the land, as if they wanted to see the country. I observ'd that the three other men had liberty to go also where they pleas'd; but they sat down all three upon the ground, very pensive, and look'd like men in despair.

This put me in mind of the first time when I came on shore, and began to look about me; how I gave my self over for lost; how wildly I look'd round me; what dreadful apprehensions I had; and how I lodg'd in the tree all night for fear of being devour'd by wild beasts.

As I knew nothing that night of the supply I was to receive by the providential driving of the ship nearer the land, by the storms and tide, by which I have since been so long nourish'd and supported; so these three poor desolate men knew nothing how certain of deliverance and supply they were, how near it was to them, and how effectually and really they were in a condition of safety, at the same time that they thought themselves lost, and their case desperate.

So little do we see before us in the world, and so much reason have we to depend chearfully upon the great Maker of the world, that He does not leave his creatures so absolutely destitute, but that in the worst circumstances they have always something to be thankful for, and sometimes are nearer their deliverance than they imagine; nay, are even brought to their deliverance by the means by which they seem to be brought to their destruction.

It was just at the top of high-water when these people came on shore, and while partly they stood parlying with the prisoners they brought, and partly while they rambled about to see what kind of a place they were in, they had carelessly staid till the tide was spent and the water was ebb'd considerably away, leaving their boat a-ground.

They had left two men in the boat, who, as I found afterwards, having drank a little too much brandy, fell a-sleep; however, one of them waking sooner than the other, and finding the boat too fast a-ground for him to stir it, hollow'd for the rest who were straggling about, upon which they all soon came to the boat; but it was past all their strength to launch her, the boat being very heavy, and the shore on that side being a soft ousy sand, almost like a quick-sand.

In this condition, like true seamen who are perhaps the least of all mankind given to fore-thought, they gave it over, and away they stroll'd abut the country again; and I heard one of them say aloud to another, calling them off from the boat, 'Why, let her alone, Jack, can't ye, she will float next tide'; by which I was fully confirm'd in the main enquiry, of what countrymen they were.

All this while I kept myself very close, not once daring to stir out of my castle, any farther than to my place of observation, near the top of the hill; and very glad I was, to think how well it was fortify'd. I knew it was no less than ten hours before the boat could be on float again, and by that time it would be dark, and I might be at more liberty to see their motions, and to hear their discourse, if they had any.

In the mean time, I fitted my self up for a battle, as before; though with more caution, knowing I had to do with another kind of enemy than I had at first: I order'd Friday also, who I had made an excellent marksman with his gun, to load himself with arms: I took my self two fowling-pieces, and I gave him three muskets. My figure indeed was very fierce; I had my formidable goat-skin coat on, with the great cap I have mention'd, a naked sword by my side, two pistols in my belt, and a gun upon each shoulder.

It was my design, as I said above, not to have made any attempt till it was dark: but about two a clock, being the heat of the day, I found that in short they were all gone straggling into the woods, and, as I thought, were laid down to sleep. The three poor distressed men, too anxious for their condition to get any sleep, were however set down under the shelter of a great tree, at about a quarter of a mile from me, and, as I thought, out of sight of any of the rest.

Upon this I resolv'd to discover my self to them, and learn something of their condition. Immediately I march'd in the figure as above, my man Friday at a good distance behind me, as formidable for his arms as I, but not making quite so staring a spectre-like figure as I did.

I came as near them undiscover'd as I could, and then, before any of them saw me, I call'd aloud to them in Spanish, 'What are ye, gentlemen?'

They started up at the noise, but were ten times more confounded when they saw me, and the uncouth figure that I made. They made no answer at all, but I thought I perceiv'd them just going to fly from me, when I spoke to them in English: 'Gentlemen,' said I, 'do not be surpriz'd at me; perhaps you may have a friend near you when you did not expect it.' 'He must be sent directly from heaven then,' said one of them very gravely to me, and pulling off his hat at the same time to me, 'for our condition is past the help of man.' 'All help is from heaven, sir,' said I. 'But can you put a stranger in the way how to help you, for you seem to me to be in some great distress? I saw you when you landed, and when you seem'd to make applications to the brutes that came with you, I saw one of them lift up his sword to kill you.'

The poor man, with tears running down his face, and trembling, looking like one astonish'd, return'd, 'Am I talking to god or man! Is it a real man, or an angel!' 'Be in no fear about that, sir,' said I, 'if God had sent an angel to relieve you, he would have come better cloath'd, and arm'd after another manner than you see me in; pray lay aside your fears, I am a man, an English-man, and dispos'd to assist you, you see; I have one servant only; we have arms and ammunition; tell us freely, can we serve you? — What is your case?'

'Our case,' said he, 'sir, is too long to tell you, while our murtherers are so near; but in short, sir, I was commander of that ship, my men have mutinied against me; they have been hardly prevail'd on not to murther me, and at last have set me on shore in this desolate place, with these two men with me, one my mate, the other a passenger, where we expected to perish, believing the place to be uninhabited, and know not yet what to think of it.'

'Where are those brutes, your enemies,' said I, 'do you know where they are gone?' 'There they lye, sir,' said he, pointing to a thicket of trees; 'my heart trembles, for fear they have seen us, and heard you speak; if they have, they will certainly murther us all.'

'Have they any fire-arms?' said I. He answered they had only two pieces, and one which they left in the boat. 'Well then,' said I, 'leave the rest to me; I see they are all asleep, it is an easie thing to kill them all; but shall we rather take them prisoners?' He told me there were two desperate villains among them, that it was scarce safe to shew any mercy to; but if they were secur'd, he believ'd all the rest would return to their duty. I ask'd him which they were. He told me he could not at that distance describe them; but he would obey my orders in any thing I would direct. 'Well,' says I, 'let us retreat out of their view or hearing, least they awake, and we will resolve further'; so they willingly went back with me, till the woods cover'd us from them.

'Look you, sir,' said I, 'if I venture upon your deliverance, are you willing to make two conditions with me?' He anticipated my proposals, by telling me that both he and the ship, if recover'd, should be wholly directed and commanded by me in every thing; and if the ship was not recover'd, he would live and dye with me in what part of the world soever I would send him; and the two other men said the same.

'Well,' says I, 'my conditions are but two. 1. That while you stay on this island with me, you will not pretend to any authority here; and if I put arms into your hands, you will upon all occasions give them up to me, and do no prejudice to me or mine upon this island, and in the mean time be govern'd by my orders.

'2. That if the ship is or may be recover'd, you will carry me and my man to England passage free.'

He gave me all the assurances that the invention and faith of man could devise, that he would comply with these most reasonable demands, and besides would owe his life to me, and acknowledge it upon all occasions as long as he liv'd.

'Well then,' said I, 'here are three muskets for you, with powder and ball; tell me next what you think is proper to be done.' He shew'd all the testimony of his gratitude that he was able; but offer'd to be wholly guided by me. I told him I thought it was hard venturing any thing; but the best method I could think of was to fire upon them at once, as they lay; and if any was not kill'd at the first volley, and offer'd to submit, we might save them, and so put it wholly upon God's providence to direct the shot.

He said very modestly, that he was loath to kill them, if he could help it, but that those two were incorrigible villains, and had been the authors of all the mutiny in the ship, and if they escaped, we should be undone still; for they would go on board, and bring the whole ship's company, and destroy us all. 'Well then,' says I, 'necessity legitimates my advice; for it is the only way to save our lives.' However, seeing him still cautious of shedding blood, I told him they should go themselves, and manage as they found convenient.

In the middle of this discourse, we heard some of them awake, and soon after we saw two of them on their feet. I ask'd him if either of them were of the men who he had said were the heads of the mutiny. He said, no. 'Well then,' said I, 'you may let them escape, and Providence seems to have wakned them on purpose to save themselves. Now,' says I, 'if the rest escape you, it is your fault.'

Animated with this, he took the musket I had given him in his hand and a pistol in his belt, and his two comerades with him, with each man a piece in his hand. The two men who were with him, going first, made some noise, at which one of the seamen who was awake turn'd about, and seeing them coming, cry'd out to the rest; but it was too late then; for the moment he cry'd out, they fir'd; I mean the two men, the captain wisely reserving his own piece. They had so well aim'd their shot at the men they knew, that one of them was kill'd on the spot, and the other very much wounded; but not being dead, he started up upon his feet, and call'd eagerly for help to the other; but the captain stepping to him, told him, 'twas too late to cry for help, he should call upon God to forgive his villany, and with that word knock'd him down with the stock of his musket, so that he never spoke more. There were three more in the company, and one of them was also slightly wounded. By this time I was come, and when they saw their danger, and that it was in vain to resist, they begg'd for mercy. The captain told them he would spare their lives, if they would give him any assurance of their abhorrence of the treachery they had been guilty of, and would swear to be faithful to him in recovering the ship, and afterwards in carrying her back to Jamaica, from whence they came. They gave him all the protestations of their sincerity that could be desir'd, and he was willing to believe them, and spare their lives, which I was not against, only that I oblig'd him to keep them bound hand and foot while they were upon the island.

While this was doing, I sent Friday with the captain's mate to the boat, with orders to secure her and bring away the oars and sail, which they did; and by and by, three straggling men that were (happily for them) parted from the rest, came back upon hearing the guns fir'd, and seeing their captain, who before was their prisoner, now their conqueror, they submitted to be bound also; and so our victory was compleat.

It now remain'd that the captain and I should enquire into one another's circumstances. I began first, and told him my whole history, which he heard with an attention even to amazement; and particularly at the wonderful manner of my being furnish'd with provisions and ammunition; and indeed, as my story is a whole collection of wonders, it affected him deeply; but when he reflected from thence upon himself, and how I seem'd to have been preserv'd there on purpose to save his life, the tears ran down his face, and he could not speak a word more.

After this communication was at an end, I carry'd him and his two men into my apartment, leading them in just where I came out, viz. at the top of the house, where I refresh'd them with such provisions as I had, and shew'd them all the contrivances I had made during my long, long inhabiting that place.

All I shew'd them, all I said to them, was perfectly amazing; but above all, the captain admir'd my fortification, and how perfectly I had conceal'd my retreat with a grove of trees, which having been now planted near twenty years, and the trees growing much faster than in England, was become a little wood, and so thick that it was unpassable in any part of it, but at that one side where I had reserv'd my little winding passage into it. I told him this was my castle and my residence, but that I had a seat in the country, as most princes have, whither I could retreat upon occasion, and I would shew him that too another time; but at present, our business was to consider how to recover the ship. He agreed with me as to that; but told me he was perfectly at a loss what measures to take; for that there were still six and twenty hands on board, who having entred into a cursed conspiracy, by which they had all forfeited their lives to the law, would be harden'd in it now by desperation; and would carry it on, knowing that if they were reduce'd, they should be brought to the gallows, as soon as they came to England, or to any of the English colonies; and that therefore there would be no attacking them with so small a number as we were.

I mus'd for some time upon what he had said, and found it was a very rational conclusion; and that therefore something was to be resolv'd on very speedily, as well to draw the men on board into some snare for their surprize, as to prevent their landing upon us, and destroying us; upon this it presently occurr'd to me, that in a little while the ship's crew, wondring what was become of their comrades and of the boat, would certainly come on shore in their other boat, to see for them, and that then perhaps they might come arm'd, and be strong too for us; this he allow'd was rational.

Upon this, I told him the first thing we had to do was to stave the boat which lay upon the beach, so that they might not carry her off; and taking everything out of her, leave her so far useless as not to be fit to swim; accordingly we went on board, took the arms which were left on board out of her, and whatever else we found there, which was a bottle of brandy, and another of rum, a few bisket cakes, a horn of powder, and a great lump of sugar in a piece of canvas; the sugar was five or six pounds; all which was very welcome to me, especially the brandy and sugar, of which I had had none left for many years.

When we had carry'd all these things on shore (the oars, mast, sail, and rudder of the boat were carry'd away before, as above) we knock'd a great hole in her bottom, that if they had come strong enough to master us, yet they could not carry off the boat.

Indeed, it was not much in my thoughts that we could be able to recover the ship; but my view was that if they went away without the boat, I did not much question to make her fit again, to carry us away to the Leeward Islands, and call upon our friends, the Spaniards, in my way, for I had them still in my thoughts.

While we were thus preparing our designs, and had first by main strength heav'd the boat up upon the beach, so high that the tide would not fleet her off at high-water-mark; and besides, had broke a hole in her bottom, too big to be quickly stopp'd, and were sat down musing what we should do; we heard the ship fire a gun, and saw her make a waft* with her antient, as a signal for the boat to come on board; but no boat stirr'd; and they fir'd several times, making other signals for the boat.

At last, when all their signals and firing prov'd fruitless, and they found the boat did not stir, we saw them, by the help of my glasses, hoist another boat out, and row towards the shore; and we found as they approach'd that there was no less than ten men in her, and that they had fire-arms with them.

As the ship lay almost two leagues from the shore, we had a full view of them as they came, and a plain sight of the men, even of their faces, because the tide having set them a little to the east of the other boat, they row'd up under shore, to come to the same place where the other had landed, and where the boat lay.

By this means, I say, we had a full view of them, and the captain knew the persons and characters of all the men in the boat, of whom he said that there were three very honest fellows, who he was sure were led into this conspiracy by the rest, being over-power'd and frighted.

But that as for the boatswain, who it seems was the chief officer among them, and all the rest, they were as outragious as any of the ship's crew, and were no doubt made desperate in their new enterprize, and terribly apprehensive he was that they would be too powerful for us.

I smil'd at him, and told him that men in our circumstances were past the operation of fear: that seeing almost every condition that could be, was better than that which we were suppos'd to be in, we ought to expect that the consequence, whether death or life, would be sure to be a deliverance. I ask'd him what he thought of the circumstances of my life, and whether a deliverance were not worth venturing for. 'And where, sir,' said I, 'is your belief of my being preserv'd here on purpose to save your life, which elevated you a little while ago? For my part,' said I, 'there seems to be but one thing amiss in all the prospect of it.' 'What's that?' says he. 'Why,' said I, ''tis that as you say, there are three or four honest fellows among them, which should be spar'd; had they been all of the wicked part of the crew, I should have thought God's providence had singled them out to deliver them into your hands; for depend upon it, every man of them that comes a-shore are our own, and shall die or live as they behave to us.'

As I spoke this with a rais'd voice and chearful countenance, I found it greatly encourag'd him; so we set vigorously to our business. We had, upon the first appearance of the boat's coming from the ship, consider'd of separating our prisoners, and had indeed secur'd them effectually.

Two of them, of whom the captain was less assur'd than ordinary, I sent with Friday and one of the three (deliver'd men) to my cave, where they were remote enough, and out of danger of being heard or discover'd, or of finding their way out of the woods, if they could have deliver'd themselves. Here they left them bound, but gave them provisions, and promis'd them if they continu'd there quietly, to give them their liberty in a day or two; but that if they attempted their escape, they should be put to death without mercy. They promis'd faithfully to bear their confinement with patience, and were very thankful that they had such good usage as to have provisions and a light left them; for Friday gave them candles (such as we made our selves) for their comfort; and they did not know but that he stood sentinel over them at the entrance.

The other prisoners had better usage; two of them were kept pinion'd indeed, because the captain was not free to trust them; but the other two were taken into my service upon their captain's recommendation, and upon their solemnly engaging to live and die with us; so with them and the three honest men, we were seven men, well arm'd; and I made no doubt we shou'd be able to deal well enough with the ten that were a coming, considering that the captain had said there were three or four honest men among them also.

As soon as they got to the place where their other boat lay, they run their boat in to the beach, and came all on shore, haling the boat up after them, which I was glad to see; for I was afraid they would rather have left the boat at an anchor, some distance from the shore, with some hands in her to guard her; and so we should not be able to seize the boat.

Being on shore, the first thing they did, they ran all to their other boat, and it was easy to see that they were under a great surprize, to find her stripp'd as above, of all that was in her, and a great hole in her bottom.

After they had mus'd a while upon this, they set up two or three great shouts, hollowing with all their might, to try if they could make their companions hear; but all was to no purpose. Then they came all close in a ring, and fir'd a volley of their small arms, which indeed we heard, and the ecchos made the woods ring; but it was all one, those in the cave we were sure could not hear, and those in our keeping, though they heard it well enough, yet durst give no answer to them.

They were so astonish'd at the surprize of this, that as they told us afterwards, they resolv'd to go all on board again to their ship, and let them know that the men were all murther'd, and the long-boat stav'd; accordingly they immediately launch'd their boat again, and gat all of them on board.

The captain was terribly amaz'd and even confounded at this, believing they would go on board the ship again, and set sail, giving their comrades for lost, and so he should still lose the ship, which he was in hopes we should have recover'd; but he was quickly as much frighted the other way.

They had not been long put off with the boat, but we perceiv'd them all coming on shore again; but with this new measure in their conduct, which it seems they consulted together upon, viz. to leave three men in the boat, and the rest to go on shore, and go up into the country to look for their fellows.

This was a great disappointment to us; for now we were at a loss what to do; for our seizing those seven men on shore would be no advantage to us, if we let the boat escape; because they would then row away to the ship, and then the rest of them would be sure to weigh and set sail, and so our recovering the ship would be lost.

However, we had no remedy but to wait and see what the issue of things might present. The seven men came on shore, and the three who remain'd in the boat put her off to a good distance from the shore, and came to an anchor to wait for them; so that it was impossible for us to come at them in the boat.

Those that came on shore kept close together, marching towards the top of the little hill under which my habitation lay; and we could see them plainly, though they could not perceive us. We could have been very glad they would have come nearer to us, so that we might have fir'd at them, or that they would have gone farther off, that we might have come abroad.

But when they were come to the brow of the hill, where they could see a great way into the valleys and woods, which lay towards the north-east part, and where the island lay lowest, they shouted and hollow'd till they were weary; and not caring it seems to venture far from the shore, nor far from one another, they sat down together under a tree, to consider of it. Had they thought fit to have gone to sleep there, as the other party of them had done, they had done the jobb for us; but they were too full of apprehensions of danger to venture to go to sleep, though they could not tell what the danger was they had to fear neither.

The captain made a very just proposal to me, upon this consultation of theirs, viz. that perhaps they would all fire a volley again, to endeavour to make their fellows hear, and that we should all sally upon them, just at the juncture when their pieces were all discharg'd, and they would certainly yield, and we should have them without blood-shed. I lik'd the proposal, provided it was done while we were near enough to come up to them, before they could load their pieces again.

But this event did not happen, and we lay still a long time, very irresolute what course to take; at length I told them, there would be nothing to be done in my opinion till night, and then if they did not return to the boat, perhaps we might find a way to get between them and the shore, and so might use some stratagem with them in the boat to get them on shore.

We waited a great while, though very impatient for their removing; and were very uneasy, when after long consultations, we saw them start all up and march down toward the sea. It seems they had such dreadful apprehensions upon them of the danger of the place, that they resolv'd to go on board the ship again, give their companions over for lost, and so go on with their intended voyage with the ship.

As soon as I perceiv'd them go towards the shore, I imagin'd it to be as it really was, that they had given over their search, and were for going back again; and the captain, as soon as I told him my thoughts, was ready to sink at the apprehensions of it; but I presently thought of a stratagem to fetch them back again, and which answer'd my end to a tittle.

I order'd Friday and the captain's mate to go over the little creek westward, towards the place where the savages came on shore when Friday was rescu'd; and as soon as they came to a little rising ground, at about half a mile distance, I bad them hollow as loud as they could, and wait till they found the seamen heard them; that as soon as ever they heard the seamen answer them, they should return it again, and then keeping out of sight, take a round, always answering when the other hollow'd, to draw them as far into the island, and among the woods, as possible, and then wheel about again to me, by such ways as I directed them.

They were just going into the boat, when Friday and the mate hollow'd, and they presently heard them, and answering, run along the shore westward, towards the voice they heard, where they were presently stopp'd by the creek, where the water being up, they could not get over, and call'd for the boat to come up and set them over, as indeed I expected.

When they had set themselves over, I observ'd that the boat being gone up a good way into the creek, and as it were, in a harbour within the land, they took one of the three men out of her to go along with them, and left only two in the boat, having fastned her to the stump of a little tree on the shore.

This was what I wish'd for, and immediately leaving Friday and the captain's mate to their business, I took the rest with me, and crossing the creek out of their sight, we surpriz'd the two men before they were aware; one of them lying on shore, and the other being in the boat; the fellow on shore was between sleeping and waking, and going to start up; the captain, who was foremost, ran in upon him and knock'd him down, and then call'd out to him in the boat to yield, or he was a dead man.

There needed very few arguments to perswade a single man to yield, when he saw five men upon him, and his comrade knock'd down; besides, this was, it seems, one of the three who were not so hearty in the mutiny as the rest of the crew, and therefore was easily perswaded, not only to yield, but afterwards to joyn very sincerely with us.

In the mean time, Friday and the captain's mate so well manag'd their business with the rest, that they drew them by hollowing and answering, from one hill to another, and from one wood to another, till they not only heartily tyr'd them, but left them where they were very sure they could not reach back to the boat before it was dark; and indeed they were heartily tyr'd themselves also by the time they came back to us.

We had nothing now to do but to watch for them in the dark, and to fall upon them, so as to make sure work with them.

It was several hours after Friday came back to me, before they came back to their boat; and we could hear the foremost of them long before they came quite up, calling to those behind to come along, and could also hear them answer and complain how lame and tyr'd they were, and not able to come any faster, which was very welcome news to us.

At length they came up to the boat; but 'tis impossible to express their confusion, when they found the boat fast a-ground in the creek, the tide ebb'd out, and their two men gone. We could hear them call to one another in a most lamentable manner, telling one another they were gotten into an inchanted island; that either there were inhabitants in it, and they should all be murther'd, or else there were devils and spirits in it, and they should be all carry'd away and devour'd.

They hallow'd again, and call'd their two comerades by their names a great many times, but no answer. After some time, we could see them, by the little light there was, run about wringing their hands like men in despair; and that sometimes they would go and sit down in the boat to rest themselves, then come ashore again, and walk about again, and so over the same thing again.

My men would fain have me give them leave to fall upon them

at once in the dark; but I was willing to take them at some advantage, so to spare them, and kill as few of them as I could; and especially I was unwilling to hazard the killing any of our own men, knowing the other were very well armed. I resolved to wait to see if they did not separate; and therefore to make sure of them, I drew my ambuscade nearer, and order'd Friday and the captain to creep upon their hands and feet as close to the ground as they could, that they might not be discover'd, and get as near them as they could possibly, before they offered to fire.

They had not been long in that posture, but that the boatswain, who was the principal ringleader of the mutiny, and had now shewn himself the most dejected and dispirited of all the rest, came walking towards them with two more of their crew; the captain was so eager, as having this principal rogue so much in his power, that he could hardly have patience to let him come so near as to be sure of him; for they only heard his tongue before: but when they came nearer, the captain and Friday, starting up on their feet, let fly at them.

The boatswain was kill'd upon the spot, the next man was shot into the body and fell just by him, tho' he did not die 'till an hour or two after; and the third run for it.

At the noise of the fire, I immediately advanc'd with my whole army, which was now 8 men, viz. my self generalissimo, Friday my lieutenant-general, the captain and his two men, and the three prisoners of war, who we had trusted with arms.

We came upon them indeed in the dark, so that they could not see our number; and I made the man we had left in the boat, who was now one of us, call to them by name, to try if I could bring them to a parley, and so might perhaps reduce them to terms, which fell out just as we desir'd: for indeed it was easy to think, as their condition then was, they would be very willing to capitulate; so he calls out as loud as he could, to one of them, 'Tom Smith, Tom Smith!' Tom Smith answered immediately, 'Who's that, Robinson?' for it seems he knew his voice. T'other answered, 'Ay, ay; for God's sake, Tom Smith, throw down your arms and yield, or you are all dead men this moment.'

'Who must we yield to? where are they?' says Smith again. 'Here they are,' says he, 'here's our captain, and fifty men with him, have been hunting you this two hours; the boatswain is kill'd, Will Frye is wounded, and I am a prisoner; and if you do not yield, you are all lost.'

'Will they give us quarter then,' says Tom Smith, 'and we will yield?' 'I'll go and ask, if you promise to yield,' says Robinson; so he ask'd the captain, and the captain then calls himself out, 'You, Smith, you know my voice, if you lay down your arms immediately, and submit, you shall have your lives all but Will. Atkins.'

Upon this, Will. Atkins cry'd out, 'For God's sake, captain, give me quarter, what have I done? They have been all as bad as I'; which by the way was not true neither; for it seems this Will. Atkins was the first man that laid hold of the captain, when they first mutiny'd, and used him barbarously, in tying his hands and giving him injurious language. However, the captain told him he must lay down his arms at discretion, and trust to the governour's mercy, by which he meant me; for they all call'd me governour.

In a word, they all laid down their arms, and begg'd their lives; and I sent the man that had parley'd with them, and two more, who bound them all; and then my great army of 50 men, which, particularly with those three, were all but eight, came up and seiz'd upon them all, and upon their boat, only that I kept my self and one more out of sight, for reasons of state.

Our next work was to repair the boat, and think of seizing the ship; and as for the captain, now he had leisure to parley with them, he expostulated with them upon the villany of their practices with him, and at length upon the farther wickedness of their design, and how certainly it must bring them to misery and distress in the end, and perhaps to the gallows.

They all appear'd very penitent, and begg'd hard for their lives; as for that, he told them, they were none of his prisoners, but the commander's of the island; that they thought they had set him on shore in a barren uninhabited island, but it had pleased God so to direct them, that the island was inhabited, and that the governour was an English man; that he might hang them all there, if he pleased; but as he had given them all quarter, he supposed he would send them to England to be dealt with there as justice requir'd, except Atkins, who he was commanded by the governour to advise to prepare for death; for that he would be hang'd in the morning.

Though this was all a fiction of his own, yet it had its desired effect; Atkins fell upon his knees to beg the captain to intercede with the governour for his life; and all the rest begg'd of him for God's sake, that they might not be sent to England.

It now occur'd to me that the time of our deliverance was come, and that it would be a most easy thing to bring these fellows in to be hearty in getting possession of the ship; so I retir'd in the dark from them, that they might not see what kind of a governour they had, and call'd the captain to me; when I call'd, as at a good distance, one of the men was order'd to speak again, and say to the captain, 'Captain, the commander calls for you'; and presently the captain reply'd, 'Tell his Excellency, I am just a coming.' This more perfectly amused them; and they all believed that the commander was just by with his fifty men.

Upon the captain's coming to me, I told him my project for seizing the ship, which he lik'd of wonderfully well, and resolv'd to put it in execution the next morning.

But in order to execute it with more art, and secure of success, I told him we must divide the prisoners, and that he should go and take Atkins and two more of the worst of them, and send them pinion'd to the cave where the others lay: this was committed to Friday and the two men who came on shore with the captain.

They convey'd them to the cave, as to a prison; and it was indeed a dismal place, especially to men in their condition.

The other I order'd to my bower, as I call'd it, of which I have given a full description; and as it was fenc'd in, and they pinion'd, the place was secure enough, considering they were upon their behaviour.

To these in the morning I sent the captain, who was to enter into a parley with them, in a word to try them, and tell me whether he thought they might be trusted or no, to go on board and surprize the ship. He talk'd to them of the injury done him; of the condition they were brought to; and that though the governour had given them quarter for their lives as to the present action, yet that if they were sent to England, they would all be hang'd in chains, to be sure; but that if they would join in so just an attempt as to recover the ship, he would have the governour's engagement for their pardon.

Any one may guess how readily such a proposal would be accepted by men in their condition; they fell down on their knees to the captain, and promised, with the deepest imprecations, that they would be faithful to him to the last drop, and that they should owe their lives to him, and would go with him all over the world, that they would own him for a father to them as long as they liv'd.

'Well,' says the captain, 'I must go and tell the governor what

you say, and see what I can do to bring him to consent to it.' So
he brought me an account of the temper he found them in; and
that he verily believ'd they would be faithful.

However, that we might be very secure, I told him he should
go back again, and choose out those five and tell them, they
might see that he did not want men, that he would take out those
five to be his assistants, and that the governour would keep the
other two, and the three that were sent prisoners to the castle
(my cave), as hostages for the fidelity of those five; and that if
they prov'd unfaithful in the execution, the five hostages should
be hang'd in chains alive upon the shore.

This look'd severe, and convinc'd them that the governour
was in earnest; however, they had no way left them but to accept
it; and it was now the business of the prisoners, as much as of the
captain, to perswade the other five to do their duty.

Our strength was now thus ordered for the expedition: 1. The
captain, his mate, and passenger. 2. Then the two prisoners of
the first gang, to whom, having their characters from the
captain, I had given their liberty, and trusted them with arms.
3. The other two who I had kept till now in my bower, pinion'd;
but upon the captain's motion, had now releas'd. 4. These five
releas'd at last: so that they were twelve in all, besides five we
kept prisoners in the cave, for hostages.

I ask'd the captain if he was willing to venture with these
hands on board the ship; for as for me and my man Friday, I did
not think it was proper for us to stir, having seven men left
behind; and it was employment enough for us to keep them
assunder and supply them with victuals.

As to the five in the cave, I resolv'd to keep them fast, but
Friday went in twice a day to them, to supply them with
necessaries; and I made the other two carry provisions to a
certain distance, where Friday was to take it.

When I shew'd my self to the two hostages, it was with the
captain, who told them I was the person the governour had
order'd to look after them, and that it was the governour's
pleasure they should not stir any where, but by my direction;
that if they did, they should be fetch'd into the castle, and be
lay'd in irons; so that as we never suffered them to see me as
governour, so I now appear'd as another person, and spoke of
the governour, the garrison, the castle, and the like, upon all
occasions.

The captain now had no difficulty before him, but to furnish his two boats, stop the breach of one, and man them. He made his passenger captain of one, with four other men; and himself, and his mate, and five more, went in the other: and they contriv'd their business very well; for they came up to the ship about midnight. As soon as they came within call of the ship, he made Robinson hale them, and tell them they had brought off the men and the boat, but that it was a long time before they had found them, and the like; holding them in a chat 'till they came to the ship's side; when the captain and the mate, entring first with their arms, immediately knock'd down the second mate and carpenter with the but-end of their muskets, being very faithfully seconded by their men; they secur'd all the rest that were upon the main and quarter decks, and began to fasten the hatches to keep them down who were below, when the other boat and their men, entring at the fore chains, secur'd the forecastle of the ship, and the scuttle which went down into the cook-room, making three men they found there prisoners.

When this was done, and all safe upon deck, the captain order'd the mate with three men to break into the round-house where the new rebel captain lay, and having taken the alarm, was gotten up, and with two men and a boy had gotten fire arms in their hands; and when the mate with a crow split open the door, the new captain and his men fir'd boldly among them, and wounded the mate with a musket ball, which broke his arm, and wounded two more of the men but kill'd no body.

The mate, calling for help, rush'd however into the round-house, wounded as he was, and with his pistol shot the new captain thro' the head, the bullet entring at his mouth, and came out again behind one of his ears, so that he never spoke a word; upon which the rest yielded, and the ship was taken effectually, without any more lives lost.

As soon as the ship was thus secur'd, the captain order'd seven guns to be fir'd, which was the signal agreed upon with me, to give me notice of his success, which you may be sure I was very glad to hear, having sat watching upon the shore for it till near two of the clock in the morning.

Having thus heard the signal plainly, I laid me down; and it having been a day of great fatigue to me, I slept very sound, 'till I was something surpriz'd with the noise of a gun; and presently starting up, I heard a man call me by the name of Governour,

Governour, and presently I knew the captain's voice, when climbing up to the top of the hill, there he stood, and pointing to the ship, he embrac'd me in his arms. 'My dear friend and deliverer,' says he, 'there's your ship, for she is all yours, and so are we and all that belong to her.' I cast my eyes to the ship, and there she rode within little more than half a mile of the shore; for they had weighed her anchor as soon as they were masters of her; and the weather being fair, had brought her to an anchor just against the mouth of the little creek; and the tide being up, the captain had brought the pinnace in near the place where I at first landed my rafts, and so landed just at my door.

I was at first ready to sink down with the surprize. For I saw my deliverance indeed visibly put into my hands, all things easy, and a large ship just ready to carry me away whither I pleased to go. At first, for some time, I was not able to answer him one word; but as he had taken me in his arms, I held fast by him, or I should have fallen to the ground.

He perceived the surprize, and immediately pulls a bottle out of his pocket, and gave me a dram of cordial, which he had brought on purpose for me; after I had drank it, I sat down upon the ground; and though it brought me to my self, yet it was a good while before I could speak a word to him.

All this while the poor man was in as great an extasy as I, only not under any surprize, as I was; and he said a thousand kind tender things to me, to compose me and bring me to my self; but such was the flood of joy in my breast, that it put all my spirits into confusion; at last it broke out into tears, and in a little while after I recovered my speech.

Then I took my turn, and embrac'd him as my deliverer; and we rejoyc'd together. I told him I look'd upon him as a man sent from heaven to deliver me, and that the whole transaction seemed to be a chain of wonders; that such things as these were the testimonies we had of a secret hand of Providence governing the world, and an evidence that the eyes of an infinite power could search into the remotest corner of the world, and send help to the miserable whenever He pleased.

I forgot not to lift up my heart in thankfulness to Heaven; and what heart could forbear to bless Him, who had not only in a miraculous manner provided for one in such a wilderness, and in such a desolate condition, but from whom every deliverance must always be acknowledged to proceed.

When we had talk'd a while the captain told me he had brought me some little refreshment, such as the ship afforded, and such as the wretches that had been so long his master had not plunder'd him of. Upon this he call'd aloud to the boat, and bid his men bring the things ashore that were for the governour; and indeed it was a present, as if I had been one not that was to be carry'd away along with them, but as if I had been to dwell upon the island still, and they were to go without me.

First, he had brought me a case of bottles full of excellent cordial waters, six large bottles of Madera wine; the bottles held two quarts a-piece; two pound of excellent good tobacco, twelve good pieces of the ship's beef, and six pieces of pork, with a bag of pease, and about a hundred weight of bisket.

He brought me also a box of sugar, a box of flower, a bag full of lemons, and two bottles of lime-juice, and abundance of other things. But besides these, and what was a thousand times more useful to me, he brought me six clean new shirts, six very good neckcloaths, two pair of gloves, one pair of shoes, a hat, and one pair of stockings, and a very good suit of cloaths of his own, which had been worn but very little: in a word, he cloathed me from head to foot.

It was a very kind and agreeable present, as any one may imagine to one in my circumstances: but never was any thing in the world of that kind so unpleasant, awkard, and uneasy, as it was to me to wear such cloaths at their first putting on.

After these ceremonies past, and after all his good things were brought into my little apartment, we began to consult what was to be done with the prisoners we had; for it was worth considering, whether we might venture to take them away with us or no, especially two of them, who we knew to be incorrigible and refractory to the last degree; and the captain said, he knew they were such rogues, that there was no obliging them, and if he did carry them away, it must be in irons, as malefactors to be delivered over to justice at the first English colony he could come at; and I found that the captain himself was very anxious about it.

Upon this, I told him that if he desir'd it, I durst undertake to bring the two men he spoke of, to make it their own request that he should leave them upon the island. 'I should be very glad of that,' says the captain, 'with all my heart.'

'Well,' says I, 'I will send for them up, and talk with them for you'; so I caused Friday and the two hostages, for they were now discharg'd, their comrades having perform'd their promise; I say, I caused them to go to the cave, and bring up the five men pinion'd, as they were, to the bower, and keep them there 'till I came.

After some time, I came thither dress'd in my new habit, and now I was call'd governour again; being all met, and the captain with me, I caused the men to be brought before me, and I told them I had had a full account of their villanous behaviour to the captain, and how they had run away with the ship, and were preparing to commit farther robberies, but that Providence had ensnar'd them in their own ways, and that they were fallen into the pit which they had digged for others.

I let them know that by my direction the ship had been seiz'd, that she lay now in the road; and they might see by and by that their new captain had receiv'd the reward of his villany; for that they might see him hanging at the yard-arm.

That as to them, I wanted to know what they had to say, why I should not execute them as pirates taken in the fact, as by my commission they could not doubt I had authority to do.

One of them answer'd in the name of the rest, that they had nothing to say but this, that when they were taken, the captain promis'd them their lives, and they humbly implor'd my mercy; but I told them I knew not what mercy to shew them; for as for my self, I had resolv'd to quit the island with all my men, and had taken passage with the captain to go for England; and as for the captain, he could not carry them to England, other than as prisoners in irons to be try'd for mutiny and running away with the ship; the consequence of which, they must needs know, would be the gallows; so that I could not tell which was best for them, unless they had a mind to take their fate in the island; if they desir'd that, I did not care, as I had liberty to leave it, I had some inclination to give them their lives, if they thought they could shift on shore.

They seem'd very thankful for it, said they would much rather venture to stay there, than to be carry'd to England to be hang'd, so I left it on that issue.

However, the captain seem'd to make some difficulty of it, as if he durst not leave them there. Upon this I seem'd a little angry with the captain, and told him that they were my prisoners, not his; and that seeing I had offered them so much favour, I would be as good as my word; and that if he did not think fit to consent to it,

I would set them at liberty, as I found them; and if he did not like it, he might take them again if he could catch them.

Upon this they appear'd very thankful, and I accordingly set them at liberty, and bad them retire into the woods to the place whence they came, and I would leave them some fire arms, some ammunition, and some directions how they should live very well, if they thought fit.

Upon this I prepar'd to go on board the ship, but told the captain that I would stay that night to prepare my things, and desir'd him to go on board in the mean time, and keep all right in the ship, and send the boat on shore the next day for me; ordering him in the mean time to cause the new captain who was kill'd to be hang'd at the yard-arm that these men might see him.

When the captain was gone, I sent for the men up to me to my apartment, and entred seriously into discourse with them of their circumstances; I told them I thought they had made a right choice; that if the captain carry'd them away, they would certainly be hang'd. I shewed them the new captain hanging at the yard-arm of the ship, and told them they had nothing less to expect.

When they had all declar'd their willingness to stay, I then told them I would let them into the story of my living there, and put them into the way of making it easy to them. Accordingly I gave them the whole history of the place, and of my coming to it; shew'd them my fortifications, the way I made my bread, planted my corn, cured my grapes; and in a word, all that was necessary to make them easy. I told them the story also of the sixteen Spaniards that were to be expected; for whom I left a letter, and made them promise to treat them in common with themselves.

I left them my fire arms, viz. five muskets, three fowling pieces, and three swords. I had above a barrel and half of powder left; for after the first year or two, I used but little, and wasted none. I gave them a description of the way I manag'd the goats, and directions to milk and fatten them, and to make both butter and cheese.

In a word, I gave them every part of my own story; and I told them I would prevail with the captain to leave them two barrels of gun-powder more, and some garden-seeds, which I told them I would have been very glad of; also I gave them the bag of pease which the captain had brought me to eat, and bad them be sure to sow and encrease them.

Having done all this, I left them the next day, and went on board the ship; we prepared immediately to sail, but did not weigh that night. The next morning early, two of the five men came swimming to the ship's side, and making a most lamentable complaint of the other three, begged to be taken into the ship, for God's sake, for they should be murthered, and begg'd the captain to take them on board, tho' he hang'd them immediately.

Upon this the captain pretended to have no power without me; but after some difficulty, and after their solemn promises of amendment, they were taken on board, and were some time after soundly whipp'd and pickl'd; after which, they prov'd very honest and quiet fellows.

Some time after this, the boat was order'd on shore, the tide being up, with the things promised to the men, to which the captain at my intercession caused their chests and cloaths to be added, which they took, and were very thankful for; I also encourag'd them, by telling them that if it lay in my way to send any vessel to take them in, I would not forget them.

When I took leave of this island, I carry'd on board for reliques the great goat's-skin-cap I had made, my umbrella, and my parrot; also I forgot not to take the money I formerly mention'd, which had lain by me so long useless, that it was grown rusty, or tarnish'd, and could hardly pass for silver till it had been a little rubb'd and handled; as also the money I found in the wreck of the Spanish ship.

And thus I left the island, the nineteenth of December as I found by the ship's account, in the year 1686, after I had been upon it eight and twenty years,* two months, and 19 days; being deliver'd from this second captivity the same day of the month that I first made my escape in the barco-longo, from among the Moors of Sallee.

In this vessel, after a long voyage, I arriv'd in England, the eleventh of June, in the year 1687, having been thirty and five years absent.

When I came to England, I was as perfect a stranger to all the world, as if I had never been known there. My benefactor and faithful steward, who I had left in trust with my money, was alive, but had had great misfortunes in the world; was become a widow the second time, and very low in the world. I made her easy as to what she ow'd me, assuring her I would give her no trouble; but on the contrary, in gratitude to her former care and faithfulness to me, I reliev'd her as my little stock would afford, which at that time would indeed allow me to do but little for her; but I assur'd her I would never forget her former kindness to me; nor did I forget her, when I had sufficient to help her, as shall be observ'd in its place.

I went down afterwards into Yorkshire; but my father was dead, and my mother, and all the family extinct, except that I found two sisters, and two of the children of one of my brothers; and as I had been long ago given over for dead, there had been no provision made for me; so that in a word, I found nothing to relieve or assist me; and that little money I had, would not do much for me, as to settling in the world.

I met with one piece of gratitude indeed, which I did not expect; and this was that the master of the ship, who I had so happily deliver'd, and by the same means sav'd the ship and cargo, having given a very handsome account to the owners of the manner how I had sav'd the lives of the men, and the ship, they invited me to meet them and some other merchants concern'd, and altogether made me a very handsome compliment upon the subject, and a present of almost two hundred pounds sterling.

But after making several reflections upon the circumstances of my life, and how little way this would go towards settling me in the world, I resolv'd to go to Lisbon, and see if I might not come by some information of the state of my plantation in the Brasils, and of what was become of my partner, who I had reason to suppose had some years now given me over for dead.

With this view I took shipping for Lisbon, where I arriv'd in April following; my man Friday accompanying me very honestly in all these ramblings, and proving a most faithful servant upon all occasions.

When I came to Lisbon I found out by enquiry, and to my particular satisfaction, my old friend the captain of the ship, who first took me up at sea, off of the shore of Africk. He was now grown old, and had left off the sea, having put his son, who was far from a young man, into his ship, and who still used the Brasil trade. The old man did not know me, and indeed, I hardly knew him; but I soon brought him to my remembrance, and as soon brought my self to his remembrance, when I told him who I was.

After some passionate expressions of the old acquaintance, I enquir'd, you may be sure, after my plantation and my partner. The old man told me he had not been in the Brasils for about nine years; but that he could assure me, that when he came away my partner was living, but the trustees, who I had join'd with him to take cognizance of my part, were both dead; that however, he believ'd that I would have a very good account of the improvement of the plantation; for that upon the general belief of my being cast away and drown'd, my trustees had given in the account of the produce of my part of the plantation, to the procurator fiscal, who had appropriated it, in case I never came to claim it; one third to the king, and two thirds to the monastery of St Augustine, to be expended for the benefit of the poor, and for the conversion of the Indians to the Catholick faith; but that if I appear'd, or any one for me, to claim the inheritance, it should be restor'd; only that the improvement, or annual production, being distributed to charitable uses, could not be restor'd; but he assur'd me, that the steward of the king's revenue (from lands) and the proviedore, or steward of the monastery, had taken great care all along, that the incumbent, that is to say my partner, gave every year a faithful account of the produce, of which they receiv'd duly my moiety.*

I ask'd him if he knew to what height of improvement he had brought the plantation, and whether he thought it might be worth looking after, or whether on my going thither I should meet with no obstruction to my possessing my just right in the moiety.

He told me he could not tell exactly to what degree the plantation was improv'd; but this he knew, that my partner was grown exceeding rich upon the enjoying but one half of it; and that to the best of his remembrance, he had heard that the king's third of my part, which was it seems granted away to some other monastery or religious house, amounted to above two hundred moidores a year; that as to my being restor'd to a quiet possession of it, there was no question to be made of that, my partner being alive to witness my title, and my name being also enrolled in the register of the country; also he told me that the survivors of my two trustees were very fair honest people, and very wealthy; and he believ'd I would not only have their assistance for putting me in possession, but would find a very considerable sum of money in their hands, for my account; being the produce of the farm while their fathers held the trust, and before it was given up as above, which, as he remember'd, was for about twelve years.

I shew'd my self a little concern'd and uneasy at this account, and enquir'd of the old captain how it came to pass that the trustees should thus dispose my effects, when he knew that I had made my will, and had made him, the Portuguese captain, my universal heir, &c.

He told me, that was true; but that as there was no proof of my being dead, he could not act as executor, until some certain account should come of my death, and that besides, he was not willing to intermeddle with a thing so remote; that it was true he had registred my will, and put in his claim; and could he have given any account of my being dead or alive, he would have acted by procuration, and taken possession of the *ingenio*, so they call'd the sugar-house, and had given his son, who was now at the Brasils, order to do it.

'But,' says the old man, 'I have one piece of news to tell you, which perhaps may not be so acceptable to you as the rest, and that is, that believing you were lost, and all the world believing so also, your partner and trustees did offer to accompt to me in your name, for six or eight of the first years of profits, which I receiv'd; but there being at that time,' says he, 'great disbursements for encreasing the works, building an *ingenio*, and buying slaves, it did not amount to near so much as afterwards it produced: however,' says the old man, 'I shall give you a true account of what I have received in all, and how I have disposed of it.'

After a few days' farther conference with this ancient friend, he brought me an account of the six first years' income of my plantation, sign'd by my partner and the merchant trustees, being always deliver'd in goods, viz. tobacco in roll, and sugar in chests, besides rum, molossus, &c., which is the consequence of a sugar work; and I found by this account, that every year the income considerably encreased; but as above, the disbursement being large, the sum at first was small. However, the old man let me see that he was debtor to me 470 moidores of gold, besides 60 chests of sugar, and 15 double rolls of tobacco which were lost in his ship; he having been ship-wreck'd coming home to Lisbon about 11 years after my leaving the place.

The good man then began to complain of his misfortunes, and how he had been obliged to make use of my money to recover his losses, and buy him a share in a new ship. 'However, my old friend,' says he, 'you shall not want a supply in your necessity; and as soon as my son returns, you shall be fully satisfy'd.'

Upon this, he pulls out an old pouch, and gives me 160 Portugal moidores in gold; and giving me the writing of his title to the ship, which his son was gone to the Brasils in, of which he was a quarter part owner, and his son another, he puts them both into my hands for security of the rest.

I was too much mov'd with the honesty and kindness of the poor man, to be able to bear this; and remembring what he had done for me, how he had taken me up at sea, and how generously he had used me on all occasions, and particularly, how sincere a friend he was now to me, I could hardly refrain weeping at what he said to me. Therefore, first I asked him if his circumstances admitted him to spare so much money at that time, and if it would not straiten him. He told me, he could not say but it might straiten him a little; but however it was my money, and I might want it more than he.

Every thing the good man said was full of affection, and I could hardly refrain from tears while he spoke. In short, I took 100 of the moidores, and call'd for a pen and ink to give him a receipt for them; then I returned him the rest, and told him, if ever I had possession of the plantation, I would return the other to him also, as indeed I afterwards did; and that as to the bill of sale of his part in his son's ship, I would not take it by any means; but that if I wanted the money I found he was honest enough to pay me; and if I did not, but came to receive what he gave me reason to expect, I would never have a penny more from him.

When this was pass'd, the old man began to ask me if he should put me into a method to make my claim to my plantation. I told him I thought to go over to it my self. He said I might do so if I pleas'd; but that if I did not there were ways enough to secure my right, and immediately to appropriate the profits to my use; and as there were ships in the river of Lisbon, just ready to go away to Brasil, he made me enter my name in a publick register, with his affidavit, affirming upon oath that I was alive, and that I was the same person who took up the land for the planting the said plantation at first.

This being regularly attested by a notary, and a procuration affix'd, he directed me to send it with a letter of his writing, to a merchant of his acquaintance at the place, and then propos'd my staying with him till an account came of the return.

Never any thing was more honourable than the proceedings upon this procuration; for in less than seven months I receiv'd a large packet from the survivors of my trustees the merchants, for whose account I went to sea, in which were the following particular letters and papers enclos'd.

First, there was the account current of the produce of my firm or plantation, from the year when their fathers had ballanc'd with my old Portugal captain, being for six years; the ballance appear'd to be 1,174 moidores in my favour.

Secondly, there was the account of four years more while they kept the effects in their hands, before the government claim'd the administration, as being the effects of a person not to be found, which they call'd civil death; and the ballance of this, the value of the plantation encreasing, amounted to [38,892] cruisadoes, which made 3,241 moidores.

Thirdly, there was the prior of the Augustin's account, who had receiv'd the profits for above fourteen years; but not being to account for what was dispos'd to the hospital, very honestly declar'd he had 872 moidores not distributed, which he acknowledged to my account; as to the king's part, that refunded nothing.

There was a letter of my partner's, congratulating me very affectionately upon my being alive, giving me an account how the estate was improv'd, and what it produced a year, with a particular of the number of squares or acres that it contained; how planted, how many slaves there were upon it; and making two and twenty crosses for blessings, told me he had said so many *Ave Marias* to thank the blessed Virgin that I was alive; inviting me very passionately to come over and take possession of my own; and in the mean time to give him orders to whom he should deliver my effects, if I did not come my self; concluding with a hearty tender of his friendship, and that of his family, and sent me, as a present, seven fine leopards' skins, which he had it seems received from Africa, by some other ship which he had sent thither, and who it seems had made a better voyage than I. He sent me also five chests of excellent sweet-meats, and an hundred pieces of gold uncoin'd, not quite so large as moidores.

By the same fleet my two merchant trustees shipp'd me 1,200 chests of sugar, 800 rolls of tobacco, and the rest of the whole accompt in gold.

I might well say, now indeed, that the latter end of Job was better than the beginning. It is impossible to express here the flutterings of my very heart, when I look'd over these letters, and

especially when I found all my wealth about me; for as the Brasil
ships come all in fleets, the same ships which brought my letters
brought my goods; and the effects were safe in the river before
the letters came to my hand. In a word, I turned pale, and grew
sick; and had not the old man run and fetch'd me a cordial, I
believe the sudden surprize of joy had overset nature, and I had
dy'd upon the spot.

Nay after that, I continu'd very ill, and was so some hours,
'till a physician being sent for, and something of the real cause
of my illness being known, he order'd me to be let blood;* after
which I had relief, and grew well: but I verily believe, if it had
not been eas'd by a vent given in that manner to the spirits, I
should have dy'd.

I was now master, all on a sudden, of above 5,000*l.* sterling in
money, and had an estate, as I might well call it, in the Brasils, of
above a thousand pounds a year, as sure as an estate of lands in
England: and in a word, I was in a condition which I scarce
knew how to understand, or how to compose my self for the
enjoyment of it.

The first thing I did was to recompense my original benefactor,
my good old captain, who had been first charitable to me in my
distress, kind to me in my beginning, and honest to me at the end. I
shew'd him all that was sent me; I told him, that next to the
providence of Heaven, which disposes all things, it was owing to
him; and that it now lay on me to reward him, which I would do a
hundred fold. So I first return'd to him the hundred moidores I
had receiv'd of him, then I sent for a notary, and caused him to
draw up a general release or discharge for the 470 moidores,
which he had acknowledg'd he ow'd me in the fullest and firmest
manner possible; after which, I caused a procuration to be drawn,
impowering him to be my receiver of the annual profits of my
plantation, and appointing my partner to accompt to him, and
make the returns by the usual fleets to him in my name; and a
clause in the end, being a grant of 100 moidores a year to him,
during his life, out of the effects, and 50 moidores a year to his son
after him, for his life; and thus I requited my old man.

I was now to consider which way to steer my course next, and
what to do with the estate that Providence had thus put into my
hands; and indeed I had more care upon my head now, than I had
in my silent state of life in the island, where I wanted nothing but
what I had, and had nothing but what I wanted: whereas I had

now a great charge upon me, and my business was how to secure it. I had ne'er a cave now to hide my money in, or a place where it might lye without lock or key, 'till it grew mouldy and tarnish'd before any body would meddle with it: on the contrary, I knew not where to put it, or who to trust with it. My old patron, the captain, indeed was honest, and that was the only refuge I had.

In the next place my interest in the Brasils seem'd to summon me thither; but now I could not tell how to think of going thither, 'till I had settled my affairs, and left my effects in some safe hands behind me. At first I thought of my old friend the widow, who I knew was honest and would be just to me, but then she was in years, and but poor, and, for ought I knew, might be in debt; so that in a word, I had no way but to go back to England my self, and take my effects with me.

It was some months, however, before I resolved upon this; and therefore, as I had rewarded the old captain fully, and to his satisfaction, who had been my former benefactor, so I began to think of my poor widow, whose husband had been my first benefactor, and she, while it was in her power, my faithful steward and instructor. So the first thing I did, I got a merchant in Lisbon to write to his correspondent in London, not only to pay a bill, but to go find her out, and carry her in money an hundred pounds from me, and to talk with her, and comfort her in her poverty, by telling her she should, if I liv'd, have a further supply. At the same time I sent my two sisters in the country each of them an hundred pounds, they being, though not in want, yet not in very good circumstances; one having been marry'd and left a widow, and the other having a husband not so kind to her as he should be.

But among all my relations or acquaintances, I could not yet pitch upon one to whom I durst commit the gross of my stock, that I might go away to the Brasils, and leave things safe behind me; and this greatly perplex'd me.

I had once a mind to have gone to the Brasils, and have settled my self there; for I was, as it were, naturaliz'd to the place; but I had some little scruple in my mind about religion, which insensibly drew me back, of which I shall say more presently. However, it was not religion that kept me from going there for the present; and as I had made no scruple of being openly of the religion of the country, all the while I was among them, so neither did I yet; only that now and then having of late thought more of it than formerly when I began to think of living and dying among them, I began to regret my having profess'd my self a Papist, and thought it might not be the best religion to die with.

But, as I have said, this was not the main thing that kept me from going to the Brasils, but that really I did not know with whom to leave my effects behind me; so I resolv'd at last to go to England with it, where, if I arrived, I concluded I should make some acquaintance or find some relations that would be faithful to me; and according I prepar'd to go for England with all my wealth.

In order to prepare things for my going home, I first, the Brasil fleet being just going away, resolved to give answers suitable to the just and faithful account of things I had from thence; and first to the prior of St Augustine I wrote a letter full of thanks for their just dealings, and the offer of the 872 moidores which was indisposed of, which I desir'd might be given, 500 to the monastery and 372 to the poor, as the prior should direct, desiring the good padres' prayers for me, and the like.

I wrote next a letter of thanks to my two trustees, with all the acknowledgment that so much justice and honesty call'd for; as for sending them any present, they were far above having any occasion of it.

Lastly, I wrote to my partner, acknowledging his industry in the improving the plantation, and his integrity in encreasing the stock of the works, giving him instructions for his future government of my part, according to the powers I had left with my old patron, to whom I desir'd him to send whatever became due to me, 'till he should hear from me more particularly; assuring him that it was my intention, not only to come to him, but to settle my self there for the remainder of my life. To this I added a very handsom present of some Italian silks for his wife and two daughters, for such the captain's son inform'd me he had; with two pieces of fine English broad cloath, the best I could get in Lisbon, five pieces of black bays, and some Flanders lace of a good value.

Having thus settled my affairs, sold my cargoe, and turn'd all my effects into good bills of exchange, my next difficulty was, which way to go to England. I had been accustomed enough to the sea, and yet I had a strange aversion to going to England by sea at that time; and though I could give no reason for it, yet the difficulty encreas'd upon me so much, that though I had once shipp'd my baggage in order to go, yet I alter'd my mind, and that not once, but two or three times.

It is true, I had been very unfortunate by sea, and this might be some of the reason; but let no man slight the strong impulses of his own thoughts in cases of such moment. Two of the ships which I had singl'd out to go in, I mean, more particularly singl'd out than any other, that is to say, so as in one of them to put my things on board, and in the other to have agreed with the captain; I say, two of these ships miscarry'd, viz. one was taken by the Algerines, and the other was cast away on the Start near Torbay, and all the people drown'd except three; so that in either of those vessels I had been made miserable; and in which most, it was hard to say.

Having been thus harass'd in my thoughts, my old pilot, to whom I communicated every thing, press'd me earnestly not to go by sea, but either to go by land to the Groyne,* and cross over the Bay of Biscay to Rochell, from whence it was but an easy and safe journey by land to Paris, and so to Calais and Dover; or to go up to Madrid, and so all the way by land thro' France.

In a word, I was so prepossess'd against my going by sea at all, except from Calais to Dover, that I resolv'd to travel all the way by land; which as I was not in haste, and did not value the charge, was by much the pleasanter way; and to make it more so, my old captain brought an English gentleman, the son of a merchant in Lisbon, who was willing to travel with me: after which, we pick'd up two more English merchants also, and two young Portuguese gentlemen, the last going to Paris only; so that we were in all six of us, and five servants; the two merchants and the two Portuguese contenting themselves with one servant between two, to save the charge; and as for me, I got an English sailor to travel with me as a servant, besides my man Friday, who was too much a stranger to be capable of supplying the place of a servant on the road.

In this manner I set out from Lisbon; and our company being all very well mounted and armed, we made a little troop, whereof they did me the honour to call me captain, as well because I was the oldest man, as because I had two servants, and indeed was the original of the whole journey.

As I have troubled you with none of my sea-journals, so I shall trouble you now with none of my land-journal: but some adventures that happen'd to us in this tedious and difficult journey I must not omit.

When we came to Madrid, we being all of us strangers to Spain,

were willing to stay some time to see the court of Spain, and to see
what was worth observing; but it being the latter part of the
summer, we hasten'd away, and set out from Madrid about the
middle of October: but when we came to the edge of Navarre, we
were alarm'd at several towns on the way, with an account that so
much snow was fallen on the French side of the mountains, that
several travellers were obliged to come back to Pampeluna, after
having attempted, at an extream hazard, to pass on.

When we came to Pampeluna it self, we found it so indeed; and
to me that had been always used to a hot climate, and indeed to
countries where we could scarce bear any cloaths on, the cold was
insufferable; nor indeed was it more painful than it was
surprising, to come but ten days before out of the Old Castile,
where the weather was not only warm but very hot, and
immediately to feel a wind from the Pyrenean mountains, so very
keen, so severely cold, as to be intollerable, and to endanger
benumbing and perishing of our fingers and toes.

Poor Friday was really frighted when he saw the mountains all
cover'd with snow, and felt cold weather, which he had never seen
or felt before in his life.

To mend the matter, when we came to Pampeluna, it continued
snowing with so much violence, and so long, that the people said
winter was come before its time, and the roads which were
difficult before were now quite impassable: for in a word, the
snow lay in some places too thick for us to travel; and being not
hard frozen, as is the case in northern countries, there was no
going without being in danger of being bury'd alive every step. We
stay'd no less than twenty days at Pampeluna; when (seeing the
winter coming on, and no likelihood of its being better; for it was
the severest winter all over Europe that had been known in the
memory of man) I propos'd that we should all go away to
Fonterabia, and there take shipping for Bourdeaux which was a
very little voyage.

But while we were considering this, there came in four French
gentlemen, who having been stopp'd on the French side of the
passes, as we were on the Spanish, had found out a guide, who
traversing the country near the head of Languedoc, had brought
them over the mountains by such ways, that they were not much
incommoded with the snow; and where they met with snow in
any quantity, they said it was frozen hard enough to bear them
and their horses.

We sent for this guide, who told us he would undertake to carry us the same way with no hazard from the snow, provided we were armed sufficiently to protect our selves from wild beasts; for he said, upon these great snows, it was frequent for some wolves to show themselves at the foot of the mountains, being made ravenous for want of food, the ground being covered with snow. We told him we were well enough prepar'd for such creatures as they were, if he would ensure us from a kind of two-legged wolves, which we were told we were in most danger from, especially on the French side of the mountains.

He satisfy'd us there was no danger of that kind in the way that we were to go; so we readily agreed to follow him, as did also twelve other gentlemen, with their servants, some French, some Spanish; who, as I said, had attempted to go, and were oblig'd to come back again.

Accordingly, we all set out from Pampeluna, with our guide, on the fifteenth of November; and indeed, I was surpriz'd, when instead of going forward, he came directly back with us on the same road that we came from Madrid, above twenty miles; when being pass'd two rivers, and come into the plain country, we found our selves in a warm climate again, where the country was pleasant, and no snow to be seen; but on a sudden, turning to his left, he approach'd the mountains another way; and though it is true, the hills and precipices look'd dreadful, yet he made so many tours, such meanders, and led us by such winding ways, that we were insensibly pass'd the height of the mountains, without being much incumber'd with the snow; and all on a sudden he shew'd us the pleasant fruitful provinces of Languedoc and Gascoign, all green and flourishing; tho' indeed it was at a great distance, and we had some rough way to pass yet.

We were a little uneasy, however, when we found it snow'd one whole day and a night, so fast that we could not travel; but he bid us be easy, we should soon be past it all. We found indeed, that we began to descend every day, and to come more north than before; and so depending upon our guide, we went on.

It was about two hours before night, when our guide being something before us, and not just in sight, out rushed three monstrous wolves, and after them a bear, out of a hollow way, adjoyning to a thick wood; two of the wolves flew upon the guide, and had he been half a mile before us, he had been devour'd indeed, before we could have help'd him. One of them fastned upon his horse, and the other attack'd the man with that violence, that he had not time, or not presence of mind enough, to draw his pistol, but hollow'd and cry'd out to us most lustily; my man Friday being next me, I bid him ride up and see what was the matter; as soon as Friday came in sight of the man, he hollow'd as loud as t'other, 'O master! O master!' but like a bold fellow, rode directly up to the poor man, and with his pistol shot the wolf that attack'd him into the head.

It was happy for the poor man that it was my man Friday; for he having been us'd to that kind of creature in his country, had no fear upon him, but went close up to him, and shot him as above; whereas any of us would have fir'd at a farther distance, and have perhaps either miss'd the wolf, or endanger'd shooting the man.

But it was enough to have terrify'd a bolder man than I, and indeed it alarm'd all our company, when with the noise of Friday's pistol, we heard on both sides the dismallest howling of wolves, and the noise redoubled by the echo of the mountains, that it was to us as if there had been a prodigious multitude of them; and perhaps indeed there was not such a few, as that we had no cause of apprehensions.

However, as Friday had kill'd this wolf, the other, that had fastned upon the horse, left him immediately, and fled; having happily fastned upon his head, where the bosses of the bridle had stuck in his teeth, so that he had not done him much hurt. The man indeed was most hurt; for the raging creature had bit him twice, once on the arm, and the other time a little above his knee; and he was just as it were tumbling down by the disorder of his horse, when Friday came up and shot the wolf.

It is easy to suppose that at the noise of Friday's pistol, we all mended our pace, and rid up as fast as the way (which was very difficult) would give us leave, to see what was the matter; as soon as we came clear of the trees, which blinded us before, we saw clearly what had been the case, and how Friday had disengag'd the poor guide; though we did not presently discern what kind of creature it was he had kill'd.

But never was a fight manag'd so hardily, and in such a surprizing manner, as that which follow'd between Friday and the bear, which gave us all (though at first we were surpriz'd and afraid for him) the greatest diversion imaginable. As the bear is a heavy, clumsey creature, and does not gallop as the wolf does, who is swift and light; so he has two particular qualities, which generally are the rule of his actions. First, as to men, who are not his proper prey; I say, not his proper prey, because tho' I cannot say what excessive hunger might do, which was now their case, the ground being all cover'd with snow; but as to men, he does not usually attempt them, unless they first attack him: on the contrary, if you meet him in the woods, if you don't meddle with him, he won't meddle with you; but then you must take care to be very civil to him, and give him the road; for he is a very nice gentleman, he won't go a step out of his way for a prince; nay, if you are really afraid, your best way is to look another way, and keep going on; for sometimes if you stop, and stand still, and look steadily at him, he takes it for an affront; but if you throw or toss any thing at him, and it hits him, though it were but a bit of a stick as big as your finger, he takes it for an affront, and sets all his other business aside to pursue his revenge; for he will have satisfaction in point of honour; that is his first quality. The next is, that if he be once affronted, he will never leave you, night or day, till he has his revenge; but follows at a good round rate, till he overtakes you.

My man Friday had deliver'd our guide, and when we came up to him he was helping him off from his horse; for the man was both hurt and frighted, and indeed the last more than the first; when on the sudden we spy'd the bear come out of the wood, and a vast monstrous one it was, the biggest by far that ever I saw. We were all a little surpriz'd when we saw him; but when Friday saw him, it was easy to see joy and courage in the fellow's countenance. 'O! O! O!' says Friday three times, pointing to him; 'O master! You give me te leave! Me shakee te hand with him: me make you good laugh.'

I was surpriz'd to see the fellow so pleas'd. 'You fool you,' says I, 'he will eat you up.' 'Eatee me up! Eatee me up!' says Friday, twice over again; 'me eatee him up: me make you good laugh: you all stay here, me show you good laugh'; so down he sits, and gets his boots off in a moment, and put on a pair of pumps, as we call the flat shoes they wear, and which he had in his pocket, gives my other servant his horse, and with his gun away he flew swift like the wind.

The bear was walking softly on, and offer'd to meddle with no body, till Friday coming pretty near, calls to him, as if the bear could understand him; 'Hark ye, hark ye,' says Friday, 'me speakee wit you.' We follow'd at a distance; for now being come down on the Gascoign side of the mountains, we were entred a vast great forest, where the country was plain, and pretty open, though many trees in it scatter'd here and there.

Friday, who had, as we say, the heels of the bear, came up with him quickly, and takes up a great stone, and throws at him, and hit him just on the head; but did him no more harm than if he had thrown it against a wall; but it answer'd Friday's end; for the rogue was so void of fear, that he did it purely to make the bear follow him, and show us some laugh as he call'd it.

As soon as the bear felt the stone and saw him, he turns about and comes after him, taking devilish long strides, and shuffling along at a strange rate, so as would have put a horse to a middling gallop; away runs Friday, and takes his course as if he run towards us for help; so we all resolv'd to fire at once upon the bear and deliver my man; though I was angry at him heartily for bringing the bear back upon us, when he was going about his own business another way; and especially I was angry that he had turn'd the bear upon us, and then run away; and I call'd out, 'You dog,' said I, 'is this your making us laugh? Come away, and take your horse, that we may shoot the creature.' He hears me, and crys out, 'No shoot, no shoot, stand still, you get much laugh.' And as the nimble creature run two foot for the beast's one, he turn'd on a sudden on one side of us, and seeing a great oak-tree, fit for his purpose, he beckon'd to us to follow, and doubling his pace he gets nimbly up the tree, laying his gun down upon the ground, at about five or six yards from the bottom of the tree.

The bear soon came to the tree, and we follow'd at a distance; the first thing he did, he stopp'd at the gun, smelt to it, but let it lye, and up he scrambles into the tree, climbing like a cat, though so monstrously heavy. I was amaz'd at the folly, as I thought it, of my man, and could not for my life see any thing to laugh at yet, till seeing the bear get up the tree we all rode nearer to him.

When we came to the tree, there was Friday got out to the small end of a large limb of the tree, and the bear got about half way to him; as soon as the bear got out to that part where the limb of the tree was weaker, 'Ha,' says he to us, 'now you see me teachee the bear dance'; so he falls a jumping and shaking the bough, at which the bear began to totter, but stood still, and begun to look behind him, to see how he should get back; then indeed we did laugh heartily. But Friday had not done with him by a great deal; when he sees him stand still he calls out to him again, as if he had suppos'd the bear could speak English, 'What, you no come farther? pray you come farther'; so he left jumping and shaking the bough; and the bear, just as if he understood what he said, did come a little further, then he fell a jumping again, and the bear stopp'd again.

We thought now was a good time to knock him on the head, and I call'd to Friday to stand still, and we would shoot the bear; but he cry'd out earnestly, 'O pray! O pray! No shoot, me shoot, by and then'; he would have said, 'by and by.' However, to shorten the story, Friday danc'd so much, and the bear stood so ticklish, that we had laughing enough indeed, but still could not imagine what the fellow would do; for first we thought he depended upon shaking the bear off; and we found the bear was too cunning for that too; for he would not go out far enough to be thrown down, but clings fast with his great broad claws and feet, so that we could not imagine what would be the end of it, and where the jest would be at last.

But Friday put us out of doubt quickly; for seeing the bear cling fast to the bough, and that he would not be perswaded to come any farther, 'Well, well,' says Friday, 'you no come farther, me go, me go; you no come to me, me go come to you'; and upon this, he goes out to the smallest end of the bough, where it would bend with his weight, and gently lets himself down by it, sliding down the bough, till he came near enough to jump down on his feet, and away he run to his gun, takes it up, and stands still.

'Well,' said I to him, 'Friday, what will you do now? Why don't you shoot him?' 'No shoot,' says Friday, 'no yet, me shoot now, me no kill; me stay, give you one more laugh'; and indeed so he did, as you will see presently; for when the bear see his enemy gone, he comes back from the bough where he stood; but did it mighty leisurely, looking behind him every step, and coming backward till he got into the body of the tree; then with the same hinder end foremost, he came down the tree, grasping it with his claws, and moving one foot at a time, very leisurely; at this juncture, and just before he could set his hind feet upon the ground, Friday stept up close to him, clapt the muzzle of his piece into his ear, and shot him dead as a stone.

Then the rogue turn'd about, to see if we did not laugh, and when he saw we were pleas'd by our looks, he falls a laughing himself very loud. 'So we kill bear in my country,'* says Friday. 'So you kill them,' says I, 'why you have no guns.' 'No,' says he, 'no gun, but shoot great much long arrow.'

This was indeed a good diversion to us; but we were still in a wild place, and our guide very much hurt, and what to do we hardly knew; the howling of wolves run much in my head; and indeed, except the noise I once heard on the shore of Africa, of which I have said something already, I never heard any thing that filled me with so much horrour.

These things, and the approach of night, called us off, or else, as Friday would have had us, we should certainly have taken the skin of this monstrous creature off, which was worth saving; but we had three leagues to go, and our guide hasten'd us, so we left him, and went forward on our journey.

The ground was still cover'd with snow, tho' not so deep and dangerous as on the mountains, and the ravenous creatures, as we heard afterwards, were come down into the forest and plain country, press'd by hunger to seek for food; and had done a great deal of mischief in the villages, where they surpriz'd the country people, kill'd a great many of their sheep and horses, and some people too.

We had one dangerous place to pass, which our guide told us, if there were any more wolves in the country, we should find them there; and this was in a small plain, surrounded with woods on every side, and a long narrow defile or lane, which we were to pass to get through the wood, and then we should come to the village where we were to lodge.

It was within half an hour of sun-set when we entred the first wood; and a little after sun-set when we came into the plain. We met with nothing in the first wood, except that in a little plain within the wood, which was not above two furlongs over, we saw five great wolves cross the road, full speed one after another, as if they had been in chase of some prey, and had it in view; they took no notice of us, and were gone and out of our sight in a few moments.

Upon this our guide, who by the way was a wretched faint-hearted fellow, bid us keep in a ready posture; for he believed there were more wolves a coming.

We kept our arms ready, and our eyes about us, but we saw no more wolves, 'till we came thro' that wood, which was near half a league, and entred the plain; as soon as we came into the plain we had occasion enough to look about us. The first object we met with was a dead horse; that is to say, a poor horse which the wolves had kill'd, and at least a dozen of them at work; we could not say eating of him, but picking of his bones rather; for they had eaten up all the flesh before.

We did not think fit to disturb them at their feast, neither did they take much notice of us: Friday would have let fly at them, but I would not suffer him by any means; for I found we were like to have more business upon our hands than we were aware of. We were not gone half over the plain, but we began to hear the wolves howl in the wood on our left, in a frightful manner, and presently after we saw about a hundred* coming on directly towards us, all in a body, and most of them in a line, as regularly as an army drawn up by experienc'd officers. I scarce knew in what manner to receive them; but found to draw ourselves in a close line was the only way: so we form'd in a moment. But that we might not have too much interval, I order'd that only every other man should fire, and that the others who had not fir'd should stand ready to give them a second volley immediately, if they continued to advance upon us, and that then those who had fir'd at first should not pretend to load their fusees again, but stand ready with every one a pistol; for we were all arm'd with a fusee and a pair of pistols each man; so we were by this method able to fire six volleys, half of us at a time; however, at present we had no necessity; for upon firing the first volley, the enemy made a full stop, being terrify'd as well with the noise as with the fire; four of them being shot into the head, dropp'd; several others were wounded, and went bleeding off, as we could see by the snow. I found they stopp'd, but did not immediately retreat; whereupon remembring that I had been told that the fiercest creatures were terrify'd at the voice of a man, I caus'd all our company to hollow as loud as we could; and I found the notion not altogether mistaken; for upon our shout, they began to retire and turn about; then I order'd a second volley to be fir'd in their rear, which put them to the gallop, and away they went to the woods.

This gave us leisure to charge our pieces again, and that we might loose no time, we kept going; but we had but little more than loaded our fusees, and put ourselves into a readiness, when we heard a terrible noise in the same wood, on our left, only that it was farther onward the same way we were to go.

The night was coming on, and the light began to be dusky, which made it worse on our side; but the noise encreasing, we could easily perceive that it was the howling and yelling of those hellish creatures; and on a sudden, we perceiv'd 2 or 3 troops of wolves, one on our left, one behind us, and one on our front; so that we seem'd to be surrounded with 'em; however, as they did not fall upon us, we kept our way forward, as fast as we could make our horses go, which, the way being very rough, was only a good large trot; and in this manner we came in view of the entrance of a wood, through which we were to pass, at the farther side of the plain; but we were greatly surpriz'd, when coming nearer the lane or pass, we saw a confus'd number of wolves standing just at the entrance.

On a sudden, at another opening of the wood, we heard the noise of a gun; and looking that way, out rush'd a horse, with a saddle and a bridle on him, flying like the wind, and sixteen or seventeen wolves after him, full speed; indeed, the horse had the heels of them; but as we suppos'd that he could not hold it at that rate, we doubted not but they would get up with him at last, and no question but they did.

But here we had a most horrible sight; for riding up to the entrance where the horse came out, we found the carcass of another horse, and of two men, devour'd by the ravenous creatures, and one of the men was no doubt the same who we heard fir'd the gun; for there lay a gun just by him, fir'd off; but as to the man, his head and upper part of his body was eaten up.

This fill'd us with horror, and we knew not what course to take, but the creatures resolv'd us soon; for they gather'd about us presently, in hopes of prey; and I verily believe there were three hundred of them. It happen'd very much to our advantage, that at the entrance into the wood, but a little way from it, there lay some large timber trees, which had been cut down the summer before, and I suppose lay there for carriage; I drew my little troop in among those trees, and placing our selves in a line behind one long tree, I advis'd them all to light, and keeping that tree before us for a breast work, to stand in a triangle, or three fronts, enclosing our horses in the center.

We did so, and it was well we did; for never was a more furious charge than the creatures made upon us in the place; they came on us with a growling kind of a noise (and mounted the piece of timber, which, as I said, was our breast work) as if they were only rushing upon their prey; and this fury of theirs, it seems, was principally occasion'd by their seeing our horses behind us, which was the prey they aim'd at: I order'd our men to fire as before, every other man; and they took their aim so sure, that indeed they kill'd several of the wolves at the first volley; but there was a necessity to keep a continual firing; for they came on like devils, those behind pushing on those before.

When we had fir'd our second volley of our fusees, we thought they stopp'd a little, and I hop'd they would have gone off; but it was but a moment; for others came forward again; so we fir'd two volleys of our pistols, and I believe in these four firings we had kill'd seventeen or eighteen of them, and lam'd twice as many; yet they came on again.

I was loath to spend our last shot too hastily; so I call'd my servant, not my man Friday, for he was better employ'd; for with the greatest dexterity imaginable, he had charg'd my fusee and his own, while we were engag'd; but as I said, I call'd my other man, and giving him a horn of powder, I bad him lay a train all along the piece of timber, and let it be a large train; he did so, and had but just time to get away, when the wolves came up to it, and some were got up upon it; when I, snapping an uncharg'd pistol close to the powder, set it on fire; those that were upon the timber were scorcht with it, and six or seven of them fell, or rather jump'd in among us, with the force and fright of the fire; we dispatch'd these in an instant, and the rest were so frighted with the light, which the night, for it was now very dark, made more terrible, that they drew back a little.

Upon which I order'd our last pistol to be fir'd off in one volley, and after that we gave a shout; upon this, the wolves turn'd tail, and we sally'd immediately upon near twenty lame ones, who we found struggling on the ground, and fell a cutting them with our swords, which answer'd our expectation; for the crying and howling they made was better understood by their fellows, so that they all fled and left us.

We had, first and last, kill'd about three score of them; and had it been day-light, we had kill'd many more. The field of battle being thus clear'd, we made forward again; for we had still near a league to go. We heard the ravenous creatures houl and yell in the woods as we went, several times; and sometimes we fancy'd we saw some of them, but the snow dazling our eyes, we were not certain; so in about an hour more, we came to the town where we were to lodge, which we found in a terrible fright, and all in arms; for it seems that the night before, the wolves and some bears had broke into the village in the night, and put them in a terrible fright; and they were oblig'd to keep guard night and day, but especially in the night, to preserve their cattle, and indeed their people.

The next morning our guide was so ill, and his limbs swell'd with the rankling of his two wounds, that he could go no farther; so we were oblig'd to take a new guide there, and go to Thoulouse, where we found a warm climate, a fruitful pleasant country, and no snow, no wolves, or any thing like them; but when we told our story at Thoulouse, they told us it was nothing but what was ordinary in the great forest at the foot of the mountains, especially when the snow lay on the ground: but they enquir'd much what kind of a guide we had gotten, that would venture to bring us that way in such a severe season; and told us it was very much we were not all devour'd. When we told them how we plac'd our selves, and the horses in the middle, they blam'd us exceedingly, and told us it was fifty to one but we had been all destroy'd; for it was the sight of the horses which made the wolves so furious, seeing their prey; and that at other times they are really afraid of a gun; but the being excessive hungry, and raging on that account, the eagerness to come at the horses had made them sensless of danger; and that if we had not by the continu'd fire, and at last by the stratagem of the train of powder, master'd them, it had been great odds but that we had been torn to pieces; whereas had we been content to have sat still on horseback, and fir'd as horsemen, they would not have taken the horses for so much their own, when men were on their backs, as otherwise; and withal they told us, that at last, if we had stood altogether, and left our horses, they would have been so eager to have devour'd them, that we might have come off safe, especially having our fire arms in our hands, and being so many in number.

For my part, I was never so sensible of danger in my life; for seeing above three hundred devils come roaring and open mouth'd to devour us, and having nothing to shelter us, or retreat to, I gave my self over for lost; and as it was, I believe I shall never care to cross those mountains again; I think I would much rather go a thousand leagues by sea, though I were sure to meet with a storm once a week.

I have nothing uncommon to take notice of in my passage through France; nothing but what other travellers have given an account of, with much more advantage than I can. I travell'd from Thoulouse to Paris, and without any considerable stay, came to Callais, and landed safe at Dover, the fourteenth of January, after having had a severely cold season to travel in.

I was now come to the center of my travels, and had in a little time all my new discover'd estate safe about me, the bills of exchange which I brought with me having been very currently paid.

My principal guide and privy councellor was my good antient widow, who in gratitude for the money I had sent her, thought no pains too much, or care too great, to employ for me; and I trusted her so entirely with every thing, that I was perfectly easy as to the security of my effects; and indeed, I was very happy from my beginning, and now to the end, in the unspotted integrity of this good gentlewoman.

And now I began to think of leaving my effects with this woman, and setting out for Lisbon, and so to the Brasils; but now another scruple came in my way, and that was religion; for as I had entertain'd some doubts about the Roman religion, even while I was abroad, especially in my state of solitude; so I knew there was no going to the Brasils for me, much less going to settle there, unless I resolv'd to embrace the Roman Catholick religion, without any reserve; unless on the other hand I resolv'd to be a sacrifice to my principles, be a martyr for religion, and die in the Inquisition; so I resolv'd to stay at home, and if I could find means for it, to dispose of my plantation.

To this purpose I wrote to my old friend at Lisbon, who in return gave me notice that he could easily dispose of it there: but that if I thought fit to give him leave to offer it in my name to the two merchants, the survivors of my trustees, who liv'd in the Brasils, who must fully understand the value of it, who liv'd just upon the spot, and who I knew were very rich; so that he believ'd they would be fond of buying it; he did not doubt, but I should make 4 or 5,000 pieces of eight the more of it.

Accordingly I agreed, gave him order to offer it to them, and he did so; and in about 8 months more, the ship being then return'd, he sent me account that they had accepted the offer, and had remitted 33,000 pieces of eight to a correspondent of theirs at Lisbon, to pay for it.

In return I sign'd the instrument of sale in the form which they sent from Lisbon, and sent it to my old man, who sent me bills of exchange for 32,800 pieces of eight, for the estate; reserving the payment of 100 moidores a year to him, the old man, during his life, and 50 moidores afterwards to his son for his life, which I had promised them, which the plantation was to make good as a rent-charge. And thus I have given the first part of a life of fortune and adventure, a life of Providence's chequer-work, and of a variety which the world will seldom be able to show the like of: beginning foolishly, but closing much more happily than any part of it ever gave me leave so much as to hope for.

Any one would think that in this state of complicated good fortune I was past running any more hazards; and so indeed I had been, if other circumstances had concurr'd; but I was inur'd to a wandring life, had no family, not many relations, nor, however rich, had I contracted much acquaintance; and though I had sold my estate in the Brasils, yet I could not keep the country out of my head, and had a great mind to be upon the wing again; especially I could not resist the strong inclination I had to see my island, and to know if the poor Spaniards were in being there, and how the rogues I left there had used them.

My true friend, the widow, earnestly diswaded me from it, and so far prevail'd with me, that for almost seven years she prevented my running abroad; during which time I took my two nephews, the children of one of my brothers, into my care. The eldest having something of his own, I bred up as a gentleman, and gave him a settlement of some addition to his estate, after my decease; the other I put out to a captain of a ship; and after five years, finding him a sensible bold enterprising young fellow, I put him into a good ship, and sent him to sea: and this young fellow afterwards drew me in, as old as I was, to farther adventures my self.

In the mean time I in part settled my self here; for first of all I marry'd, and that not either to my disadvantage or dissatisfaction, and had three children, two sons and one daughter: but my wife dying, and my nephew coming home with good success from a voyage to Spain, my inclination to go abroad, and his importunity, prevailed and engag'd me to go in his ship, as a private trader to the East Indies. This was in the year 1694.

In this voyage I visited my new collony in the island, saw my successors the Spaniards, had the whole story of their lives, and of the villains I left there; how at first they insulted the poor Spaniards, how they afterwards agreed, disagreed, united, separated, and how at last the Spaniards were oblig'd to use violence with them, how they were subjected to the Spaniards, how honestly the Spaniards used them; a history, if it were entred into, as full of variety and wonderful accidents as my own part; particularly also as to their battles with the Caribbeans, who landed several times upon the island, and as to the improvement they made upon the island it self, and how five of them made an attempt upon the main land, and brought away eleven men and five women prisoners, by which, at my coming, I found about twenty young children on the island.

Here I stay'd about 20 days, left them supplies of all necessary things, and particularly of arms, powder, shot, cloaths, tools, and two workmen, which I brought from England with me, viz. a carpenter and a smith.

Besides this, I shar'd the island into parts with 'em, reserv'd to my self the property of the whole, but gave them such parts respectively as they agreed on; and having settled all things with them, and engaged them not to leave the place, I left them there.

From thence I touch'd at the Brasils, from whence I sent a bark, which I bought there, with more people to the island, and in it, besides other supplies, I sent seven women, being such as I found proper for service, or for wives to such as would take them. As to the English men, I promis'd them to send them some women from England, with a good cargoe of necessaries, if they would apply themselves to planting, which I afterwards perform'd. And the fellows prov'd very honest and diligent after they were master'd and had their properties set apart for them. I sent them also from the Brasils five cows, three of them being big with calf, some sheep, and some hogs, which, when I came again, were considerably encreas'd.

But all these things, with an account how 300 Caribbees came and invaded them, and ruin'd their plantations, and how they fought with that whole number twice, and were at first defeated, and three of them kill'd; but at last a storm destroying their enemies' canoes, they famish'd or destroy'd almost all the rest, and renew'd and recover'd the possession of their plantation, and still liv'd upon the island; all these things, with some very surprizing incidents in some new adventures of my own, for ten years more, I may perhaps give a farther account of hereafter.

NOTES

---

p. 4 the wise man: Solomon. The reference is to Proverbs 30, 8.

p. 5 meer: absolute, complete; 'nothing but my fate.' The meaning has since slid into something more casual and derogatory.

p. 8 roads: sheltered waters.

p. 9 sheet anchor: an extra anchor carried in case the regular or 'bower' anchors fail.

better end: bitter end. That end of the anchor cable that remains around the anchor post, or 'bitt.' The original sense has been obscured by common metaphorical use: 'hang on to the bitter end.'

p. 11 Winterton Ness: Winterton, Norfolk, is noted for its vicious currents and treacherous sands. When Defoe went there, he noted that most of the houses in the area were built from the timbers of wrecks, as he described later in *A Tour Thro' the Whole Island of Great Britain.*

p. 15 calenture: spanish: *calentura*, fever.

Sallee: Sale, just north of Rabat.

p. 16 Maresco: from the Italian, 'a moor.'

p. 17 antient: sometimes spelled 'ancient.' Corruption of 'ensign.'

p. 19 twist: crotch. One meaning of 'twist' is 'a divided object,' i.e. where the body divides.

p. 21 the hands of lyons and tygers: there are no true tigers in Africa, but the word has long been generalized to include large felines: jaguar (*tigre* in South American Spanish), cougar, panther.

p. 27 perspective-glasses: telescopes.

p. 34 Oronoque: one of many alternative spellings for 'Orinoco.'

p. 38 strangled: the original sense of 'killing by constriction' used to extend to 'killing by stopping the breath.'

turn'd off: from the phrase 'to turn off the ladder,' to hang.

p. 41 rack: arrack. Sweet, fermented drink.

p. 46 runlets: sort of cask. 'Large runlets appear to have varied between 12 and 18.5 gallons, small ones between a pint or quart and 3 or 4 gallons' (OED).

p. 58 shoal: alternative for 'shallow.'

p. 59 seals: there are no seals in the tropics. But they do live in Selkirk's island in the Juan Fernandez group.

p. 61 flaggs: a 'flag' is now a sort of iris. Used in the plural, in Defoe's time it meant coarse grass.

p. 63 oakum: 'off-combings,' twists of old rope.

p. 66 stark: extremely, absolutely, as in 'stark naked.'

p. 77 the line: usually, the Equator. Here, Defoe muddles it with the date-line, which runs down the Pacific.

p. 100 search: searce, originally a cloth made of bristles.

p. 102 periagua: dug-out. One of two dozen or more alternatives for 'piragua,' from the Carib.

p. 104 grutches: begrudges.

p. 109 twenty-six year: should be twenty-seven. An example of Defoe's hasty writing.

p. 122 frog: loop. Originally, a tuft of wool or cotton. From the Latin *floccus*.

p. 138 abated: abetted, increased. 'Abated,' i.e. diminished, makes no sense.

p. 142 naked: the sense of 'unarmed' has now disappeared.

p. 144 chark: abbreviation of 'charcoal.'

p. 145 wild-fire: a combination of inflammable substances. Tinder, in this case gunpowder.

p. 149 nicest: one meaning of 'nice' is 'finely discriminative.'

p. 150 Muschatoes: Moustache. Another common spelling was 'Mustachio'.

p. 153 motion: emotion.

  naturalists: those who follow nature rather than revelation.

p. 155 bolt-sprit: alternative form of 'bowsprit,' the difference in spelling and pronunciation suggests an origin unconnected to 'bow,' in the sense of the fore-end of a ship.

p. 156 succades: from the French. 'Fruit preserves in sugar.'

p. 158 moydor: or 'moidore.' Corruption of the Portuguese 'moeda d'ouro,' 'money of gold,' a gold coin worth about 27 shillings.

p. 176 'O': from the Christian form of address in prayer: 'O Lord . . . '

p. 179 affection: emotion.

p. 185 fustic: two kinds of wood used in dyeing yellow. Here, the Venezuelan sumac.

  Nicaragua wood: a species of Caesalpinia tree that produces a red dye.

p. 189 fetch'd a compass: made a circle.

p. 198 sixteen: three pages later, Defoe has 'fourteen.'

p. 201 oak: an unlikely find on a Caribbean island. Most oaks grow in temperate and high-altitude conditions.

p. 202 writing: suddenly, Crusoe has ink; yet earlier he gave up his journal when it ran low.

p. 211 waft: a waving motion.

p. 226 eight and twenty years: Defoe has his sums wrong again. It is actually twenty-seven years (1659–86).

p. 228 moiety: share.

p. 232 let blood: bleeding, or blood-letting (phlebotomy), was a standard treatment for many diseases.

p. 235 the Groyne: Then, the English name for Corunna, northwest Spain.

p. 241 bear in my country: there are no bears in lowland Venezuela or Guyana.

p. 243 a hundred: mass attack by wolves is a popular subject in fiction, but it is based on a myth. Wolves hunt in small packs, but a head-on assault on humans is unknown.

DEFOE AND HIS CRITICS

Charles Gildon (1665–1724): *The Life and Strange Surprizing Adventures of Mr D . . . De F . . ., of London, Hosier*, 1719.

> *D[anie]l.* Hum, hum . . . well, and what are your complaints of me?
> *Cru[soe].* Why, that you have made me a strange whimsical, inconsistent Being, in three Weeks losing all the Religion of a Pious Education; and when you bring me again to a Sense of the Want of Religion, you make me quit that upon every Whimsy; you make me extravagantly Zealous, and as extravagantly Remiss . . . Therefore, I say, *Friday*, prepare to shoot.
> *Fri[day].* No shoot yet Master, me have something to say, he much Injure me too.
> *Dl.* Injure you too, how the Devil have I injur'd you?
> *Fri.* Have injure me, to make me such a Blockhead, so much contradiction, as to be able to speak *English tolerably well* in a Month or two, and not to speak it better in Twelve years after.

Alexander Pope (c. 1729):

> The first part of *Robinson Crusoe*, good. Defoe wrote many things, and none bad, though none excellent.

From the article on Defoe, *Lives of the Poets* (1753), attributed to a 'Mr Cibber' – Theophilus Cibber (1703–58). It is probably mainly by Robert Shiels, a friend of Dr Johnson:

> His imagination was fertile, strong and lively, as may be collected from his many works of fancy, particularly his *Robinson Crusoe*, which was written in so natural a manner, and with so many probable incidents, that for some time after its publication, it was judged by most people to be a true story. It was indeed written upon a model entirely new.

Jean-Jacques Rousseau (1712–78): *Emile, ou de l'éducation* (1762).

> Since books are absolutely necessary, there is one which to my taste supplies the happiest introduction to natural education. This will be the first book my Emile will read. For a long time it will constitute his entire library by itself, and it will always retain a distinguished place there. It will be the text on which all our discussion of the natural sciences will be merely a gloss. It will serve as a check on the state of our judgement as we proceed, and in so far as our taste remains unspoilt, we shall always take pleasure in reading it. What is this wonderful book, then? Is it Aristotle, or Pliny, or Buffon? No – it is *Robinson Crusoe*. (Translated by Pat Rogers.)

Dr Samuel Johnson (1709–84): from Boswell's *Life*.

> His *Robinson Crusoe* is enough of itself to establish his reputation.

Johnsonian Miscellanies (ed. G. B. Hill, 1897).

> Was there ever yet anything written by mere man that was wished longer by its readers, excepting Don Quixote, Robinson Crusoe, and the *Pilgrim's Progress*.

Sir Walter Scott (1771–1832), *The Miscellaneous Works of Sir Walter Scott, Bart* (Edinburgh, 1834).

> It cannot be the beauty of the style which thus commands the reader's attention . . . In general the language is loose and inaccurate, often tame and creeping, and almost always that of the lower classes of society. Neither does the charm depend upon the character of the incidents . . . Neither can it be the artful conducting of the story, by which we are so much interested. De Foe seems to have written too rapidly to pay the least attention to these circumstances . . . To what, then, are we to ascribe the general charm attached to the romances of De Foe? We presume to answer, that it is chiefly to be ascribed to the unequalled dexterity with which our author has given an appearance of REALITY to the incidents which he narrates.
>
> There scarce exists a work so popular as *Robinson Crusoe*. It is read eagerly by young people; and there is hardly an elf so devoid of imagination as not to have supposed for himself a solitary island in which he could act *Robinson Crusoe*, were it but in the corner of the nursery.

Walter Wilson (1781–1847), *Memoirs of the Life and Times of Daniel De Foe* (1830).

> The fine sentiments that abound in *Crusoe*, its delicate touches, and pure morality, are not the least parts of its beauties . . . While it instructs us in the development of the human powers, under the guidance of natural reason, it points to the Almighty as the source from whence man derives his capacities.

George Borrow (1803–81), *Lavengro* (1851).

> Reader, is it necessary to name the book [*Robinson Crusoe*] . . . whose very prints, feeble expounders of its wondrous lines, had produced within me emotions strange and novel? Scarcely, for it was a book . . . to which, from the hardy deeds which it narrates, and the spirit of strange and romantic enterprise which it tends to awaken, England owes many of her astonishing discoveries both by sea and land, and no inconsiderable part of her naval glory.

Karl Marx (1818–83), *Das Kapital* (1867).

> Since Robinson Crusoe's experiences are a favourite theme with political economists, let us take a look at him on his island. Moderate though he be, yet some few wants he has to satisfy, and must therefore do a little useful work of various sorts . . . Of his prayers and the like we take no account, since they are a source of pleasure to him, and he looks upon them as so much recreation . . . Necessity itself compels him to apportion his time accurately between his different kinds of work . . . This our friend Robinson soon learns by experience, and having rescued a watch [ed: Crusoe had no watch – this is a piece of wishful thinking by Marx], ledger, and pen and ink from the wreck, commences, like a true-born Briton, to keep a set of books. His stock-book contains a list of the objects of utility that belong to him . . . [and] of the labour time that definite quantities of those objects have, on the average, cost him . . . those relations contain all that is essential to the determination of value.

Sir Leslie Stephen (1832–1904), *Hours in Library* (1874, revised 1892).

> We may infer, what is probable from other cases, that a man living 15 years by himself, like Crusoe, would either go mad or sink into the semi-savage state . . . [Defoe] gives a very inadequate picture

of the mental torments to which his hero is exposed . . . His stay on the island produces the same state of mind as might be due to a dull Sunday in Scotland . . . [It] is a book for boys rather than men . . . it falls short of high intellectual interest.

An unsigned review, *Cornhill Magazine*, 1871.

Robinson Crusoe stands out from its companions [Defoe's other novels] like a noble mountain amidst a range of stunted hillocks; it is a book so manly in tone, so feminine in sweetness, so Christian in feeling, that it deserve a place on the same shelf with the *Faery Queene* and the *Pilgrim's Progress*.

William Minto, *Daniel Defoe* (1879).

If he had never chanced to write *Robinson Crusoe*, he would now have a very obscure place in English literature . . . The vast mass of Defoe's writings received no kindly aid from distinguished contemporaries to float them down the stream; everything was done that bitter dislike and supercilious indifference could do to submerge them. *Robinson Crusoe* was their sole life buoy.

SUGGESTIONS FOR FURTHER READING

Curtis, Laura, *The Elusive Daniel Defoe*, Vision, and Barnes and Noble, 1984.

Dobrée, Bonamy, *English Literature in the Early 18th Century 1700–40*, OUP, 1959.

Hunter, J. Paul, *The Reluctant Pilgrim*, Johns Hopkins Press, 1966.

Leavis, Q. D., *Fiction and the Reading Public*, Chatto and Windus, 1968.

Novak, Maximillian, *Defoe and the Nature of Man*, OUP, 1963.

Richetti, John, *Defoe's Narratives*, OUP, 1975.

Rogers, Pat, ed., *Defoe: The Critical Heritage*, Routledge and Kegan Paul, 1972.

Sill, Geoffrey, *Defoe and the Idea of Fiction*, University of Delaware Press, 1983.

Starr, G. A., *Defoe and Spiritual Autobiography*, Princeton, 1965.

Sutherland, James, *Daniel Defoe: A Critical Study*, Harvard University Press, 1971.

Watt, Ian, *The Rise of the Novel*, Penguin, 1963.

TEXT SUMMARY

The desert-island heart of the story is preceded by a series of adventures that provide an introduction to the hero and his character.

Crusoe, the third son of a trader, refuses to consider the responsible, stay-at-home life his father suggests. Instead, filled with the heedless impetuosity of an eighteen-year-old, he insists on going to sea. This disobedience to the God-like guidance of his father will doom him to misery.

No sooner is he on board than his father's words are fulfilled. He is almost drowned in two violent storms. He recognizes his error, but then, when the wind abates, forgets all about repentance. 'My ill Fate pushed me on,' to London, and to sea.

On his next voyage, to Africa, he learns navigation and the basics of trade. Embarking again, his ship is seized by Moorish pirates. He is enslaved. One of his tasks is to help his master fishing. After two years, he makes a well-planned escape with a local boy, Xury, who becomes his slave. After weeks sailing along the African coast, with a number of exotic contacts with tribes and wild animals, the two are picked up by a passing ship and taken to Brazil. On the way, Crusoe sells Xury.

In Brazil, Crusoe sets himself up with a plantation. Again, security and prosperity beckon. Again, Crusoe is tempted by travel, to buy slaves in Africa. In the Caribbean, off the mouth of the Orinoco, the ship hits a storm, and is wrecked.

This is the start of the real story. Crusoe is 28, an experienced sailor, prudent in business, but with hardly a serious thought in his head.

He finds himself cast up on the sand, a sole survivor. He has nothing but a knife and some tobacco. After a night spent in a tree, in case of attack by wild animals, he sees the wreck. He makes the first of a dozen trips, builds a raft, and takes off a huge store of equipment, food, clothing and ammunition, working from a make-shift camp. This takes two weeks.

Exploring further, he finds a living site, a hollow beside a hill. Here he builds a defence of stakes, hauls in his goods, and then burrows a cave from the rock. He also ventures out hunting.

After weeks of labour, his thoughts begin to expand. Why this odd combination of misfortune and providential luck? Consideration leads him to keep records: a post notched to count days, a journal to record his progress.

Gradually he masters new skills. After throwing away some husks, he finds a small harvest of barley growing, and begins to farm.

A bout of fever induces a terrible dream of impending death. He remembers his father's warning, and for the first time examines the meaning of his life and what role God might have in it. Recovering, he begins to read his Bible, and to pray. He has been on the island ten months, and we are one-third through the book.

Now he begins to explore. He finds a valley, with wild fruit. Here he makes a second place to live, and after a year crosses the island. He improves his life by tilling, planting, basket-weaving, raising goats, pot-making, baking. He already has animal companions – a dog and several cats – and now acquires a parrot, which learns to talk. Time runs more easily (the second year is covered in ten pages). All things considered, it is a comfortable life, and he gives thanks for it.

Once secure in his new life, he begins to think of escape by dug-out canoe. Making it becomes such an obsession that he never thinks of its weight. When it is done, he cannot move it – a warning against the thoughtless creation of luxury and ingratitude for the 'long series of miracles' that have saved him so far.

Like Adam in Eden, he is acquiring knowledge, and Adam-like makes clothes, out of goat-skins.

Five years pass.

He makes a better canoe, which he fits with lockers and a sail, and again attempts escape. It almost ends in disaster when a strong current carries him away from land, until a favourable wind blows him back again. Shocked, he resolves 'to lay aside all thoughts of my Deliverance by my boat.'

Time passes, carrying him into a timeless state of control and contentment as 'Lord of the whole Island,' confident he could last there forty years if necessary.

After fifteen years on the island, and almost exactly half way through the book, this idyll is shattered. He sees a footprint on the beach. Realizing he is not alone, fearing he is about to encounter cannibals, he undergoes a crisis.

In a panic, he redoubles security and re-orders his life.

With good cause. Two years later, he finds the remains of a cannibal feast. He dreams of destroying the 'savages,' until wiser thoughts prevail.

Their savagery is not his responsibility. If they reappear, he will stay clear.

His twenty-fourth year on the island brings another crisis. He sees a sail. The ship is wrecked. There are no survivors, and Crusoe realizes how desperate he is for company. He even dreams of encountering the cannibals and saving one of the victims. Fear and longing become his constant companions. He concludes his only way to escape is 'to get a Savage into my Possession.'

All this prepares the way – physically, emotionally, dramatically – for the actual appearance of cannibals, two-thirds of the way through the book. One of the victims escapes. Crusoe saves him from his pursuers.

Crusoe feeds him, clothes him and names him Friday. Friday becomes devoted to his saviour. Seeing that Friday has the intelligence and feelings to match his own, Crusoe teaches him English, shows him how to work, and instructs him in religion (though not easily: Friday challenges Crusoe with puzzling questions – 'Why God no kill the Devil?')

For three years, they live 'perfectly and compleatly happy.'

Still, though, there looms the dream of escape. Friday builds a sea-going canoe. Opportunity comes when the cannibals return, this time with a European victim. There is a battle. Crusoe and Friday save the man, a Spaniard, and another intended victim, who turns out to be Friday's father.

As he wryly observes, Crusoe now has a society of subjects in miniature: a pagan, a Catholic and a Protestant (Friday). The Spaniard is one of a party on the mainland. Crusoe sends the Spaniard and Friday's father off in the canoe to summon the other Europeans in their ship.

In fact, the next arrival is an English ship. Mutineers beach, with their captain a prisoner. Crusoe and Friday save him, and take several prisoners. After a battle, Crusoe's little army takes the ship. They sail away, leaving the mutineers stranded, but with the benefits of Crusoe's years of labour.

The book concludes with thirty pages of epilogue in which Crusoe re-establishes contact with home, moves to Lisbon, finds out that his Brazilian estates have prospered, takes his profits and returns home by land, with adventures along the way that include a dramatic flight from wolves in the Pyrenees. A final brief mention of a return to the island hints at a sequel to come.

CLASSIC FICTION
IN EVERYMAN

**The Impressions of
Theophrastus Such**
GEORGE ELIOT
*An amusing collection of character
sketches, and the only paperback
edition available*
£5.99

Frankenstein
MARY SHELLEY
*A masterpiece of Gothic terror in
its original 1818 version*
£3.99

East Lynne
MRS HENRY WOOD
*A classic tale of melodrama,
murder and mystery*
£7.99

**Holiday Romance and
Other Writings for Children**
CHARLES DICKENS
*Dickens's works for children,
including 'The Life of Our Lord'
and 'A Child's History of England',
with original illustrations*
£5.99

The Ebb-Tide
R. L. STEVENSON
*A compelling study of ordinary
people in extreme circumstances*
£4.99

The Three Impostors
ARTHUR MACHEN
*The only edition available
of this cult thriller*
£4.99

Mister Johnson
JOYCE CARY
*The only edition available of this
amusing but disturbing twentieth-
century tale*
£5.99

The Jungle Book
RUDYARD KIPLING
*The classic adventures of Mowgli
and his friends*
£3.99

Glenarvon
LADY CAROLINE LAMB
*The only edition available of the
novel which throws light on the
greatest scandal of the early nineteenth century – the infatuation of
Caroline Lamb with Lord Byron*
£6.99

**Twenty Thousand Leagues
Under the Sea**
JULES VERNE
*Scientific fact combines with
fantasy in this prophetic tale
of underwater adventure*
£4.99

All books are available from your local bookshop or direct from:
Littlehampton Book Services Cash Sales, 14 Eldon Way, Lineside Estate,
Littlehampton, West Sussex BN17 7HE (*prices are subject to change*)

To order any of the books, please enclose a cheque (in sterling) made payable to
Littlehampton Book Services, or phone your order through with credit card details (Access,
Visa or Mastercard) on 01903 721596 (24 hour answering service) stating card number
and expiry date. (*Please add £1.25 for package and postage to the total of your order.*)

In the USA, for further information and a complete catalogue call 1-800-526-2778

CLASSIC NOVELS
IN EVERYMAN

The Time Machine
H. G. WELLS
*One of the books which defined
'science fiction' – a compelling
and tragic story of a brilliant
and driven scientist*
£3.99

Oliver Twist
CHARLES DICKENS
*Arguably the best-loved of
Dickens's novels. With all the
original illustrations*
£4.99

Barchester Towers
ANTHONY TROLLOPE
*The second of Trollope's
Chronicles of Barsetshire,
and one of the funniest of all
Victorian novels*
£4.99

The Heart of Darkness
JOSEPH CONRAD
*Conrad's most intense, subtle,
compressed, profound and
proleptic work*
£3.99

Tess of the d'Urbervilles
THOMAS HARDY
*The powerful, poetic classic
of wronged innocence*
£3.99

Wuthering Heights and Poems
EMILY BRONTË
*A powerful work of genius – one of
the great masterpieces of literature*
£3.99

Pride and Prejudice
JANE AUSTEN
*Proposals, rejections, infidelities,
elopements, happy marriages –
Jane Austen's most popular novel*
£2.99

North and South
ELIZABETH GASKELL
*A novel of hardship, passion
and hard-won wisdom amidst the
conflicts of the industrial revolution*
£4.99

The Newcomes
W. M. THACKERAY
*An exposé of Victorian polite
society by one of the nineteenth-
century's finest novelists*
£6.99

Adam Bede
GEORGE ELIOT
*A passionate rural drama enacted
at the turn of the eighteenth
century*
£5.99

All books are available from your local bookshop or direct from:
Littlehampton Book Services Cash Sales, 14 Eldon Way, Lineside Estate,
Littlehampton, West Sussex BN17 7HE (*prices are subject to change*)

To order any of the books, please enclose a cheque (in sterling) made payable to
Littlehampton Book Services, or phone your order through with credit card details (Access,
Visa or Mastercard) on 01903 721596 (24 hour answering service) stating card number
and expiry date. (*Please add £1.25 for package and postage to the total of your order.*)

In the USA, for further information and a complete catalogue call 1-800-526-2778

SHORT STORY COLLECTIONS
IN EVERYMAN

The Strange Case of Dr Jekyll and Mr Hyde and Other Stories
R. L. STEVENSON
An exciting selection of gripping tales from a master of suspense
£1.99

Nineteenth-Century American Short Stories
edited by Christopher Bigsby
A selection of the works of Henry James, Edith Wharton, Mark Twain and many other great American writers
£6.99

The Best of Saki
edited by MARTIN STEPHEN
Includes Tobermory, Gabriel Ernest, Svedni Vashtar, The Interlopers, Birds on the Western Front
£4.99

Souls Belated and Other Stories
EDITH WHARTON
Brief, neatly crafted tales exploring a range of themes from big taboo subjects to the subtlest little ironies of social life
£6.99

The Night of the Iguana and Other Stories
TENNESSEE WILLIAMS
Twelve remarkable short stories, each a compelling drama in miniature
£4.99

Selected Short Stories and Poems
THOMAS HARDY
Hardy's most memorable stories and poetry in one volume
£4.99

Selected Tales
HENRY JAMES
Stories portraying the tensions between private life and the outside world
£5.99

The Best of Sherlock Homes
ARTHUR CONAN DOYLE
All the favourite adventures in one volume
£4.99

The Secret Self 1: *Short Stories by Women*
edited by Hermione Lee
'A superb collection' The Guardian
£4.99

All books are available from your local bookshop or direct from:
Littlehampton Book Services Cash Sales, 14 Eldon Way, Lineside Estate,
Littlehampton, West Sussex BN17 7HE (*prices are subject to change*)

To order any of the books, please enclose a cheque (in sterling) made payable to
Littlehampton Book Services, or phone your order through with credit card details (Access,
Visa or Mastercard) on 01903 721596 (24 hour answering service) stating card number
and expiry date. (*Please add £1.25 for package and postage to the total of your order.*)

In the USA, for further information and a complete catalogue call 1-800-526-2778

CHARLES DICKENS
IN EVERYMAN

*The Everyman Dickens is the most comprehensive paperback
edition available, with all the original illustrations*

Bleak House
lited by Andrew Sanders
great mystery unravelled
£5.99

Great Expectations
edited by Robin Gilmour
*From Newgate prison to society
drawing rooms – Pip's hopes and
dreams of becoming a gentleman*
£3.99

Hard Times
edited by Grahame Smith
*Dickens's bleak vision of
mid-Victorian England*
£3.99

Oliver Twist
edited by Steven Connor
*An innocent's journey through
London's underworld*
£4.99

Martin Chuzzlewit
edited by Michael Slater
*Classic examination of greed
and hypocrisy, by turns disturbing
and hilarious*
£4.99

Nicholas Nickleby
edited by David Parker
*An exciting tale of the young
Nicholas making his way in
the world*
£5.99

The Old Curiosity Shop
edited by Paul Schlicke
*A story that has provoked more
extreme responses than anything
else Dickens wrote*
£5.99

A Tale of Two Cities
edited by Norman Page
*The classic English evocation
of the French Revolution*
£3.99

**Holiday Romance and Other
Writings for Children**
edited by Gillian Avery
'Holiday Romance', The Life of
Our Lord', 'A Child's History
of England', *available only in
Everyman*
£5.99

All books are available from your local bookshop or direct from:
Littlehampton Book Services Cash Sales, 14 Eldon Way, Lineside Estate,
Littlehampton, West Sussex BN17 7HE (*prices are subject to change*)

To order any of the books, please enclose a cheque (in sterling) made payable to
Littlehampton Book Services, or phone your order through with credit card details (Access,
Visa or Mastercard) on 01903 721596 (24 hour answering service) stating card number
and expiry date. (*Please add £1.25 for package and postage to the total of your order.*)

In the USA, for further information and a complete catalogue call 1-800-526-2778

AMERICAN LITERATURE
IN EVERYMAN

The Marble Faun
NATHANIEL HAWTHORNE
The product of Hawthorne's two years in Italy, the thrilling story of young Americans in Europe
£5.99

The Portrait of a Lady
HENRY JAMES
A masterpiece of psychological and social examination, which established James as a major novelist
£5.99

Billy Budd and Other Stories
HERMAN MELVILLE
The compelling parable of innocence destroyed by a fallen world
£4.99

The Red Badge of Courage
STEPHEN CRANE
A vivid portrayal of a young soldier's experience of the American Civil War
£3.99

Leaves of Grass and Selected Prose
WALT WHITMAN
The best of Whitman in one volume
£6.99

The Age of Innocence
EDITH WHARTON
A tale of the conflict between love and tradition by one of America's finest women novelists
£4.99

Nineteenth-Century American Short Stories
edited by Christopher Bigsby
A selection of the works of Henry James, Edith Wharton, Mark Twain and many other great American writers
£6.99

Selected Poems
HENRY LONGFELLOW
A selection spanning the whole of Longfellow's literary career
£7.99

The Last of the Mohicans
JAMES FENIMORE COOPER
The tale that shaped American frontier myth
£5.99

The Great Gatsby
F. SCOTT FITZGERALD
Much loved story of passion and betrayal, glamour and the powerful allure of the American dream
£4.99

All books are available from your local bookshop or direct from:
Littlehampton Book Services Cash Sales, 14 Eldon Way, Lineside Estate,
Littlehampton, West Sussex BN17 7HE (*prices are subject to change*)

To order any of the books, please enclose a cheque (in sterling) made payable to
Littlehampton Book Services, or phone your order through with credit card details (Access,
Visa or Mastercard) on 01903 721596 (24 hour answering service) stating card number
and expiry date. (*Please add £1.25 for package and postage to the total of your order.*)

In the USA, for further information and a complete catalogue call 1-800-526-2778

DRAMA
IN EVERYMAN

The Oresteia
AESCHYLUS
*New translation of one of the
greatest Greek dramatic trilogies
which analyses the plays in
performance*
£5.99

**Everyman and Medieval
Miracle Plays**
edited by A. C. Cawley
*A selection of the most popular
medieval plays*
£4.99

Complete Plays and Poems
CHRISTOPHER MARLOWE
*The complete works of this great
Elizabethan in one volume*
£5.99

Restoration Plays
edited by Robert Lawrence
*Five comedies and two tragedies
representing the best of the
Restoration stage*
£7.99

**Female Playwrights of the
Restoration: Five Comedies**
edited by Paddy Lyons
*Rediscovered literary treasures
in a unique selection*
£5.99

**Plays, Prose Writings
and Poems**
OSCAR WILDE
*The full force of Wilde's wit
in one volume*
£4.99

**A Dolls House/The Lady from
the Sea/The Wild Duck**
HENRIK IBSEN
introduced by Fay Weldon
*A popular selection of Ibsen's
major plays*
£4.99

**The Beggar's Opera and
Other Eighteenth-Century Plays**
JOHN GAY et. al.
Including Goldsmith's She Stoops
To Conquer *and Sheridan's* The
School for Scandal, *this is a volume
which reflects the full scope of the
period's theatre*
£6.99

**Female Playwrights of the
Nineteenth Century**
edited by Adrienne Scullion
*The full range of female nineteenth-
century dramatic development*
£6.99

All books are available from your local bookshop or direct from:
Littlehampton Book Services Cash Sales, 14 Eldon Way, Lineside Estate,
Littlehampton, West Sussex BN17 7HE *(prices are subject to change)*

To order any of the books, please enclose a cheque (in sterling) made payable to
Littlehampton Book Services, or phone your order through with credit card details (Access,
Visa or Mastercard) on 01903 721596 (24 hour answering service) stating card number
and expiry date. *(Please add £1.25 for package and postage to the total of your order.)*

In the USA, for further information and a complete catalogue call 1-800-526-2778